The Chronicles of Elantra
by
New York Times bestselling author

Michelle Sagara

CAST IN SHADOW
CAST IN COURTLIGHT
CAST IN SECRET
CAST IN FURY
CAST IN SILENCE
CAST IN CHAOS
CAST IN RUIN
CAST IN PERIL
CAST IN SORROW
CAST IN FLAME
CAST IN HONOR
CAST IN FLIGHT
CAST IN DECEPTION

And
"Cast in Moonlight"
found in
HARVEST MOON,
an anthology with Mercedes Lackey and Cameron Haley

Look for the next story in
The Chronicles of Elantra,
coming soon from MIRA Books.

MICHELLE SAGARA

CAST IN CHAOS

mira

For my uncle Shoichi, with gratitude

AUTHOR NOTE

There are, in fantasy, two types of series. One is the extended single story that, with multiple viewpoints and various plot threads, spreads out over several volumes. The other is a connected series of stand-alone stories that feature more or less the same characters facing different situations; mysteries are characteristically this type of series. The Chronicles of Elantra is the second type of series, as well. Kaylin Neya, the main character, is an Elantran police officer, and her job is to investigate crimes and solve them—although both the problems and the solutions in a world with winged mortals, Dragons and large furred Leontines tend to be less mundane than the problems a real-world precinct would generally face. I hope that someone picking up any volume of the series would be able to follow the story and the characters from the beginning of the book to the end.

But.

In this second type of series, the individual story arcs are often small; it's the *character* arcs that have room to grow, because ideally what your characters experience for good or ill causes trickle-down changes that continue on into the future. The Kaylin of *Cast in Shadow* (the first of The Chronicles of Elantra) and the Kaylin of the book you now hold in your hands is substantially the same person, but she has learned to let go of some of her earlier prejudices because of the events of subsequent books (for example, *Cast in Secret*, in which she confronts her visceral dislike of the Tha'alani, the racial telepaths).

Some of the events of previous books also cause emotional ripples in her life, and while she *is* facing an entirely different threat in *Cast in Chaos*, she's come far enough to begin to acknowledge some of them. If this is the first time you've joined her, welcome to Elantra; if you've been following her all along, my heartfelt thanks.

CAST IN CHAOS

CHAPTER 1

The Halls of Law occupied real estate that the merchants' guild salivated over every time discussion about tax laws came up, and for that reason, if no other, Private Kaylin Neya was proud to work in them. The building sat in the center of the city, its bulk overshadowed by three towers, atop which—in the brisk and heavy winds of the otherwise clear day—flags could be seen at the heights. It was the only building, by Imperial decree, which was allowed this much height; the Emperor considered it a personal statement. She would probably have been slightly prouder if she'd managed to make Corporal, but she took what she could get.

What she could get, on the other hand, could be a bit disconcerting on some days. She approached the guards at the door—today Tanner and Gillas were at their posts—and stopped before she'd passed between them. They were giving her funny looks, and she was on time. She'd been on time for four days running, although one emergency with the midwives' guild had pulled her off active duty in the middle of the day, but the looks on their faces didn't indicate a lost betting pool.

"What's up?" she asked Tanner. She had to look up to ask

it; he was easily over six feet in height, and he didn't slouch when on duty.

"You'll find out," he replied. He was almost smirking.

The problem with coming to the Hawks as an angry thirteen-year-old with a lot of attitude was that the entire force felt as if they'd watched you grow up. This meant the entire damn force took an interest in your personal business. She cursed Tanner under her breath, and left his chuckle at her back.

It was only about ten feet from her back when she ran into Corporal Severn Handred. Who just happened to be loitering in the Aerie, under the shadows of the flying Aerians, who were practicing maneuvers that no other race on the force could achieve without a hell of a lot of magic, most of which would require postmaneuver paperwork that would keep them grounded for weeks. The Emperor was not a big fan of magic that wasn't under his personal control.

Kaylin, her wrist weighted by a few pounds of what was ostensibly gold, knew this firsthand. The bracer—studded with what were also ostensibly gemstones, and in and of itself more valuable than most of the force on a good day, which would be a day when their Sergeant wasn't actively cursing the amount of money being wasted employing their sorry butts—was also magical. It was older than the Empire.

No one knew how it worked—or at least that's what was claimed—but it kept random magic neutralized. Kaylin had been ordered to wear it, and on most days, she did.

Severn looked up as she approached him. "You're on time," he said, falling into an easy step beside her.

"And the world hasn't ended," she replied. "Betting? It's four days running." It was a betting pool she'd been excluded from joining.

He grinned, but didn't answer, which meant yes, he was betting, and no, he hadn't lost yet.

"If you win, you can buy me lunch."

He raised a brow. "You're scrounging for lunch this early in the month?"

"Don't ask."

He laughed.

"Instead," she continued, "tell me why you're here."

"I work here."

"Ha, ha. You don't usually loiter in the Aerie, waiting for me to walk by." In fact, if it was something that was a matter of life or death, or at least keeping her job, he was more proactive: he'd show up at her apartment and throw her out of bed.

"Loitering and waiting are not considered—"

"Tanner was smirking."

Severn winced. "An official courier came by the office this morning."

"Official courier?"

"An Imperial Courier."

"Please tell me it had nothing to do with me," she said, without much hope.

"You want me to lie?"

She snorted. "Is Marcus in a mood?"

"Let's just say he didn't seem overly surprised." Which wasn't much of an answer if the one you wanted was No.

Teela was in the office and at her desk, which was generally a bad sign. She was also on break, which meant she was lounging on a chair that was balanced on its back two legs, and watching the door. Tain was somewhere else, which meant Kaylin only had to deal with one of the Barrani Hawks she sometimes counted as friends. On this particular morning, she couldn't remember why, exactly.

The fact that Teela rose—gracefully, because it was impossible for a Barrani not to be graceful—the minute she laid emerald eyes on Kaylin made it clear who she'd been watching for. The fact that she was smiling as she sauntered across the usual chaos of the office meant she was amused. This didn't mean that the news for Kaylin was good, on the other hand.

"Good morning, Private Neya," the window said. "It is a bright and sunny day, but rain is expected in the late afternoon. Please dress accordingly while you are on duty."

Teela took one look at Kaylin's raised brows and laughed out loud.

Kaylin said a few choice words in Leontine.

"Please be aware that this is a multiracial office, and the terms that you are using might give offense to some of your coworkers," the same window chided.

Kaylin's jaw nearly hit the floor.

"Apparently," Teela said, as her laugh trailed off into a chuckle, "the mage that designed the window to be a cheerful, talking timepiece, was not entirely precise in his use of magic."

"Which means?"

"Off the record? Someone tampered with Official Office equipment."

"This is worse. The old window didn't greet us by name. What the hells were they trying to do?"

"Get it to shut up without actually breaking it."

"Which seems to be almost impossible. The breaking-it part."

"So does the shutting-it-up part, if it comes to that." Teela grinned. "We've started a new betting pool."

"Hell with the pool—we should just make the Hawklord stay in this damn office. The window would be gone in less than a week." She started to head toward her very small desk.

"Private Neya," the window said, "you have not checked

today's duty roster. Please check the roster to ascertain your current rounds."

Teela burst out laughing because Kaylin's facial expression could have soured new milk. She did, however, head toward the roster because she couldn't actually break the window, and she was pretty damn certain it would nag her until she checked.

Elani street had been penciled, in more or less legible writing, beside Kaylin's name. Severn was her partner. There were no investigations in progress that required her presence, although there were two ongoing. The shift started in half an hour. She took note of it as obviously as possible, and then returned to her desk, by way of Caitlin.

"Good morning, dear," Caitlin said, looking up from a small and tidy pile of papers.

Kaylin nodded, and then bent slightly over the desk. "What happened to the window?"

The older woman frowned slightly. "We're not officially certain, dear." Which meant she wouldn't say. "Sergeant Kassan is aware that the enchantment on the window is causing some difficulty. I believe he is scheduled to speak with the Hawklord."

"Thank the gods," Kaylin replied. The window, during this discussion, was in the process of greeting yet another co-worker. "Does it do this all day?"

Caitlin nodded. "You weren't here yesterday," she added. Her frown deepened. "It not only greeted the employees by name, it also felt the need to greet every person who walked into—or through—the office in the same way."

"But—"

Caitlin shrugged. "It's magic," she finally said, as if that explained everything. Given how Kaylin generally felt about magic, it probably did.

She tried to decide whether or not to ask about the Imperial Courier. Caitlin was the best source of information in the office, but if she felt it wasn't important or relevant to the questioner, she gave away exactly nothing. Since she was bound to find out sooner or later—and probably sooner— she held her tongue.

"Private Neya!" The low, deep rumble of Leontine growl momentarily stilled most of the voices in the office. Marcus, as she'd guessed, was not in the best of moods. "Caitlin *has* work to do, even if you don't."

"Sir!" Kaylin replied.

"He's in the office more than anyone else who works here," Caitlin whispered, by way of explanation. "And I believe the window likes to have a chat when things are quiet."

Kaylin grimaced in very real sympathy for Old Ironjaw.

"In particular, I think it's been trying to give him advice."

Which meant it wasn't going to last the week. Thank the gods.

"Oh, and, dear?" Caitlin added, as Kaylin began to move away from her desk, under the watchful glare of her Sergeant.

"Yes?"

"This is for you." She held out a small sheaf of paper.

Kaylin, who had learned to be allergic to paperwork from a master—that being Marcus himself—cringed reflexively as she held out a hand. "Am I going to like this?"

"Probably not," Caitlin said with very real sympathy. "I'm afraid it isn't optional."

Kaylin looked through the papers in her hands. "This is a class schedule."

"Yes, dear."

"But—Mallory's gone—"

"It's not about his request that you take—and pass—all of the courses you previously failed, if that's helpful. The Hawklord vetoed that, although I'm sorry to say Mallory's suggestion did meet with some departmental approval."

It was marginally helpful. "What's it about, then?"

Caitlin winced. "Etiquette lessons. And I believe that Lord Sanabalis has, of course, requested that your magical education resume."

"Is there any good news?"

"As far as we know, nothing is threatening to destroy either the City or the World, dear."

Kaylin stared glumly at the missive in her hands. "This is your subtle way of telling me not to start doing either, isn't it?"

Caitlin smiled. "They're just lessons. It's not the end of the World."

"So," Severn said, when she joined him and they began to head down the hall, "did you speak with Caitlin?"

"Yes. Let me guess. The entire office already knows the contents of these papers."

"Betting?"

"No."

He laughed. "Most of the office. How bad is it?"

"Two days a week with Sanabalis."

He raised a brow.

"With *Lord* Sanabalis."

"Better. Isn't that the same schedule you were on before the situation in the fiefs? You both survived that."

"Mostly. I think he broke a few chairs."

"He'd have to." Severn grinned. "Gods couldn't break that table."

It was true. The table in the West Room—which had been given a much more respectful name before Marcus's time, which meant Kaylin had no idea what it was—was harder than most sword steel. "Three *nights* of off-duty time with the etiquette teacher."

"Nights?"

She nodded grimly.

"Is the teacher someone the Hawks can afford to piss off?"

"I hope so."

"Who's teaching?"

"I don't know. It doesn't actually say."

"Where?"

She grimaced. "The Imperial Palace."

He winced in genuine sympathy. "I'm surprised Lord Grammayre approved this."

Kaylin was not known for her love of high society. The Hawklord was not known for his desire to have Kaylin and high society anywhere in the same room. Or city block. Which meant the dictate had come from someone superior to the Hawklord.

"It's not optional," Kaylin said glumly. "And the worst part is, if I pass, I probably get to do something big. Like meet the Emperor."

"I'd like to be able to say that won't kill you."

"You couldn't, with a straight face."

He shrugged. "When do you start?"

"Two days. I meet Sanabalis—*Lord* Sanabalis—for Magical Studies—"

"Magical Studies? Does it actually say that?"

"Those are the exact words. Don't look at me, I didn't write it—in the afternoon tomorrow." She dropped the schedule into her locker with as much care as she generally dropped dirty towels.

Elani street was not a hub of activity in the morning. It wasn't exactly deserted, but it was quiet, and the usual consumers of love potions and extracts to combat baldness, impotence, and unwanted weight were lingering on the other side of storefronts. Remembering her mood the last time she'd walked this beat, Kaylin took care not to knock over offending sandwich boards. On the other hand, she also took the same care not to read them.

"Kaylin?"

"Hmm?" She was looking at the cross section of charms in a small case in one window—Mortimer's Magnificent Magic—and glanced at her partner's reflection in the glass.

"You're rubbing your arms."

She looked down and realized he was right. "They're sort of itchy," she said.

He raised one brow. "Sort of itchy?"

The marks that adorned most of the insides of her arms were, like the ones that covered her inner thighs and half of her back, weather vanes for magic. Kaylin hesitated. "It doesn't feel the way it normally does when there's strong magic. It's—they're just sort of itchy."

"And they've never been like that before."

She frowned. She'd had fleas once, while cat-sitting for an elderly neighbor. The itch wasn't quite the same, but it was similar.

She started to tell him as much, and was interrupted midsentence by someone screaming.

It was, as screams went, a joyful, ecstatic sound, which meant their hands fell to their clubs without drawing them. But they—like every other busybody suddenly crowding the streets—turned at the sound of the voice. It was distinctly male, and probably a lot higher than it normally was. Bouncing a glance between each other, they shrugged and headed toward the noise.

The scream slowly gathered enough coherence to form words, and the words, to Kaylin's surprise, had something to do with hair. And having hair. When they reached the small wagon set up on the street—and Kaylin made a small note to check for permits, as that was one of the Dragon Emperor's innovations on tax collection—the crowds had formed a thin wall.

The people who lived above the various shops in Elani street had learned, with time and experience, to be enormously cynical. Exposure to every promise of love, hair, or sexual prowess known to man—or woman, for that matter—tended to have that effect, as did the more esoteric promise to tease out the truth about the future and your destined greatness in it. They had pretty much heard—and seen—it all.

And given the charlatans who masqueraded as merchants on much of the street, both the permanent residents and the officers of the Law who patrolled it knew that it wasn't beyond them to hire an actor to suddenly be miraculously cured of baldness, impotence, or blindness.

Kaylin assumed that the man who was almost crying in joy was one of these actors. But if he was, he was damn good. She started to ask him his name, stopped as he almost hugged her, and then turned to glance at the merchant whose wagon this technically was.

He looked...slack-jawed and surprised. He didn't even bother to school his expression, which clearly meant he was new to this. Not new to fleecing people, she thought sourly, just new to success. When he took a look at the Hawk that sat dead center on her tabard, he straightened up, and the slack lines of his face tightened into something that might have looked like a grin—on a corpse.

"Officer," he said, in that loud, booming voice that demanded attention. Or witnesses. "How can I help you on this fine morning?" He had to speak loudly, because the man was continuing his loud, joyful exclamations.

"I'd like to see your permits," Kaylin replied. She spoke clearly and calmly, but her voice traveled about as far as it would have had she shouted. It was one of the more useful things she'd learned in the Halls of Law. She held out one hand.

"But that's—that's *outrageous!*"

"Take it up with the Emperor," Kaylin replied, although she did secretly have some sympathy for the man. "Or the merchants' guild, as they supported it."

"I am a member in good standing of the guild, and I can assure you—"

She lifted a hand. "It's not technically illegal for you to claim to be a member in good standing of a guild," she told him, keeping her voice level, but lowering it slightly. "But if you're new here, it's really, really *stupid* to claim to be a member of the *merchants'* guild if you're not." Glancing at his wagon, which looked well serviced but definitely aged, she shrugged.

"I am *not* new to the city," the man replied. "But I've been traveling to far lands in order to bring the citizens of Elantra the finest, the most rare, of mystical unguents and—"

"And you still need a permit to sell them here, or in any of the market streets or their boundaries." She turned. Lifting her voice, she said, "Okay, people, it's time to pack it in. Mr.—"

"Stravaganza."

The things people expected her to be able to repeat with a straight damn face. Kaylin stopped herself from either laughing or snorting. "Mr. *Stravaganza* is new enough to the City that he's failed to acquire the proper permits for peddling his wares in the streets. In order to avoid the *very* heavy fines associated with the lack of permit, he is now closed for business until he makes the journey to the Imperial Tax Offices to acquire said permit."

Severn, on the other hand, was looking at the bottle he'd casually picked up from the makeshift display. It was small, long, and stoppered. The merchant started to speak, and then stopped the words from falling out of his mouth. "Please, Officer," he said to Severn. "My gift to a man who defends our city." He even managed to say this with a more or less straight face.

Severn nodded and carefully pocketed the bottle. As he already *had* a headful of hair, Kaylin waited while the merchant packed up and started moving down the street. Then she looked at her partner. "What gives?" she said, gesturing toward his pocket.

"I don't know," was the unusually serious reply. "But that man wasn't acting. I'd be willing to bet that he actually thinks the fact that he now has hair is due to the contents of this bottle."

"You can't believe that," she said, voice flat.

Severn shrugged. "Let's just make sure Mr. Stravaganza crosses the border of our jurisdiction. When he's S.E.P., we can continue our rounds."

The wagon made it past the borders and into the realm of Somebody Else's Problem without further incident. Kaylin and Severn did not, however, make it to the end of their shift in the same way. They corrected their loose pattern of patrol once they returned to the street; as the day had progressed, Elani had become more crowded. This was normal.

Some of the later arrivals were very richly clothed, and came in fine carriages, disembarking with the help of their men; some wore clothing that had been too small a year ago, with patches at elbows and threads of different colors around cuffs and shoulders.

All of them, rich, poor, and shades in between, sought the same things. At a distance, Kaylin saw one carriage stop before the doors of Margot. Margot, with her flame-red hair, her regal and impressive presence, and her damn charisma. Margot's storefront was, like the woman whose name was plastered in gold leaf across the windows, dramatic and even—Kaylin admitted grudgingly—attractive. It implied wealth, power, and a certain spare style.

To Kaylin, it also heavily implied fraud—but it wasn't the type of fraud for which the woman could be thrown in jail.

The doors opened and the unknown but obviously well-heeled woman entered the shop. This wasn't unusual, and at least the woman in question *had* the money to throw away; far too many of the clientele that frequented Elani street in various shades of desperation didn't.

Severn gave Kaylin a very pointed look, and she shrugged. "She's got the money. No one's going hungry if she throws it away on something stupid." She started to walk, forcing Severn to fall in beside her. Her own feelings about most of Elani's less genuine merchants were well-known.

She slowed, and after a moment she added, "I know there are worse things, Severn. I'm trying."

His silence was a comfortable silence; she fit into it, and he let her. But they hadn't reached the corner before they heard shouting, and they glanced once at each other before turning on their heels and heading back down the street.

The well-dressed woman who had entered Margot's was in the process of leaving it in high, high dudgeon. Margot was—even at this distance—an unusual shade of pale that almost looked bad with her hair. Kaylin tried not to let the momentary pettiness of satisfaction distract her, and failed miserably; Margot was demonstrably still healthy, her store was still in one piece, and at this distance it didn't *appear* that any Imperial Laws had been broken.

"Please, Lady," Margot was saying. "I assure you—"

"I am *done* with your assurances, *Margot,*" was the icy reply. The woman turned, caught sight of the Hawks, and drew herself to her full height. "Officers," she said coldly. "I demand that you arrest this—this woman—for slander."

"While we would dearly love to arrest this woman in the course of our duties," Kaylin said carefully, "most of what she says is confined to private meetings. Nor is what she says to her clients maliciously—or at least publicly—spread."

"No?" The woman still spoke as if winter were language. "She spoke—in public—"

"I spoke in private," Margot said quickly. "In the confines of my own establishment—"

"You spoke in front of your other clients," the woman snapped. "When my father hears of this, you will be *finished* here, do you understand? You will be languishing in the Imperial jail!"

It was too much to hope that she would climb the steps to the open door of her carriage and leave. She turned once again to Kaylin; Severn was, as usual, enjoying the advantage of having kept his mouth shut. It was a neat trick, and Kaylin wished—for the thousandth time—that she could learn it. Or, rather, had *already* learned it.

"You will arrest this—this charlatan *immediately.*"

"Ma'am, we need to have something to arrest her *for.*"

"I've already told you—"

"You haven't told us what she said," Kaylin replied. Given the heightening of color across the woman's cheeks, the fact that this was required seemed to further enrage her.

"Do you know who I am?"

It was the kind of question that Kaylin most hated, and it was the chief reason that her duties were not *supposed* to take her anywhere where it could, with such genuine outrage, be asked. "No, ma'am, I'm afraid I haven't had the privilege."

Her eyes rounded, and out of the corner of her eye, Kaylin saw that Margot was wincing.

"Who, may I ask, are you?" the woman now said.

"Private Neya, of the Hawks."

"And you are somehow supposed to be responsible for safeguarding the people of this fair city when you clearly fail to recognize something as significant as the crest upon this carriage?"

Kaylin opened her mouth to reply, but a reply was clearly no longer desired—or acceptable.

"Very well, *Private*. I will speak with Lord Grammayre *myself*." She spoke very clear, pointed High Barrani to her driver, and then stomped her way up the step and into the carriage. Had she been responsible for closing its door herself, it would have probably shattered. As it was, the footman did a much more careful job.

They watched the carriage drive away.

"I suppose there's not much chance that she's just going to go home and stew?" she asked Severn.

"No."

"Is she important enough to gain immediate audience with the Hawklord?"

Margot sputtered before Severn could answer, but that was fine. Severn's expression was pretty damn clear. "She is Lady Alyssa of the Larienne family. Did you *truly* not recognize her?"

Larienne. Larienne. Like most of the wealthy families in Elantra, they sported a mock-Barrani name. Something about it was familiar. "Go on."

"Her father is Garavan Larienne, the head of the family. He is *also* the Chancellor of the Exchequer."

Kaylin turned to Severn. "How bad is it going to be?"

"Oh, probably a few inches of paper on Marcus's desk."

She wilted. "All right, Margot. Since I'm going to be on report in a matter of hours—"

"Hour," Severn said quietly.

"What the hell did you say that offended her so badly?"

"I'd prefer not to repeat it."

Kaylin sourly told her what she could do with her preferences.

"So let me get this straight. Lady Alyssa comes to you for advice about her love life—"

"She is Garavan's only daughter." Margot was now subdued. She was still off her color. "And she's been a client for only a few months. She is, of course, concerned with her greater destiny."

"I'm not. What I'm concerned with is the statement Corporal Handred has taken from some of your other clients. You told Lady Alyssa that her father was going to be charged with embezzlement, and the family fortunes would be in steep decline? *You?*"

Margot opened her mouth, and nothing fell out of it. Kaylin had often daydreamed about Margot at a loss for words; this wasn't *exactly* how she'd hoped it would come about.

"I—" Margot shook her head. "I had no intention of saying any such thing, Her father's business is not her business, and she doesn't *ask* about him."

"Then what in the hells possessed you to do it now?"

"She—she sat in her normal chair, and she asked me if—if I had any further insight into her particular situation."

"And *that* was your answer? Come *on*, Margot. You've

been running this place—successfully—for too damn many years to just open your mouth and offend someone you consider important."

"That was my answer," was the stiff reply. "I felt—strange, Private. I felt as if—I could *see* what would happen. As if it were unfolding before my eyes. I didn't mean to speak the words. The words just came." She spoke very softly, even given the lack of actual customers in her storefront; she had sent them, quietly, on their way. Apparently, whatever it was that was coming out of her mouth was not to be trusted, and she was willing to lose a full day's worth of income to make sure it didn't happen again.

"So. A cure for baldness that worked—instantly—and a fortune-teller's trick that might *also* be genuine."

"I'd keep that last to yourself."

She shrugged. "I think it's time we visited all of the damn shops on Elani, door-to-door, and had a little talk with the proprietors."

Severn, who didn't dislike Margot as much as Kaylin, had been both less amused at her predicament and less amused by the two incidents than Kaylin. Kaylin let her brain catch up with her sense of humor, and the grin slowly faded from her face, as well. "Come on," she told him.

"Where are we starting?"

"Evanton's. If we're lucky, that'll take up the remainder of the shift, and then some. I'm not looking forward to signing out tonight."

CHAPTER 2

Evanton's apprentice, Grethan, opened the door before Kaylin managed to touch it. He looked as if he hadn't slept in three days, and judging from his expression, Kaylin and Severn were part of his waking nightmare.

"Are you shutting up for the day?" Kaylin asked, keeping her voice quiet and low.

He looked confused, and then shook himself. "No," he told her. "I was just—going out. For a walk," he added quickly.

She didn't ask him how Evanton was; he'd pretty much already answered that question. But she did walk into the cluttered, gloomy front room, and she stopped as she crested the opening between two cases of shelving. The light here was brilliant.

Evanton was wearing his usual apron, and it was decorated with the usual pins and escapee threads of the variety of materials with which he worked. But his eyes were, like the lights in the room, a little too bright. He glanced at her, his hands pulling thread through a thick, dark fabric that lay in a drape across his spindly lap. "I was wondering," he said, although it was somewhat muffled, given the pins between his lips, "when you would show up."

"The Garden—"

"Oh, the Garden's fine. Whatever you did in the fiefs a couple of weeks ago was enough to calm it. It looks normal. No, the Garden is not your problem." He removed the pins and stuck them carefully into one of a half-dozen oddly shaped pincushions by his left arm. "I've almost finished with your cloak," he added, "if you want to try it on."

She had the grace to redden. "Not now," she told him. "I'm on duty."

He raised a brow. "Have you two been on patrol all morning?"

Kaylin nodded.

"Notice anything unusual?"

She nodded again, but this time more slowly. *Note to self: visit Evanton's first, next time you're in Elani.* "What is it, Evanton? We're just about to make a sweep of the street to see if anything else unusual turns up."

"I hope you've got a lot of time," the old man replied. He rose and folded the cloth in his lap into a careful bundle. "I'd offer you tea, but the boy's forgotten to fill the bucket."

"I can fill it—"

"No. That won't be necessary."

She frowned.

"It's not only in the rest of the street that the unusual is occurring," he told her. "This morning, when he came in with the water, the water started to speak to him."

"Evanton—"

"Yes. He was born deaf, by the standards of the Tha'alani. He has always been *mind* deaf, but he is *still* Tha'alani by birth. In the Elemental Garden, he can hear the water's voice, and through it, some echo of the voice of his people. This is the first time it's happened outside of the Garden, and the water was in buckets. It is not, sadly, still in those buckets. I can't get him to drink a glass of water at the moment. He sits and stares at it instead." He frowned. "I had heard rumors that you were studying magic with Lord Sanabalis."

"From who?"

"Private, please. I gather from your sour expression that the rumors are true. You might wish to speak with Lord Sanabalis about the events on Elani at your earliest convenience. If we are lucky, he will be unaware of the difficulties you might encounter."

"And if we're not?"

"He will already know, and it will mean that the difficulties are present across a much wider area of the city."

"What will it mean to him?"

"What it *should* mean to you, if you've been studying for any length of time," was the curt reply. But Evanton did relent. "There has been a significant and sudden shift in the magical potential of an area that is at least as broad as Elani."

Kaylin froze. "Severn, are you thinking what I'm thinking?"

"I'm thinking that our sample size—of three—is more than enough for the day. We should return to the office immediately."

Evanton frowned, although with his face it was sometimes difficult to tell. "Something unusual happened outside of the confines of this particular neighborhood."

"Yes. An enchantment laid against some of the windows in the Halls of Law has developed a more commanding and distinct personality than it possessed a few days ago."

Evanton closed his eyes. "Go, Private, Corporal. Speak with the Hawklord *now*."

Speaking with the Hawklord was not at the top of Kaylin's list of things to do before the end of her shift. Or at all. He was—they all were—aware of the shortcomings in an education that didn't include the rich and the powerful on this side of the Ablayne. For one, power in the fiefs usually meant brute force; manners were what you developed when you wanted to avoid pissing off the brute force in question. Marcus had once told her that manners in the rest of Elantra were exactly the same thing, but Kaylin knew they weren't. In the fiefs, the best manners were often either silence or total invisibility.

Here, you were actually expected to talk and interact. Without obvious groveling or fawning, and without obvious fear.

Severn caught her hand.

"What?"

"Stop rubbing your arm like that. You'll take your skin off."

"Like that would be a bad thing." But she did stop. "I should have known," she added. "You suspected?"

"I wondered."

The Halls loomed in a distance that was growing shorter as they walked; they weren't patrolling, so there was no need for a leisurely pace. They also weren't running because running Hawks made people nervous.

Tanner took one look at her face and stepped to one side. "Trouble?" he asked them both.

"Possible trouble," Kaylin replied. They breezed through the Aerie and the halls that led to the office that was Kaylin's second home. Marcus was at his desk, and he roared when he caught sight of them. Kaylin cringed.

"Here. *Now*."

Only a suicidal idiot would have ignored that tone of voice. Or the claws that were adding new runnels to scant clear desk surface. Both she and Severn made their way to the safe side of his desk—the one he wasn't on. Kaylin lifted her chin, exposing her throat. Marcus actually glowered at it as if he was considering his options; his eyes were a very deep orange, and about as far from his usual golden color as they could get when death wasn't involved.

"In your rounds in Elani today did you happen to encounter anyone significant?" he growled, his voice on the lower end of the Leontine scale. The office had fallen—mostly—silent; total silence would probably occur only in the event of the deaths of everyone in it.

"Alyssa Larienne."

"*Lady* Alyssa Larienne. She is the daughter of one of the oldest—and wealthiest—human families in Elantra. Her father is a member of significance in the human Caste Court. Her mother is the daughter of the castelord. If you wanted to make my life more difficult when dealing with the human Caste Court, you couldn't have chosen a better person to offend."

Well, there is her father. This time, Kaylin kept her mouth shut.

"I expect there to be a good explanation for this."

"I wasn't the one who actually offended her, if that helps."

He snarled, which meant it didn't. "What happened?"

"She's a client of Margot's."

"You're telling me—with a straight face and your job on the line—that Margot offended her."

"Yes, sir."

"How?"

"That's part of why we're here—"

"Stick with this part, for now. Report on the rest later."

"Yes, sir." She took a deep breath. "*Lady* Alyssa arrived for her usual appointment. Today, Margot chose to tell her that her father, Garavan Larienne, was to be arrested for embezzlement."

Breathing would have made more noise than the combined contents of the office now did.

"Let me get this straight. *Margot* told Alyssa Larienne that the Chancellor of the Exchequer was to be arraigned for embezzlement."

"Yes, sir."

"And your part in this was?"

"Lady Alyssa demanded that I arrest Margot for slander. I personally would love to arrest Margot for anything she could possibly—"

Marcus flexed his claws. Kaylin took this as a sign that she should answer his questions, and only his questions. "I asked Lady Alyssa what Margot had said. She declined to repeat it. She did not decline to repeat her demand."

Marcus's eyes were still orange.

"She did, however, take offense at the idea that I didn't immediately recognize the crest on her carriage or her own import, since obviously either of those would lead me to arrest Margot on the spot, and said she would take it up with Lord Grammayre personally."

Marcus growled. "This is *extremely* unfortunate. I would like you to request that Margot come into the office for debriefing."

Kaylin's jaw nearly dropped. "What?"

"Which part of that sentence wasn't clear?"

Severn cleared his throat. "When would you like us to request Margot's cooperation with the Halls of Law?"

"After you finish speaking with Lord Grammayre. You're early," he added, his eyes narrowing. "Please tell me there is no *other* emergency in Elani." Oddly enough, when he said this, his eyes began to shade into a more acceptable bronze.

Severn was notably silent.

"It would save me paperwork and ulcers if I just chained you to a desk, Private. Go talk to the Hawklord. Now."

"Private," Kaylin whispered, as they walked quickly up the spiral staircase. "As if you weren't there at all."

"You seem to be fairly good at attracting trouble in spite of your assigned partner," Severn replied, with a faint smile.

"If Margot has somehow blown things for an ongoing investigation…" She didn't finish, because they reached the Hawklord's tower door. They'd bypassed his office, but Kaylin didn't expect him to be in his office; he rarely conducted his meetings there. For one, it was as crowded and cluttered as any busy person's office. It also wasn't as imposing as the more austere and architecturally impressive tower itself.

"This," Kaylin muttered, as Severn placed his palm firmly across the doorward of the closed tower doors, "is worse than magic. This is politics."

"On the bright side," Severn replied, as the door swung inward, "this is probably making etiquette lessons look a lot more inviting."

The Hawklord was standing in front of his perfect, oval mirror. In and of itself, this was not a bad sign. The mirror, however, reflected no part of the room, which meant he was accessing Records. Kaylin could see nothing but a blank, black surface. He glanced over his shoulder as she and Severn walked into the room, and she stopped almost immediately.

His eyes were blue.

Blue, in the Aerians, like blue in the Barrani, was not a good sign. With luck, it meant anger. With less luck, it meant fury. In either case, it meant tread carefully. Likewise, the Hawklord's wings were high above his shoulders. They weren't fully extended; they were loosely gathered. She'd seen loosely gathered Aerian wings strike and break bone exactly once.

She offered the Hawklord a perfect salute. Severn, by her side, did likewise.

"Alyssa Larienne came to this tower just over an hour ago,"

he said without preamble. "Sergeant Kassan attempted to detain her by taking a detailed report of the incident which had angered her."

Kaylin winced.

"As a result she left the Halls some fifteen minutes before your arrival." The Hawklord's wings twitched. His eyes were still a very glacial blue. "She did not appreciate the filing of an incident report. I was assured that Sergeant Kassan was polite and respectful."

"She probably doesn't have much to do with Leontines on a daily basis," Kaylin pointed out. "She might not have been able to tell."

"That," the Hawklord said, and he did grimace, "is my profound hope. What happened in Elani street, Private Neya?"

Kaylin stared straight ahead. She wanted to at least look at Severn, because she could read minute changes in his expression well enough to be guided by them. But in the Hawklord's current mood that might be career-limiting.

"We're not entirely sure, sir. We cut our patrol short to report," she told Lord Grammayre. "After we visited Evanton."

The Hawklord's face became about as inviting and open as the stone walls that enclosed them. "Continue."

"There were three incidents in the space of a few hours of which we're aware. With your permission, we'll canvass the merchants and residents of the street tomorrow to see how many others we missed."

"Incidents?"

She hesitated; he marked it. But he waited. "The first was a man selling a cure for baldness that actually appeared to work—instantly."

He raised one pale brow. "It *is* Elani street."

"Sir." This time she did glance at Severn; his chin dipped

slightly down. "We took the merchant's name. Corporal Handred acquired a sample of the tonic."

"You...believe that this was genuine."

"Much as I hate to admit it, yes."

"Go on."

"The second incident of note, you've already heard about. Alyssa Larienne."

"Lady Alyssa Larienne is young, idealistic, and convinced of her own importance."

Severn cleared his throat.

"Corporal?"

"I would say that she is young, insecure, and in need of someone to convince her of that import."

"She throws her weight around—" Kaylin broke in.

"If she was certain she had that weight, she wouldn't need to throw it."

Kaylin shrugged. "For *whatever* reason, she's been a client of Margot's for many months."

"Margot Hemming?"

"The same."

"Margot Hemming is not, to my knowledge, and to the knowledge of Imperial Records, a mage. She has no training, and no notable talent or skill. She is, by human standards, striking. She is forty years of age—"

"She can't be forty."

"She is forty years of age," he repeated, spacing the words out thinly and evenly. "And she has twice been charged with fraud in the last twenty-five. She is not violent, she has no great pretensions, and for the last decade, she has settled into the life of a woman of modest, respectable means."

Kaylin glanced at the flat surface of a mirror that reflected nothing, and the Hawklord continued. "She has no known

criminal ties, she is despised by the merchants' guild, she do-
nates money to the Foundling Halls."

Kaylin's brows disappeared into her hairline. "She *what?*"

"She can afford it."

"That's not the point."

"No. It is not. She has very few clients of any significant
political standing. Garavan Larienne does not travel to her
shop, nor does his wife. She supports no political causes that
we are aware of, and believe that I have demanded every
possible legal record that she might be associated with, however distantly. But she has, today, single-handedly caused
the Hawks—and the Swords, and possibly indirectly, the
Wolves—more difficulty than the Arcanum has in its entire history."

Kaylin closed her eyes.

"What did Margot Hemming do, Private?"

"She told a fortune, more or less."

"I am aware of the fortune's contents." He turned. "The
other difficulties?"

"After the incident with Margot, we paid a visit to Evanton's. Evanton said that...there was an incident in the store,
involving his apprentice."

"Did it also involve the future of arguably the most politically powerful human in Elantra?"

"No, sir."

"Then I am not interested in the details at this present moment. Continue."

"It was also of a magical nature. Evanton thinks—
thought—that there is an unusually strong flux in the magical potential of a specific area, and it's causing things to go
completely out of whack."

"His words?"

"Not exactly."

"What, exactly, were his words?"

"He thought I should speak with Sanabalis—"

"Lord Sanabalis."

"Lord Sanabalis. Now."

"Far be it from me to ignore the urgent advice of so important a man," the Hawklord replied.

"He thinks it could be disastrous if we don't—"

"It has already been almost disastrous. At this particular moment in my career, I fail to see how it could be worse. Take Corporal Handred with you, avoid *any* discussion of Larienne, and avoid, as well, any men who obviously bear his colors. Go directly to Lord Sanabalis, make your report, and return directly here. If I am absent, wait."

"Sir."

The Imperial Palace, home of future etiquette lessons, loomed in the distance of carriage windows like the cages outside of Castle Nightshade. The flags were, as they almost always were, at full height, and the wind at that height was impressive today; it buffeted clouds.

Severn, seated across from Kaylin, glanced at her arms. It wasn't a pointed glance, but she rolled back one sleeve, exposing the heavy, golden bracer that bracketed her wrist. The unnatural gems, socketed in a line down its length, gleamed in the darkened interior of the carriage. He nodded, and she rolled her sleeve down, covering it. By Imperial Edict, and by the Hawklord's command—which were in theory the same thing—she wore it all the time.

It prevented the unpredictable magic she could sometimes use from bubbling to the surface in disastrous ways. It unfortunately also prevented the more predictable—to Kaylin—magic that was actually helpful from being used, so it didn't *always* reside on her wrist, edict notwithstanding. Her magic could be used to heal the injured, and it was most often used when the midwives called her in on emergencies.

But it was this wild magic, and the unpredictable and unknown nature of it, that was at the root of the Magical Studies classes she was taking with Sanabalis. The Imperial Court reasoned that if she could use and channel magic like actual working mages did, she would be in control of it. And, in theory, the Court would be in control of her, because indirectly they paid her salary, and she liked to eat.

It was also the magic that was at the heart of etiquette lessons. The Dragon Emperor was not famed for his tolerance and sense of humor. He was, in fact, known for his lack of both. But Sanabalis, Tiamaris, and even the ancient Arkon who guarded the Imperial Library as if it was his personal hoard—largely because it was—all felt that she would soon have to come to Court and spend time in the presence of the Dragon who ruled them all. They wanted her to survive it, although Sanabalis on some days seemed less certain.

The carriage rolled to a halt in the usual courtyard. It was not an Imperial Carriage; most Hawks who didn't have *Lord* somewhere in their name didn't have regular use of those. It did bear the Hawk symbol, and a smaller version of the Imperial Crest, but it also needed both paint and a good, solid week's worth of scrubbing.

Still, it did the job. The men who always stood in the courtyard opened the side doors, but they didn't offer her either the small step that seemed to come with most fancy carriages, or help getting out of the seat that was so damn uncomfortable on long, bumpy rides. They just opened the door, peered briefly in, and got out of the way.

She handed one of them the letter Caitlin had written. Marcus had signed it with a characteristic bold paw print under a signature that was—if you knew Leontines—mostly legible. Caitlin, on the other hand, had done the sealing. Marcus didn't care for wax.

He hadn't much cared for her destination, either, but only barely threatened to rip out her throat if she embarrassed the department, which was bad; it meant he had other things on his mind. His eyes had never once shaded back to their familiar gold.

The man who had taken the sealed letter returned about fifteen minutes later, accompanied by a man she recognized, although not by name.

"Lord Sanabalis," this man said, with a stiff bow, "will see you. Please follow me."

She started to tell him she knew the way, and bit her tongue.

Sure enough, she did know the way, because he took her to Sanabalis's personal meeting room. It wasn't an office; there was no sign of a desk, or anything that looked remotely business-like—besides the Dragon Lord himself—in the room. And it had windows that did not, in fact, give out lectures on decorum, dress, and the use of racially correct language to random passersby. The windows here, on the other hand, were impressive, beveled glass that looked out on one of the best views of the Halls of Law in the city.

"If this," he told Kaylin, indicating one of the many chairs positioned in front of the one he occupied, "is about your class schedule, I will be tempted to reduce you to ash on the spot." As his eyes were the familiar gold that Marcus's hadn't been since she'd returned to the office, she assumed this was what passed for Dragon humor, and she took a chair.

Severn did likewise.

"It's not about the class schedule, although if you want my opinion—"

Sanabalis raised a pale, finely veined hand. It looked like

an older man's hand, but it could, in a pinch, probably drive a dent into solid rock. Dragons could look like aged wise men, but it was only ever cosmetic. They were immortal, like the Barrani. They lacked Barrani magnetism, and their unearthly beauty and grace, but Kaylin assumed that was because they didn't actually *care* what the Barrani or the merely mortal thought of them. At all.

"I believe, given previous exposure to your opinions, I can derive it from first principles."

Severn coughed. Kaylin glared at the side of his face, because for Severn, this was laughter that he'd only barely managed to contain. "There was an incident in Elani street today."

So much for gold. His eyes started the shade-shift into bronze the minute she mentioned the street. "I take it," she added, "you heard."

"We were informed—immediately—by Lord Grammayre, yes. I am not at liberty to discuss it at the moment. I am barely at liberty to have this meeting," he added. "But in general, you come to the Palace with information that is relevant, and often urgent. Do not, however, waste my time."

"I didn't cause the incident. I caused outrage because I didn't immediately obey the orders of a pissed-off noble."

"Understood. You have information on what did cause the incident?"

"Not directly."

He snorted. Small plumes of smoke left his nostrils, which was unusual. "Evanton sent me," she said quickly.

"The Keeper sent you?"

She nodded. "He started to talk about magical potential, and the sudden surge he felt in Elani."

Sanabalis was silent. It wasn't a good silence.

"He—the incident with Alyssa Larienne—he thought the magical potential shift was responsible for it somehow."

"Let me reverse my earlier position," he said quietly. "What were the *other* incidents?"

She told him.

His eyes were now the color of new copper. "And these incidents," he finally said, rising and turning his face toward the window. "Did they all occur within roughly the same area?"

It was Severn who answered. "We aren't entirely certain of that."

"How uncertain are you, and why?"

"You are no doubt aware that Sergeant Mallory made a few changes to the official office out of which the Hawks operate. One of those changes was—"

"The window, yes. I can tell you his requisition raised a few eyebrows in the Order."

"The window is perhaps not the most popular addition to the office. It is, however, impervious to most casual attempts to harm it."

"Go on."

"Someone attempted to dampen or neutralize the magic on the window—or so we believed."

"Tampering with official property?"

"As I said, that was our belief at the time. Given the nature of the enchantment—"

"It would be entirely believable. What happened?"

"The window now greets visitors—and staff—by name. Among other things. Its lectures have become more directed."

"The names could possibly have been carried over from any connection with Records, and I assume, given the requisition request, that connection would be mandatory."

"That was the theory. The window began, however, to greet visitors by name, as well, and some of those visitors don't exist in our Records. None of the Hawks are mages. We naturally assumed, given the nature of the original enchantment, that the attempt to disenchant the window had simply skewed it."

Sanabalis raised a hand, not to silence Severn, but to touch the window that separated them from high, open sky. Kaylin's hair began to stand on end.

The window darkened instantly, shutting out both sunlight and the sight of the Halls of Law. The bars that separated the panes seemed to melt into the surface of what had once been glass until the entire bay looked like a smooth, featureless trifold wall.

"Records," Sanabalis said, and the blackness rippled at the force of the single word. So, Kaylin swore, did the ground. He was using his dragon voice. The mirror—such as it was—rippled again, and this time light coalesced in streaks of horizontal lines. Sanabalis inhaled. Kaylin lifted her hands to cover her ears. Severn caught them both in his and pulled them down as the dragon spit out a phrase that Kaylin could literally feel pass through her.

"When you finally get called to Court," Severn told her, when it was silent again, "you won't be able to do that. Not more than once."

"They'll…" She grimaced. "I just assumed they'd be speaking High Barrani." She swallowed, nodded, and wondered how bad a Court meeting would be if she couldn't actually *hear* anything after the first few sentences.

Severn released her hands; they both turned to face the image that Sanabalis had called so uncomfortably into being. It was, to Kaylin's surprise, a map. "We," the Dragon Lord said, without looking away from the lines that now stretched, in different shades, and in different widths, across the entire surface area, "are here." A building seemed to dredge itself out of the network of lines, assuming solid shape and texture; it was, however, small.

"The Halls, as you can see, are here." A miniature version of the Halls also seemed to grow *out* of the surface of the map.

"The Keeper's responsibility is here." He gestured, and a third building rose out of the map. Kaylin frowned as it did. She walked past Evanton's shop at least a dozen times a day when she was sent to Elani on patrol. That shop and the one that now emerged at Sanabalis's unspoken command had *nothing* in common.

"Private, is there some difficulty?"

She turned to Severn. "Severn, does that look like Evanton's place to you?"

"No."

Sanabalis frowned. "It is a representation of—" The frown deepened, cutting off the rest of his words. His eyes narrowed and he leaned toward the emerging building. He needn't have bothered; the building that had started out in miniature began to expand, uprooting the lines that were meant to represent streets or rivers as if they were dusty webs.

The dragon spoke, loudly, at the image. It froze in place.

"It appears," he said softly—or at least softly compared to his previous words—"that we have a serious problem."

CHAPTER 3

When a Dragon of Sanabalis's power uses the word *problem* in that tone of voice, you start to look for two things: a good weapon, and a place to hide, because, when it comes right down to it, the weapon's going to be useless. Kaylin, aware of this, did neither.

"Problem?" she said, staring at the malformed map. Sanabalis didn't appear to have heard her. Clearing her throat, she said, "What are the distances from the Palace to the Halls, the Halls to Elani and the Palace to Elani?"

"I would prefer, at this point, not to ask," he replied. "Suffice it to say it is not an insignificant distance. The full length of Elani itself would not have been an insignificant distance, given the perturbations you've described. I am now assuming that either Margot or the young Alyssa Larienne drew upon the waiting potential and used it. That they did so entirely without intent…

"Come," he told them both, and turned away from the mirror.

"Where are we going?"

"You are going to the courtyard. I will meet you there with an Imperial Carriage."

"Why?"

"I would prefer not to use magic at this point. I would also prefer to have no one *else* use it. Word of this zone, if we can even deduce its boundaries, will spread. We cannot afford to have it touched or used by the wrong people."

Kaylin stilled. "People can deliberately use it?"

"Not without effort, and not without unpredictable results. Mages are likely to find their spells much more powerful in that zone, and if they are not prepared for it and they are using the wrong spells, it could prove fatal. It is not, however, for the mages that I am concerned."

"This has happened before," she said, voice flat.

"Yes, of course it has. Magic is not easily caged or defined. It has not, however, happened over an area this large in any recent history."

"How recent is recent?"

"The existence of our current Empire."

Immortals.

If Kaylin had any curiosity about where Sanabalis had gone in the brief interval before he met them in the courtyard, it was satisfied before they left the Palace: she could hear the thunderous clap of syllables that was the equivalent of dragon shouting. The Imperial guards, to give them their due, didn't even blink as she and Severn walked past.

But if Dragons were immortal, an emergency was still an emergency; they waited for maybe fifteen minutes in total before Sanabalis, looking composed and grim, met them. "Do not," he said, although Kaylin hadn't even opened her mouth, "ask." He glared at the carriage door, and it opened, although admittedly it opened at the hands of footmen.

The ride was grim, silent, and fast. Imperial Carriages were built for as much comfort as a carriage allowed, and people got out of its way. Sanabalis had the door open when it hit the Halls' yard; the Halls, unlike the Palace, expected people to more or less do things for themselves. He waited until the precise moment someone else had a hand on the horse's jesses, and then jumped down. Kaylin and Severn did the same, following him as quickly as they could without breaking into a run.

Sanabalis wasn't running, of course.

There was what wouldn't pass for a cursory inspection at the front doors; Sanabalis gave his name, but the formality of crossed polearms failed to happen because Sanabalis also didn't stop moving. They didn't have time to send a runner ahead, at least not on foot, but there were Aerians practicing maneuvers in the Aerie that opened up just behind the front doors, and Kaylin noticed the way at least one shadow dropped out of formation.

Lord Grammayre was, uncharacteristically, not in his Tower when they finally crested the last corner and hit the office proper. Nor was Marcus behind his desk. The two of them were standing more or less in the space in front of Caitlin's desk, which was what passed for a reception area this deep into the Halls itself. They turned to greet Sanabalis as he walked briskly toward them.

"Lord Sanabalis," the Hawklord said, bowing.

"Lord Grammayre. I have need of your Hawks."

"Of course."

"Let us repair to the West Room. We can discuss the nature of their deployment—and their new schedule."

Marcus didn't even blink.

"For reasons which will become clear, I would like to shut down the use of Records except in emergencies." He turned to the small mirror on the wall. "Records," he said. Which would clearly make this an emergency.

Lord Grammayre lifted his left wing, and then nodded.

"I have spoken with the Imperial Order of mages. The Emperor is currently evaluating the possibility of a quarantine on the Arcanum. Map, Elantra."

A map that was in no way the equal of the one he'd called on in the Palace shimmered into view. For one, it occupied a much smaller surface. Reaching out, Sanabalis touched three points on the map; they were familiar to Kaylin.

"A quarantine?" the Hawklord asked, watching the map shift colors where the Dragon Lord had touched it.

Sanabalis nodded grimly. "I will," he added, "speak with the Lord of Swords when I am finished here. If it is possible, it will be his duty to see that it is enforced."

"That is not likely to make the Emperor more popular with the Arcanists."

"Nothing short of his disappearance would do that. The Arcanists *are* a concern, but they are not the cause of the current difficulty. They are merely the most obvious avenue for turning it into a disaster. Here," he added. "Here, and here. At the moment, they are sites in which what I will call leakage for the purpose of discussion has been known to occur. The leakage in your office—the windows—is not as severe as the incidents that occurred in Elani street.

"It does not, however, matter. People's expectations during this unfortunate leakage guide some of its effects. Our historical Records are, as might be expected, veiled. The Arkon is looking over them now."

"Are there historical Records that would be relevant, Lord Sanabalis?"

"There are. They are not exactly fonts of optimism, however. What we need the Hawks to do is, as Private Neya would colloquially put it, 'hit the streets.' We need to ascertain what the boundaries of the area are. Look for the unusual. Look for the miraculous. Take note of the usual crimes or deaths, but examine them for any...unexplained...phenomenon. This has to start now," he added.

"The Emperor himself will speak to the Master Arcanist. He has been summoned to Court as a precaution. At the moment however, the Arcanum sits squarely outside of the area marked by the three geographical incidents. With luck, it will remain that way.

"Sergeant Kassan," Sanabalis added, "you may assure your Hawks that they will be adequately reimbursed for their extra duties."

Marcus looked as though he had just swallowed something more unpleasant than a week's worth of unforwarded reports. "Several of the Hawks are involved in the current investigation into the Exchequer."

"It pains me to say this, Sergeant Kassan, but both duties—the more subtle and now-endangered investigation, and the much less predictable magical one—must be fully discharged.

"As Private Neya is not currently involved in the former, I suggest you deploy her in the latter. I have taken the liberty of arranging an appointment with the Oracular Halls, as she had some success in not offending the man who runs it on her previous visit. I would recommend that you send both her and her current partner."

"I have—" Kaylin began.

"Private Neya will, however, be excused her classes."

Kaylin shut her mouth.

"Or rather," Sanabalis continued, "her classes under *my* tutelage. I was unable to shift the class schedule for the etiquette lessons, and it is vital that she not offend that teacher." He turned to Kaylin. "If anything is untoward or of particular interest in the Oracular Halls, you will return to the Palace to report to me."

Kaylin glanced at Marcus, who nodded stiffly, and managed not to growl. Given the state of his hair, much of which was standing on end, it was surprising. In a good way.

As if he could read that stray thought, the Sergeant added, "And you'll report back at the Halls after you've been debriefed at the Palace."

"But—"

"I don't care how late it is. From the sounds of it, the office will be operating under extended hours." He grimaced, which in Leontine involved more fur and ears than actual facial expression. "I'll mirror my wives and let them know."

She didn't envy him that call.

The appointment with the Oracular Halls was, ironically enough, one hour in the future. Sanabalis handed Kaylin a very official document with the unmistakable seal of the Eternal Emperor occupying the lower left quarter, where words weren't.

"Take the Imperial Carriage. Master Sabrai will be expecting you," he told her. "He did not, of course, have time to respond to or question the request, and he did not look terribly surprised to receive it, which is telling."

What it told Sanabalis, Kaylin wasn't sure; Sabrai *was* an oracle, after all, and they were supposed to be able to thresh glimpses of the future out of the broken dreams and visions of the Halls' many occupants. "What am I supposed to discuss as the official representative of the Imperial Court?"

"I'm sure you'll think of something. Given the lack of disaster during your last visit—in spite of your many attempts to contravene the rules for visitors to the Halls—I am willing to trust your discretion in this matter."

Someone cursed, loudly, in Leontine. Kaylin recognized the voice: it was Teela's.

"Well," she told Sanabalis, "Severn and I will head there immediately." She managed to make it out of the office as other voices, mostly Barrani, joined Teela's. Marcus had apparently already started the who-hates-the-duty-roster-most game, and while the Barrani in the office were Hawks first, they were still Barrani. Barrani in a foul mood were a very special version of Hell, which, if you were lucky, you survived intact.

Given the way the day had started, she didn't feel particularly lucky.

"It isn't cowardice," Severn said, with a wry grin, because he understood her sudden desire for punctuality. "It's common sense."

The Oracular Halls, as befitted any mystical institution that labored in service to the Eternal Emperor, was imposing. Constructed of stone in various layers that suggested a very sharp cliff face, it was surrounded on all sides by a fence that looked as if it would impale any careless bird that landed on it. The posts were grounded by about three feet of stone that was at least as solid as the walls it protected; it wasn't going to be blown over by a storm, a mage, or an angry Leontine.

A Dragon, on the other hand, wouldn't have too much trouble.

In the center of the east side of the fence, which fronted the wide streets that led up to and around it, was a guardhouse. It was late in the day, but the hour did not lead to *less* guards; there seemed to be more than the last time she'd visited at the side of Lord Sanabalis. She counted eight visible men, and those eight wore expensive, very heavy armor. They also carried swords.

Severn glanced at her as the carriage came to a halt, but said nothing.

The guards didn't meet the carriage itself; they waited until it disgorged its occupants. Said occupants walked—in much less heavy armor—to the wide, very closed, doors that led to the grounds. To Kaylin's surprise, the guards didn't demand her name or her business. Then again, the first thing she did was hand them the paper that Sanabalis had handed her.

A lot of clanking later, the doors opened.

"Master Sabrai is waiting," one of the men told her. "He will meet you when you enter."

The rules that governed visitors to the Oracular Halls were pretty simple: Don't speak to anyone. Don't touch anyone. Don't react if someone screams and runs away at the sight of you.

The first time Kaylin had come up against these rules they had been confusing right up until the moment she'd entered the building. She understood them better now, and wasn't surprised when she entered the Halls and saw a young girl teetering precariously on the winding steps that punctuated the foyer, singing to herself in a language that almost sounded like Elantran if you weren't trying to make any sense of it.

Master Sabrai was, as the guard had suggested, waiting to greet them. Kaylin tendered him a bow; Severn tendered him a perfect bow. He nodded to each in turn, and Kaylin remembered, belatedly, that all visitors to *these* Halls were called supplicants.

Master Sabrai looked every inch the noble. His hair was iron-gray, and his beard was so perfectly tended it might as well have been chiseled. He wore expensive clothing, and if his hands weren't entirely bejeweled, the two rings he did wear were very heavy gold with gems that suited that size.

He had the bearing and posture of a man who was used to being obeyed.

Once that would have bothered Kaylin. In truth, in another man, it would have set her teeth on edge now.

"Private Neya," Master Sabrai said. "Your companion?"

"Corporal Handred, also of the Hawks."

"You have apprised him of the rules for visitors?"

"I have." She grimaced, and added, "He's better at following rules than I generally am. He'll cause no trouble here."

"Good. I am afraid that your visit here was not unexpected, and it is for that reason that I am here. Sigrenne is at the moment attempting to quiet two of the children, one of whom you met on a previous visit."

"Everly? But he doesn't talk—"

"No. He doesn't. I was speaking of a young girl."

Kaylin remembered the child, although she couldn't remember the name. "She's the one who saw—" She stopped. "She's upset?"

"She had planted herself firmly in the door and would only be moved by force. She was not notably upset until her removal. I believe she was looking forward to reading you. Those were her exact words. She also," he added, glancing at the covered mirrors that adorned part of the foyer, "attempted to decorate. She seemed to be afraid of the mirrors, which is not, with that child, at all the usual case. Come, please. Let us go to the Supplicant room."

Sigrenne, still large and still intimidatingly matronly in exactly the same way as Marrin of the Foundling Hall—but without the attendant fur, fangs, and claws—was waiting for Master Sabrai in the Supplicant room. She was not on guard duty, so she didn't resemble an armor-plated warrior, unless you actually paid attention to her expression.

That expression softened—slightly—when she caught sight of Kaylin. "You're the Supplicant?" she asked.

"Well, sort of. One of the Supplicants, at any rate."

"How is Marrin?"

"Doing really well. I swear, someone rich left all their money to the Foundling Halls. I've never heard so few complaints from her."

"It's probably the new kit."

"You heard about him?"

"I saw him." Sigrenne's face creased in a smile that made her look, momentarily, friendly. "She brought him here when she came for her usual suspicious flyby."

Some of the orphans left on the steps of the Foundling Halls ended up with the Oracles. Marrin, as territorial as any Leontine, still considered them her responsibility in some ways, so she made sure they were eating, dressing, and behaving as well as one could expect in the Oracular Halls.

Master Sabrai raised a brow at Sigrenne, and then threw his hands in the air, a gesture entirely at odds with both his dress and his generally reserved manner.

Sigrenne took this as permission to speak about matters that concerned the Oracles more directly. "You're the only Supplicant we're entertaining today. And that would mean you're here by Imperial Dictate." The last two words were spoken with very chilly and suspicious capitals.

Kaylin stiffened. "The other Supplicants?"

"Meetings have been postponed."

"For how long?"

"Indefinitely. You can imagine how popular this has made Master Sabrai."

If the Oracles did, indeed, see into the future—or the past—they often spoke in a way that made no bloody sense to anyone who couldn't also see what they were seeing. Some of the Oracles didn't speak at all, although that was rarer. But since the Emperor himself consulted with the Oracular Halls from time to time—and funded them—many powerful men and women thought they could gain some advantage by visits to the Oracles.

Those visits weren't free, and they weren't cheap. Kaylin, who sneered at the charlatans in Elani on a weekly basis, found the so-called real thing just as troubling, but for different reasons. She was mostly certain that the Supplicants who came with their questions couldn't make heads or tails of the answers they actually got, and she couldn't figure out *why* they'd spend the money at all.

But people with that much money could be really, really difficult if disappointed. She glanced at Sabrai. "Why have the Halls been closed to visitors?" she asked, in the no-nonsense tone she'd adopted while on formal Hawk business.

"I would imagine," he replied, "that you have some suspicion, or Lord Sanabalis wouldn't have sent you."

"Is it like the last time?"

"No. Or at least, not yet."

She waited.

So did he. And since he was used to dealing with people who could forget a conversation before they'd even finished a sentence, he won. "What do you mean when you say not yet?"

"There were a number of disturbing incidents today."

"Were there any visual Oracles offered?"

"There were. They are not...unified, but there is a similarity of theme in some of them. It is not the visual that is of concern, and until we isolate the possible cause, we would prefer not to deal with the more trivial questions that cross this threshold. Why did the Emperor send you?"

"There were marked unusual disturbances in parts of the city today."

"Unusual?"

"You could call them miraculous, given that we were on Elani."

"How?"

"Some of the daily garbage that passes for magic on Elani actually seemed to work," she replied.

He was silent for a few moments, staring just to the left of Kaylin's shoulder.

"Master Sabrai," Sigrenne said firmly.

He blinked, and shook his head. "My pardon, Sigrenne. I was...thinking." His gaze became more focused, and his expression sharper. "And did incidents of this nature occur elsewhere?"

"Yes. I'm wondering, at this point, if they occurred here."

"No. Or at least not in a fashion that would appear un- usual to either myself or the caretakers. What question do you have for us?"

"I'll get to that in a minute," she replied, with a confidence she didn't feel, because she didn't actually *have* a question she wanted to hand to the Oracles. "Can you describe the un- usual verbal incidents you've been experiencing?"

He hesitated for just a moment, and then said, "Let me see the letter you're carrying." It wasn't what she was expect- ing, but she had no trouble handing it over. He, on the other hand, read it with care before he returned it.

"We have transcripts on hand," he finally said. "They are less...useful...than normal, but in the past two days, a pat- tern seems to be emerging. The pattern involves fear—of monsters, of armies, of invasions. And," he added, with a frown, "of doors."

She watched the glance that passed between Master Sabrai and Sigrenne.

"There's more."

Master Sabrai nodded and massaged the bridge of his nose. "Everly is painting."

CHAPTER 4

Everly wasn't painting. He was stretching a canvas. He worked, as he always did, in silence; the only noises he made were the usual grunts physical effort produced. The canvas, however, was taller than he was, and it was almost as wide as it was tall. Kaylin looked at it, and then turned to Master Sabrai.

"When did he start?"

"Approximately two hours ago. We keep wood, nails, and canvas in the corner of his gallery." The gallery in question was also the room he slept and lived in.

"He hasn't done any drawings at all?"

"No. Not one. Whatever it is he's painting, the image is strong enough—and large enough—that he feels compelled to begin immediately."

From tone alone, Kaylin understood that this was not a good thing in the opinion of Master Sabrai.

"It is seldom that his large canvases are used for trivial affairs, but it does happen. The very large image of Lord Sanabalis might be considered one such event."

That image, as Master Sabrai called it, occupied the wall directly opposite the door. It was the largest painting in the room, and as Kaylin wasn't much of an artist, one of the largest she'd seen. The Halls of Law did boast some sculpture and some tapestry, but it was mostly for show, and therefore tucked away where only important visitors could see it.

"He will work until he's done," Master Sabrai added. "Inform Lord Sanabalis when you report to him. He has always expressed a clear interest in Everly's work." He paused and then added, "If you wish to remain, Private, you may remain to observe."

She watched Everly for another fifteen minutes, and then said, "We'll come by tomorrow or the day after."

It was raining when they left the Oracular Halls. Master Sabrai was kind enough to hand them the transcriptions of the other possible Oracles, and he was foresightful enough to mention that anything discovered while under the auspices of the Imperial Court, however indirectly, could be legally discussed only with members of said Court.

Then again, foresight—for a definition of foresight that included garbled confusion and mute painters—was his specialty, so it didn't come as much of a surprise. The carriage was still waiting, the horses looked a little more bedraggled, and the streets had half emptied, which at this time of day— closing in on sunset—was about as much as you could hope for this side of the Ablayne.

But as they drove toward the Imperial Palace, the rain changed. Kaylin thought at first it had just gotten heavier, because visibility plummeted sharply as they turned a corner. This pleasant bit of mundane wrongheadedness didn't last, in part because the street around the carriage suddenly got a whole lot louder. People were shouting, screaming, and running for cover—not all at once, and not necessarily in that order.

She glanced at Severn; Severn had already unlatched the

door on his side of the carriage by the time the carriage rolled to a halt. The streets weren't empty enough to negotiate while people were running all over the place in blind panic.

Kaylin stepped into the rain and immediately understood why people were screaming.

It was raining blood.

Blood this watery and this red was usually warm; the rain was no exception. The clouds that were shedding it looked like normal green-gray storm clouds; there was no lightning and no thunder. Given the nature of what there was, on the other hand, the lack was probably a blessing in disguise.

It was the only one they were likely to get.

Kaylin headed straight for an actual store, tried hard not to drip on the bolts of cloth that seemed to take up most of its available space, and borrowed a mirror. She let Severn talk the establishment's occupants down from the ceiling, because frankly, he was better at it.

The mirror rippled, losing her reflection—and gaining, sadly, a sticky, wet palm print, which, given the cost of the mirror, was going to cause ructions—and Caitlin's face swam into view, solidifying after a few seconds. Her usually calm expression stiffened instantly, and her eyes widened.

"No, no—it's fine, Caitlin. The blood's not mine." Realizing that this would not, in fact, calm the office mother down, she added, "We're having a bit of trouble down on Lattimar road, near Gorran, and we need Swords out here. Now. Can you get Marcus?"

The image froze on silence. When it began to move again, Caitlin said, "You're not the only place that's having trouble, dear." At least she looked less shocked about the blood. Her image froze again. Kaylin waited until it started moving and said, "How large an area is this rain falling in?"

"A large one, dear. Sergeant Kassan is here."

Ironjaw's eyes were orange, and he was bristling. He was not, however, angry at Kaylin, and even if he were, she was well out of reach. "You said you were at Lattimar and Gorran?"

She nodded. "It was at Lattimar and Gorran that the rain went…strange, sir."

"Get your butt back outside and see whether or not there's a clear line of so-called strange."

"People are running around screaming in total panic."

Eyebrows rose; the tufts of Leontine ears were standing on end. "The Swords are already out in the streets, Private. It's covered. Now get out there and get me some *useful* information."

There was a clear line of so-called strange, a point at which blood gave way to water. It wasn't instant, but the blur between the two could be seen both on the ground and in the air itself. They had followed Lattimar past Gorran, heading toward the wall, and when they found the five yards of blur, Kaylin actually muttered what she hoped sounded like thanks to any possible deity who might be eavesdropping.

It was wet, and the rain was cold; the blood-rain wasn't, but in this case, Kaylin was willing to settle for cold. While the rain lasted, Kaylin and Severn followed its line, and marked the streets where clear water gave way to red fluid. Neither of them had the means to take more than a very small sample of this altered rain, if you didn't count what could be wrung out of their clothing.

They didn't manage to trace the periphery of the area, which seemed to be roughly circular in shape, before the rain petered out. It was perhaps the only time she could think of that she cursed lack of rain—and in two languages, at that.

But they'd circled a large enough part of the city, sans carriage, before they made their way back to the Halls.

There were guards at the doors, which wasn't unusual—even in the midnight hours, these doors were manned. But these guards had clearly not only seen the effects of the rain; they'd also been standing in it. They didn't even lift a brow at the reddened mess that was Kaylin's clothing. Nor did they engage in anything like small talk; they were silent in that grim, worried way, and they waved both Hawks through the unlocked doors.

The Aerie was as crowded as it was during training maneuvers, and Kaylin glimpsed familiar wings in the artificial light that radiated down from the heights. Aerian shadows looked a lot like giant fish against the stone floors, and she watched them—briefly—before Severn tapped her shoulder.

"Sorry," she told him, as she picked up her walking speed.

The office was not, as one would expect at this time of the day, empty. But the foul temper the orders from on high had caused had dissipated the way it always did when there was a distinct and obvious emergency. If people weren't thrilled to be there—and judging from some expressions, they weren't—they were awake and focused.

They were all also, almost to a man—and one shockingly matted Leontine—in various shades of red. Patches of dried blood lay across the office floor, making a visible track between desks and mirrors; it looked as if Marcus had gone berserk.

"Private!"

Speaking of berserk... Kaylin headed straight to the Sergeant's desk, and stood at attention, which was hard because he looked like a drowned cat. But huge. "Reporting in, Sir."

"Well?"

"We have some street coordinates. We gathered the information we could before the rain stopped."

He turned and shouted at the mirror closest to his desk, not that it mattered much; all of the office mirrors were alive. The window, sadly, was *also* alive, and it reminded people that it was time to leave, that they had to clock out, that they had to check the duty roster before they left, and that they should be careful in case of rain. Kaylin stared at it.

"Every ten minutes," Marcus growled. "And it has special commentary on the hour." He added, "Map, center city, low detail." The mirror rippled, as it often did, and the image that had occupied it before his curt command receded until it was part of a larger network of lines.

"Special commentary?" She walked over to the mirror, looked at her hands, and let them drop to the side.

"It has," he continued, ignoring the interruption, "stopped attempting to correct 'obscene' language." He gestured to the mirror, stepping out from behind his desk to do so.

Since even Mallory had never attempted to rein in what was politely referred to as local color, Kaylin grimaced. She hated to think that something could be more uptight than Mallory. "I'll wash up," she told him.

"Don't bother. No one else has." To drive this point home, he ran a claw lightly over the mirror's surface. It stopped at the intersection of Lattimar and Gorran. "You mirrored from here."

"A bit down the road, but yes, that was the general area."

Severn stepped up to the mirror, to the left of their Sergeant. "Magnify. Center Lattimar and Gorran." The mirror obeyed, and Kaylin found herself holding her breath as the buildings came into view. But they didn't leap out of the mirror's surface, and they didn't turn into something monstrous or strange, which was good because she needed to exhale.

Severn pinpointed the boundary—and the boundary's width. The point just beneath his finger began to glow; gold for the outer bounds, bright pink for the inner. When she snorted, he said, "I don't choose the colors."

Marcus growled, which was tired Leontine for Shut the Hell Up. Since it was aimed at Kaylin, Severn continued to call cross streets. The map would blur and shift, he'd add two points, and then repeat the process. When he was done, he called "Map" again, and this time the line of dots—in gold and pink—formed a pattern. To emphasize this, a line, in each color, ran between the points, terminating at the start and the finish of their trek.

It was a third of a circle, give or take some math.

Marcus actually purred. If you had very little experience with Leontines, it sounded a lot like growling. "Good work," he said. He barked an order, and the map began to extrapolate, from their coordinates, the perimeter of these two circles; the theoretical portions were in slightly dimmed colors, which in the case of the pink, was a distinct improvement.

"Good work, Private Neya, Corporal Handred." He turned and then bellowed at the rest of the office. "No, *don't* crowd around this mirror. Use the ones closest. Teela, Tain—you were out on the eastern edge. If what we've got is inaccurate, mark it. The same goes for the rest of you." He turned to her and added, "What did Lord Sanabalis say about your report?"

Kaylin froze. "We were on our way to the Palace when it started to rain blood, Sir."

"And you didn't head there before you reported in."

"No, sir. You said—"

"I *know* what I said, Private." He growled. Because Kaylin *did* have experience with Leontines she couldn't tell herself it was a purr. But he didn't bite her head off, and he didn't demand that she expose her throat, although she'd already started to lift her chin. "Did you get anything from the Halls?"

"Gibberish, mostly."

"Useful gibberish?"

"I'll tell you in a month or two."

He did chuckle at that. "I'll mirror Lord Sanabalis. You two, hop in a carriage."

"The yard's closed."

"I didn't tell you to use one of ours."

"Sir."

"The department," he added, "will reimburse you." Which meant he really was pleased.

Severn had enough money to pay the driver; Kaylin didn't.

Severn shook his head as they parked themselves on opposite benches. "You can't be paid so little that you're scrounging for meals for the last week or two of every month."

"Clearly, I can."

"I live in a larger apartment than you do, and I can afford to eat."

"My point. You're a Corporal. You get paid more."

"Some, yes, but I have the larger expense. I realize now is not the time for this discussion, but if you sat down and ran some numbers, you could plan out a month in advance."

"What do you mean?"

"Budget."

She snorted. "You need money to budget."

"You have money. At the start of the month."

"You've been to my place—it's not like I'm spending it on anything. It just doesn't last."

It wasn't exactly an old argument, but the few times they'd had it, it sounded the same, although admittedly sometimes there were more actual Leontine words thrown in.

He raised a brow, and then said, "Maybe you should cut back on the betting, given how often you lose."

This, on the other hand, was new. He might as well have told her to stop *speaking*. She opened her mouth and no words came out. That lasted for about a minute, and she gave up on the effort and turned to look out the window instead. It was dark now. There were puddles in small dips in the road, but their color wasn't immediately obvious.

Given a combination of Records, the rest of the Hawks, and their own trek into and out of warm, red rain, they now had a roughly circular area. Elani fit easily within its parameters; the Halls of Law and the Imperial Palace were close to the edges, albeit on opposite sides. The circle didn't encompass the Arcanum, for which they could all be momentarily thankful.

The carriage pulled up the road that led to the Palace; it was met before the courtyard. Kaylin jumped out; Severn followed. It was *not*, inasmuch as they existed, visiting hours for the Emperor or the Imperial Staff. On the other hand, like the Hawks, the Palace Guards had seen their share of blood-rain, and they didn't blink at the sight of either Kaylin or Severn.

Kaylin wished she'd had time to clean up, anyway.

"We're here to see Lord Sanabalis," she began.

"We know," was the curt reply. "He's been expecting you."

She wilted.

"For the past two hours."

Sanabalis was not, however, waiting at the front doors. A pinched-face, somewhat harried man was. He was obviously aware that there'd been some difficulty outdoors, because he didn't even blink at the state of their tabards. Or hair. Or, Kaylin thought, clasping her hands behind her back, their fingernails.

"You are Private Neya?"

She nodded.

"Corporal Handred?"

"I am."

"Good. Lord Sanabalis is waiting for both of you. Please follow me."

"We know the way——"

"He is not waiting for you in his usual chambers," was the clipped reply. "He is waiting for you in the Library."

It seemed a bit unfair that she could piss off both Sanabalis and the Arkon at the same damn time when she was only doing her job; she had no doubt whatsoever that the Arkon had *also* been waiting. For two hours. She glanced at Severn, whose expression had fallen into a state of grim which offered no comfort.

The man led them through the halls at a speed that was almost a run. Since the Library was not close to the entrance halls or any of the rooms that appeared to be used as semi-public meeting space, it took a while. But at this speed, Kaylin didn't have time to let the usual height of ceilings and random finery intimidate her. Nor did she have time to try to recognize the almost-familiar halls.

She did not, however, have any problems recognizing the Library doors. They were huge, and they were warded. They were also closed.

Any hope that their escort would open the door himself, sparing her the momentary pain of placing her own palm against the ward, was instantly dashed as he performed a curt, but mostly respectful, bow. "I will leave you both and return to my post."

"It's your turn," Kaylin told Severn when she was certain the man was far enough away he couldn't hear them.

He chuckled. Easy for him to do; the first time she'd touched the door, alarms had sounded—and she'd been expected. But he lifted his hand and placed it firmly across the ward. Blue light spread in an instant uniform layer across the face of both doors, twitching slightly.

"This is...different," he said.

They waited until the light faded, but the doors remained closed. Kaylin cursed under her breath, which meant she had to settle for the slightly inferior Elantran words she knew. She lifted a hand and pressed it firmly against the ward. This time, there was no loud noise, and she didn't *feel* as though she'd been struck by lightning. The same blue light covered the doors like a translucent, fitted sheet, fading slowly.

The doors, however, didn't open.

"I don't suppose we could tell them we've been trying to get in for two hours?"

"No. Here, help me push them open."

She put her shoulder into the motion; the doors were large and, more important, they were heavy.

The Arkon was standing about ten yards from the door, looking as if he'd swallowed whatever was left of the storm clouds that had caused so much panic. Beside him, less obviously annoyed—or at least less surprised—was Sanabalis.

"Sorry," Kaylin began.

"While I'm sure it would be amusing to hear your excuse this time," Sanabalis broke in, "it would probably take at least another half an hour."

She shut up.

"We've set up a mirror in the Library," he added, as the Arkon's eyes narrowed. "There are containment fields in the Library which are stronger than any other such enchantments to which we have immediate access. Sergeant Kassan has kindly sent some preliminary reports of your evening's work." He turned and began to walk away, by which Kaylin understood he meant them to follow.

The Arkon, however, said, "I have volunteered to cede some space in my collection for use by the Dragon Court, so that we might deal with the difficulties that this current crisis has caused. I will not regain that space until the crisis is deemed to be concluded."

Which would, Kaylin thought, explain some of his mood.

They passed through the largest of the Library rooms—in which the books were placed on shelves so high there were rolling ladders to accommodate people who were still about half a foot taller than Kaylin—and into another hall. This in turn led to a room with multiple doors nesting against one wall that seemed to be curved stone.

She had seen a similar room before, and wondered, briefly, if it was the same one; she didn't visit the Library unless she was pretty much ordered to do so. It was, for one, huge; it contained many sculptures and odds and ends—scrolls, armor bits, what was left of armor bits, odd weapons, carpets, clothing—much of which was delicate, and all of which the Arkon guarded zealously. For two, it was the Arkon's hoard, and while Kaylin didn't understand the subtleties of hoard law at all, there wasn't much that was subtle about the parts she did understand: touch my stuff and die was pretty straightforward.

There was, however, no stuff here, where *here* was a room that looked very familiar: rounded walls, a long, flat—and uncluttered—table in the room's center, around which were placed six chairs. None of those chairs were occupied.

But first appearances were deceiving. The Arkon was last into the room, and when he closed the door at their backs, it vanished into the wall. It left no seams and no trace of its previous existence at all. Kaylin looked at the curved gray

of walls; there were wall sconces set at regular intervals—
six—about six feet off the ground, but instead of torches,
they contained stones. There did not appear to be much *else*
in the room.

She glanced at Sanabalis.

Sanabalis walked over to the top of the unadorned table,
placed his palm across its surface, and spoke a few words. They
were High Barrani, and they were softly spoken.

The surface of the table rippled beneath his steady palm, as
if the wood grain had turned, in that instant, to water. The
table, Kaylin realized, was a mirror.

CHAPTER 5

It was more than a little disconcerting to watch the surface of the table re-form. Why it was worse than watching an actual mirror do it, Kaylin wasn't certain. "Why is the table a mirror?"

Sanabalis lifted his hand. "Almost any surface can be used, in theory. In practice, some surfaces dampen magic. They don't conduct it well. The table, or more particularly, the wood out of which it is constructed, would be considered one such surface.

"It therefore requires a great deal more power to initialize the contact between the table's surface and the whole of Imperial Records. It takes more power, in theory, to maintain that connection. It does not, however," he added, casting a glance toward the Arkon as if it were a protective charm, "destroy the table."

"The table is the Arkon's?"

"It is a very old table. If you look at the legs, you will find—"

"I would prefer," the Arkon broke in, in a chilly voice,

"that she not make the attempt. I would, in fact, insist that she not touch the mirror at all."

Kaylin lifted her hands. "Not touching," she told the Arkon.

This didn't improve his mood much.

"The table is taken from the wood of the West March," Sanabalis told her. "Some of the trees there are highly prized for their magical properties. They are also zealously guarded."

"Which is why you weren't speaking Dragon."

"Indeed. There are some things that we can do, and some things we can't. The wood itself resists much." He passed a palm over the table, and then said, again in High Barrani, "Map."

The image shifted into a very familiar-looking map; she'd last seen it in the office. The more elegant lines of the much larger city that Sanabalis had roared into being across a bank of windows were gone. The central image now displayed showed the two concentric circles that neatly enclosed one section of the city; all of the streets external to the outer circle were in pale gray lines.

"Sergeant Kassan said that the preliminary boundaries— and the conjectured extrapolation—were due to your efforts." He glanced up at her. "For this reason, we will overlook the hour of your arrival. I did, however, speak with Master Sabrai, and he was under the impression that you had information to report."

She nodded, frowning. "You spoke about a magical-potential leak," she said, looking at the streets contained by the inner circle.

"I did."

"Is it significant that it fades out in this pattern? The Palace, here—" she let her finger hover over the streets that surrounded the Palace without actually touching them "—and the Halls, here, are almost at the edge of the circle. But Elani—where we first noticed the incidents—is almost directly at its center.

"Is that position significant? Does your leak, or any leak of this nature, grow weaker as you move away from its core?" Her frown deepened. "And is it just me, or does it look awfully close to Evanton's shop?"

Sanabalis nodded, as if this were a classroom and she had just done well on the first of a series of grueling questions. "Our direct experience—"

"*Your* direct experience," the Arkon interjected.

"—is very limited. The difficulties in the Palace to date have been confined to irregularities in Records. And one difficulty elsewhere, which was not disastrous and cannot be spoken about. The only known difficulty the Halls of Law have experienced appears to involve a window."

"A talking bloody window that gets offended by 'curse' words."

"That was not how it was described. I believe your explanation is more concise."

"The rain hit everyone."

"It did. I have taken the liberty of sending out a small team of Imperial mages. They are in Elani now."

"What are they looking for?"

"The source of the leak," he replied.

"Why mages? If magic is amplified in a bad way—"

"Mages have a much more rigid intellectual structure for thinking about the use of magic. Without solid control and concentration, they cannot use it. With solid control and concentration, and with an awareness of the potential growth, they can confine what they *do* use to the correct parameters. I believe that mages—not Arcanists—will have more luck at avoiding careless invocation or unusual wish fulfillment than the undereducated."

"Meaning people like me."

He didn't bother to answer. "What occurred at the Oracular Halls?"

"I was taken to see Everly," she replied. "He was stretching canvas. It was not a *small* one."

"I...see."

"I'll check in again tomorrow or the day after, depending on what Marcus has me doing."

"Private Neya," the Arkon said quietly. Very quietly. But he was the Arkon; it carried anyway.

She gave him her immediate—and respectful—attention. "Arkon."

"When you visit Everly, take Lord Sanabalis with you."

Sanabalis bowed, and held that bow while the Arkon swept out of the room. He then rose. "At times like this," he told Kaylin, with a grimace, "I miss the presence of Lord Tiamaris. The Arkon, like many of the eldest and wisest of *any* race, has a store of impatience he reserves for the young, and if it is spent on the young, it is exhausted."

"And you're now young?"

"Compared to the rest of the Dragon Court, no. Compared to the Arkon, yes. I will meet you in the morning— first thing in the morning—at the Halls of Law."

"When do you think the mages of the Imperium will make their report?"

"As soon as they either have definitive information, or one of them manages to commit suicide in a remarkable and unusual fashion."

It was late enough that Kaylin decided to go straight home, because first thing in the morning by Dragon definition skirted the edge of dawn. Probably from the wrong side. The streets between the Palace and her apartment were decidedly empty for this time of night; it reminded her of living in the fiefs, although there were no Ferals. The rain had gone on for long enough, and had caused—she assumed—enough panic that no one wanted to be exposed to sky.

Fair enough. She didn't particularly care for a repeat, either.

But when she made her way up the stairs and through her door, she saw her mirror flashing. She had bread and cheese and meat in the basket that Severn had given her, and if she disliked magic—and she did—it was still damn useful. The bread wasn't stale enough to cut herself on, and the cheese hadn't dried out. Nor was the meat likely to be sour enough to poison her. She grabbed all of those, and headed to the mirror; it was her personal mirror, after all, and no one could dress her down for leaving fingerprints on it.

She lost most of her appetite when the screen's image solidified and the familiar face of Marya took up most of the frame. Marya was as close to head of the midwives' guild as made no difference, and she looked haggard. The circles under her eyes—which were often there because her sleep hours were worse than Kaylin's—had almost overtaken her cheekbones.

She wasn't speaking; the mirror wasn't active; this was just a placeholder to indicate she'd tried to reach Kaylin earlier. Kaylin, around a mouthful of meat, muttered Marya's name. The mirror twitched twice, and took its sweet time connecting, but it finally did.

Marya's face swam into view.

"Kaylin!" Marya, who was probably in her sixties although it wasn't safe to ask her actual age, looked horrified.

The midwives' guild was not, Kaylin suddenly remembered, within the circle in which rain had turned to blood.

She cursed, briefly and quietly, just before she swallowed the overly ambitious mouthful she'd just bitten off. "I'm sorry, Marya," she said quickly. "It's not what it looks like. I'm not bleeding, I wasn't in a fight for my life, and I didn't kill anyone else."

Marya's expression shifted from pale horror to something almost as bad.

"You need me to go somewhere." It wasn't a question.

"I need—I'm not sure what we need. But, Kaylin—" she shuddered "—things are—things are going wrong with some of the births in a way we've never seen. And one or two pregnancies. I—"

"You want me there? Or do you want to give me an address?"

Marya bit her lip. Marya *never* did something as impractical and quavering as biting her lip. Kaylin lost her appetite.

"Come here," the midwife finally said. "I've got the other addresses, and…and I don't want to send you out there for nothing, but I don't— Just, come here."

It didn't rain. The sky was the kind of clear that threatens rain, but doesn't quite deliver. That was about as much as Kaylin noted on her run to the midwives' guild. She was aware that it might be a long damn night, and she had forced herself to eat, which was never much fun when anxiety made one's stomach actively revolt. She also changed her clothing, peeling herself out of things that were way more sticky than they should have been. She wouldn't have bothered, given Marya's tone and expression—but if she was sent out to help anyone, showing up covered in dried blood wasn't likely to make her job any easier.

She made it to the guild on foot, glancing briefly at the

visible moon and wondering how much it had shifted its position. The guild's doors were open. Lights were on, and could be seen through the slightly opaque windows.

As a building, the guildhall was not terribly impressive; it didn't boast the size—or the expensive stairs, doors, and decorative bits that stuck out at all levels—of something like the merchants' guild. It also didn't boast the same prime real estate, but at the moment it was situated outside of the Circle From Hell, closer to the Ablayne, on Kirri street. The street was one of the oldest of the Imperial streets, and the name on the very few signs that marked it was actually about ten paragraphs longer than Kirri, which is why it deserved a diminutive.

Kaylin hurried in.

Marya was in the office, such as it was. She had a large desk—it was half again as large as Marcus's—but there were no other desks in the room. There were cupboards, and a long counter that ran the length of the wall opposite the window, breaking only for the door. There were two standing shelves as well, and these were the repository of a number of books, but they also held bottles, jars, and assorted dried herbs. At least that's what Kaylin assumed they were. She recognized some of them; bitterroot for fever, worry-not to prevent pregnancy; most of them she didn't know.

There were three mirrors in the room, none of them full-length; one sat on the right-hand side of Marya's desk, its lion claw iron legs ensuring that nothing short of serious effort would knock it over. Marya appeared to be seriously considering it. She looked up as Kaylin entered.

Her first words reassured Kaylin.

"There've been no deaths. If it had been—if we'd really

needed you, we'd've been able to find you. Your Sergeant's been good about that, I admit it. I didn't expect it, but—he's been good."

Kaylin exhaled, because she'd been holding her breath and it was well past stale. "Okay," she said. "No emergencies."

"There were two births. One was a first child, but in either case the delivery was not considered a terrible risk. I had Mellan attend the first birth."

Kaylin nodded. It made sense; Mellan was one of the younger midwives, but she'd been the midwife in charge at a number of births for the past three months.

"The baby was born. A boy. He was healthy." She hesitated, and then said, "He had three eyes."

"Pardon?"

"Three eyes. They were infant eyes in every other respect, but he has an eye in the center of his forehead just above the bridge of his nose."

"Where was the birth?" Kaylin asked quietly. "What was the address?"

"Sauvern, near Bitton."

The child had been born within the confines of the circle.

The rain of blood had been bad; the Swords were probably still out in the streets enforcing a certain rationality upon people who'd been caught in the torrent. A demonstrably secret, ongoing investigation into one of the most powerful humans in the city had been totally compromised by a cheap, charlatan fortune-teller.

But with this new bit of information, it was suddenly, completely damn serious. "How were the parents?"

"The parents, thank the gods, are followers of Iravatari."

When Kaylin failed to nod as if the sentence seemed relevant, Marya rolled her eyes. "The goddess of wisdom and enlightenment? Tall, robed lady?"

"Sorry."

"Never mind. Iravatari *has* three eyes. It was a shock to the parents, yes—and I think a shock to young Mellan—but when they recovered, they were not unhappy."

Kaylin nodded.

"The second birth was more problematic."

And tensed. "How?"

"The second birth was attended by Helen. You know Helen?"

Kaylin frowned for just a minute, and then nodded. "Older woman, this tall, brown eyes, hair down to her knees?"

"She doesn't wear her hair down when she's working," was the severe reply. "But yes, that would be Helen. She attended the second birth. The second birth was a first child, a girl."

"The child was also…different?"

"The child, at two minutes out of her mother's womb, could speak."

"Speak?"

"Yes. In complete sentences. There may well be a god of speech, but in this *particular* case, the parents were *not* thrilled. I believe they were confused, but the child's grandmother insisted that the baby had been possessed by evil spirits. She did not attempt to harm the infant—"

"Not if Helen was there, she didn't."

"—but she insisted that the child be exorcised. Formally. The child had other ideas, and some argument ensued."

"Where is the child now?"

"Helen is still there. The grandmother, however, is not. The mother is…not happy. The father is confused."

"Tell me where this child was born," Kaylin said, in a tone

of voice that indicated she had a good idea. Marya's answer confirmed her suspicions. "Can I use your mirror?" she asked, although she'd already walked behind the desk and tapped it with her palm.

"Yes, but use it *quickly*. Given the incidents tonight, I want an entirely open channel."

Kaylin nodded. She waited for the mirror to blur, and when the image shifted from reflection to communication, she saw that Marcus was, as she suspected he would be, still in the office. So was Caitlin. So, she thought, were a number of Hawks, although it looked like they were mostly Barrani. The Barrani didn't exactly *need* sleep.

"Marcus—"

"Where the hell are you?"

"Midwives' guild."

"You went to the Palace?"

"Yes. And I'm due in at the office first thing to head back to the Oracles' Hall. With Sanabalis."

"First thing?"

"Yes. I'm considering skipping sleep entirely." She caught Caitlin's expression, and added, "Just joking. But I need you to send something across to *this* mirror, now."

Marcus looked as tired and frazzled as Kaylin felt, and he bared his fangs at the tone of her voice. But that was all he did; he didn't even give her a knee-jerk refusal. Instead, he said, "Please don't tell me that this is affecting births."

"If you don't want to hear it, I'll write it up when I make my report."

"I'll have to read that."

"Eventually." She glanced pointedly at the piles that could be seen teetering on his desk in the distance. "I need Marya to have a map, so she'll have a good idea of where things are likely to—to go bad."

"Done. It is not to be transmitted beyond the guild's mirror."

Marya, who had wedged herself into the frame's view beside Kaylin, nodded, and the mirror instantly blanked in that way that implied something more pleasant than angry Leontine face was about to appear. What did appear was the city map, complete with two circles. "Make the inner circle brighter," Kaylin told the mirror.

The mirror complied.

Reaching out, she hit the two places on the map where the unusual births had occurred. "Mark and record."

"What is the circle?" Marya asked softly.

"No one's certain. You were probably busy enough to miss the whole rain of blood thing. I wasn't," she added.

"That's why you looked as if—"

"I'd fallen into an abattoir? Yeah. It caused a lot of panic, no surprise. The Swords are still patrolling the streets within this boundary. Things have happened within the boundary that imply that there's some kind of—of—wild magic." Kaylin, who didn't entirely understand the concept of a "potential leak" was not up to explaining it to anyone else.

"Is it going to grow?"

The thought had occurred to Kaylin. "I don't know. We know it's been in place for at least a day. We have no idea how large the area was when the…unusual disturbances started. We wouldn't actually know for certain how large the circle was if it weren't for the rain, so we're grateful for it. The Swords, on the other hand, have no reason for gratitude, and I imagine they aren't."

She moved away from the mirror to give Marya some space to actually sit down; Marya did, pulling a ledger from a desk drawer and flipping it open. "How many women are going to give birth in that circle within the next, say, two weeks?"

"I'm looking at the next four weeks at the moment," Marya replied, without looking up. She flipped back and forth between pages, made notes, and added her own square fingerprints to the map's image, pausing to magnify streets where it became necessary. "Within four weeks," she finally said, "this is what we've got."

Not every pregnant woman came to the guildhall, but most did; the guildhall received its share of donations, and it could afford to do work for next-to-nothing. "Twelve?"

"Ten. You're counting the two you marked."

"Good. Can you get them out of there?"

Marya lifted the ledger. "Ahead of you there. Do you think this magic has affected the actual pregnancy, or does it just manifest itself at birth?"

"I honestly don't know, but we've got nothing to lose by relocating them. If it's the pregnancy, they're still in the same predicament. If it's the birth, they're safe."

"My thinking, as well." She looked tired. "Will you be home if something goes wrong?"

"Yes. But the first thing I do in the morning is meet with a Dragon Lord."

"Your morning?"

"No, sadly. The real morning. We'll be leaving the Halls of Law immediately, and heading out to the Oracles. If anything comes up—anything at all—mirror there."

To say that she was tired when the Halls of Law appeared around the corner would have been so inaccurate she didn't bother. She made one stop on her jog to the Halls, and came away with three stuffed buns from a baker's stall. That, and enough change to throw into a wishing well without worrying about lost money.

She'd had the usual restless sleep that occurs between the hours of way-too-damn-late and dawn. Because she knew that Sanabalis would be seriously pissed off if she was late, the mirror's chime actually woke her.

Sanabalis was waiting in the office. She was bleary-eyed enough that she didn't actually note who was on door duty.

"Kaylin?" Caitlin said from her desk nearest the office doors. "Were you at the guild last night?"

Kaylin nodded.

Clearly, it was the wrong kind of nod. "There were problems?"

"Yes." She headed straight for Marcus's desk, and only in part because Sanabalis was seated, more or less quietly, in front of it. The Dragon Lord looked up as she came to stand just in front of him.

"Sergeant."

Marcus had seen her enter the office. "What happened last night?"

"We had two births. One baby born with three eyes. One born speaking. In full sentences."

"None born with two heads?" Sanabalis asked. She didn't appreciate his sense of humor and turned to tell him as much, but when she caught sight of his expression, she bit back the unfortunate words just before they could leave her mouth.

"Why are you asking? What have you found?"

"I found nothing that might point in that direction," he replied. "The Arkon, however, has spent the entirety of the evening poring over some of his private collection, and he extracted some information that might be of use to us."

"Two-headed babies?"

"Yes. They were not, however, human, if that's any comfort."

"Not really." She paused. "What were they?"

"Barrani."

"What happened to them? No, never mind. I really don't want to know." She turned back to her Sergeant. "Marya's moving any of the women who are pregnant and might go into labor. She can only move the ones she knows about."

He nodded. "You have an appointment with the Oracles."

"Could you—"

"I'll mirror Marrin and let her know about the possibility of abandoned newborns."

She exhaled. "Thanks. I'd mirror her myself but—"

"Go."

When the carriage—which, as promised, was the usual heavy, Imperial model—was in motion, Kaylin leaned back and closed her eyes. "When were the two-headed babies born?"

"The exact date is not known."

"Meaning the Arkon doesn't know it, or it's not known by the Barrani, either?"

Sanabalis raised a brow.

"Forget I asked. Why did he think it was relevant? He doesn't even know about the midwives' guild report yet."

"No. He was looking for reports of anomalous and unusual manifestations of magic in concentrated geographical areas. Leaving out the usual anomalies that might occur in or around what is now the heart of the fiefs, and discounting transformations that could be directly traced to shadow storms, he found two possible events."

She didn't like the way he said the last word. "Events?"

"The perturbations continued for a small period of time—

the exact period is uncertain, but it is not more than a month, and not less than three days."

"What happened to end them?"

"Whatever buildup of magical potential had occurred was discharged."

"Sanabalis, what *happened?*"

"The conjecture at the moment, and it is simple conjecture— we do not have enough physical evidence to make a definitive statement—indicates one of two possibilities."

If he had been human, he would have been dragging his answer out on purpose, to be irritating. He was a Dragon. Like the Barrani, they *had* forever, and could usually be counted on to make someone who didn't, really feel it. She watched the streets crawl by, glancing up at the sky to see if it looked as if there might be something as ominous as rain in the near future. The sky, however, was clear. And pink.

"The two possibilities? Before we reach the Oracular Halls?"

"Very well. The *reason* we have so little information about a possible event of this nature is because anything within a ten-mile radius—or possibly larger—was destroyed. It could not have been *instantly* destroyed, or there would be no information at all."

She stared at him. "You think the magical buildup destroyed an area that size *almost* instantly?"

He pinched the bridge of his nose. "If you would like an immediate answer—not precisely. If you would, however, like the longer and more thoughtful answer I was *attempting* to give, you will *cease* your interruptions."

She tried. It lasted about ten buildings. "Not precisely?"

"The intensity of the effect seems to be confined. We are attempting to monitor its spread—and I will say that the rain itself was a blessing, however it started, in that regard—and we have begun to draw up plans to evacuate much of the central area. For obvious reasons, neither the Palace nor the Halls will be evacuated. There are also other buildings that we cannot afford to empty."

"What was the second possibility?"

"The second possibility does not—exactly—negate the first. But... In the wake of one of these geographically confined events, the first evidence of your ancestors was found."

CHAPTER 6

"P-pardon?"

"Humans are not native to this world, as I believe we've mentioned before."

"But—" She stopped talking for a few minutes. It wasn't hard; there were too many words trying to get out the door at the same time, and the collision made her seem speechless. She dealt with the mess as quickly as possible.

He raised a brow. "If you have some disagreement to offer, attempt to apply both rationality and historicity." His lips curved in a grin, and he added, "I will live forever. If you require some tutoring and study in either of these, I can be persuaded to wait."

"Can I just mention that the *history* of humans offered in class—such as it was—involved the Caste Courts, their separate laws, and their role in the politics of the Empire? Nowhere, in any lesson, was Origin of Species covered. I would have been interested in *that*."

"And not in the rest?"

"The rest was relevant. If you go back and look at my transcripts, I passed that part."

"Indeed," he replied, with a nod to Dragon memory.

"However, you passed in a fashion that was less than laud-able." He lifted a hand before she could speak again. "Hu-mans are not native to our world. If you need proof of that, you have only to examine what you know of species that were created in, and of, the world itself.

"It is why the Arkon strongly believes in the overlapping world theory. The spontaneous creation of an entire species—or three—is otherwise lacking in credibility. Not when they are, to all intents and purposes, sentient."

Since this was about as complimentary as the Immortals generally condescended to be when discussing the merely mortal, Kaylin managed to stay silent.

"There are one or two scholars who disagree with this commonly held view," he added. "And if you wish to peruse their papers, the Arkon can point them out to you. They are in the normal section of the Library, in which it is much, much more difficult to earn his ire."

His abuse of the word *commonly* was about as bad as Kay-lin's abuse of the word *punctual*.

"So...humans arrived here, heralded by freak storms and two-headed Barrani babies."

"That is not exactly what I said, but it will do."

"How did they arrive?"

"That," he replied, "is the question. We have no solid in-formation from that period. It was not recent, and much of the information we had was lost."

"Lost?"

"Lost," he replied, in a tone of voice that approximated the sound of a very heavy door slamming. "If the Arkon's conjecture—and it is a tentative conjecture—proves true, we will have an answer."

"And you expect we'll also have a large crater in the mid-dle of the city."

"That is, unfortunately, one of our fears, yes. The Emperor has already called an emergency meeting with the Lord of Swords and the Lord of Hawks. I believe the Lord of Wolves is also involved, but in an advisory capacity."

It made sense; evacuating even a small building in times of emergency generally required the Swords. Evacuating blocks and blocks of small buildings—many of them somewhat upscale—would probably require an army. "You can't move Evanton," she said.

"No. The Keeper, however, is likely to survive whatever occurs. He is not our concern."

She nodded. "If it's close to where he is, though, could he do something to *stop* it?"

"If it is necessary, perhaps."

"You don't think so."

"No. And it is my belief that it would pose a risk to the Garden should he try."

"Making the cure more deadly than the disease." She glanced out of the window as the carriage turned up the drive to the Halls. The guards that stopped the carriage stopped it for a matter of seconds; Sanabalis was a recognized visitor, and even had he not been, the carriage was marked all over with signs of Imperial ownership. "I don't suppose the human Caste Hall has any useful libraries?"

"Compared to the Imperial ones? No. And I would thank you not to repeat that question in the Arkon's hearing." The carriage pulled to a stop very close to the guarded doors. "Come. Master Sabrai is expecting us."

Master Sabrai was, in fact, waiting at the doors. He looked, at first glance, as if he'd gotten about as much sleep as Kaylin; she wondered what was keeping his eyes open. Hers were now running on the certainty of impending doom. He executed an enviable, perfect bow as Sanabalis crossed the threshold. "Lord Sanabalis."

"Master Sabrai," the Dragon replied, returning the bow with a nod. He waited until Master Sabrai had straightened out to as much of his full height as a bleary-eyed, clearly exhausted man could attain before he added, "The evening was eventful?"

"Let us just say," Master Sabrai replied, with a wince, "that your inquiries were not untimely."

"How bad was it?"

"It has not—yet—reached the proportions of the previous incident. Not all of our Oracles are almost sharing the same dreams or visions, and we have not—yet—reached the point where those who can live off grounds are also simultaneously entering a vision state."

"You expect it." Flat words, no question in them.

"If last night was any indication, Lord Sanabalis, yes. I do. Some preparations are being made. They are being handled by Sigrenne and her assistant. I have some written reports, mostly taken by Sigrenne and two of the other attendants. I was...otherwise occupied or I would have seen to it myself."

Sanabalis grimaced, a clear indication that he did not consider Sigrenne's transcription to be of the highest quality. "Have you examined them?"

"I have not had the chance to examine all of them, no. If you are looking for an estimate of convergence, I cannot give you one that would meet the standards of the Oracular Halls."

"What estimate would you hazard, if you were not held to those standards?"

It was clearly the question that Sabrai had been both expecting and dreading. "Everly did not sleep at all last night. He has been painting like a possessed man."

"How serious an attempt did you make to stop him?"

"It's only the first day," was the evasive reply. "It is not, yet, a matter of safety. He will eat, if food is provided, and he drinks when water is provided. But he does not otherwise interact with anything but the painting."

"Not a good sign," the Dragon Lord said softly. He glanced at Kaylin.

"No."

"What is his subject?"

"That, I believe, you will have to see for yourself," was the quiet reply. "I cannot describe it."

"It's not, in your opinion, trivial?" Kaylin asked, speaking for the first time.

"No, sadly, it is not."

Everly's room smelled of paint; it was the first thing Kaylin noticed when the door was open, in large part because she wasn't as tall as either Sabrai or Sanabalis and she couldn't actually see past their bulk into the gallery that served as the boy's room. They stood in the door for that little bit too long before finally moving through it and out of her way.

The canvas that Everly had been stretching with such focus now sat on a large set of wooden legs. The back of the painting, as usual, faced the door, obscuring the artist himself; the windows at Everly's back provided the light by which he was, in theory, working. Kaylin wished, for a moment, that the office could be more like this; usually work was punctuated with little things like obscenities, gossip, and the damned window, which never, ever, shut up.

Master Sabrai approached the side of the painting, and disappeared behind its edge; Sanabalis, after a pause, did the same. Five minutes of silence later, Kaylin repented: she had heard funerals which were more lively. She didn't wait for an invitation; she also took a small detour around the edge of

Everly's canvas, but chose the opposite side. The small, flat table that held his palette, paints, brushes, various cloths, and a box of charcoal sticks of varying widths and lengths happened to be on that side; she almost ran into it, and managed to dodge collision at the last second.

Everly had clearly been working without stop. The edges of the canvas were almost blank; some sketching had been done, and what looked like flat representations of nearly familiar buildings rose in black and gray against a white sky, like inverted ghosts. No obvious signs or flags marked those buildings; they were clearly abstracted from an Elantran street, but Kaylin, who was more than passingly familiar with most of them, couldn't immediately place which one.

And placement was made urgent by what Everly *had* painted.

A cloud made of night hovered above cobbled stones that were clearly colored by the sun at its height. Its edges were blurred and indistinct, but this wasn't just smudging of paint or color sketching. Stars could be seen, and the livid glow of something that seemed either red moon or blood sun hung close to the blurred edge itself. The cloud was contained in what seemed almost a garish, ornate door frame, absent a door.

He had worked on that odd, messy frame, in which daytime colors overlapped in startling contrast with night colors; he had taken care to paint stars and a haze of mist that twisted, like an incongruously delicate veil, across a foreign sky. He had taken care to paint its height, and seeing that, she almost flinched; it was as tall as some of the unpainted buildings, and if it was in any perspective at all, it swallowed the road.

But at its center was white space. He had done no sketching there.

Everly, oblivious to his audience, continued to work. He

was using the darker spectrum of his palette, applying paint here and there as carelessly as Kaylin applied words, but achieving the effortless effect of a slowly coalescing reality that Kaylin's careless words couldn't.

"Given the speed at which he's painted this," Kaylin said quietly, "we'll have some idea of what's going to emerge tomorrow. Or later tonight."

"It is not...small, if the area he's left is indeed something that emerges and not further scenery."

"It's not really the center we need, anyway."

Sanabalis raised a brow.

She pointed to the buildings that lined either side of the street in their frustrating lack of detail. "We need to know where—roughly—this vision takes place."

"It is *not* a concrete representation of place, Private," Master Sabrai said curtly. "That is not the way Oracles work."

"I've been the subject of one of his Oracles," she replied, just as curtly. "And I think the clues will be there if we can read 'em. We need them."

Sanabalis cleared his throat. Loudly. The sound was enough to cause Everly to lift his head for a few seconds as if he were testing the air. Speech, however, failed to hold his attention, and he went back to his quick, light movements. "Master Sabrai *is* correct in this, Private. What he paints is not predictive in the sense you hope for. You cannot direct him. What he finishes, he finishes."

But she looked at the space that he had not yet started to touch, and she felt cold, although she was standing in sunlight. "Tonight," she told Sanabalis quietly.

"I concur. I do not think, however, that it will be necessary to stand here for the entire eight hours while he paints. We now have other things to examine." He turned to Master Sabrai. "If you will deliver the transcripts of the dreams that interrupted the Halls last eve, we will begin to attempt to make some overarching sense of the impending difficulty. Thank you," he added, in a more clipped tone.

Master Sabrai shook his head as if to clear it. "As you say, Lord Sanabalis. If you will return to my office, I will give you what I've managed to transcribe."

"I am willing to deal with Sigrenne's less than perfect penmanship."

Not reminding Sanabalis of this definitive statement was difficult, because it would sound smug; Sigrenne's hand was neither neat nor precise, and Sanabalis had clearly not spent as much time deciphering human scribbles as Kaylin had. Most of the Hawks were not in the running for world's best penman.

Sanabalis sat in the carriage opposite Kaylin; smoke drifted from his nostrils and the corner of his lips, and his eyes were a decided shade of orange. Given the way he glared at the pile of papers—and the paper was by no means uniform in size or shape, which made it ungainly—Kaylin was half-surprised they hadn't gone up in that smoke.

Every so often he glared over the top of a curling fold. At least one session was partially illegible because either someone with wet hands had picked it up, or it had been put down, briefly, in water. Or worse.

To prevent Kaylin from being too amused, Sanabalis handed her the occasional bit he couldn't read. She took them with gratitude, since it was better than doing nothing, and safer than mocking a Dragon Lord. Especially given the lack of sleep. Kaylin, reading the various notes, cringed. She had an easier time interpreting Sigrenne's scrawl, but because she had no context, it was hard to guess what the words she *couldn't* read meant.

But she understood enough. In many of these dreams, there were visitors. Some were monsters. Some were ghosts. Some were—she thought the words were *stray kittens,* which caused some head scratching.

"How the hell does Sigrenne know that it's an Oracle and not a normal dream?" she muttered.

"She probably doesn't," was the curt reply. "Which means she has to take as many notes as possible. It isn't all Sigrenne's writing. Some of it is probably Notann's. The one that looks like a series of ink blots is almost certainly Weller's. When the Oracles dream like this, one person is not going to get to all of them in time. I have another door-locker."

She glanced across the carriage. "No, that's the same one. That's Tylia. Her name's up in the left corner." She caught a few words, and added, "but that's more detailed than she was. There's a door but no walls. Oh."

"Oh?"

"Well, the lack of walls means the sky is falling, and Tylia can't find a roof to hide under. See, there. That lines up with Everly's painting."

"Possibly. This is merely our attempt to understand why, and perhaps where, some future difficulty must be intercepted. I will let you out at your own Halls. I would take you to the Palace, but the Arkon dislikes interruption and you are not the quietest of visitors. You possibly also have a job, or several, to do."

The guards at either set of doors were tense enough that the usual good-natured mockery failed to occur. Kaylin missed it.

The office wasn't quiet. The window wasn't impressed; it was hard to tell which was louder. Marcus was bristling, which, given the state of emergency, was expected. Caitlin was quiet and grim. Not a single groundhawk could be seen in the office, not even Severn.

"Neya!" Marcus shouted.

She walked past the duty roster, glanced at it, and shuddered. The fact that she could read it at all, given that there were now more changes than there had been original postings, was due to thirteen years of experience with the way Marcus's writing was affected by his moods. One thing was clear: all of the Hawks were out on patrol, and it was a very tight patrol: it centered in the section of city that featured Elani at its core.

"The Swords," Marcus told her, as she approached his desk, "have been ordered to begin evacuation." He stabbed a piece of paper on his desk. It was the map of the streets that lay within the two circles. There were holes at the corners of a square area within the circle itself. "They're starting at Strathanne, between Highpost and Delbaranne. They're clearing straight through to Lattimar."

She opened her mouth in order to let at least one question out; he flexed his claws. It was one of his more serious versions of *shut up*. He did, however, answer the question. "While you were out, Lord Diarmat of the Dragon Court mirrored. The Imperial Order of Mages tendered the report from their initial exploratory investigation."

"Good or bad?"

"If you're a member of the Imperial Order's scouting forces, bad."

She closed her eyes. "How many did they lose?"

"One death. Three casualties."

His tone of voice made death seem like the better deal. She schooled her expression. "Did they transmit the Imperial Records information here?"

"No. Lord Diarmat didn't feel it was necessary, and frankly, it is *not* my problem. I don't need to worry about mages right now. The Arcanists are, in theory, the Swords' problem. Teela has gone, by way of the Barrani High Halls, to deliver the news."

"What news?"

"We're sealing off the portion of the city the Swords are now evacuating. We've set up roadblocks and guards on all routes in and out. Evacuation should take three days at the outside. Teela is at the Halls. Tain and the rest of our crew are spread out among the Swords."

The Swords were going to love *that*.

"Why?"

"Because the Arcanists are now interested, and one or two of them are causing the Swords some difficulties. While I'd like to resolve it by jailing them," he said in a tone of voice that made jail and death synonymous, "we are understaffed. If it were up to the Lord of Swords, we'd be extending the blockade to the full perimeter of the outer circle."

"We can't," she said, voice flat.

"Funny, that's what I told him. The perimeter would include the Halls and the Palace. The Emperor declined the Swordlord's request, and this is the compromise. I can see why he doesn't like it. We can keep the Arcanists out of this area. We have no hope of keeping them out of the circle. The Emperor had implied that he'd just keep them locked in their damn tower."

"On what charges?"

"Not my problem."

She snorted. It would be, if they tried. Still, the Arcanists would be vastly less likely to cause trouble for Barrani Hawks, and if they were babysitting the Swords, the roadblock would probably not spontaneously—and conveniently—combust. Kaylin nodded grimly. "Where do you want me?"

"You're up on the roster."

She bit her lip; it prevented suicidal words from emerging. "I'll check now," she told him. She was relatively certain it wouldn't take too damn long to find her name in the hideous mess of ink and pencil marks.

"Good. Go." He paused, and then added, "You might want to remove your bracer and toss it somewhere."

She'd found her name. It was beside Severn's, and was, in fact, their regular Elani beat. "You're sure?"

"We have Imperial Permission," the Leontine replied, and she caught the brief flash of teeth that was their version of black humor. "Lord Diarmat looked like he'd just found out he'd been put on a vegetarian diet when he delivered it."

Leontines, in theory, held Dragons in high regard. It was no wonder that fact had come as a huge surprise to Kaylin, because Marcus did not. "Lord Diarmat was difficult?" she asked.

"Stop gabbing, and get moving."

Kaylin had once or twice in her seven years with the Hawks—admittedly most of them as unofficial mascot—seen roadblocks and quarantines within Elantra. They were mostly put in place to contain outbreaks of summer wasting sicknesses, but not always. Occasionally the Arcanists on the Wolf hit list didn't bother to make a break for the outer walls or the fiefs; they headed into extremely crowded areas and attempted to hold out by using sorcery, with whole city blocks as hostages.

This was like the latter case, except there were no Arcanists you could kill to end the threat.

The roadblock was going up when she slid through. On this side of the square, the Arcanists wouldn't be a problem, so there were no Hawks here. She nodded, briefly, and headed straight for Elani.

Since she had no way of signaling Severn when she reached Elani, she did a quick perusal of the street. The Swords had arrived, and they were, even now, knocking on doors. One Sword carried a very long, very ornate roll, around which was wrapped a long scroll. The writing on the scroll itself couldn't be clearly seen at this distance, but the illuminated bits for the capital letters *could*. The scroll looked impressive, expensive, and Official.

It was, of course.

The Sword in question wore her weapon around her waist, but carrying it was optional; she was flanked by Swords who had nothing better to carry. Kaylin sometimes envied the Swords their jobs, because for the most part, their jobs *were* easy. But riot duty and evacuation duty made envy pretty damn hard, and the situation was dire enough that petty satisfaction was just as hollow. She cringed when she heard a door slam, because she would have bet money it had just slammed *in* their faces.

But Elani was close to the center of the circular area that rain had allowed them to map; here, there was no leeway possible. She wondered how many people would leave their homes voluntarily, and how many would have to be carried, or thrown, out.

It wasn't just homes, of course; some of the merchants didn't live above their storefronts, choosing instead to rent them out. The boarders were, like any other resident, being ordered to leave; the merchants were *also* being ordered to leave. Kaylin was just petty enough to smile at the sound of Margot's operatic rage as she hurried toward Evanton's.

There were no Swords at Evanton's door. The door itself

was ajar, and Kaylin could see Grethan standing in the window and staring, eyes rounded, at the commotion that Elani had become. She walked in, and Grethan jumped.

"I'm not here to throw you out," she said quietly. Glancing around the empty store, she added, "Where's Evanton?"

"He's in the Garden," Grethan replied. "With your partner."

Grethan had a natural affinity for the Elemental Garden, or rather, for entering it. It wasn't, however, necessary.

"It's not locked," he told Kaylin, half-apologetically. "Not when he's *in* it."

"Hmm. Have you considered locking it behind him when he's in a mood?"

Grethan's eyes rounded slightly, which was a definite No. On the other hand, if Evanton got *out* of the locked Garden, the minor hilarity of trapping him in it probably wouldn't be worth the consequences. But the young apprentice's eyes narrowed again as he grinned. "There's only one key."

The itchy feeling that covered most of Kaylin's body—not coincidentally the *same* portions that were also covered by glyphs—was almost painfully intense as she stood in front of the rickety, narrow door that led into Evanton's Elemental Garden.

She touched it. It wasn't warded—she was half-certain that attempting to ward this door would just destroy it, because the wood would probably collapse under any attempt to enchant it—but her palm suddenly *hurt*, and she withdrew it almost instantly.

Suspicious, she examined the door as Grethan's slow steps retreated. But there was no rune or mark on it, certainly not where her palm had touched it. To make matters worse, the flesh on her arms was now goose-bumping. She grimaced, but still, she hesitated. Since her own hesitations annoyed her, she shook them off and opened the door.

"All right, door," she muttered under her breath, "take me to the heart of the Elemental Garden."

The door didn't open into a gale that would have sunk ships in the harbor if it had happened on the outside of the Garden.

Given the last time she'd visited, this came as a relief. She walked into the Garden, leaving the door open at her back; she didn't walk very far. The Garden itself seemed, in composition, to be in its rest state: she could see the small shrines and candelabras, the shelves and reliquaries, clumped together in at least three areas.

She could see the surface of the small pond that was water's domain, and she frowned as the light slid across it. What she couldn't see was Severn or Evanton. She started forward; the grass was soft, short, and smooth. She even cast the normal shadow one would expect when the sun was at this height. Lifting her face, she felt no breeze. In the Garden, that was rare. But maybe the Elemental Air was calm today.

She headed toward the small pond in the Garden's center. It was there, as it always was, and moss beds lay against the flat, large stones to one side. There was a small mirror that lay facedown on the stone, as if it had been casually lifted and set aside; she didn't touch it.

But...the pond looked wrong. She stood at its edge, her toes almost touching the water. The water was still, and it was clear. But some of the darkness that hinted at its endless depth was...missing. Bending, Kaylin touched the ground. It felt like, well, grass with a bit of dirt underneath.

In fact, the Garden itself felt like the cozy, quiet retreat of a rich eccentric. Which was, of course, what was wrong with it. That, and she could see no sign of Severn or Evanton at all. It was as if she'd taken a turn through the wrong damn door and ended up in something that *looked* like Evanton's Garden, without any of its substance or life.

It was not a comforting thought.

Turning, she headed back in the direction she'd come. The door stood slightly ajar, and she stopped five feet from the narrow glimpse of hall, resting her hands lightly on her hips. She realized, as she looked at it, that there had never *been* a door out without Evanton, something she should have bloody well considered before she'd entered. But here it was, and it looked, from this vantage, to be the same door into the same dim hall, lined with the same bookcases, half of which were so packed they looked as if they were about to dump their contents on the poor fools who wandered by at the wrong time.

This was wrong. It felt wrong. She took a step toward the door anyway, and felt the hair on the back of her neck begin to rise. The fact that the Garden was magical was known. The fact that she felt magic only here, this close to the door, was bad. And, of course, she hadn't yet removed the bracer that existed to confine her own magic. She had no idea— at all—if the damn thing would follow Severn home, the way it normally and inexplicably did, if she took it off and dropped it here.

Cursing in Leontine, which sounded unnaturally loud in the sudden and suspicious silence of this Garden, she pulled up her sleeves, exposing the gemstones that lay in a vertical line on the inner side of the thick, golden manacle. She pressed them in sequence, and waited until she heard the familiar click. Prying it off her wrist, she looked at the grass, the Garden, and the now-distant pond, and then she shoved it into her tunic, above her belt.

She reached out to touch the door, and her hand froze just

before it made contact. The air around her hand was *wavering*. The closest thing she'd ever seen was a heat mirage, but heat mirages generally didn't come with color, and, aside from the sweat the heat itself caused, didn't cause sensation.

Something intensely uncomfortable passed through the whole of her body, like a moving, permeable wall. She grimaced, jumped back, and found that the distance didn't cause the sensation to stop. But it did change the perspective through which she viewed the door, or rather, the hall on the other side of said door.

What had been the span of a door frame away now seemed to be visible through a long, long tunnel. The tunnel itself was not door-shaped; it seemed to have no shape at all. It was as if the frame and the world to which it was attached had been sundered, and what lay between them was a gap into sky, or cloud, or unbound space.

Walking through it to the door was *almost* not an option. She glanced over her shoulder at flat, empty garden, and wondered where it was, truly; it seemed, for a moment, as substantial as the space that now existed between the frame of the door and Evanton's shop. Color was here, yes, and the grass was not dry or dead. It looked right, but everything else about it was missing.

Note to self, she thought, clenching her jaw. *Do not enter Elemental Garden when magic is unpredictable right next-damndoor.* On the other hand? There weren't any shadows here; it wasn't as if she'd walked into the heart of the fiefs on an aimless stroll. At the moment, whatever might kill her—and given the total chaos of unpredictable magic that wasn't even her own, that could be anything—was likely to be starvation if she didn't leave. The shelf-lined hall was not getting any closer.

Backing up, she tensed, bent into her knees, and approached the door at a sprint. Passing through the frame was easy. Getting to the other side, not so much. There was solid ground beneath her feet, but running across it was like running across soft sand; it ate momentum. She couldn't see what lay beneath her boots; it seemed to exist without any visual component.

And that, of course, was magic; the marks along the insides of her thighs, arms and the back of her neck were now aching in that all-skin-scraped-off way. She clenched teeth, gave up on sprinting, and walked instead. She could walk quickly. The hall on the other side, however, seemed to be moving, and it wasn't moving in the right direction.

Come on, legs. Come on. Widening her stride, she tried to gain speed; she managed to gain enough that she wasn't losing ground. But she wasn't gaining any, either. A pace like this, she could keep up all day. But magic in its infuriating lack of predictability probably wouldn't *give* her all damn day, and if the sight of those damn bookshelves suddenly faded, she'd be stranded in the middle of a nowhere that was ancient and totally unknown.

Because she was certain it *was* ancient. The only place she had encountered anything similar was in the heart of a Tower in the fiefs, and those Towers had been constructed by gods. When the rest of the city had started their decline into crumbling ruins, the Towers had mimicked them—but nothing destroyed them. Nothing broke them.

They, on the other hand, were perfectly capable of destroying the people who wandered through their doors. She walked. The hall receded, as if it were teasing her. But it was the kind of teasing that caused tears and heartbreak.

"Severn! Evanton!"

Her voice was clear, strong, and completely steady; she

was proud of the last one. There was no echo, no subtle resonance that indicated either geography or architecture in the distance to either side. The only clear reality loomed ahead, always ahead.

She had no idea how long she'd been walking; she broke into a run every so often, but the run was almost as slow as the walk, and it was more tiring. Her arms and legs still ached, and at length she rolled her sleeves as high as they would go because the cloth brushing her skin was almost agonizing.

It didn't surprise her much to see that the runes were glowing. Their color, on the other hand, did: it was gray, almost an absence of color, in keeping with the rest of her environment. It made the runes seem, for a moment, like windows into the Other, and windows were not meant to grace the arms of living people. She let her arms drop back into the wide pumping swing of a brisk walk, and then stopped and lifted them again.

Severn.

No answer. No answer at all. She tried again, gazing at the only reality she could see. Silence. Turning, she dared one backward glance over her shoulder. There was no frame, no door, no Garden; the gray of this nonplace had swallowed them.

The hairs on the back of her neck rose so sharply they might as well have been quills. She turned instantly, and then stopped moving. She had taken her eyes off her destination, and the destination had, like the Garden, vanished.

CHAPTER 7

Kaylin had had nightmares like this, but they didn't usually start someplace bucolic. They didn't usually end in a gray, empty space, either. They ended, frequently, with the voice-of-pissed-off-Leontine on the other end of an active mirror. She didn't panic, largely because she wasn't in pain, didn't appear to be close to death by starvation, and, more important, it wouldn't do her any damn good.

Instead, she kept moving forward. There wasn't anything to move toward, anymore, and the movement didn't appear to be doing any good, but she still hoped. And cursed. There was an awful lot of Leontine cursing where no one could hear it; she also practiced her Aerian, and her translation of either into common.

Since there was no sun, and none of the usual geographic markers by which she told time, she had no idea how much had passed. It could have been very slow minutes—and probably was—but it felt like hours. And hours. And hours. The whole lot of nothing began to wear on her nerves, and she let it. More time passed.

And more.

And more.

She could jog with her eyes closed, because there wasn't anything to trip over, run into, or avoid. Sometimes it helped, because the darkness beneath lids felt natural, and this was as close to a dream—albeit boring and featureless—as anything real generally came. Unfortunately, dreams had a way of taking sharp turns or steep drops into nightmare. She opened her eyes.

When her stomach growled, she was almost grateful, because it gave her some sense that time—in a decent interval—was passing, not that she wasn't often unreasonably hungry at random times throughout the day. But when she heard the second growl—a distinctly external one, she froze. Her legs and arms still ached; nothing short of getting away from this damn place was going to solve that.

She fell silent, listening; she wondered if her stomach's growl could produce the echoes her natural voice—in tones of Leontine, even—couldn't. Funny, how little she appreciated the answer. The growl—the only other evidence that someone else was also in this space, seemed to come from somewhere below her feet.

She stopped cursing. Which meant she stopped speaking at all, and started to *move*.

She could hear the sound of deep and even breathing. Sadly, it wasn't hers; hers was now shorter and sharper. And quieter. There was no obvious wind—but it felt, now, as if the gray, amorphous endless space was a living thing, and she was trapped inside it. She left off the specifics of where, because it didn't seem to have anatomy, and any answer she came up with was not good.

She stopped jogging. Stopped running. She kept moving, because it was better, for the moment, than standing still. The bracer was now warm against her stomach, and she thought about tossing it away. Thought about what the Emperor would say—possibly even to her—if it failed to reappear again, ever. Or the Arkon. She had some suspicion that it came, indirectly, from his hoard.

Then again, that would mean he'd parted with it, so maybe that was inaccurate.

She crouched, pressed her hand against the ground. Her palm passed through it, as if it didn't exist. She *hated* magic. Her feet, clearly, were being supported by something; her hands, however, couldn't touch it. She stood, took a step forward, and fell.

So much for exploration.

Falling was like flying without options.

She didn't scream; it wouldn't have done any good. But she held her breath for an uncomfortable length of time while she waited for the ground—or what passed for ground here—to rise up and splatter her. When it failed to happen—or at least, when that breath ran out—she swallowed air and opened her eyes. She'd closed them when the ground had suddenly dropped out from under her. It hadn't made much difference.

The sickening sensation of stomach being pressed up against throat diminished; instead of falling she was now floating. But the growling grew slowly louder, and almost instinctively she began to jog again. Falling stopped, and not the usual way, which involved ground and pain. This was good. But the growling had changed or shifted; it wasn't directional, and it seemed to bypass her ears and head straight for the base of her spine, where it then traveled up and down like a hysterical child.

Severn!

The silence was worse, this time; it hit harder. The growl that answered—that seemed to answer—the silent invocation was now louder. She spun, hands dropping to daggers, but could see the same nothing she'd seen since she'd arrived.

Severn...

No answer.

This time, she realized that no answer would come. He would look for her, if he knew—but the chances are, he *didn't*. He was with Evanton, and the real Garden, in some other place. He hadn't known that she was coming; he therefore didn't know that she hadn't arrived. She had given him *her* name, it was true: the name she had taken for herself from the Barrani stream of life. But she'd taken no name for him; what he gave her, as always, was acceptance.

She didn't have his name.

If he called hers, she might hear it—she wasn't certain, because she had no damn idea where she was. But...he had never used it. He understood that in some ways it felt wrong, to her; it wasn't *her*, it wasn't what she knew of herself. He let her approach. He let her speak, in the silent and private way that Barrani names conferred, and he didn't pull back, didn't hide, didn't offer her fear.

But he didn't *call* her. He didn't invoke what was so foreign and inexplicable.

She swallowed. The growling was louder and thicker; it was one sound, but it seemed to come from everywhere. Closing her eyes, she whispered a single word.

Calarnenne.

Silence. She opened her eyes, and the world was still gray, still formless, still empty. Her marks were the same shade of empty, but the edges of each rune were glowing softly, not that the light was necessary. She looked up, down, and shuddered once as the only other sound she'd heard since she arrived repeated itself.

It wasn't Feral growling; it wasn't angry dog; it wasn't the Leontine sound that meant you were a few seconds away from needing a new limb or a new throat. She'd dreaded all of these in her life, but the sound she heard now?

It was death.

Kaylin personally preferred a civilized, more or less human personification of death, which was the one that usually got into the stories she'd heard as a child. Hells, as an adult. She drew her daggers for the first time since entering the nonworld. They looked pathetic in her hands, but they were all she had, and they were better than nothing.

She began to curse the growling noise in soft, steady Leontine—because that seemed to make no difference, either, and it made her feel better. A little. She threw in an Aerian curse or two, and dropped a few brittle words of High Barrani into the mix; she saved the most heartfelt of her curses for later use.

But cursing, she finally heard something that wasn't a growl, although it was, in its own fashion, as deadly, as dangerous, and ultimately, as unknown.

Kaylin.

She froze. She had just enough experience with the Lord of the fief of Nightshade to know when he wasn't particularly pleased by something she'd done, and she'd had twelve years in the fief he ruled to develop a visceral and instinctive fear of his anger.

But she'd had seven living well away from Nightshade, and if her automatic reaction was to drop or hide, she could fight through it and remain more or less calm. Less, today, but she didn't usually have conversations like this while standing in the middle of nothing.

Nightshade.

You…called me.

She swallowed. *I did. I can't—I didn't—*

You did not mean to compel.

She hadn't even tried. In theory, she could, if she were strong enough. She held his name. But she'd always doubted that she would be strong enough, and if she weren't, and she tried, she'd be dead.

I only wanted to get your attention.

Ah. And now that you have it?

There's a difficulty in Elantra. She swallowed. It was habit; she wasn't actually speaking. But if she had stopped, the growling hadn't, and she heard it clearly.

Kaylin. His voice shifted, the sound simultaneously sharpening and losing some of its edge. *Where are you?*

Funny thing, she began, as the growl grew louder.

Kaylin. Sharper, sharper. *Wherever you are, leave. Now.* When she didn't answer, he added, *This is not a joke. It is not a matter for your mortal sense of humor. You are in danger. You must leave.*

I... I don't know how. It was hard, to say it. To admit it. Especially to Nightshade. Ignorance was weakness.

No, she thought. Ignorance was only weakness if you clung to the damn thing. Obviously, hours in gray nowhere had unsettled her, and Nightshade's voice pretty much always had that effect; they weren't a good combination.

But he could hear her. She thought he was possibly the only person she knew who would.

I can hear you, he continued. *But I cannot see where you are. I cannot see what you see.*

Kaylin. Call me.

Running, she closed her eyes and she called his true name again, putting a force into the syllables that she never spoke aloud. And this time, she felt the syllables resist her; she felt them slide to one side or the other, their pronunciation—

if you could even call it that, because she didn't open her mouth—shifting or changing as they struggled to escape.

Again.

She ignored the urge to point out who held whose name, because there was, in the absolute intensity of the command, the hint of desperation. That, and the damn growling had finally reached a level where she could feel it. Not as strongly as she could feel Nightshade's voice, though. It almost seemed—

Whatever it is—it can hear you. It can hear you clearly, she told him. And then, before he could answer, she struggled with his name. Struggled to say it, while he pulled back, while he fought her. Because she suddenly understood what the point of the seemingly pointless exercise was. When she struggled for control of the syllables, when she struggled to force them to snap into place, she could feel him pushing back against them; she could feel the way they slid when he exerted his will.

But more significant, she could feel, for just the moment she encountered each small act of resistance, the direction from which it came.

It can hear me. It is surprising that it cannot clearly hear you. Come, Kaylin. Come to me.

She called his name once more, and this time she let the syllables slide as far as they could without losing them; she existed for as long as she could in the moment of the struggle, as if conflict were the only road home.

Opening her eyes, she saw, in the gray folds of nothing ahead, something dark that wavered around the edges. It wasn't Nightshade, but it was *something.*

Closer. Closer, Kaylin. Be ready.

For what? She didn't ask.

But he heard it anyway. *You will not have long. I do not know*

*how you came to be where you must be—but I cannot join you. I
can hold a window open. You must take it.*

The growling—

*Yes. A very small window. I am sorry. I have neither the resources
nor the ability to offer more.*

The dark patch of space became larger and more distinct
as she approached it, and she saw, standing at its heart, the
Lord of Nightshade, his eyes almost black in the shadows,
both hands extended to the sides as if, by physical force, he
had ripped a hole in the world. His arms were shaking with
the effort.

The gray beneath her feet began to ripple, as if it were the
back of a horse that was trying, with unexpected savagery,
to unseat her. Spikes formed, like stalagmites made of cloud,
glittering although there was no source of light. She dodged
them, because she could, but the ground directly beneath her
feet still felt like soft sand.

Soft, hot sand. Or miles of flesh.

She pivoted sideways between two growing, jagged spikes;
one clipped the inside of her arm. She bled. Where blood
struck ground, it sizzled.

She felt Nightshade's curse. It had the force of Marcus in
fury, although it was entirely subvocal; High Barrani lacked
the words to encompass it. But she kept running. Nightshade
didn't recede the way the halls of Evanton's shop had, and she
knew that if she lost sight of him now, it would be because
he couldn't hold.

She felt his response; he didn't form words around it. He
was not, however, pleased at the doubt the thought implied.
You had to love Barrani arrogance.

And at the moment, she *did*.

She stopped trying to say his name. She stopped trying to
do anything but reach him. He didn't offer her a hand; he

couldn't. The weight of the world—as if strange, shapeless clouds could have weight—wasn't something he could support with one hand.

But all she could see was Nightshade: Nightshade and darkness. There was no hall behind him, no stone floors beneath his feet, no glimmer of torches or lamps; even his hair seemed to blend with the background, highlighting pale skin and sapphire eyes by contrast.

Kaylin—quickly. Quickly.

Gods, the ground was thick now. She'd run across mud that had less give—and that had been ankle bloody deep.

Kaylin!

She tensed, grinding her teeth as she felt something sharp cut the back of her left calf. She heard roaring; the growling had clearly escalated into something that could handle primal rage. Dragon roars were just as loud, but far less threatening.

She saw the wavering shape of this hole in the middle of nothing begin to collapse, and although she wasn't close enough to make a clean leap through what was left of it, she tried anyway. *Nightshade—*

She felt his curse; he didn't speak. But more than that? She felt the mark on her cheek begin to burn. She felt the hairs on the back of her neck straighten as if they were made of fine quills, and she felt the inside of her thighs and her arms almost freeze in sudden protest.

Magic. His magic. The momentum the ground and her own legs couldn't give her, his power could. She cleared what was left of the dwindling rent in space, her arms and right shoulder hitting his chest and driving them both back. His own arms fell instantly; he grabbed hold of her, and he pulled.

Which was good, because something began to pull from the other side. She could feel it grab her legs, and the wound in her calf ached and burned with the unexpected solidity of its grip. She didn't want to lose her leg.

But she knew that Nightshade didn't care if it was *only* her leg that was lost; she could feel the thought, absent words to shape or form it. All that mattered now was that she remain here, with him. He lifted his face; she felt his chin rise, although hers was pretty much plastered to the front of his robes. She could almost see what he saw: the small gap in space, through which her legs had yet to emerge, and the edges of the place she was trying so hard to escape. Closing her eyes didn't help; the sudden disorientation, the unwelcome glimpse of Barrani vision and Barrani sight, made her head and her stomach do the same hideously unpleasant lurch that Castle Nightshade's portal did.

But even as she began to spin into the nausea of portal passage, she saw what now existed on the other side of the rapidly shrinking tear: darkness, broken by stars and the borealis of a foreign sky. And in it, some shape that was not shadow as she understood it; it was far too solid, far too real, for that. She could see no eyes, no mouth, nothing that made it look like the monsters of her nightmares—but in the lack of those things, she thought the darkest of nightmares lay waiting. And it needed no form, no face, no pathetic rendering of *shape* to devour.

No, it just needed her damn legs.

I am sorry, Kaylin, she heard Nightshade say. Knew that he meant to cut those legs off at midcalf. Knew, as well, that she couldn't allow it—how could she be a Hawk without legs? How could she patrol, how could she run, how could she do the only things that defined her? She cried out in anger and fear and even the darkness on the other side of life—which was death, all death—didn't look so bad.

But she was spinning, disoriented, even while clinging so

tightly to him that her hands crushed the fabric of his shirt and his hair. She kicked, struggling to pull herself free. His magic enveloped her, and she felt his desire to preserve her life over what her life *meant* to her, and she spoke a single word of denial.

It was not, however, an Elantran word. It wasn't a Barrani word. It wasn't Leontine, or Aerian or Dragon, the last of which would have been impossible anyway. It was a true word.

And true words, she discovered, like true names, had power.

She heard, for the first time, something rise out of the roar at her back that sounded like language. It had syllables, the shape and texture of words, the small dips and rises in tone; it had the elements of voice, which had always been important to Kaylin. It had the force of will behind it, a force just as visceral as hunger or desire—she knew, because it had those, too.

What it didn't have, what she couldn't hear, were actual *words,* and she was grateful for it. She spoke again, and this time—this time she heard Nightshade raise a cry of alarm; she felt his arms slide away from her as if she could no longer be safely held.

But for a minute more of her weight was on the right damn side of the portal. She kicked, and fell free. It would have helped if there had been anything to land on.

"Kaylin."

She pushed herself up off the ground, and saw, as she opened her eyes a crack, that she was looking at gleaming, polished marble. She wanted to heave, she really did. Which was not outside of the norm, because she recognized this room: it was the foyer that graced Castle Nightshade. She had never arrived through the front door feeling human.

This time, she hadn't even bothered with the portal.

Nightshade was considerate, as always; he waited until she

could lever herself off the ground and stand—very shakily—on her own two feet. He hadn't, however, dimmed the damn lights, and they stabbed her vision in a very unpleasant way. She exchanged a few words of Leontine with their bleeding bright haloes; they didn't respond.

"Kaylin," Nightshade said, when the last of the syllables had stopped echoing.

She looked up. His eyes were a shade of green that was almost, but not quite, blue. This was about as safe as he ever got. Waiting until the last of the nausea subsided would mean she'd be silent for another hour. Keeping her head very still, she said, "Thank you."

He raised a dark brow, and offered her the briefest of smiles. It didn't really reach his eyes. "I admit," he said quietly, "that I was surprised."

"That I called you?"

"Ah, no. That you have not, since the fief of Tiamaris was founded, returned to Nightshade. One would think it was almost deliberate."

The problem with portals, and with Castle Nightshade's portal in particular, was that she arrived feeling like she'd mixed alcohol on an all-night drinking binge. It wasn't the best state of mind in which to have a conversation with her friends; it was a dangerous state of mind in which to have a conversation with the fieflord whose mark she bore. "It was deliberate," she told him, because she knew he knew it anyway.

"May I ask why?"

She stopped herself from shrugging, and then met his eyes for a second time. "Do you mind if I sit down?"

"No. Forgive my lack of hospitality. Let us repair to a more useful set of rooms." He hesitated, and then added, "Take my arm."

"Pardon?"

"My arm, Kaylin. The Castle will be slightly more difficult for you to traverse at the moment than is the norm."

Given what the Castle was normally like, this said something. He offered Kaylin his arm, in High Court style, and
she placed her hand on it. It was difficult not to also place
a large part of her weight on it. She made the effort. "Why
will it be harder?" She asked, because it gave her something
to focus on that wasn't her nausea or his nearness, both of
which were difficult for entirely different reasons.

He ignored her question as he led her along a hallway that
seemed familiar.

They stepped through doors into the safety of a very large,
and as usual, sparsely, but finely, furnished room. Only when
the doors closed did Kaylin release his arm and step away.
While the halls seemed to expand or collapse with no warning and no rhyme or reason, she had never seen the rooms
change around her.

She made her way to the long couch, and sat heavily on
cushions that were that little bit too soft. Nightshade remained
standing. He had the decency not to offer her either food or
drink. Her cheek was warm; the rest of her skin felt cold.

"How did I travel through the portal? Did you carry me?"

"No."

"Did I walk?"

"No."

*Are we going to play twenty bloody questions while my head
pounds and I want to throw up?*

She didn't say the last out loud. It didn't make much difference; his smile was very chilly when he offered it.

"You dislike the portal of Castle Nightshade. I would have
thought, given how deep that dislike is, that you might recognize it when you see it."

"Oh, I do." She paused as her thoughts, such as they were, caught up with her mouth.

"You were standing *in* the portal when you found me."

Very good.

She closed her eyes. It helped, a little. Portal travel was bad enough to make her queasy—or worse—but it usually passed a lot faster. At the moment she wanted to fall over onto her side and curl her knees into her chest. Maybe sleep a little. Instead, she was having a conversation with Lord Nightshade.

"I was at Evanton's," she said, speaking slowly and clearly. "I walked into his Garden. Or I thought I walked into his Garden. But it wasn't. It looked the same. It wasn't the same."

He nodded.

"So I tried to leave it. I ended up...nowhere. I could see his shop—but I couldn't reach it. And eventually, I couldn't see it, either."

"That is when you...called me?"

She nodded. "You know where I was." Not a question.

"I have some suspicion. Don't rearrange your face in that expression. I am a Barrani Lord, Kaylin. I am not more, or other."

"What was chasing me?"

He said nothing.

"Nightshade—"

"I have no definitive answer for you. I will not condescend to pointless conjecture." He wasn't quite lying; he was certainly not telling the truth. Which was about as much as anyone sane could expect from the Barrani, although given the turn the afternoon had taken, Kaylin wasn't certain she qualified as sane. "But I could not find you by conventional means. I chose a...less conventional approach, through the Castle's portal. It would not be an approach open to many. Perhaps the High Lord, or another fieflord—but only if you held their name."

She opened her eyes. "What happened in Evanton's store?"

"The Keeper's domain is bound by many, many magics. Most of those are older than any known Empire. I cannot say for certain what happened. You might wish to speak with him, but I am not sure he will be able to enlighten you. May I suggest, for the duration of the current crisis, that you avoid wandering in his shop when he is not actively present?"

She grimaced, and then her eyes narrowed. "Current crisis?"

"I believe you are suffering from rains of blood, among other difficulties." He raised a brow. "Come, Kaylin. You did not honestly think a difficulty of that magnitude would stay across the Ablayne?"

"I wasn't thinking about it much at all. It's not fief business."

"Not yet, no. But I believe that your difficulty in the city and the difficulty you encountered in the Keeper's abode are linked. "Remain here. I will return with food and water, now that you are somewhat more settled."

Kaylin drifted off while Nightshade was absent. The room was quiet, the couch too comfortable. She was cold, here, and there were no convenient throws that she wanted to touch; she felt too damn grubby, and even at its simplest, Castle Nightshade was out of her league. But her stomach had settled enough that the complaints it now issued were the usual ones. She *was* hungry, damn it.

Nightshade had implied that he'd had to go to the portal to find her. Which said something about the portal. One of the many things it said? Entering it at the moment was probably not a great idea, so leaving might prove difficult.

But one of the other things it implied was that the portal existed in an entirely different space than the rest of the Castle. Or at least the rest of the fief. She turned that one over for a few minutes. What did she know about the Castle, after all? Its well, if you fell all the way down to the bottom and miraculously survived, contained a cavern with a vast lake that the Elemental Water could actually reach out and touch; its basement contained a literal forest of trees that seemed sentient—certainly more sentient than the Hawks when they'd been out drinking all night and had work the next day; somewhere beyond that forest, there was a huge cavern that was covered in runes that were very similar to the ones that adorned half of her skin.

She grimaced. What else?

There was a throne room. She'd seen it once. It contained statues of almost every living race in the Empire, and when Nightshade desired it, those statues came to life. Were, in fact, in some way, always alive. He'd said he used the power of the Castle to create them, but made it clear that he had started from flesh. But...how? How had he used that power? What had he told it to *do?*

She stood, found that her knees no longer wobbled, and began to pace in a rectangle around the low table.

What *was* the Castle, at heart? It was not the Tower of Barren. Or rather, of Tiamaris. It didn't speak, or think, or plan, or love.

Or did it?

"No," was the quiet reply.

CHAPTER 8

Nightshade stood in the open doors, a tray in his hands. Or rather, between the open palms he held to either side. She hesitated, and then walked quickly over to where he stood and lifted the tray the normal way. Watching the Lord of the fief play servant *always* unsettled her.

He raised a dark brow; his eyes were still the shade that exists just before emerald falls into sapphire. His hair, unbound, draped across both shoulders; his skin was pale. The tray shook in her hands; she looked at what was on it. Water, or a liquid just as clear and colorless, fruit, cut cheese, meat. No bread. She carried the tray to the table. He followed in silence.

She was always aware of where, in a room, Nightshade was. It might have been because of the mark; it might have been because she knew his true name. But she thought she'd have been just as aware if she'd had neither. Even his silences demanded attention. She could more easily ignore the Dragon Lords whose company she kept than the Lord of Nightshade.

He knew. It amused him. Which annoyed her. "Why doesn't Castle Nightshade speak?" she asked, veering away from both annoyance and compulsion.

"I think you know the answer to that better than I."

Clearly, if she were interested in forcing the conversation into safer channels, she was going to have to carry most of it. "You were there. You were there when the Tower of—of Tiamaris—woke."

"I was there for only some part of it. My knowledge of the Towers at that time—and it was not without significance—was based in its entirety on their nascent forms. I understood, however," he added, voice softer, gaze fixed on her face, "that I was not to be bored. I had encountered a mortal—a mortal with the unfortunate manners of a wild human, or a coveted one—and she bore my mark." His glance brushed the sleeves of her shirt, and his eyes flared—literally.

Magic caused her skin to tingle and the hair on the back of her neck to rise. Before she could speak or move, the ties at her sleeves fell open, and those sleeves were rolled, end over end, up her arms until the inside of those arms were exposed. Both arms, simultaneously. It was a neat trick, for a value of neat that was also distinctly uncomfortable.

"You bore, as well, the marks of the Chosen. And you seemed both powerless and ignorant, in the main, of what those marks might mean to you should you survive them."

"But the Tower—" she began, attempting to control the conversation. Or anything, really.

"The Tower of Tiamaris heard you," was his reply. "As did I. You were there when his Tower woke. You were not, however, *here*. Nor were you in the other fiefs in which such Towers woke and found they were powerless. What you touched, Kaylin, you changed. You have not touched the heart of Castle Nightshade, and before you ask—if you are so foolish as to entertain the notion—no, you *will not* wake the Castle's heart."

But as he said it, she felt both the force of his declaration, and the tremor of uncertainty that lay beneath it. He wasn't sure that she could be kept from it if she wanted to go to the heart.

"You are wrong," was the cool reply. "But the only certainty is your death, and I am reluctant, at this moment, to kill you."

"But at this moment," she replied, half touching his thoughts, half speaking them as if they were also her own, "you *can* kill me. And you're not certain that's always going to be true."

One brow rose, revealing more of the blue his eyes had become. He didn't deny it, however; there wasn't any point. Not that he wouldn't have lied if there was any chance it would be effective; the burden of truth for any Barrani was decided by the gullibility of the audience, and the possible consequences of the lie itself *to* said Barrani.

She glanced at her arms.

"Yes," he said quietly.

"You knew. You knew I would live in Nightshade. You knew it centuries ago."

"I knew," was the quiet reply, "that you would be born in the fief of Nightshade. I knew that you would grow here. I also knew that until the moment you were old enough, there would be no way to distinguish you from any other motherless human urchin."

The words, and the callous sentiment that informed them so perfectly, caused Kaylin's jaws to ache.

"I knew, when Severn Handred came to my Castle for the first time, that the long wait was almost done. Barrani are immortal, but we are not famed for our patience. I was not, initially, absorbed by the boredom and frustration of waiting. There was much, indeed, that I had to discover, much to achieve, before your arrival."

"You knew that the Outcaste—the Dragon—would be here."

"No. That, I did not know, not immediately." He stepped toward her, and she stood her ground, tensing slightly as he raised his hand to touch her cheek. It was, oddly enough, the cheek that was unmarked. "I was not, then, the man I am now. What I could read from you—and I did try—was not so complete.

"But I waited, Kaylin."

"You marked me."

"Yes."

"But you never said a word."

"No. I knew, when we first met, that the time for speech would follow. But I did not wish to influence or change what might occur in the Tower in my past and your future. Had I, who knows what might have occurred in the darkness there? We might have no fieflord, no Tiamaris, and the shadows might now be spilling across the Ablayne, and from there, to the whole of the Empire.

"I interfered very, very little in your life. I knew very little of my role in it. I learned, for instance, that you would go to the High Halls, that you would face the test of the Tower there. You are not guarded or careful with your knowledge. Perhaps, if you lived to be my age, you would learn this caution.

"But perhaps not." His fingers stroked her cheek; his eyes were a blue that spoke of sky, not cobalt. She didn't know what it meant, and didn't want to know. "I have been careful. I have been cautious.

"But the fief of Tiamaris now exists. The moment our paths crossed at that Tower in your timeline, I was free. I am no longer constrained by the possible future. I am no longer constrained by any attempt to meet the future as promised, by a single day, in the past.

"I understood," he continued, "when Illien fell, what the significance of that long-ago meeting might be. I understood what the fall of Illien might presage. And I understood, as well, that you might face death when you returned, after centuries, to the Tower you had wakened."

"That's why you were there?"

"It is why I took that risk. Understand that I have played many games in the long stretch of years between our first meeting and that one. I explored, as Lord Tiamaris explored, and I learned what was possible for one with my abilities to learn. The Castle was not entirely expected, but I had explored such buildings before. I could not be certain that you would survive *this* entry into the Tower."

"I might not have."

"No. But I could no more join you in Illien's Tower than Illien could join you in mine."

"Would the Tower have known?"

"That I am bound to another? Yes."

She wanted to ask how he knew. She didn't.

"And in truth I would not risk my fief in the attempt. Had the Tower fallen, or had you fallen in the Tower, the shadows at the heart of the fief would now have two borders to my lands, and my power and ability to defend what I have taken—and held—would be taxed. Possibly to the point of failure." He let his hand trail down to the underside of her jaw, and then, slowly, let it drop.

"But Tiamaris now exists. I feel his name as strongly as I have ever felt Illien's or Liatt's. In truth," he added with a grimace, "it is stronger. He will never again venture across this border, and I fear that any forays I make across his will be instantly known."

She took a deep breath, because now that his hand was not

so close to her skin, she could. "Why does Castle Nightshade *have* a portal? The Tower doesn't."

"Tiamaris's tower...does not?"

She mentally kicked herself. "No. The Tower's Avatar thought it wasn't needed."

He raised a dark brow. "You mean, the Tower's Avatar felt that you disliked them enough that she chose not to have one where you might be forced to use it." Not a question.

Since it was more or less true, Kaylin shrugged. It was a fief shrug.

"It will compromise her security," Nightshade offered, his eyes darkening into a more familiar shade of annoyance at the gesture itself. "But if you think there are no portals in her domain, you are mistaken. There *will* be at least one. She cannot be so foolish as to leave her heart unguarded."

"I know what lies at the heart of that Tower," Kaylin replied.

"I know. But there will be a portal somewhere within the Tower. You might never see it, although I think it unlikely that you will be able to avoid it entirely. The Tower trusts you, inasmuch as it is allowed to trust one not its Lord." He walked over to the low table, and lifted a silver goblet. The contents absorbed some of his attention. "You gambled, Kaylin. It is an interesting gamble.

"A Dragon has never, to my knowledge, been fieflord before. It will also be interesting." He sat, slowly, on the couch opposite Kaylin, who stood, motionless, to one side of the low table. "You cannot know how you intrigued me, the first time we met.

"You, dirty and underslept mortal urchin, bearing marks of power that even now you do not understand. Severn, who bears a weapon that whispers if you are aware of how to listen, accompanied you, and Tiamaris, Dragon Lord, was by your side but clearly *not* your master.

"I had spent much of my life in the West March, and some of it at Court. I had endured—and passed—the test of Name. I had survived my family and my extended family's particular exuberance for political power plays. It is something that whiled away time, and I learned to excel at it."

No surprises there.

"But the entry into the Tower made the first meeting almost unremarkable. The Tower's voice... I can still hear it. I can see her wings," he added softly, "and see the obsidian glint of her skin as she landed and took the throne itself."

"I can still see the bodies," Kaylin replied, and this time, she did sit.

"You could see those before the Tower," he answered. "The Tower did not tell you anything you did not already know. She helped you, in a fashion, to unburden yourself. Not more, and not less."

Kaylin nodded; it was true. She was uncomfortable here, in this room, and she couldn't really tell herself it was because of the portal transition—if that's what it was—because she didn't believe it. Nightshade's gaze was now upon her face; it was as if there was nothing at all between his eyes and hers. Honesty with Severn, she could manage.

Honesty with a Barrani had never been desired—either by Kaylin or by the Barrani she knew. "You waited. For me."

"I waited."

"Why?" As she asked the word, she *listened*. She listened through the tenuous connection of his true name; she listened through a different, but equally tenuous connection, because the mark on her face was as warm as the touch of his palm.

His answer, when it came, seemed to belong to a different question. "To my kin, to my people, history is not story. But we have stories. We dignify them by calling them legend, where it is appropriate to refer to them among outsiders, but we have words for story in High Barrani that we do not speak among outsiders. I do not know if Dragons have similar words in their own tongue—in my youth I would have denied even the possibility.

"Now? I feel they must. But it is of little consequence. The stories that we have, the stories that we tell, we tell seldom. Human stories are like human gossip and human greeting. Human religion is often the same. It skirts the surface of things, but it has no heart."

Kaylin didn't bridle. She'd spent enough years around Barrani to understand that this particular type of arrogance was proof against all merely mortal annoyance.

He felt the annoyance she hadn't bothered to vocalize. But because she hadn't, he took no offense. "You tell stories to children," he said quietly. "We do not. If the Barrani can be said to have crimes in any mortal sense of the word, telling these stories to our children would be one of them."

"Why?"

His silence was both verbal and internal; she felt the lull, and knew to wait until he had gathered the words he cared to gather.

"The Dragons feel," he finally began, "that they are the only ones with any memory of, and knowledge of, the oldest of tongues, the ancient words."

His words, once offered, took root quickly, like fire spreading through the floorboards and joists of a dry, wooden building. "These…stories…are in the language of the Old Ones?" She thought of the Leontines, then.

"They are," he said softly. "And they are told nowhere but the West March. It is why the West March is ruled by a Barrani High Lord who is attached by blood to the High Halls. When—and if—we pass the test of the High Halls, we journey to the West March, and there, we listen."

"Could you speak the words?"

He lifted a brow. "No. Not I, Kaylin. And I have heard them. Mortal memory is a cracked vessel. Whatever it holds leaks quickly away, and in little time. Barrani memory, like Dragon memory, is immortal. But there are some things that our thoughts cannot easily contain. Very, very few of our kind can hold those words, and use them. It is my belief that the Dragons have more success, but it is not a popular opinion among my sundered kin." His smile was sharp and bitter, although he was genuinely amused.

"Why do you make this journey? I mean, why do you listen at all?"

"Some of us will hear the words, see them, feel them, and remain unmoved by what they contain. Others will be... transformed...in some fashion. The language is harsh," he added, "and it is almost imperative."

"And children?"

"Irrevocably changed." There was no doubt in the words; they were dark. She wanted to ask him how he knew this.

"It was tried," he replied, because she didn't have to ask the actual words, not now. He was as close to her as he had ever been, even given the table between them.

"The change itself isn't bad."

"It is not always bad, no. It is considered another rite of passage, and those who can adapt to the tale gain both power and prestige. It is why some felt we would gain in our wars with the Dragons if we exposed our young to the tale.

"But that is not what happened. They were not anchored in kin and custom. They were not, yet, wholly themselves. Nor were they ever destined to become so." He lifted a hand. "And that dark bit of our history was not the purpose of this tale. I will not address it now, and if you are lucky, you will never hear it addressed." He drank quietly, watching her.

She waited for his words, breaking no silence, because in some ways, there was no silence to break. His mute but constant presence was, in its own way, too loud to be ignored.

"Such stories, we call the *Regalia*. We encounter them once."

Nodding, she lifted her own glass. She brought it to her lips; felt the cold, silver lip of the goblet against the dryness of her own.

"You asked me why I waited," he said, reminding her because mortal memory was so ephemeral, and her attention was now wholly upon the fate of those unknown Barrani children.

She drank.

"In you, centuries ago, in the heart of what is now the fief of Tiamaris, I heard the beginning of a *Regalia*, Kaylin."

She choked.

His smile was slightly malicious and slightly smug; he had, of course, expected her reaction. He waited, his eyes once again a clearer, paler blue than Barrani blue generally was, until she could breathe normally again; her eyes however were still tearing.

"It was subtle. I fear your companions are also listening to the tale, and they are being tested—and transformed—by it, although I do not believe they are aware of its significance."

She shook her head. "That makes no sense," she finally managed.

"Oh?"

"Your...stories...your *Regalia*...they're in a language I can't even *speak*. I don't know them. I don't have any goal here. I just want to do my job. At the end of the day, I want to eat and sleep. I want to complain about the office and the bureaucrats that sometimes interfere in our work."

He shrugged. "I waited for you, Kaylin, because the tale

had only barely begun. I will hear the rest of it, I will be tested by it, and I will test it. But now, I will do so without fear of somehow distorting or destroying its beginning in the process.

"And I think it not a coincidence that it is the first Tower claimed by a Dragon Lord, and that the Dragon Lord is one of your companions. *Ravellon* is waking, Kaylin. It was waking before you were born. It has its champion, also a Dragon Lord, and of the Dragons, one of considerable power before his transformation." He set his goblet upon the table, beside the food she couldn't bring herself to touch.

"My actions were, in all ways, constrained by what little information I took from that first encounter. I knew two things—that you bore my mark, and that you held my name. The latter was far more disturbing than the former, although the former was…unsettling. I might," he added quietly, "have changed my own past had you no knowledge of my name.

"I admit," he continued, rising and leaving the confines of the couch, "that I was curious. I was not certain how *you* could *take* my name. The mark was inconsequential. I was surprised at how easily it was laid upon you. I had not expected that. You had no defenses at all." His smile was odd.

"You had no defenses when you first entered my portal. You had no defenses when you visited my Castle, and when you at last came to the forest at its heart.

"I did not…expect…what occurred on that day. You woke the voices and the presence of the Ancients. Kaylin…you were almost destroyed while I watched.

"And then I understood. There was only one way to preserve you, and it was the answer to my question. You did not *take* my name. I gave it."

"You did," she said. And this time, it was almost a revelation. Nightshade had *given* her his name. She hadn't asked. She had barely understood what it meant. No, she thought with a grimace, she hadn't understood it at all. Not until she had gone to the High Court. Perhaps not even then.

She had Nightshade's name. She never thought about it when she could avoid it, which was most of the time. She almost never attempted to use it; today was the first time since the High Halls.

Yes, he replied.

All conversations with Nightshade were going to be like this. Her thoughts, the things she struggled not to put into words, were just as clear to him as the words she did say. Maybe clearer. She grimaced again. Lifted her hand to her cheek.

Why did you take the risk?

I told you, Kaylin. You were the beginning of an ancient tale, a true tale, the like of which I have heard only once. And to reach that beginning, you had to survive.

"Did you take the fief of Nightshade because you were waiting for me?"

"Not entirely, no. But I understood, when the opportunity arose, what I was meant to do. No, it is not, and was not, a matter of *fate.* That is Dragon fare, or misguided mortal belief. The Barrani do not believe in fate or destiny."

She said nothing. Tried to think of nothing. Managed to think of Teela, which, given Teela, sort of proved his point. He drifted toward her, his feet utterly silent against the carpeted floor. She started to take a step back, felt the edge of the couch against her calves, and stopped moving.

He was now standing so close to her she could reach up and touch his face. "Will you keep Nightshade?"

"I will."

"Even if—"

"It is as much part of me as my name, Kaylin. Death will part me from the fief and the Castle. Nothing else. In that, I am a traditionalist. I am not a Dragon, but there are similarities. I keep what is mine." He cupped her unmarked cheek in the bend of his palm; his hand was warm, but dry.

Kaylin's mouth was dry; she wanted to close her eyes. "When you marked me—"

"Yes," he said, his voice soft and that little bit too close to her ear, "I marked you because you were, in my past, marked. I understood that it would bind us. I did not know when you would take my name, or how, and I wanted at least that binding. I found the thread of the tale again, when I at last met you, and I was not willing to relinquish it easily to accidental death or loss."

"And now?"

"Now, you are here, and you are alive. You have survived what even my kin have seldom survived—an encounter with one of the most powerful of the living Dragon Lords. You are Chosen, but you are only beginning to understand what that means, and I have no intention of freeing you now."

"What do you want from me?"

"I told you—"

"You told me only part of the truth."

His brow rose. His eyes darkened a shade. She would never have thought that dark blue was safer, but in some ways, it was. For her. "Very good," he said softly, his tone sharper and colder.

She opened her mouth to speak, and he swallowed the words, almost literally. His lips caught hers, and his hands, which were warm and smooth and dry tightened almost imperceptibly around her cheek and the line of her jaw, holding her face in place.

She felt desire; she couldn't even be certain it wasn't her own, it was so tangled up in the mark and the name and the nearness of him. But she couldn't move, and didn't, not to draw back, not to push him away. This much, she had in her because this much had never happened, not in Barren, and not in the nightmares that Barren had left her.

But when his hands moved, when he shifted, when his body was fully flush against hers, she stiffened. Desire gave way to something darker and colder and wilder—but it was the wildness of a cornered animal. She froze, opened her eyes, saw the lights in the room dimming.

He froze with her, and then very carefully stepped back before she could push him away. His eyes were that odd shade of blue, and they were clear and unblinking.

"I see," he said, and his voice was lower, rougher. He lifted his hand, touched her cheek—the marked cheek, this time—before withdrawing. Heat left the mark as he moved toward the low table, turning his back. She had no words to offer. Nothing to say.

She tried.

He shook his head as she struggled with even the first of the words. "I should have killed Barren," he said. "I should have killed him, but I was not certain that would not destroy the future in which we first met.

"I am willing to wait, Kaylin. Unlike your mortal, I *have* forever."

She was almost shocked at the words, because she couldn't avoid feeling what lay beneath their surface: a grim possessiveness, a violent desire, anger, disappointment. All things she knew well. All things she had experienced, time and again, in the White Towers of Barren after her first—and her only—betrayal of the man who had called the fief his own.

But the fieflord of Nightshade had withdrawn, and stood at a distance, all motion stilled; he didn't look at her, didn't allow her to see his expression—not that that made much of a difference with the Barrani, in the end. He didn't ask her what she wanted, didn't ask her *if* she wanted, didn't ask her when she *might*.

He asked *nothing*. It was not what she expected. Not from a fieflord. Not from Lord Nightshade. His hands were curved like scythes by his sides. After a few minutes had passed, he said, "You will, of course, want to leave."

CHAPTER 9

"There may be some difficulty," he added. When he turned, his eyes were sapphire, and it wasn't the depth of the blue that alarmed, but the hardness. "The portal," he added, when she failed to reply.

She swallowed, nodded, remembered where the day had actually started, and why she had gone to Evanton's in the first place. It was surprisingly difficult. "Do you—did I tell you why I was there?"

"In the Keeper's domain, or the echo of it?"

She nodded.

"I believe you did. And I will say, now, that you have cause for concern. You went to visit the Oracular Halls, did you not?"

"I did." She hesitated. "I don't think the fief is in any danger."

He raised a dark brow. "Perhaps. Perhaps not. I have heard tales—tales only—of the endless way. I have heard, as well, of the Devourer."

"Devourer."

"They are stories, Kaylin. Some would dignify them with the word *histories*. I was not one of them, until this afternoon, and were it not guaranteed to be…interesting… I would have preferred to remain skeptical. But what you did—"

"I didn't *do* anything!"

"What you did in the Keeper's domain implies that those tales are indeed based in some part in truth, and I do not have the resources at my disposal to ascertain how much truth. It is possible, however, that you know someone who might."

"Who?"

"The Arkon of the Royal Library."

She winced.

"Or the Avatar of the Tower of Tiamaris."

"I admit I like that one better," she replied. "But what exactly are these tales I'm supposed to ask about? I don't think I've ever heard of a Devourer—"

"No, you possibly haven't. But if you study some of the oldest of your human religions, I can almost guarantee that there will be some mention of exactly that in their Genesis stories."

"I like this less and less." According to Sanabalis, humans weren't native to this world. It had only barely occurred to her to wonder how they'd got here. And from where. "Is there any other way out of the Castle?" she asked, without much hope.

The answer was no. It was a silent, cool no, with a hint of disapproval for the very strong desire to never cross the portal threshold again in her life. But he led her out of the room, offering her his arm at the door.

She took it; she didn't need another warning about the Castle's fickle geography. She just needed to leave; to get back to Severn before Marcus shredded all possibility of the promotion she'd been chasing for two years. She needed to speak with Tara and Tiamaris; she needed—although she really disliked the idea— to speak with the Arkon.

And she needed to do all of this before her early-evening appointment with Everly in the Oracular Halls. She tried not to resent the banks of endless gray nothing that had eaten up so much of her day, and failed miserably.

But when Lord Nightshade reached the foyer and the closed door that led to the outside world, he glanced down. "I will never be your Tara," he said quietly. "I will never expose my-self as she has done, nor will I lessen the ability of the Castle to protect itself by having so much of it rooted firmly in the outer world.

"But I will not send you through the portal alone today, nor will I summon you through it again until the...current difficulty...is resolved. Come, Kaylin," he added.

He scooped her off her feet; she had time to stiffen, time to breathe, time to throw her arms lightly around his neck and turn her face toward his chest before he began to walk.

Try not to listen, he told her.

She didn't ask him what he meant, because as they passed into the surface of the door, all light shattered, flying out in irregular shards into the blackness of the Castle's portal. The darkness shuddered and undulated; she felt it as if it were a living thing, pressing in on all sides. And she heard it roar. Or she heard *something* roar. Lifting her hands, she covered her ears.

She felt Nightshade's chuckle. *I fear,* he told her, as the roar came again, broken this time into what sounded like the dis-carded refuse of syllables from too many known languages, *that that is perhaps not the most effective way not to listen in this space.* The anger and the desire had ebbed from his voice; it was velvet again. Velvet over the usual cold steel.

She almost found it comforting. No, she *did* find it com-forting. And any day, any series of events, that could make *that* comfortable didn't bear thinking about for long.

He laughed. He seldom laughed. She clung to the sound because it was strange, welcome, and infinitely better than the other voice that currently occupied the same damn space.

But when they emerged, she felt no disorientation, no rebellion from her stomach; the world didn't lurch and spin as her eyes tried to reorient her vision to something resembling reality.

"No," he said, as he set her gently down on her feet. "You passed through the portal in my sphere. I think, until the current difficulty is better understood, I will meet you on this side of the portal."

"Why?"

"I am not entirely certain you will exit the portal in the appropriate place, otherwise." He smiled. "Your discomfort is mildly amusing. Your loss would be less so. Give my regards to Lord Tiamaris," he added.

The sun was lower than Kaylin had expected it would be, which was good; although she felt as if she'd spent half an eternity in the middle of nowhere, she hadn't. Either that or she'd emerged on the wrong day. Nightshade hadn't mentioned time one way or the other, and she hadn't thought to ask. Nor was she about to try now. She knew where she was; she knew it wasn't anywhere close to dark, and she knew where the nearest border crossing was.

Before she'd cleared the walk that led to the Castle—which was now missing the hanging cages that had been such a despised and terrifying symbol of power in her childhood—she ran into Lord Andellen. Sadly, head slightly bowed, thoughts on, of all things, geography, that was literal. He managed to catch her before she bounced; she'd been walking quickly, and he wore armor.

She grimaced. "Sorry," she said, slightly red-faced. "I didn't see you there." The Barrani guards of Nightshade had always worn real chain or even plate, unlike the more common mortal thugs, who often made do with cheap and dirty leather. Andellen however was not dressed as one of Nightshade's guards. He wore a tabard that she'd never seen before, and he wore both a helm and a plate chest that looked as though they should have been in a display case. They were golden.

What kind of idiots tried to make armor out of gold? Probably no one. And if it was Barrani, it probably only looked that way. But then again, what kind of idiots tried to make armor that *looked* like gold?

"You were no doubt preoccupied," was Andellen's grave reply. He bowed. "Lord Kaylin." When he rose, the gravity was heavier. "The High Lord bids me tell you, should I encounter you, that there is some difficulty occurring near the heart of the outer city."

She almost laughed. Didn't. "You were at Court?"

"I was. You might recall that the High Lord convened Court during the difficulty in the fief formerly known as Barren."

"Well, yes, but that was weeks ago."

He raised a brow. "I begin to understand why you were given permission to absent yourself. It was, indeed, a scant *few* weeks ago. And the session itself has not yet come to a close."

"But—"

"Yes?"

"But...you're here."

He nodded, still grave. "You appear to be in a hurry. May I assume that the warning that was to be offered, should I encounter you in person, is no longer necessary?"

She nodded. "We've had days of it. I've spent several hours at the Oracles' Hall, and I'm due back there this evening.

I've also spent several hours walking through a literal rain of blood, among other things. Speaking of which..."

"Perhaps I will offer escort, if you are leaving the fief."

"I am."

He fell in beside her. His stride was not her stride, but he slowed his step in such a way that he didn't outpace her. "The matter of Shadow storm was much discussed," he continued, when she didn't immediately begin to speak. "As was the matter of a Dragon fieflord." His smile was slight, but wry. "Apparently, a Dragon fieflord is of more concern than either an undying Lord or an Outcaste one."

"Did they discuss Illien at all?"

"Only briefly. Illien has not...returned to Court. As far as we are aware, what is left of Lord Illien still resides within the Tower of Tiamaris. Lord Tiamaris has not seen fit to make overtures of any kind to the High Halls, although the High Lord is aware that Lord Tiamaris is still considered a member of the Imperial Dragon Court.

"It is not, entirely, to the liking of the Barrani High Court."

It wouldn't be. Kaylin frowned and then took a right at Kiln road, and Andellen paused. "Lord Kaylin?"

She looked back. "What?"

"You are perhaps too preoccupied. The Ablayne is this way."

She started to tell him she wasn't heading toward the Ablayne and remembered—before she spoke—that the borders in the fief were unstable in unpredictable ways. It was faster, if nothing went wrong, to go the way she'd intended, but given the day? She decided she'd try wisdom, instead of haste.

The bridge that led across the Ablayne and into the fief that had been called Barren for most of Kaylin's life wasn't empty, and she thought better of wisdom when she saw the three wagons waiting on something at the bridge's far end. It wasn't a wide bridge, but she could squeak past the wagons by turning sideways and scraping bridge rails with her butt. Which was not how she wanted to spend the next fifteen minutes. On the other hand, walking through the water in her kit didn't seem like a terrific option, either. She glanced at Andellen in his plate. It was Barrani plate, and probably wouldn't notice an influx of Ablayne.

On the other hand, wearing the Hawk on this side of the bridge actually did serve a useful function; none of the milling and slightly annoyed merchants—or their guards—tried to elbow her over said rails and into the river when she had to push them, more or less politely, out of the way. Since no one who was actually breathing would attempt to elbow a Barrani in any gear over the rail, they made it across the bridge in only ten minutes.

The idea that a *wider* bridge was needed *into* the fiefs was as foreign as native Dragon, to Kaylin. But clearly she could still learn something new every damn day.

Andellen paused at the fiefside foot of the bridge. "These are?"

"Carpenter things," she replied vaguely. "I think."

He raised a brow. "I believe I am capable of recognizing some of the loads. What I meant was, what is the intended destination?"

"Gods know. Tiamaris planned on constructing a Dragon's version of a 'proper' market somewhere in the fief."

"Some rumor about the reorganization of the fief has, of course, reached Nightshade," Andellen said, as he turned away from the bridge and toward Kaylin. "But I highly doubt that the mortals are donating these materials out of the goodness of their hearts."

He spoke the last phrase in Elantran, and Kaylin laughed. The Barrani had no similar phrase, and even saying the words in Barrani would probably have completely slaughtered all of their meaning. She shrugged and turned, as well. "Who knows? I'm not a financial genius." It wasn't something she would have said, had Severn been in earshot; she was still stinging from the lecture about budgeting. "But he's clearly getting it from somewhere."

"And you don't apparently disapprove."

"Possibly because I don't know where," she said with a grimace. "But it's not just the outsiders who are working. He's got his own citizens working on the various projects, as well." She hesitated again, and then added, "This fief lost a lot of people to the Shadows. It's as secure as it's going to get now, but whole buildings melted into something other than stone or ash nearer the interior border—with all the people *in* them. At least we've stopped finding corpses," she added.

"'We'?"

She shrugged. "This way."

The Tower rose at the junction of the newly renamed Avatar Road and the equally newly renamed Garden Row. While Kaylin could understand Avatar—which had been Tiamaris's choice—she privately thought the Dragon Lord should have overruled Garden Row. It might work in the outer city in certain districts, but in the fiefs it just felt wrong. Tiamaris had not, however, overruled the Lady, as she was called.

She and Morse had an ongoing bet about how long it would take for the Lady to ask for *anything* that he'd either deny or overrule. So far, there were no winners, but as Morse had bet Never, it wasn't really something Kaylin could collect on, anyway.

Andellen, however, didn't blink when Kaylin grudgingly acknowledged the names on the *very prominent* street signs erected so close to the Tower.

"I don't know how much Nightshade—"

"Lord Nightshade." He offered the correction while his gaze traveled up to the Tower's impressive, pale—and faintly shiny—height, where a flag struggled against the wind.

"Lord Nightshade, then. How much did he tell you?"

"Very little. It may come as a surprise to you, Private Neya," he added, in a perfectly serious tone, "but I seldom cross the bridges—or the walls—into other fiefs, nor do most occupants of other fiefs enter Nightshade. Information about Tiamaris would not, therefore, be useful. We will never be at war."

"Well," she said, as she turned up the walk, with its singular absence of surrounding fences, gates, or a gatehouse, "try not to step on the carrots or the tomatoes, and try not to bring up the subject of gardening. At all."

"Carrots?" he said, and this time his brow did ripple in confusion.

"The Avatar thinks gardening and farming mean more or less the same thing. Or thinks they should."

"The Avatar."

"Yes. I call her Tara. But everyone else calls her the Lady. If Tiamaris gives you permission, and you take a look at what he's been building around the fief, you'll hear her name. A lot. They think she has eyes everywhere."

He raised a brow.

"I didn't say they were stupid."

Andellen stepped on nothing, of course. Even though his feet were larger than Kaylin's, he still managed to avoid the great, messy leaves that were already encroaching on the path to the blessedly normal doors—and he did it without breaking stride. Catching her expression, he smiled.

"I spent many years in the West March," he said, as if that

explained something. When the explanation had obviously failed to enlighten, he added, "There are groves in the interior of the West March that you do not so much as breathe on. Stepping on any part of any plant would generally be considered suicide."

"To the Barrani?"

He nodded.

"I never want to see their trees."

"It is my suspicion that you will not be overly fond of the insect life, either." He stopped at the foot of the stairs that led to the double doors, both of which were closed. Kaylin glanced over her shoulder at the visible acres of garden; she was well aware that some portion of the garden was in the glasshouse, and some of it was out of line of sight. But the breeze seemed to be the only thing that was moving the plants at the moment. When Tara was at work in the garden itself, it was impossible to miss her.

Kaylin then strode over to the doors and knocked. Andellen joined her slowly as the doors rolled inward. Tara stood in their center, and she beamed; she was wearing dirty gardening gloves and a kerchief that didn't look much cleaner. It kept her hair out of her face. She didn't have to worry about sun, though; they'd discovered that nothing seemed to change her complexion.

"Kaylin!" She ran the two steps and enfolded Kaylin in a hug. Then, arms still wrapped around the Hawk, she glanced at Andellen. "Who's this?"

"Lord Andellen," Kaylin said, returning the hug briefly before she disentangled herself. "Lord Andellen, I'd like you to meet the Avatar of the Tower of Tiamaris."

Andellen stared at Tara for a full minute longer than was comfortable—for Kaylin. Tara had a very odd notion of what was—or was not—polite, and Kaylin had learned to be grateful for it very quickly, as it saved Tiamaris from actually having to eat people or reduce them to ash. Stares did not discomfit her; nor did silences like this one, or their opposite—an endless stream of babble.

She was, in some ways, like a child: she viewed the whole outside world with wonder, and often had to be pulled away from the cracks in the cobbles where weeds grew, or the small birds that congregated wherever there was even the faintest possibility of crumbs. Kaylin wanted to be with her the first time she saw snow.

She stepped back from Kaylin, and then said, to Andellen, "You're of Nightshade."

He'd recovered himself enough to bow, and it wasn't a shallow gesture. "I am, Lady," he replied, as he straightened.

Her frown was slight, and she turned to the open doors as Morse stepped out into the sunlight. Morse was armed. Kaylin realized, with surprise, that it had been a while since she'd seen Morse holding daggers. "He's with me," she said quickly.

"You brought him *here?*"

"Well, technically, yes."

"Why?"

"He's a member of the High Court," Kaylin replied. "And the High Court has some reservations about Tiamaris."

"What kind of reservations?" Morse said, in exactly the wrong tone of voice.

"He's a Dragon. They've got a complicated history." Kaylin shrugged. "But for what it's worth, I trust Andellen, and I trust Tiamaris, so I didn't expect it would be a problem to have them meet."

"It'll be a problem today, unless you want to head back to the market."

"He's out?"

Morse nodded. "We were just about to head out, as well."

"To the garden."

"Oh—no." Morse glanced at Tara's clothing and cringed. "We're due at the construction near the interior border. There are still some…difficulties there, and the Lady can always tell where they are, and how far we can safely go. She can also make it safer, so we don't start without her. Why did you drop by?"

"I'm having a totally different problem," Kaylin replied. "And I wanted to ask Tara a few questions about it. We can walk with you, if you're late." Tara's sense of time, like Kaylin's, was not precise. On the other hand, no one threatened to dock the Tower's pay.

Tara turned to Kaylin. "What problem?" she asked, in her gravest of tones.

Kaylin hesitated, trying to choose her words with care—not so much for Tara's sake, but for Morse's. "I was on Elani street—and while I was visiting a friend, I kind of fell out of the world."

Morse said, "What the fuck is that supposed to mean?"

But Tara frowned, and her eyes darkened. Although she looked human, her eyes, like the eyes of many other Elantran races, shifted in color as her mood did. "You reached the edge of the world?"

"I don't know where I reached—it looked like a whole lot of nothing. But I opened a familiar door, entered a—a very large room. When I tried to leave, the door didn't open into the hallway anymore—it opened into…nothing."

Tara turned to Morse. "I think," she said quietly, "that we will be a little late today." Turning, she waved toward the open doors as Morse muttered something inaudible under her breath. "Come, Kaylin. Lord Andellen?"

"If you permit it, Lady, I will accompany Lord Kaylin."

Tara wrinkled her nose at the title.

"Don't look at me," Kaylin said with a grimace. "I don't think it suits me, either, and *I* can't get him to stop."

Kaylin had spent very little time in the Tower of Tiamaris, not because she disliked it, but because Tiamaris himself spent so little time here. But she did recognize the front foyer, which was very different from that of Castle Nightshade. Some Barrani influences existed, but the Tower belonged to a Dragon now, and that showed. The doors, for one, were very wide, and they were always doubled; the floors were solid stone. In some places, carpets ran the length of the halls—but they didn't run the length of the hall that Tara now opened, again with a wave of her hand.

This hall was as tall as anything in the Imperial Palace, but it was wider; the walls were largely unadorned. Doors could be seen along either side, and doors lay like tiny statements at the far end. But between that end and the one they now stood in, a Dragon could walk. He couldn't fly, not here— but Kaylin would have bet every copper she owned that there were vast, vast caverns beneath these halls in which he could.

"There are," Tara said, cheerfully.

Andellen glanced at Kaylin, who shrugged. "It's not like I'm not used to visiting fieflords and having my thoughts plucked out of thin air. Are we going to the end of the hall?"

"We are," Tara replied.

Kaylin hesitated, and Tara marked it.

"There is no danger to you, here," she said quietly.

"I...might have a bit of a problem with portals, if we need to enter one."

Tara stopped walking then. "Why?"

"I'm not sure—but I got out of nowhere with the help of Lord Nightshade."

"Impossible," was the flat reply. "He cannot travel to where I believe you might have been."

"He didn't exactly travel there," Kaylin replied. "He went into the portal of Castle Nightshade, and he—he made a rip in the world. He pulled me through that. And he didn't think it was a good idea for me to use his portal, afterward—I don't think he thought I'd get to someplace I wanted to go. I'm thinking that probably applies to any portals that you've made, as well."

Tara was quiet—and motionless—for what felt like a long damn time. Andellen, taking his lead from the Lord of this Tower as if she were Lord Nightshade, stilled, as well, which left Kaylin feeling distinctly fidgety. "Did he send you here?" Tara finally asked.

"Not exactly. But—he implied that everything about what I did, or what I experienced, is ancient, and it's ancient in a way that he has no access to. And I thought—you were created when the world was ancient. But *you* can talk in a way that his Castle can't. Or won't," she added quickly.

"There is a possibility," Tara replied, without a trace of annoyance, "that you could touch Castle Nightshade. It would not have the same effect it had on me, because the Castle has been awake for centuries with no sense of who, or what, you are—but I believe, if you tried, it would hear you."

"And I'd survive?"

The Tower's eyes darkened into perfect obsidian orbs. They even reflected light. "You would survive," she said, her voice, like her eyes, both dark and cool. It was disturbing, because she was still wearing her smudged and dirty gardening clothing—and none of it actually *looked* out of place. "I am not entirely certain what such communication would do to the current fief-lord, and I assume he has forbidden the attempt."

Kaylin nodded slowly, remembering—because it was so easy to forget—that the Tower could be damn scary.

"But it is not entirely necessary for you to retreat to the interior of the Tower, and perhaps not wise." She turned once again and began to walk down the hall. Kaylin joined her and listened to the echoing fall of their steps in the acoustically unforgiving heights until they reached the doors—which were no longer all that tiny. Tara waved them open, a fact which made Kaylin love her even more, and they rolled into a room that was both huge, round, and almost empty.

Almost referred to the large, circular pool of water that lay in the center of the floor. It was surrounded by about ten feet of stone on all sides, and while the walls had no obvious lights and no obvious magic—at least none that Kaylin could feel in the usual aching tingle of her skin—and there didn't *seem* to be a window at the top of the curved ceiling, the whole of the room was lit as if it were a public fountain near the Imperial Palace at midday.

Tara's chin, as she approached the still water without hesitation, began to glow, and Kaylin realized that the light was coming from the water itself. She started to follow, but Tara lifted a hand in the universal gesture for "stop." Kaylin stopped.

In theory, Tara didn't have eyes in the back of her head; in practice, she didn't need them. She could, with very little effort, see most of what was happening anywhere within the boundaries of the fief, let alone the Tower itself. She lifted her head and raised her arms, and as she did, Kaylin saw the faint, translucent outline of delicate wings rising above her shoulders. They *really* looked odd considering the rest of what she was wearing.

She spoke, and as she did, the stone of the walls began to crumble. It was a slow, delicate crumble, as if rock were being turned to sand—or dust. But it wasn't all of the wall; it was very selective bits. Kaylin watched as a gentle breeze came and brushed those aside, until what was left was a wall engraved with familiar runes.

"Tara—"

"No, it is not a danger," Tara replied. But the words felt murky to Kaylin, almost muffled. "These are not what lies at the heart of me. I do not need to show you those," she added, and her voice softened as she spoke, losing the hard edge of perfect, ancient knowledge, and returning, for a brief moment, to the soft vulnerability of a young girl.

Andellen glanced at Kaylin, raising a brow.

Tara replied, "No, she wrote them. Or rewrote them."

The Barrani Lord's eyes widened.

"But they're not the ones she wants now," Tara continued. "And even if they were, she can't read them without help anyway." She took a deep breath—there was some question about whether this was an affectation or a necessity on her part—and then spoke.

Or sang.

It was hard to tell the difference.

What was not hard to tell was the effect it had. One by one, the newly engraved words that rested within the confines of the circular walls beyond the edge of the glowing pool, began to glow with a bright, azure light.

CHAPTER 10

Show me, Tara said.

Kaylin, staring at the blue light that now blazed across the walls as if it were fire, shook herself and turned to face Tara. Tara had taken two steps to the edge of the pool, lowering her arms to her sides. Her hands, like the runes, were glowing. "Show you?"

Show me the where that you were.

"That's not normally how we say it," Kaylin replied, joining the Avatar at the edge of the still water. She caught Andellen's expression, and added, "She wants us to correct her use of what she calls idiom."

"How would you normally say this?" Tara asked, speaking out loud, as if only remembering that she could.

"We'd say 'show me where you were.' Well, actually, only the Tha'alani would be able to say that in this case. The rest of us would say, 'Tell us where you were.'"

"Show me."

Kaylin nodded hesitantly. "Uh, how?"

"The water."

"You want me to touch the water?"

"Yes."

Kaylin bent and stretched out a hand.

"No! Not like that!"

She stood again, grimacing. Her reflection was perfectly clear. "How?"

"It's a—think of it as a mirror," she said. "Like your mirrors. This is one of mine. Just—talk to it, the way you talk to your Records."

They weren't Kaylin's Records, and Kaylin had no idea how most of the information *in* Records actually *got* there. It had never occurred to her to wonder. But she nodded, as if information were now contained in...water.

"Just—think at it."

"Think at it."

"The way you think at me."

"I don't think *at* you, Tara. You hear what I'm thinking *at me*."

Then think, the Tower replied, with just a hint of frustration, *at yourself. But through the water.*

Kaylin nodded, pretending the instructions made sense. "Records," she said, automatically. Tara had, however, been as helpful as she could in the creation of this place: the surface of the water shimmered, and the light began to break.

"You can't just skip the water and take it from my thoughts?"

"No. Not as easily. There's too much and it's hard to separate what's relevant from what's constantly just there. And it's not only you who will be using my mirror," she added, with the hint of a sniff. "I'll need to show you things, as well. Maybe."

"It was just a thought. Records," Kaylin repeated, not because it was necessary—she had no idea what was necessary—but because it was familiar. Light across the surface of the pool—larger than any single mirror Kaylin had ever seen—

began to break in a way that was both familiar and disturbing. Strands of different colors began to travel across the circle, moving faster and faster, as if they were seeking something. She thought they were like prettier versions of water worms. It wasn't comforting.

They didn't so much coalesce as interweave, squirming closer and closer together until they couldn't be easily distinguished, and once they did that, the image sharpened. She knew where she was—or rather, what was being depicted: the inside of Evanton's shop, in his very crammed back hall. The door opened.

"No," she said, a little too quickly.

Tara's frown could be felt; Kaylin was desperately thinking *at* the water in an attempt to displace the open image of the Keeper's Garden, so she didn't actually look at the Avatar to catch it. The image dispersed, but Kaylin thought that had more to do with Tara than with any attempt to save her own neck on her part.

She tried again, but this time she closed her eyes and faced out from the immaculate and somehow sterile version of the wrong damn garden, through an open door which faced a rapidly receding hallway. "Records," she said, in a more subdued tone, when she was certain she had the image fixed in her mind's eye.

This time, the world unfolded in gray; the only real color was, as it had been then, the glimpse of a familiar hall. Those halls, she thought, Evanton would forgive her. The Garden, never. The image followed Kaylin's memories, probably more exactly than Kaylin herself could; the image shifted as if it had just taken a step. And then another.

"The hall?" Tara asked.

"I couldn't reach it."

"Why?"

"I couldn't run fast enough. There was no real ground—but what there was felt like dry, soft sand."

"Records," Tara now said. "Above."

Nothing except the glimpse of hallway changed. Above—and below, which was the next instruction—looked pretty much the same as straight ahead, or behind. Kaylin looked across at Tara. Her eyes were still obsidian, but some spark of light—like lightning in a storm—now crossed their small, convex surfaces.

"This is bad?" Kaylin asked, keeping her voice as even as she knew how.

"It is…not good," the Tower replied. She had lost the inflections that often made her sound like a young, excitable girl. Absent those, her voice was like a Barrani voice or a Dragon voice: the surface expression over the ancient. "How long were you—"

A low rumble entered the stillness. Tara's eyes widened, her lips opening on a total lack of words, her question forgotten. She whispered a single word—an unfamiliar word that had at least ten syllables—before she dropped to her knees. She lifted both of her hands, palms down, and placed them flat against the surface of the pool; as she did, the rumbling grew louder. Much louder, in fact, than it had been for most of Kaylin's endless, pointless walk.

Tara shook her head, and her hair flew free, caught by a nonexistent breeze in the still room. "Kaylin, where were you when this happened?" Her voice was low and urgent.

"In the—in a store—" *I hate this.* "I was in the Keeper's home."

"The Keeper?" She frowned, and then nodded. "The Elemental wild ones. You were *there*?"

"No. I was supposed to be there, but the door opened into a different place."

"Different how?"

"Looked the same, but...it was empty. There was no life in it, no real movement, no sense of...of..." She muttered something in Leontine. "I knew it wasn't the right place."

"You crossed a threshold."

"Yes."

"A portal."

"No." She grimaced, and then added, "Not like the portals in the Towers, no. It's always been a normal door. It doesn't even have door wards. It has a boring, normal key."

"It is very, very old," Tara replied. "I have...no memory of it."

"You probably weren't built—"

"I have memories of things that occurred before I was created. It is part of my function. I was created to serve a purpose. Without knowledge of *why*—all of which would have occurred before my birth—I could not do so with any competence. But I do not retain that memory. If it is a portal, it is not a portal in any modern sense."

The Tower's use of modern in this context made Kaylin want to sneeze.

"However...it must fulfill that function. You opened the door and you entered an echo-world. You were aware of it. It is often not something that is clear."

"What the hell is an 'echo-world'?"

"Irrelevant," was the curt reply. "I will speak more to the question later, if you remember to ask it." She closed her eyes, concentrating on gods only knew what. "But this...space... is the great desert. This, I retain in memory. The memories are not clear. They are mostly fragmentary."

Kaylin, who had not done particularly well in any geography that was not confined to Elantra, nonetheless knew what a desert was, and this, leaving aside the sense of sand beneath her heavy patrol boots, was not it. "Not in the normal, mortal context, it's not."

Tara frowned. "You should not have been able to reach it at all. Records," she added. "Marks of the Chosen."

The image obligingly shifted until Kaylin was looking at the insides of her arms—writ huge—as they had been when she'd inspected them after leaving the fake garden. They were, like the space that Tara called the great desert, colorless but glowing. It was more disturbing here than it had been there.

"Tara," Kaylin said, struck by a sudden thought. "Can you *read* those marks?"

"Some of them," the Tower replied, in the distracted way Kaylin sometimes answered the pestering questions of foundlings in the Foundling Halls.

"Are they responsible for—for the desert?"

"No. Nor are they entirely responsible for your presence in it. Show me."

"Show you?"

"How did you leave? How did you find your way back to here?"

"I...called Lord Nightshade."

"Called?"

"I called him."

Tara's eyes widened slightly as the import of those words sank in. But she didn't press further, not directly. Instead, she said, "And he heard you?"

"Yes. Yes, he heard me."

"If you have his—" She glanced at Andellen, pursed her lips, and said, "Perhaps this is something else we should speak of at a later time. I interrupted you. I apologize. Show me. Records cannot contain how you called him," she added. "The act is not a matter of simple elements of memory, like vision or sound."

Kaylin grimaced, nodded. "Records," she said. This word was different; it was tighter and more clipped. Tara was afraid of something, and the Tower's fear was impossible to ignore.

A small rip appeared in the fabric of nothing, shaped like an eye but sideways. In its center stood Lord Nightshade. Where the space itself was colorless, the tear in it was dark—obsidian dark. The only light it shed came from the Barrani fieflord himself. Tara said something; it was a low, low rumble of sound. Kaylin recognized it—it was Dragon.

She probably knows all the good words by now, she thought, and then felt instantly embarrassed.

Nightshade grew larger in the field of the pool's vision, and this time, Kaylin could actually look at his face, examining both his expression and the darkness of his surroundings. What had looked like simple black was not; there were elements of subtle luminescence in the darkness that framed him, like the faint flecks in black opals. She saw his hands in literal fists around whatever it was he was holding, and she noticed then that his fingers—the portions that were exposed to the nonworld—were almost translucent.

His eyes were so dark a blue they were midnight, and as the image grew, and his eyes grew with it, she could see her reflection in them. They didn't likewise reflect the gray.

She heard the roar—and apparently this pool was not as solid as a mirror, because the whole of the image rippled at the sound. Looking up, she saw Tara's eyes; they were, like Nightshade's, black. Unlike his, they still possessed no whites. Kaylin knew the moment she leaped toward the opening, and she knew the moment something wrapped itself around her legs, pulling her back.

Or trying. Nightshade held her. Nightshade, who would have cut off her legs before he allowed her to be pulled back. It was the type of salvation she didn't want.

"What happened here?" Tara's voice was so sharp it sounded entirely unfamiliar.

"Something...caught me," Kaylin said quietly.

The Avatar's hands were splayed flat against the water's meniscus, and she grimaced as the image began to turn—toward what Kaylin hadn't seen. Kaylin froze as it came into view, the edges of the portal, of Nightshade, of her own struggling body, giving way to what she had called the 'nonworld.' If she did speak to the Arkon about this, she was going to have to come up with another damn name.

And she'd speak with the damn Arkon. She'd speak with the Emperor himself, and risk immolation or being the source of brief indigestion. Because this time, she *didn't* see shapeless, endless gray. This time she could see the voracity of hunger; the sky was a face, and it was as black as Tara's eyes, as black as Nightshade's heart, as black as the Dragon Outcaste who had retreated to the heart of the fiefs. But it was larger in all ways; she felt, for a second, that its only desire was the desire to consume—everything.

Tara was frozen.

But the creature grew larger and larger, and although it had no eyes that Kaylin could *see,* she could feel them. It roared. Its roar was encased in syllables, and they shook not only the image, but the room itself; she could feel it beneath her feet. She tried to look at Andellen but she couldn't quite tear her gaze away from the mirror, and she saw that her legs, like Nightshade's fingers, had grown translucent; she could see through them.

She could see through them *except* for where the marks were.

Tara spoke again, her hands so rigid they were stone—stone of Tower, stone of form and birth, waiting for the right word to give them breath and heart—and she opened her mouth, but there were no words at all. Kaylin frowned, and then she bent, grabbing the Avatar's wrists in each of her hands. Her arms, her legs, and half the skin on her back, shrieked in sudden protest, as if some idiot was running his fingers along the slate boards, and she happened to *be* those boards.

She cursed—she thought it was in Leontine, but it was so automatic she couldn't actually tell—and yanked the Avatar's hands away from the water. Or tried. She would probably have had more luck moving Tiamaris. While he was in his Dragon form.

"Andellen," she said, although it came out in a series of grunts. "Help me. No, *don't* touch her—grab me. Pull, damn it."

The water shook. The image grew larger, the sense of hunger stronger. Kaylin thought the shape and the size of the pool couldn't contain it—and she *did not want* to know what would happen if it somehow spilled out. Magic, never the most predictable of tools, could accidentally destroy whole city blocks, and she was standing at ground zero.

The creature roared; the walls shook with the force of its words—and the horrible thing about it was they *were* words. And they weren't. In the face of them, she lost all of her own; what was left was the impulse that formed beneath speech, impelling action. The light in the room began to pulse, as if it were alive; the runes etched across the face of the circular walls flickered wildly.

Another roar, louder, closer; she thought it would crack the stone she was standing on. But this roar was different. Blessedly different. She managed—with effort—to close her eyes, and she heard the raging syllables of a familiar yet unknown language. It was Dragon.

Tiamaris had come.

He was not in Dragon form, but he wore the plated armor that appeared when Dragon scales were somehow pushed to the exterior of the human form; he wore no helm, no cloak. This much, Kaylin could see out of the corner of her eye; her eyes were still focused on the mirror, and on what it contained.

And what it contained less than ten seconds after she became aware of the Dragon Lord was his flame, his fists, a large splash, and a series of ripples that somehow made tidal waves seem like the kiddie end of the public pools near the Imperial Palace. Neat trick.

The image was gone; what remained was a glowing—and moving—pool of water, surrounded on all sides by a lip of circular stone. Which was as much as Kaylin saw before she, Andellen, and Tara all fell over in the type of straining heap you get when you play tug-of-war and the opposite side suddenly lets go of the rope. The usual tangle of limbs, and the usual bruises—because Andellen, in plate, was not exactly a cushion—occurred, and three people—well, two people and the Avatar of one damn strange building—all looked up from more or less the same vantage at the Lord of the Tower, who stood, his arms folded across his chest, his eyes a bright, blazing red that was, even as Kaylin cringed, fading to orange.

"Would someone care to explain," he said, in a voice that managed to be both icy and burning at the same time, "what *exactly* was being attempted, here?" His inner eye membranes rose, muting a color that was never a good sign, and his lips thinned slightly. "Lord Andellen?"

Andellen would have been the first to rise, but he was mostly on the bottom of the pileup, and only an idiot would have shoved at least one of the two people higher up the pile off in a big rush to stand. He managed, on the other hand, to sound like the usual dignified Lord of the Barrani High Court, regardless. "Lord Tiamaris. Forgive the intrusion."

"I may," was the quiet reply. "If I assume that you are here at the behest of Private Neya."

This wasn't technically the case, but given the color of Tiamaris's eyes, Kaylin let it pass. She slid off both the Avatar and the Barrani Lord, rolling more or less to her feet. Then she turned and offered Tara a hand. Tara took it and Kaylin lifted her; she weighed almost nothing. Then again, she could probably shift that weight as much as she wanted, at least in the confines of the Tower.

Andellen's dignity was Barrani; no one offered the Barrani that kind of help. Tiamaris waited until they were all on their feet, and then he turned to glance down at the pool of clear, still water. Kaylin noticed, however, that the runes that were carved in the surface of every inch of wall that wasn't door were still present.

"Lady," Tiamaris said gravely. "Why did you summon me?"

"Not for this," Tara replied, "but thank you."

"What did you see? What were you looking for?"

"Answers." She turned now to Lord Tiamaris. "Kaylin... traversed the dreaming road, if I understand what I saw correctly."

Tiamaris frowned. It was similar to the frown Kaylin offered, but clearly more significant. "The dreaming road?"

"There are other words for it, but there are no true words. It is not an exact description."

"And what I saw when I entered?"

"That... I fear that was the Devourer."

Again, the Dragon Lord waited, and it was slightly comforting to see that Tiamaris, who was centuries older, was at least as ignorant as Kaylin. "What is the Devourer?"

"We do not entirely understand what it is, nor did we. But it exists on the dreaming road, and it hunts for things that fill the emptiness, even in small ways. What it finds, it devours."

"Thus, the name?"

"Thus the name." She hesitated.

But Kaylin understood the hesitation, now. "It found me."

"It found you, yes. But it found you quickly, Kaylin. Too quickly. It is almost as if—"

"As if it were already sniffing around the area."

"If the dreaming road can *have* an area, then yes. There were theories," Tara added, shoving strands of her hair back beneath the kerchief that bound most of it—and which now sat lopsided on the top of her head. "But they were theories, only. Once," she added softly, "there were doors between this world and other worlds. Once.

"But not all worlds and not all doors are safe. That, we learned. The dreaming road was the space *between* worlds. You could not take doors to reach them, not the first time, perhaps not even a second. You walked in the emptiness and it either devoured you, or it led you. If it led, you would find a world similar to, and different from, the one you had left.

"Forgive me, Lord," she added, and she looked almost embarrassed. "But the information I have is...not complete. I was created with an awareness, but there was no specific instruction. The Devourer exists only on the dreaming road, but it is said that he can exist—for some time—upon other worlds, and in other places.

"And it is said, if he does, his nature will, in the end, destroy the world, or the node, upon which he stands. He will reduce a world, bit by bit, into motes of dust and light."

"And how, exactly, does he do this?" Kaylin asked, trying to keep the disrespectful edge of disbelief out of her voice— and mostly, to her surprise, succeeding.

"We do not know. But where worlds once existed before the Devourer reached them, no worlds existed after. Some said the worlds were sundered, but it was not the belief of most of the Ancients. They spoke of an end."

Tiamaris's eyes had now shaded to a pale copper, which was probably about as gold as they were going to get this afternoon. "And what you saw?"

"It is the Devourer. I am certain of it."

"And you have seen this creature before?"

"No. No memories exist of him, just stories. Just poor words, not true ones. But—his voice, I know. I felt his voice, Lord, and I *know* it."

"How does he enter a world?" Kaylin finally asked.

"I do not know. No one—nothing—would be foolish enough to invite him. He must wait for, or stalk, a traveler. Lord Nightshade perhaps did not understand what he faced. I think the Barrani and the Dragons have too little information of this kind, for they were never meant to be a race of travelers. They exist here. They are *of* this world."

"And me?" Kaylin asked, loosely clasping her hands behind her back.

"Your race was not created here. Which means at least one of you, or your kin, could walk the long road through the dreaming. And survive it. But Lord Nightshade is correct. If you can, *by accident,* fall onto the dreaming road, you must avoid portals. Mine. His. The Devourer saw you. He was aware of you. He will hunt you.

"He cannot open the portals himself. It was said he cannot create. But if a portal is open, and he can reach it somehow, he will enter that door."

Lord Andellen now bowed. "My pardon, Lord Tiamaris. Lady. I think that I must return—in haste—to my Lord. I had hoped to have some small tour of the fief of Tiamaris. The Barrani High Court, not conversant with the culture of the fiefs, has been troubled by the presence of a ruling Dragon Lord in the city—one who is not the Emperor.

"But clearly, if the time for such a tour exists, it is not now."

Tiamaris nodded. "I believe," he added, "that I, too, now have business elsewhere. Kaylin, attend me."

"Tara?"

"He's going to the Court," Tara replied. "To speak with the Arkon."

"Oh, great. That was my next stop."

Tiamaris raised a brow.

"So…" Kaylin said, as they reached the bridge—which, for the moment, had lost its wagons and their somewhat annoyed drivers and looked more or less like a normal fief bridge. "We've been having a bit of trouble in the city."

"Having, which is not the same as causing?"

"Ha, ha. I see you've picked up some of Tara's sense of humor."

Tiamaris frowned.

"She's a building, Tiamaris. She doesn't *have* one."

"Ah. And clearly, you do."

"What it was meant to imply was that you now have *more* of a sense of humor than you had before, which was less than none at all."

He raised a brow, and his lips folded in just such a way that Kaylin actually laughed out loud.

"I also know she knows how to curse in Dragon, so I intend to visit more often. Just saying."

He shook his head, and they walked a few blocks in silence. At length, he said, "She will be happy to have your company, although she has been quite busy in the fief. I would, however, appreciate that you keep the *source* of this newfound knowledge—should you be able to pronounce the words in a way that would make them recognizable—to yourself. My position in the Dragon Court is already somewhat tenuous, and at least one member would look at your acquisition of this particular part of our language as a hostile activity on my part."

"Sanabalis?"

"Ah, no. If any of my kin can be said to possess a sense of humor, it is *Lord* Sanabalis." The pause between this sentence and the next was distinct. It was also accompanied by a look that Kaylin didn't immediately recognize. "Has a teacher for your etiquette lessons been confirmed yet?"

It was hard to remember that the space between the time they'd been brought up—as utterly mandatory—and now was less than two full days. She glared. "Things have been a bit hectic—both in the Halls *and* the Imperial Palace. I imagine they're willing to let it slide."

"Things would have to be more than merely hectic for the Dragon Court to let anything, as you put it, *slide*."

"Rains of blood?"

He raised a brow. "Were they *within* the Palace?"

"No. There was a breach of magical containment in the Palace Records, if that counts."

Both of his brows rose.

"I guess that means it counts."

Both of his brows fell, and joined for a moment across the bridge of his nose. It was like Dragon sign language. On the other hand, his eyes were a fairly solid gold at this point, so the disapproval wasn't all that visceral. In a more serious tone, Kaylin continued. "I have another appointment at the Oracular Halls with Sanabalis this evening—Lord Sanabalis—and the midwives are relocating all potential live births to a section of town nowhere near the aforementioned rain of blood." Seeing his expression, she grimaced. "Don't ask. A delicate investigation—delicate enough that I never heard a word about it in the Halls—was thrown on its ear, if we're being polite—"

He lifted a hand. "I see. Very well. I will, however, indulge in an attempt to continue my culture acclimatization by offering a bet on the outcome of those lessons."

If her jaw hadn't been attached, she would have lost it when it fell off. As it was, it kind of hung there for a few seconds while her brain went in search of words. "You want to—you want to *bet?*"

He did laugh, then. It was a low, deep, very, *very* loud sound, and it cleared the street for yards in any direction, even if it didn't seem insane or maniacal. "I am attempting to absorb local color and dialect."

"You mean, without eating it first?"

"Indeed."

She watched his face, watched his expression, watched the easy way in which he walked through the streets. He looked very much like the Tiamaris she had first met months ago— but it was as if he'd grown *into* his skin, somehow, as if he was truly comfortable for the first time.

"I am not entirely certain what will occur when I enter the Palace. This will be the first time that I have appeared without an explicit command from the Emperor."

"Do you mind?"

"Are you asking me if I miss it?"

She nodded.

"No. But I do not delight in its absence, either, and this was unexpected. The Dragon Court is not entirely comfortable with my current position—which was to be expected—but over the various meetings of the past few weeks, the Dragon Lords have become less suspicious and more resigned. I am familiar with both states," he added, with a mild grimace, "because of my rebellious youth.

"They will never be entirely without suspicion, however. If I benefit from one thing, it is their assumption of my callow youth."

"All centuries of it."

"Indeed."

The Palace Guards were not in a state of high alert when Tiamaris set foot on their grounds. Then again, the Imperial Guards were human; it was *just* possible that they thought you could own your own land *and* be an upstanding citizen. Either that, or they didn't fancy pissing off a Dragon. They were their usual brand of crisply officious, and Kaylin felt discouraged because she was certain that *this* is what etiquette lessons were supposed to teach. Among other things.

But when they entered the Palace, Tiamaris was stopped by the man who often seemed to be in charge of giving directions. Seneschal? "Lord Tiamaris."

Tiamaris nodded. "If possible, we would like a moment of the Arkon's time. It is likely something he would consider urgent."

"Very good, sir." The man turned and signaled; he never raised his voice. Two of the Palace Guards now approached. "Please convey word that Lord Tiamaris has arrived, accompanied by an Imperial Hawk, to both the Arkon and Lord Sanabalis."

They didn't salute; they did nod. And they moved quickly.

To no one's surprise, Sanabalis arrived first. He didn't look entirely pleased. "Private," he said, making the word sound like an epithet, which, given he spoke his usual High Barrani, said something. "You have been absent from the office for hours under circumstances that would be considered both unusual and upsetting *at this time*. I would suggest you avail yourself of the nearest mirror to let Sergeant Kassan know you are still alive."

She glanced down the grand—and entirely mirrorless—hall.

Sanabalis was not, by any stretch of the imagination, in a good mood. "My meeting rooms should be ready by the time we reach them. I took the liberty of ordering food. Follow."

They both knew the way; they'd been there often enough at this point But they followed in wordless silence. More or less.

"We need to speak with the Arkon," Kaylin told Sanabalis as they walked.

"I'm certain a message has been sent to that effect. With luck, the person carrying the message won't suffer too much for the interruption of the Arkon's current work."

CHAPTER 11

Food, according to Kaylin's stomach, was welcome. It was also—for Imperial Food—very simple: no sauces, no strange unidentifiable bits, nothing unusual done with eggs. Kaylin didn't like to eat anything she couldn't recognize. She took her usual seat in the large room, glancing as she did through the huge bank of fancy windows that overlooked the Halls of Law. The three flags—Wolf, Sword, and Hawk—were flapping in the winds at the heights, and Aerians in larger numbers than usual were on sky patrol.

She frowned; their patrol was both lower and wider than its usual orbit of the towers. "Sanabalis?" she asked, as she watched.

The familiar sound of Tiamaris clearing his throat made her add a word as she tried again. "Lord Sanabalis?"

"Private?"

"Did something *else* happen while I was missing?"

"I believe Sergeant Kassan may have new information for you."

"Will I survive long enough to get any of it?"

"It depends. How often does your Sergeant worry when you've disappeared without warning or notice, in an obviously magical way, in the center of a locus of potential that is entirely unpredictable?"

She cringed. "Can I use a mirror here?"

"Use the mirror on the inside of the cabinet on the East wall." As she began to make her way across the room, he added, "The other East, Private."

Marcus was a bristling ball of fur. Kaylin could see that clearly, even though the face that mostly filled the mirror when she made the connection was Caitlin's. "Kaylin!"

Kaylin immediately held up both hands, palms out, in a gesture of surrender. "I'm sorry."

"You went into Evanton's shop and disappeared for several hours, dear." She spoke in a very quiet voice. Given it was Marcus, it wouldn't help.

"Marcus looks…fluffy."

"It's been a difficult few hours. We've been handed a small army of lawyers' documents, not all of which can be forwarded to the Palace to be dealt with. You disappeared—the young boy, Grethan, was *very* distraught when he mirrored—and there have been five fires within the quarantined area, all of unknown origin.

"There's also been a delegation of Arcanists ensconced in the waiting rooms for the past hour and—"

"Private!"

"Here's Sergeant Kassan, dear."

"Where the hells are you?" Marcus said. His jaw was in the position that had earned him the nickname Ironjaw, and his fangs—both sets—were on prominent display. Kaylin instantly lifted her chin, exposing her throat, which wasn't going to be all that calming, given he couldn't *actually* reach through the mirror to grab it.

She cleared said exposed throat. "I'm with Lord Sanabalis and Lord Tiamaris in the Imperial Palace."

Her location—and the probable existence of witnesses—might not make a difference given his current mood, but it couldn't hurt. His eyes were a shade of orange that was too damn close to red; she tried to pretend it was just the visual distortions of the mirror's transmission. He took a deep breath, and expelled it in a growl.

"When, exactly, did you arrive at the Palace?"

She grimaced. "Ten minutes ago."

"And you took the time to wander over to the fiefs and pick up Lord Tiamaris on your way there?"

She really, really wished his eyes would shade a little more to the gold. Or a lot. "Not exactly."

"There *is* an explanation for your sudden disappearance?"

"I'm—I'm not entirely sure."

Marcus growled. It was a low sound that caused the image in the mirror to vibrate.

"I can tell you what *happened,*" she added quickly. "I just can't explain *why.* I opened a door in Evanton's shop, and I ended up somewhere else. I couldn't get back to either his shop or anything resembling the world I know."

"But you're here."

"Yes. Nightshade found me. Don't ask. I don't understand how it worked, either. I didn't intend to disappear, Marcus."

"And you *intended* to report in and it slipped your mind?"

This was not a question she wanted to answer in the affirmative. It was not, sadly, a question that could be answered in any other way, because Kaylin was demonstrably still alive and still conscious.

"Sergeant Kassan," Sanabalis said, unexpectedly coming to her rescue. "My apologies for interfering in your discussion with Private Neya, but the Arkon has arrived, and his time is being diverted—to his grave displeasure—from studies the Emperor feels necessary to our present difficulties.

"If you could perhaps resume your disciplinary interrogation after the Arkon has concluded his brief visit, I would be grateful."

Marcus's eyes narrowed; the fur tufts on his ears were standing straight up. But he nodded, curtly, to the Dragon Lord. "I expect a full report on the entire day before you leave for the night," he added to Kaylin. The mirror went gray before she could reply.

Orange-eyed Leontines were a fact of life. They weren't a *pleasant* fact of life, but if you worked in the Halls of Law, you learned to deal with them. Orange-eyed Dragons were, sadly, becoming a fact of life, and Kaylin was considerably less sanguine about their existence.

Lord Tiamaris and Lord Sanabalis bowed, quickly, as the Arkon entered the familiar room. Kaylin did the same, but she was more careful about the speed at which she shed obsequiousness. He did *not* look happy to see her. He looked about as pleased to see Tiamaris, but he did offer Sanabalis a terse, and not terribly friendly, nod. He took a seat without preamble, and he fried a sandwich in the process. He also burned through half the table the sandwich was on. She had never seen the Arkon breathe fire before.

The table teetered, and Sanabalis caught it deftly—and without comment—before it landed, smoldering, on the carpets beneath it. He put the small flames out with his hands, again without comment, before he took a seat himself. Tiamaris waited until the two older Dragons were seated before he sat. Kaylin stood.

"I am busy," the Arkon told her, again without preamble. "No reason was given for the interruption." His tone made clear that the reason she was about to offer had better be a damn good one.

"I'm here," Kaylin said, keeping her voice cool and even, "to ask you about the Devourer."

The silence that enfolded the room in the wake of the word was entirely controlled by the Arkon. His eyes did not, in fact, shift color at all, and to make the threat in that color clear, his inner membranes now lowered completely. She swore the other two Dragons weren't even breathing.

Then again, she had never seen the Arkon angry before; maybe they had.

"The Devourer." It wasn't a question. She now had his full attention. His irritation at his interrupted research—whatever it was—seemed to have evaporated, along with the sandwich and part of the table.

She waited. It wasn't a game; she was being cautious. For Kaylin, silence had often been the best bet.

"You will now explain where you heard the word, and in what context," the Arkon said. "You will answer any questions I ask, but absent those questions, you will start at the beginning and continue—in a logical, linear fashion—until you reach the end."

She nodded carefully and, taking a small breath, began.

"The Keeper's Garden was not the Garden?"

"No."

"And you knew this how?"

"I've been in it a couple of times."

"It looked the same, to your eye."

"Yes. But that's all it did—it *looked* the same. There was no life in it."

"Continue."

"You heard a growl?"

"Yes."

"An actual growl?"

"That's what it sounded like to me."

For the first time, the Arkon looked away from Kaylin's face. "Sanabalis, I would like to access the Palace Records."

"I think it unwise," was Sanabalis's cautious reply. "If it becomes necessary, we might repair to the Library. There are stronger wards and magical precautions in place against unknown or unpredictable intrusions, there."

To Kaylin's surprise, the Arkon nodded. "If it becomes necessary." He turned back to Kaylin; he did not appear to notice that Tiamaris was in the room. Lucky Tiamaris. "Continue."

"You summoned Lord Nightshade."

"No. I called his name."

"And he heard it."

"Yes. He went into the portal between his Castle and the rest of the fiefs, and he—he ripped down part of the wall."

"That is a *very* imprecise description, Private Neya."

"It's the only description I have."

"Very well. I am considering a permanent memory crystal. For your use."

She stopped herself from grimacing or objecting. Barely.

"This hole that he ripped in the wall was visible to you from where you were standing?"

She nodded. "It was black. He was standing in it. The growling had gotten a lot louder while I'd been calling him—I don't know if that's because whatever was making the noise could hear *me* call. In theory, I know that's not possible. But practically speaking, it certainly looked that way.

"But I made it to Nightshade. He was having trouble holding the hole open. I was moving slowly. I think the landscape shifted under my feet as I tried to reach him, and I ended up jumping that last little bit. He caught me. Something else caught me, as well, from the other side."

The Arkon stared at her. "What," he finally asked softly, "did Lord Nightshade see?"

"I...don't know." As far as this went, it was entirely accurate. "But...he didn't hear what I heard, either. He didn't hear growling. I would swear he heard words."

"What were those words?"

"I don't know. I don't think he *recognized* them, either. But...when I heard what *he* heard, when I listened to what *he* was listening to—which was hard, by the way—they sounded like syllables. Like language. But not a language I knew." She hesitated, and then added, "I used my own magic, somehow. It let go."

"'Somehow'?"

This time, Kaylin did glance at Sanabalis; the Dragon Lord was watching the Arkon as closely as the Arkon had been watching her.

"I'm not entirely certain," she finally replied. "I don't always know how the magic works. If I pay attention while I'm using it, I pick up the details on a conscious level—but I don't need the details to use it."

The answer did not appear to please him; nor did it enrage. "You left the nonworld, as you call it, and you entered Castle Nightshade, in the fief of Nightshade."

"Yes."

"From there you went to the fief of Tiamaris."

She nodded.

"Continue."

She managed a brief version that left out Lord Andellen entirely, but when she reached the room with the pool, the

Arkon lifted a hand. His eyes were now a golden-brown; he was troubled, but focused. "A moment, Private."

She nodded, and glanced at the food that had not been turned to ash. Her stomach was vastly less subtle, and she heard Sanabalis snort. He didn't tell her to eat, and she wasn't stupid enough to start without the Arkon's permission.

"Lord Tiamaris."

Tiamaris nodded. Unlike Kaylin, he'd chosen to sit, and he didn't vacate his seat when his name was called. To be fair, the Arkon didn't seem to expect it, either.

"You hold the Tower in your fief."

"Indeed."

"It is, by all accounts—and those accounts are scant and very underdocumented in my opinion—unique."

Tiamaris inclined his head; Kaylin cleared her throat. The latter caused the Arkon's baleful glance to fall on her for a second. "Private?"

"I think all of the Towers are unique. I mean, I don't think generalizations will give you much useful information."

"Understood." He turned back to Tiamaris. "Your Tower has an Avatar that speaks and interacts with the people who live in the boundaries of your fief."

"Yes."

"Does the Avatar maintain the information that existed at the time of its creation?"

"Her," Kaylin inserted.

This time the Arkon failed to look at her at all.

"The events that occurred at, or after, her creation have not been relevant to the ruling of the fief," was Tiamaris's reply. He glanced at his hands as he spoke. "We have been much occupied with repairs and rebuilding. The fief took severe casualties before the borders were stabilized, and we are still uncovering evidence of damage, and attempting to recover from it."

"If this is your way of telling me that you *do not know...*"
The Arkon didn't finish the sentence; instead he lifted a hand
to his eyes. "Sanabalis," he finally said, "finish this for the
moment. I fear to become too frustrated."

Sanabalis coughed slightly. "As you wish, Arkon. Will you
retire to the Library?"

"No."

Sanabalis, however, had, in theory, years of practice dealing
with recalcitrant students. "The Tower," he said, gesturing
for Kaylin to sit, "has more freedom. She can communicate
directly with people who are not her Lord. What she did,
Private, has not been done for a very long time."

"What do you mean?"

"The creation of a water-based mirror."

Kaylin couldn't recall having seen one before. "I'd bet
money the Barrani High Halls have them."

"I would not take that bet. I did not speak of the *use* of
such mirrors, only of their creation. You did not note what
the runes on the walls were."

"No. They're Old Tongue, like my marks—but you know
I can't read them." Kaylin shrugged. "It's a *Tower,* Sanabalis."
Glancing at the Arkon, she added, "Lord Sanabalis. Tower
space, Castle space—it's *not* normal space. It shifts and changes."

"You said, however," the Arkon interjected, "that you were
not required to enter a portal to reach this particular room?"

"Yes. So?"

All three Dragons exchanged a similar glance. Sanabalis
finally said, "In fief parlance, it is a good bet that this room
exists in the here and now. Its dimensions and its functions
will not now change, unless she desires it. Beyond the portal,
you are deep in the heart of her territory, and her territory
is stable and solid only to her, and possibly to Lord Tiamaris.

But…what you have said so far is troubling, and I think you are not yet done."

"Not…quite."

"Then please, continue."

"She made me review what I'd seen. When she reversed the mirror view, when she forced me to examine what I'd managed to see through Lord Nightshade's vision, she was… upset. She touched the surface of the water itself—I think she meant to stabilize it—"

"She did not," Tiamaris said quietly.

"What was she trying to do?"

"I am not entirely certain. It was defensive," he added.

Kaylin didn't ask him how he knew. Instead, she said, "She called what she saw the Devourer. She told me to come to the Arkon."

"I think, old friend," Sanabalis told the Arkon, "that your particularly old-fashioned attachment to the Worlds theory of magic and Genesis is about to be proved indisputably true."

The Arkon, however, was now looking at Kaylin. "What did *you* see, Chosen?"

She closed her eyes, and then opened them quickly, because his question had returned a glimpse of the dark and hungering void that made a lie of any definition of *nothing* she'd ever known. "I saw what she saw. I understood why she called what she saw the Devourer."

"And this Devourer touched you."

She nodded.

"We *need* Records, Lord Sanabalis. We need them *now*." The Arkon rose swiftly, the grace and economy of his movements belying his supposed age. "Come."

"The Library?" Sanabalis asked.

"Yes."

★ ★ ★

The Arkon could *move*. His walk was generally stately and even; today it was almost a run. This silenced Tiamaris and Sanabalis—who were careful enough not to speak much when the Arkon was present anyway. Kaylin could talk, or shout, while running, but didn't bother. The Imperial Guards basically made a beeline for the nearest wall or section of hall that didn't contain three heavy Dragons.

The Library door's ward was glowing as they approached, and Kaylin flinched automatically, but this time she wasn't required to touch it; the Arkon *spoke at it* instead, and the doors practically flew to either side in their rush to avoid him. Sanabalis and Tiamaris exchanged a glance, no more, and Kaylin walked in behind them, pulling up the rear. The fact that the rear was farthest from the Arkon was purely coincidence.

He led them past the shelves with their obvious books, but this time, instead of heading to the rounded room at the end of one hall, he jogged to the right, to where the shelves and their odd rolling ladders compressed into a tangle of narrow walkways, teetering papers, and stairs. The stairs were just larger than one Dragon in width.

Kaylin wondered just how large the Arkon's collection of expensive odds and ends actually was as she dutifully followed. She hadn't been in the Library often, but suspected at this point that *Library* was not the accurate word. Or maybe it lost a lot in the translation from Dragon to Barrani. The small hall that opened at the head of the steps had the advantage of not being lined by packed, crammed shelves. It had the disadvantage—to the Dragons—of being slightly shorter than six feet in height. This didn't bother Kaylin; everyone else was crouching.

Sanabalis asked a question that Kaylin caught only around

the edges, and the Arkon grunted in response. Light brightened the hall. In this case, it wasn't that much of an improvement, because most of it was held by Sanabalis, and his back blocked it.

But they continued to walk; the hall seemed to be built at a slight incline, and it ended in yet another door. The door was the height of the hall, and it looked as if it were wooden, although bands of something like iron or steel cut across it in three places. It had, of all things, a handle, and three locks that were obviously meant for keys.

"How old is this place?" she asked. She'd never seen doors in the Imperial Palace that weren't protected by door wards; door wards could be enchanted to serve a variety of different levels of privacy, and they captured Records information about who had triggered them and who had crossed the threshold, not to mention when.

"Old enough," was the reply. It was curt. "If you refer to the absence of door wards, there is a reason for it."

"I'm in favor of absent door wards," Kaylin said quickly. "But...they're considered state of the art, and the Emperor's not exactly hurting for money or mages."

"No, he is not. This, however, is relevant to my duties, and door wards would not be beneficial here."

"Why?"

"They would be an entirely foreign source of magical energy." He pushed the door, and it opened into the type of natural darkness you get when there are no windows. This darkness didn't last long, but it was broken by dragon's breath and—of all things—torches. There were torches in a large, long basket attached to the wall. He lifted one, lit it; she could smell the oil as the fire started to burn. He passed this torch to Tiamaris, and lit two more.

None of them were offered to Kaylin.

"This," the Arkon said, his voice echoing oddly in this new, and mostly unseen, room, "is the heart of the most ancient parts of my collection. I feel the need to remind you of the rules of the Library at this juncture."

"Touch nothing, or die?" she said, in Elantran.

The Arkon's brow looked bronze in the torchlight. "A fair summation, if perhaps a bit unadorned." He nodded at the other two Dragons. "Follow me, Private. If you feel the need to examine something more closely, give me warning. I should also add that if you feel a need to discuss the contents of this room with anyone you will discuss it with Sanabalis or myself."

She thought about Marcus's final expression and grimaced. But a Dragon in your face was more of a concern than a Leontine in a mirror, so she nodded and began to walk.

She'd been in a similar dark room before, and she had assumed—at the time—that it was the repository of all things ancient; clearly the Arkon had enough of them scattered about in nooks and crannies that she'd been mistaken.

"Was this where you were working before you were interrupted?"

"By you?"

"By us," she replied, nodding in Tiamaris's direction.

"Ah. No. The light here is poor, even for Dragon eyes, and some of the items in this particular room appear to be sensitive to the use of external magic." He frowned and paused. "The last time you entered one of the more unusual artifact stores, you interacted with a skeleton and removed one or two items of value.

"The Emperor, however, felt your presence in the city necessary, or you would have taken their place. Is that understood?"

"Yes, Lord—yes, Arkon."

"Good."

This room, unlike the previous room, did not seem to be lined with shelves—although it was hard to tell, because torchlight didn't seem to extend as far as the walls. It was a much larger room, and the floors were rougher, like hewn stone, rather than the wooden planking that was common in most buildings meant to house living people.

"Tiamaris," she whispered.

He glanced at her, lifting a brow that was dark, in contrast to the Arkon's ivory.

"Please tell me this is not a cavern."

"If you insist. Is the statement meant to be accurate?"

"Why is it that so many buildings in this damn city have caverns either beneath their floors or—or wherever this is?"

"I think, if you consider the question, the answer will present itself," Lord Sanabalis interjected. "And this is perhaps the time to consider the question in silent contemplation."

"I thought the reason this city existed in *this* place was because of the fiefs and the High Halls."

"Yes. You did."

Kaylin continued to follow in the Arkon's steps, while trying to remember that, for the most part, she liked Dragons. They were straightforward when compared to the other Immortals she saw a lot of, namely the Barrani, and while they were undeniably arrogant, they didn't make too much of a point of expecting you to confirm all the reasons why they had every right to be that way, in public.

But she stopped thinking about Dragons as the Arkon slowed, because if the torchlight didn't touch walls, it did touch what he now approached. It was an altar.

Kaylin didn't spend a lot of time in churches or cathedrals. For one, murders seldom happened in them, and for two, she had never quite decided which of the various gods it would be advantageous to worship. But she had seen her share of altars, and she had long since past the age where the phrase "stone table" came to mind.

This altar, however, was different from any other that she'd seen in one respect: it was huge. The flat of it was, at best guess, about twenty feet across. Sadly, it was also at least eight feet in height—or possibly more. There was no easy way, short of climbing a ladder, to get a good look at what lay on top of it. On the other hand, there were carvings on the sides of the base, and to no one's surprise—or at least not Kaylin's—they were familiar.

"This is the Old Tongue," she said quietly.

"It is, indeed," was the Arkon's reply.

"Did you move this, or was it already here?"

"What do you think?"

"It was already here."

He nodded. "I cannot think why you were considered such a poor student."

Because none of the other teachers I had could threaten to turn me to cinders or eat me? She said nothing when Sanabalis politely coughed. "No one tried to move it before the Flight arrived here?"

"It is possible it was tried. There was no clear evidence remaining, but you will note that the rock of the floor forms the shape of a basin only here."

"Is this the reason the Palace is actually standing where it stands?"

"It is not the *only* reason, and before you ask, if you are unwise enough to do so, I am not at liberty to discuss more. I feel it is somewhat unwise to have you here at all, but the situation merits the lack of caution. You will, if you approach the altar, note the runes graved here."

She nodded.

The Arkon lifted one hand. "We will stand back," he told her. She stopped walking, and he frowned. "Perhaps my Barrani is insufficient to the task of instruction, Private Neya. *We* will stand back. You, however, will approach."

"Can I take a torch?"

"Lord Tiamaris, give her your torch. At this point, there is very little that she can damage."

Tiamaris complied. Kaylin, who hated most tests and utterly loathed impromptu ones, took the torch and obligingly approached the base of an altar that was clearly meant for giants. Well, small giants. "Did Dragons use this, do you think?" she asked the Arkon. "It's about the right height for the form."

"It is possible," was the neutral response.

"You're not certain?"

"Dragon form doesn't lend itself to finer manipulation, and most ceremonies that involve altars require that ability."

How much fine motor control did it take to dump a large carcass on an altar top? Kaylin didn't ask. As she approached the altar's side, she saw that the runes engraved there had begun to glow. This was not, in and of itself, all that surprising. What did surprise her was that specific runes began to *fade*. She stopped walking.

"Continue, Private. You are not, in fact, defacing the altar. The shift in the runes appears to be a function of the altar's magic."

She started to walk again, and as she did, the runes that remained—at least on the one side of the altar's base she could easily see—began to glow brighter; light passed from faint to bright, and it was a golden light, unlike the blue that her marks often became. There was more than one rune; she thought there were five. They grew larger.

She began to walk around the sides of this pedestal; they weren't as long, but they also contained golden runes: two. They were not the same as the ones on the front, if it was the front. She fumbled with her sleeves, while holding the torch; it took a long damn time.

"Private?"

"Just checking something." She shoved the left sleeve up to her elbow. The marks on her arms, like the marks on the altar, were glowing—but not *all* of them. "Arkon?" she asked, arms still exposed.

He nodded and approached, and after a hesitation, so did the other two Dragon Lords, who had apparently been relegated to the category of inconsequential for the moment. Tiamaris took back his torch. The Arkon caught her wrist, and she allowed it—in part because his grip reminded her a lot of stone, and the effort to shake it off would probably cost her skin, to no notable effect. The Arkon's presence didn't seem to cause the runes on the altar's side to change significantly, either.

"Does it normally do this?"

"A variant, yes," was his quiet reply. He hadn't taken his eyes off the marks on her arms. She, on the other hand, was now watching his eyes, because those were the weather vanes of the Dragons. This one indicated an upcoming storm.

"What do they say?" she finally asked.

"I am not completely certain. I would like to see your other arm. Tiamaris." His voice was flat; he was talking to a lackey, now, not a colleague. "Get the ladder on the far wall—the one with the platform. Put it on the other side of the altar."

Tiamaris, in spite of any change in status, did what any sane person would have done: he obeyed, first handing his torch to Sanabalis, who followed him. The ladder, from the sounds of raw scraping against the floor, was heavy, but Tiamaris returned with it, and she heard a different scraping as it was put into the desired position. "Arkon?"

"Don't just stand there. Come here. I want your opinion on the marks on Private Neya's arms. The glowing ones," he added, in exactly the peremptory tone of voice Kaylin most hated in any of her teachers. Clearly, several centuries had enabled Tiamaris to handle it with grace.

But Tiamaris's eyes were almost gold; the Arkon's were now orange. The younger Dragon glanced at the older Dragon's face before he spoke. "I don't recognize them."

"*Any* of them?"

"Not clearly. If you wish, we can repair to my Tower. The Lady may have more knowledge."

"We are not likely to be able to repair to your Tower *with* the altar," was the chilly reply. The Arkon was silent for a few beats before he added, "I would, however, like to visit the Avatar at a slightly more convenient time in the future. And I would also like you to take note of both the glowing marks on Private Neya's arms, and the runes on the side of the altar. If it is at all possible, as we don't have a convenient memory crystal, I would like to know what she thinks they mean."

But Tiamaris inched the sleeve up Kaylin's wrist, and frowned. "This one," he said quietly, "I've seen before. And this."

"It's not on the altar—" Kaylin began, and then bit her tongue; she couldn't see the whole damn thing. "What do you think it means?"

He smiled, and the smile was wholly Dragon. "This one? It is in the Old Tongue, of course, and the meaning may not be precise. Or rather, *our* meaning may not be precise. But it is the root of the Dragon word for Hoard."

CHAPTER 12

"The root of the Dragon word?"

"Neither Barrani—in any flavor—nor Dragon appear to come from the Old Tongue in any linguistic way. Nor, for that matter, does Aerian or the Human tongue. We can trace the developments between High and Low Barrani precisely. We can trace the disparities between Human languages, with some effort. The Leontine language does not seem to diverge greatly with geography, but there are better reasons for that."

"The Tha'alani—"

"The Tha'alani share some linguistic characteristics with Humans." Tiamaris frowned. "The style of writing, here, looks in very superficial ways to be similar with formal, High Barrani—of the archaic variety, which you will not have studied in the Halls of Law." Or outside of it, either, his tone suggested. "It is not, however. But some key concepts exist, and there is overlap."

"So this isn't the same as your theory of harmonic presentation?"

He raised a brow.

"Never mind."

"There is no larger pattern in the presentation. The runes

here are singular." He frowned, and glanced at her arm again. "There might be some pattern to the marks on your skin, but the marks there are not subject to our revision."

They had once been subject to revision, at a distance and with a dimly understood magic that involved human sacrifice. Kaylin failed to remind him.

The Arkon nodded. "That," he said, pointing to one glowing mark, "and the third rune, are familiar."

"What does the third rune mean?" she asked.

"Journey."

"Travel?"

"No."

"What about this rune?"

"That one, you've seen," was his curt reply. He started to turn away. Dragons.

"Pretend I'm mortal, with the usual fallible human memory."

He raised a dark brow, his expression indicating that this clearly wasn't an acceptable excuse, even if it was a fact. "It is the rune for Truth, the truth of a thing, the whole of a thing. It is one of the first spoken words in the Genesis of the Leontines. I would speak it, but I am already weary. If you need a more active reminder, Lord Sanabalis, I'm certain, would be pleased to aid you. He will not, however, *do it here*."

"Private, please join me at the ladder's height."

She glanced at the Arkon, hoping the ladder was as heavy as Tiamaris's movements had made it sound, and walked around to the other side of the big stone block. The opposite side of the base was also adorned with runes: five. They didn't look the same as the ones on the side facing the door, and she hoped that she wouldn't end up either rolling up her pants or stripping her shirt off.

She forgot about that as she climbed, because as she did, she saw, at last, what lay across the surface of the altar. It was, or looked like, water. She understood, then, why the Arkon had been so concerned about the Tower.

"This is a mirror," she said softly.

"It is."

"Is it attached to Imperial Records?"

"With effort, yes, it can access them."

Something about his reply was slightly wrong. "What do you access when you don't put in effort?"

"That," was his curt reply, "would be the question. What do you see when you look in it now?"

She stared at it. It seemed like faintly luminescent water. "Nothing."

"Nothing?"

"It looks like glowing water to me."

He nodded. "You might wish to cover your ears," he told her.

Grimacing, she did as bid, because he drew a loud, rattling breath—which would have been alarming had he been an ancient mortal—and began to speak in his native tongue. Covering her ears did not noticeably diminish the pain or the vibrations; even the surface of the water rippled at the force of his speech.

The water did ripple, yes. It didn't change. It looked the same to Kaylin. "Do you see anything there?" she asked. The Arkon glared at her. But the water that lay across the surface of the altar—how, she didn't know, because it didn't seem to be lying *in* stone—was otherwise unresponsive.

"It appears," he finally grudgingly said, "that the magical wards and protections currently in force in the inner sanctum of my Library are causing some interference." He glanced at Sanabalis. The younger Dragon Lord shrugged.

"The Library is yours, Arkon. The risk is yours to take."

The Arkon nodded, weighing his options. At last he said, "Lowering those wards and protections is not a risk I wish to take at this time. I will, however, try some of the less ar-tificial invocations. Private, you may take your hands away from your ears now. I will not be speaking properly."

The Arkon began to speak, and this time, Kaylin felt the hair on her neck rise. It wasn't the usual prickling discomfort caused by magic. She recognized, in the richness of his voice and the breadth and depth of his syllables, each spoken with precision, focus and care, the language of the Old Ones.

She didn't recognize the words he spoke—if he spoke more than one; she remembered Tara teaching her, by repetition and desperation, to repeat *one* rune that was over twenty syllables long. But...when Sanabalis had told his story, she had almost understood it. She started to say as much and then remembered the other thing that had happened.

She had seen the words, as he spoke them.

She saw the word that the Arkon spoke now, materializing in the air between them; it was, like the words on the altar's side, a lambent, warm gold. It stood half the ancient Dragon's height, from his waist to the peak of his head, and it floated as if it had no weight. "You're speaking the Old Tongue," she said, although it was obvious and Dragons hated that sort of thing.

"Indeed. The native enchantment upon the altar is ancient, and the words of invocation are therefore naturally in keeping with its creators. With some effort under normal conditions, the altar can be used in the regular fashion."

Kaylin nodded, but most of her attention was caught and held by the floating sigil above her. When it began to move, she said, "Is it supposed to do that?"

"Do what?"

"Move."

"We do not apprehend the words in the same way, Private, if you recall. I do not see the word as a concrete mani-festation."

She remembered. She'd had to *touch* them before they were visible to anyone else. "Do you want me to—"

"No. I would appreciate the chance to study your... interpretations...in more detail, but at a more appropriate time. The rune should descend into the water, in your paradigm of comprehension."

"Good, because that's what it's doing."

When the rune touched the water, the water shivered and absorbed it, the way it might have absorbed dust. But where dust might muddy the waters, this single rune seemed to clear them entirely; the liquid in the lake now looked like water's pristine, elemental ideal. The Arkon nodded; clearly this is what he expected.

"What do we need to do to activate it?" she asked him. "Because if we need to ask it questions in the Old Tongue, we're not going to get much."

"You would," was the slightly grim reply, "be surprised. Let me attempt to access the Palace Records now."

"But you said—"

"*If* you were paying attention to what I said and not what you incorrectly inferred—a trying habit of mortals and the young—you would know that what I said was it is difficult to *invoke*."

"Yes, Sanabalis."

He turned slightly orange eyes on her while she tried to catch the mistake that had just fallen out of her mouth. On the ground some distance away, torch in hand, Sanabalis cringed. Tiamaris, on the other hand, turned to one side, and Kaylin had the distinct impression he was laughing.

The Arkon chose not to notice either of his colleagues;

he fixed a steady and baleful glare on someone who wasn't even his student—not that she was stupid enough to point this out. She apologized under her breath, and he snorted in the smoky, literal way of irritated Dragons everywhere. Because he was irritated, he didn't bother to give her much warning when he started to speak again—and this time, he roared.

This time, however, the waters began to move and respond to his voice, images forming from the streaks of color that seeped from the edges of the rectangle toward its center in a widening spiral. She couldn't understand what he said— and if learning Dragon was to be part of her etiquette class, she'd be so deaf she'd miss Marcus shouting in her ear—but the colors solidified into very, very familiar images: her own inner arms, writ huge.

The marks were their usual dark color. When the Arkon spoke again, images of her inner thighs and her back added themselves. "These are our most recent Records. I understand that you will possibly find this uncomfortable, Private, but I now require you to disrobe."

Every word she wanted to say slammed smack against every desire she had ever had to keep her head attached to the rest of her body—but only because she'd entertained the suspicion that it would come to this on the long walk here. Pretending she was headed for the showers with Teela, she stripped off her gear and set it to one side of the platform. The room wasn't cold, and the Arkon's interest was so dry and intellectual it was like visiting a doctor.

Which, come to think, she avoided like the plague. The Arkon instructed her to turn, and then to turn again; he positioned her legs so he could examine them, his gaze flickering between the surface of the pool and the fact of flesh so rapidly Kaylin had to close her eyes in order to prevent dizziness. As he did, he spoke in his loud, bombastic mother tongue.

But she opened her eyes when Sanabalis called up from the ground. "Arkon?"

The Arkon nodded. "You may get dressed, now, Private."

She did. Quickly. When she turned back to the Arkon, the images in the pool had shifted again, shrinking in size to accommodate new images. Kaylin, who had a vested interest in these particular images, was aware that any resentment she might feel over her brief lack of clothing was misplaced; at least the Arkon hadn't insisted that the skin on which the marks resided be detached from the rest of her body.

"Private?" the Arkon said, in an uncharacteristically subdued tone. He spoke two very loud words, and the water shivered, images dispersed by small ripples. When those ripples regrouped, the only two that remained were once again huge: they were side-by-side images of the runes on her thighs. They weren't, however, identical.

"That one," she asked, in a voice that matched his, "was the last known image before today?"

He nodded. "You see it."

She did. The marks on her lower leg had changed. She didn't examine herself often—other than the usual brief perusal-and-cringe that constituted standing in front of a mirror—and she certainly didn't examine the marks for minute changes of any kind. But it was clear, examining these, that the last two rows—such as they were—were dimmer and grayer than the rest; they had somehow faded.

"You think—"

"I think," the Arkon said heavily, "that your brief encounter with your unknown pursuer in your nonworld caused the fading, yes."

Her eyes narrowed as she looked at his profile. "You think," she said, flatly, "that if it weren't for the marks, I'd be dead."

He nodded, without shifting his gaze.

"Do you think it was the use of the magic?"

"No. I would ask if you believe that previous use of your magic has caused similar...discoloration...but it is my suspicion that your answer would only annoy me."

She failed to annoy him, staring at the pale and shining water instead. The marks on her legs were basic black, except for one on the newer image, which was a softly glowing gold. Without thinking, she said, "Records, enlarge left gold mark."

The mirror obligingly complied, and Kaylin examined it with care. "Arkon, this was the one that meant journey?"

But the Arkon didn't immediately answer. She glanced at him; he was staring at her, his eyes slightly rounded. They weren't orange, which was good; they were absent inner membrane, which could go either way. She started to ask what was wrong, and then realized it on her own.

She'd spoken to the water as if it were a run-of-the-mill Office mirror, and it had responded. "Should I shut up now?"

"In my opinion, you should speak perhaps ten percent of the time you actually do," was his reply. He hesitated; she was, after all, accidentally experimenting with an ancient and clearly valuable part of his hoard. To her surprise, he finally said, "Continue. Continue, however, with caution."

She glanced at Tiamaris and Sanabalis; Tiamaris was staring at the Arkon in open surprise. Sanabalis, however, had better control of his expression.

She nodded. Turning back to the mirror, in which the rune writ large was rotating in three dimensions, she said, "Records, access information—Devourer."

"If this is your definition of caution, Private, it is a small wonder you have survived your handful of years." The Arkon's voice was dry as summer grass in a drought.

The rune was swallowed whole by a sudden vortex in the water's center; as a transition, she preferred ripples. No image came to replace the rune; the water was dull and flat. Five minutes went by. Ten. Kaylin turned to the Arkon and shrugged. "I guess there are no on-Record stories. There are supposed to be religious—"

Her words were interrupted by a *roar*.

It wasn't a Dragon roar, but it was familiar. Turning, she left the sentence dangling and looked at the altar mirror. In its center, she expected to see the hungering void that had almost terrified Tara.

She didn't. She saw, instead, a man. He wasn't human, to her eye; she thought he might be Barrani, although there was a subtle wrongness about the cast of his features; his bone structure seemed too heavy. Dragon? But he was slender, and his hair was both white and long; it fell well past his knees.

He spoke; his voice broke twice, lost to the roar in the background. She tried to see beyond him, to get a sense of where he was, but he existed entirely in isolation in the image. His eyes were ringed with dark circles; he looked exhausted. He faltered once, looking over his shoulder, his hair a spray at his back, the movement was so fast.

He turned back. He seemed to be looking at her; he was probably looking at whoever held the memory crystal that had so perfectly captured his image. "I will not make it," he said. His voice was a rasp, and it was surprisingly deep. "Enkerrikas has gone ahead, leading what remains of our number. I am here, and I will face the Devourer.

"I will be lost in the void." His eyes flashed like new copper catching sunlight on a damn clear day. He was afraid, and he took no trouble to hide it, because he was also determined. If he was immortal—and he must be, she thought, because those were *not* mortal eyes—all of the arrogance and general condescension immortals usually showed were absent.

"But I will hold him as I can. Escape, now. Send word. Our enemy is not dead, as we hoped, and the ways are now in peril." He lifted both of his hands, palms out, toward her. It was neither a plea nor a rejection; she wasn't certain what it meant. But years of watching the Barrani, the Aerians, and the Leontines had made clear that each race had different gestures for basic, simple things like *myself.* Or *Come here.*

His eyes were now bright enough that the shadows that had dogged their undersides vanished. "...with luck—both good and ill—you have seen what occurred in Ankhagorran, and you know what waits if you do not escape." His eyes flashed copper again, but he now seemed exhausted; he opened his mouth to speak, and then closed it again, because the roaring was so loud only a shout—or a scream—could overwhelm it.

The water darkened all around him, light leaking out the edges until only he remained. His expression, shorn of voice or sound, was pale and grim; he looked young, to Kaylin, and frail. She reached out to touch him, but the platform meant her hand was several feet above the water's surface, which, given the sound the Arkon made, was probably a damn good thing.

But she was still leaning toward the water, almost in free fall; gravity made her heavier and heavier as she leaned toward the pool's center and the man's eyes, as if drawn. And she was; she tried to pull back and it only sent her inches farther over the rail. "Arkon!" she shouted.

Or tried. What came out was so garbled it wasn't a word at all, just a collection of random syllables similar to the "speech" of very, very young toddlers. The Arkon shouted her name; it made her teeth rattle. But she couldn't turn and look at him; she couldn't even move her face. The eyes of the man in the pool grew until they filled the whole of it, tear ducts the size of her head touched the smaller sides; brows that were almost white, they were so blond, nestling against the length. They existed, for a moment, in darkness; there was no skin, no bridge of nose, no cheekbones, no *context*.

It would have been disturbing even without her sudden loss of control over her own movements. She heard the Arkon's intake of breath, and every hair on her body stood on end, because that particular breath was familiar to her: it usually presaged fire. This time was no exception.

But the fire, in its entirety, was aimed *at* the mirror, and when it hit the surface of water, eyes were replaced by white, hissing clouds of vapor. Only then did she stumble—and she stumbled backward, and nearly fell off the damn ladder. Would have fallen, too—but the Arkon caught her wrist in one hand. A hand, she thought, given the grip, that might as well have been chiseled from stone. Granite, maybe.

"Because I am both curious and in a *tolerant* mood," he said coldly, "I am not going to drop you." He did, however, carry her down the ladder, which was awkward, given that he didn't let go of her wrist. "Tiamaris. I am placing the Private under your care, for the moment."

Tiamaris came—quickly—to the foot of the ladder. He glanced at the Arkon, who had climbed back up to the platform, and he winced. "Arkon?"

The Arkon said nothing.

"Has damage been done?"

"I am not certain. Previous experiments have indicated that the mirror is not fragile. Attempts to tamper with its functionality have proven futile in the past."

Tiamaris said nothing. He did, however, grimace when Kaylin asked, "How many of those attempts included full

Dragon breath." He also shook her slightly by the arm as he led her back to where Sanabalis was standing.

"Well?" her only current teacher said, in a tone of voice that was suspiciously like a whisper. She'd never heard a Dragon whisper before, and would have been willing to bet it was impossible.

"I think I'll wait on the Arkon," she replied.

The Arkon did not feel that damage had been done to the altar. He was not, however, willing to let Kaylin experiment further. "And not," he told her grimly, "for the sake of the mirror. I believe that falling into the water at that juncture would have injured you far more than the artifact."

In theory, given that it was his hoard he was talking about, he should have been relieved. In practice, he was in a mood that was just a touch worse than the one he'd been in when he'd walked into Sanabalis's rooms. "Arkon," Sanabalis finally said, when they'd cleared the cramped halls and the cramped stairs and the cramped stacks and made it back to the place where the books, the desks, and the windows resided. "Neither Lord Tiamaris nor I could see what the mirror revealed."

"Could you hear it?"

The two Dragon Lords exchanged a brief glance, which the Arkon interpreted as a no. "Interesting."

Kaylin frowned. Mirrors could be keyed, which allowed only certain people to access them; Records could be keyed in the same way. It was more common to protect Records than individual mirrors, and one of these days, Kaylin would probably learn why. It was practical, so magical theory didn't touch it. Security, on the other hand, talked about the effect of either form of protection, and the reasons why protection of sensitive material might be valuable or necessary. She'd done fairly well in that class, which was beside the point.

Mirrors might not activate if the wrong people were *in* the room or in range of the mirror itself, but if they were active, they were active.

Since this particular mirror was set an annoying height above the actual ground, and was also horizontal, instead of the usual vertical that people had come to expect from a reflective surface, she hadn't expected the Dragon Lords to see what it showed. She had, however, expected them to *hear* it, because it had been bloody loud.

She hesitated. "Arkon?"

"Yes," he replied. "I saw what you saw."

"Did you recognize the man's race?"

He raised a brow.

"He looked almost Barrani. Heavier set than any of the Barrani I've met, but it's not impossible. His eyes, though—"

"Yes."

"He was all the wrong build for a Dragon, wasn't he?"

The Arkon said nothing for long enough that Kaylin wondered if the first words out of his mouth—in Dragon—would be *get out*. But what he said, instead, was, "You understood what he said, didn't you?"

She frowned. "Yes. He was speaking in High Barrani. I *know* that one, inside and out." She would have offered him class transcripts to prove the claim, but the transcripts also included the *rest* of her classes, which were spotty on a good day.

"No, Private, he was not."

"What was he speaking then?"

"I regret to say that I have no idea. If I play with the images for long enough, I can take educated guesses, because I think the structure is similar to some of what we do know. It is not, however, exact, and it is no form of ancient tongue that exists *here*. I will, however, take your transcript of what you *think* you heard."

Lord Sanabalis now cleared his throat. Since Sanabalis wasn't generally hesitant, it often amused Kaylin to see him side by side with the Arkon.

"Yes?" the Arkon said. The word was short and curt.

"Private Neya and I have an appointment—at the behest of the Imperial Court—with Master Sabrai in the Oracular Halls."

"Now?"

"Within the hour, Arkon."

"Very well. Private, I will give you paper, and you can transcribe what you remember on the way. I would take your report after the appointment, but mortal memory is so ephemeral. You may hand what you've written to Lord Sanabalis. He will see that it is personally delivered to me."

"You realize, if I'm lucky," Kaylin said, around a mouthful of sandwich cadged from the Imperial kitchens by a servant who was so well dressed he was intimidating, "Marcus will only dock me a day's pay and eat half my face while informing me about the loss of income?"

Lord Sanabalis, seated opposite Kaylin in the interior of an Imperial Carriage, looked at her and nodded almost absently. He then turned his gaze back to the streets that were moving past in the small frame of the open window. Tiamaris had been dropped off by the bridge across the Ablayne; he and Sanabalis had conversed, briefly, at the foot of that bridge, conspicuously out of the range of Kaylin's hearing. She'd taken the time to scribble down her remembrances of the vision.

She watched the older Dragon Lord's face; his inner membranes were high. "Have you slept at all in the past week?" she surprised herself by asking.

Clearly, she'd surprised him, as well. One brow rose, and had he a thicker head of hair, it would have been invisible to hairline. As it was, it was close. "I fail to see the relevance of the question, Private Neya. Dragons, like the Barrani, do not *require* sleep in any great quantity. Lack of sleep does not damage the performance of our duties."

She slid into Elantran. "It's a polite way of saying you look like hell."

"I was not aware," Sanabalis replied, failing to follow her linguistic slide, "that there *was* a polite way of saying that. If it will cause you less worry," he added, in a tone that implied this was impossible, "I am, indeed, concerned with the unfolding of events. It is my hope that the visit to Everly will provide some counterweight to what otherwise seems to be suggested."

"It's the Devourer."

"No, it is not. There have always been monsters in our midst, Private, some of whom might, in the right circumstances—and usually without intent—destroy the world. It does not, of course, fill me with joy. I am not a fool."

"Then what?"

"The magical investigation this afternoon—most of which you were absent for—implies that the boundaries of the circle have moved. They have not moved *far*, but the effects of random magic are spreading to a larger area of the city."

"Is the central area getting any worse?"

"I believe the answer to that question must be yes. Your disappearance, for one. But the nature of your disappearance is also *particularly* troubling. You understand the significance of the Keeper. If the Keeper's responsibility can be damaged—or sundered from him—*randomly*..." He shook his head. "You understand my concern."

She did. "Maybe Everly will tell us something we want to know."

"That is, sadly, my hope." He grimaced, and she understood why: hoping for comfort from Oracles was not exactly the act of a rational person. Or Dragon, if it came to that.

Master Sabrai was waiting for them at the open doors, which not even Kaylin could take as a hopeful sign. The guards at the gate didn't bother to stop the Imperial Carriage, with its obvious Dragon Lord on the inside. They didn't do more than glance at Kaylin, either, but Dragon Lords generally trumped any other occupant, given that the only Dragons in the Empire served the Emperor directly.

Sanabalis exited the carriage quickly, prompting Kaylin to do the same, and they made the front doors at something like a jog. When Dragons jogged, you *felt* it if you happened to be matching their stride. Or at least their speed.

"Lord Sanabalis," Master Sabrai said, walking down the stairs to meet them. "Private Neya." He was pale, and the dark circles under his eyes implied that if Everly had not once stopped painting since he'd first stretched canvas, Master Sabrai had not stopped watching.

"Master Sabrai," Sanabalis replied, tendering the exhausted Oracle a very correct nod.

"Please follow me."

"Is something wrong?" the Dragon Lord asked, although he did obey what was barely a request.

Master Sabrai had not, apparently, heard. Sanabalis glanced at Kaylin; it was meant as a warning, but it wasn't necessary. She knew two things, heading down the maze of oddly colorful and occupied halls. Everly always painted; that was his version of an Oracle, and he had painted many things in his short life: Dragons, altars, elementals, and deaths. Master Sabrai had seen them all, of course, because he had also been called on to tender an explanation for most of them.

His current mood was unusual; she could tell this by Sanabalis's grim silence. Which meant something else had also happened.

CHAPTER 13

If she wondered what had happened, the answer was clear before Master Sabrai had fully opened the door that led to the gallery Everly called home. Light was provided by magic and contained flame; it was evening now, and well on its way to pitch-black; the clouds had moved in sometime during the afternoon. But light wasn't necessary. Nor was sight of Everly's painting—which she could see only from the back while he worked.

No, it was his voice. Everly couldn't speak.

But he was speaking now, an endless drone of words and syllables, sometimes louder and sometimes softer.

Lord Sanabalis frowned and turned to Master Sabrai, who had taken a moment to drop his lined face into slightly shaking hands.

"Master Sabrai."

He lowered his hands, straightened his shoulders, and grimaced. It was, Kaylin thought, supposed to be a smile. "Lord Sanabalis."

"How long has he been speaking?"

"Two hours, give or take a few minutes." The Master of the Oracular Halls reached into the folds of his jacket, and withdrew a folded stack of paper. "We attempted to transcribe what he was saying."

"Did you try to speak with him at all?" Kaylin asked.

"An attempt was made."

"By who?"

"By myself and Sigrenne. Sigrenne spent some thirty minutes in the attempt. But the...speech...itself seems to be in keeping with his painting. He is neither aware of, nor receptive to, interference or interaction."

Sanabalis took the transcription.

"It is not, of course, entirely precise," Master Sabrai said, an edge to his otherwise apologetic voice. "And we have, of course, full running Records of his commentary for your perusal should it become necessary."

"No one is transcribing now."

"No. He isn't speaking in any language that Records could identify."

"He's speaking in tongues?" Kaylin asked. She hadn't taken her eyes off the back of the painting, and could see brief glimpses of Everly's arms and hands as he switched brushes or added colors to his palette.

Neither Sabrai nor Sanabalis responded, and Kaylin glanced back at them. "What?"

"Nothing, Private," Sanabalis replied curtly. "Master Sabrai?"

"Please feel free to examine what he has painted. I believe you'll be surprised."

"When do you think he'll finish?"

This was always a worry for Sabrai. Everly did not sleep, eat, or drink while working. Kaylin doubted he even went to the bathroom. "While working" covered the period from stretching a canvas until the moment he'd made his last brushstroke, and it was a *large* canvas. Sigrenne had said, privately, that food *could* be pushed into Everly's mouth while he was working if you stood on the opposite side of the painting from his palette and you never cut across his field of vision.

"Soon,' was the noncommittal reply.

Kaylin shrugged. Fair enough; it wasn't as if she wasn't standing in the room while Everly babbled and painted. She could walk a few yards, and get as much of an answer as Sabrai could provide just by looking. She did this now.

Everly's speech, such as it was, was disturbing. She'd seen insane prophets and mad drunks on the corners of various city streets for seven years' worth of patrols, so she had some experience with incoherent speeches. Everly's was different; the words had force behind them for a run of hundreds of syllables, and then would sink into a whisper; they would break with hysterical laughter, and then drop into raw fury. She listened; she couldn't help it. It was almost as if he was speaking for a crowd, but one person at a time, and capturing their words and thoughts at that moment.

Listening, she turned to look at the canvas.

"Private?" Sanabalis's familiar voice came from a long damn way away. He had not yet left Master Sabrai's side, as if he knew the Master needed more support than his Oracle.

"I know where it is," she said, in the wrong tone of voice.

"I told you," Master Sabrai began, "that representations of place do *not*—" But Sanabalis cut him off.

"Private?" he said again.

Kaylin however, stared at Everly's painting. The buildings that had been sketched in rough, coal lines, had been painted and fleshed in—to an extent. They had color, but the color was washed-out and faint, as if he were working in watercolors, and not the oils that so clearly dominated. She saw the flags of the Halls where she worked in the distance; it didn't matter.

She recognized the buildings. At the farthest left edge of the painting, Evanton's shop formed the boundary of the street's end—or as far as Everly had chosen to paint—and at the closest, the sandwich board that stood outside of Margot's, rain or shine. She recognized, on the right, a textile store—which always seemed so out of place on Elani, and at the far end, the wilting and paint-flecked storefront of Zoltan, a charm-maker who had the distinction of choosing the stupidest name in the district, in Kaylin's opinion.

Sanabalis joined her. "Private," he said. He'd used her rank three times, and each time, imbued it with the weight of his opinion.

She shifted her gaze from the familiar buildings to the center of the painting itself. In the foreground, were a handful of men. At least they looked like men, to Kaylin. But they were tall, for humans. They didn't have Barrani hair—which is to say, their hair was either short, nonexistent, or pulled back from their faces in braids or knots; she couldn't tell, because she couldn't see their backs.

They weren't Aerian, because they had no wings; they weren't Leontine, because, well. No fangs, no facial fur, and too much clothing. But...they weren't young. Or rather, the central three of the nine weren't young. Their hair was gray or white, and their faces were lined by years of exposure to sun and wind. They carried weapons that would have caused every patrol that caught a glimpse of them to stop them and question them for, oh, hours: big, bladed axes, big damn swords, and something that looked like a strung bow meant for Dragons.

But on the farther fringes of these three, the hardened and set grimness of age gave way to the lean determination of youth. Here, the lines across brows and the corners of mouths weren't yet etched there by anything but paint. Kaylin thought at least two of these younger people were women, but given the heavy clothing they wore and the weapons they carried, she wasn't certain; they were slender enough that shape could be lost to the shapeless with ease.

They looked...tired. Angry. Frightened. But they didn't look demonic or evil. They didn't look like they were going to end a world.

"Private?"

She nodded. "He hasn't finished the painting yet," she added. It was true. Behind these figures, were shadows and shapes that implied a host of people without giving them substance. No, they might not end the world. On the other hand, in numbers like these and with those weapons, they were going to either start a war or be crammed on top of each other in a jail that was in no way built to accommodate them.

She frowned and stepped closer to the painting, avoiding the area in which Everly now worked. Everly was still speaking as he painted, but this time his voice was a soft keening, like a cry. She knew better than to touch him, and because she did, she let her hand fall to her side again with effort.

"He's been talking like this for how long?"

"Since he started painting the living figures," Master Sabrai replied. The man sounded exhausted.

She nodded. Started to turn. Stopped. She couldn't understand what Everly was saying, but she didn't need to; not this time. His voice had lifted, not in pain, but in confusion; his syllables had become longer and simpler. She tried to ignore it, found it harder, and looked at the shadows cast by the combination of buildings, strangers, and the sun she couldn't directly see.

"We need a date," she said softly.

Master Sabrai cleared his throat.

"Master Sabrai?" Sanabalis prompted.

"I believe I may have a rough approximation, Lord Sanaba-

lis. It is not only Everly who has been subject to visions in the
past day."

"Are they growing in number?"

The answering silence was clearly hesitation. It was also
Sanabalis's problem. Kaylin continued to study the painting,
moving from it up Everly's arms to his face, his constantly
moving lips, as if this combination would provide all of their
much-needed answers if she could translate them.

"They are growing, in both number and strength."

Without looking up, Kaylin said, "Is it as bad as the Oracles for the tidal wave were?"

"Not yet."

"Not yet?" This time she did look up.

"If it follows the same trajectory, every Oracle in the Halls,
and everyone with the slightest hint of the Oracular gift will
be having screaming nightmares or waking visions across the
whole of the city within four days."

"So...we've got at least four days."

He stared at her as if her words made no sense. Sanabalis stepped on her foot before she could attempt to clarify
them. She grimaced; she had enough dignity not to yelp out
loud. Turning her attention back to Everly, she said, "I think
Everly's speaking for them." She pointed at the strangers that
he was continuing to bring to life. "I don't think they speak
our language, but I do think they speak whatever it is he's
been saying."

Sanabalis frowned. "With your permission, Master Sabrai, I
would like to bring a Tha'alani operative to the Halls."

Once, this would have made Kaylin's hair stand on end.
Now she simply said, "Ybelline?"

Sanabalis nodded.

"When?" Master Sabrai said. He did not appear to be overly
concerned by the request.

"I feel it most relevant to bring her now," was the Dragon
Lord's grave reply. "While Everly is still painting the strangers.
You have a safe mirror?"

"I do. In my office," he added. There were very seldom
mirrors in the rooms the Oracles occupied.

They left Kaylin in Everly's room. She grabbed a stool and
sat outside of his visual range—not that he'd notice—while
she watched him work. Had he been painting something se-
date, it would have been soothing; there was something about
the rhythm of his brushstrokes, the regularity with which he
turned to his palette, the pursing of his lips as he considered—
and discarded—splotches of color that admittedly all looked
the same to her that was a silent music of gesture.

But his babbling, his broken words, his sudden shouting,
his anger, and especially his whimpering, were harder to ignore, because she understood them. Not the actual words,
but the tone behind them. She'd heard frightened crowds
before. Most of them hadn't involved small children, which
made this harder, because she knew better than anyone but a
Sword, what a frightened crowd could easily become.

Elani street.

She glanced at the corpses she could see in the foreground
of the painting now. Maybe a dozen, if the body parts were
still attached to the rest of the bodies. Maybe more. This,
she thought grimly, could be prevented. She knew roughly
where these people would appear—if indeed she could assume that this painting represented any literal truth at all;
certainly the last painting Everly had done that was as significant as this hadn't.

The door opened, and looking up, she saw Sigrenne, a bowl
in one hand, the doorknob in the other. Sigrenne's brows
rose slightly when she realized Everly was not alone, but fell

again when she saw who was with him. She headed into the room, and toward the little painter.

"Is he almost finished?" she asked Kaylin. She was carrying what looked like a stew of some sort, everything in bite-size chunks that could be spooned into a moving mouth.

"I don't know," Kaylin replied. "I think so."

"Good. It's hard to get him to eat. It's almost impossible to get him to eat while he's—he's talking." She set the bowl down, ran a hand over her eyes, and added, "Those of us who work here would really appreciate it if you'd keep your possible disasters to a manageable scale."

"Bad?"

"It's been bad, yes. It's going to get worse. And we're understaffed." Before Kaylin could ask, Sigrenne added, "We've the funding for staff, but it's hard to find suitable candidates for work here. Most people don't last a month under normal circumstances in the Halls. I don't think they'd last a day, under these."

"I bet." The significance of these two words was lost on Sigrenne.

"We get a lot of applicants," she continued, waiting with a spoon for some break in Everly's speech, "but—" she looked very, very tired "—not everyone can work here. Not everyone can look at our Oracles and just accept them for who and what they are. And even if they could grow into that acceptance, they're not going to do it *now.*"

Moved by something she didn't understand, Kaylin said, "You do good work here."

Sigrenne raised a brow.

"I mean, important work. Necessary work."

"I know the Emperor thinks—"

"Sigrenne, if not for the Halls the last time, most of the

city would be underwater by now, and we'd have an insane Arcanist as ruler of the World."

"Off the record?" The weary matron asked.

Kaylin grimaced. "Off the record. Hopefully off the Records here, as well."

"They're recording all of his speech."

"Yes, of course they are. This would be," she added wryly, "why I'm still a Private in spite of my many career successes."

Sigrenne did chuckle at that, and if it was a weary, exhausted chuckle, it was better than nothing.

Ybelline Rabon'alani arrived and entered the room before either Sanabalis or Master Sabrai had cleared the door. She was much smaller than either, and she was neither severe nor intimidating but something about her presence demanded a certain respect. Respect for the Tha'alani, on the other hand, took many guises. She walked directly to where Kaylin stood, and as she drew close, Kaylin automatically opened her arms.

The Tha'alani castelord hugged her tightly, and stroked her forehead with the ends of her stalks as she did. *You are well?*

Kaylin, who could barely control her words, had no control whatsoever of her thoughts, and they flickered by in a "best of" or rather, "worst of" medley for Ybelline's cursory inspection. Ybelline understood, and in any case, would not have been put off by simple thoughts, no matter what their content was, but she did stop Kaylin when Kaylin at last thought of Everly.

These images, these impressions, the Tha'alani castelord studied carefully, as if Kaylin were a memory crystal.

You've touched Everly before? Kaylin asked.

I have, although it is not always I who comes here. The Oracles have their own fears, but they are not so accessible or so clear that they cause damage to touch or read.

Then why did they summon you?

She felt Ybelline's wry grin a moment before it touched her lips. *I believe both Master Sabrai and you, yourself, find my presence less alarming. Lord Sanabalis is an astute observer of human nature, when it suits him.*

And, she added, becoming more serious, *if, as you suspect, Everly is somehow channeling an entire language, or snippets of one, it's possible that whoever does absorb Everly's thoughts will have to work with linguists and translators in order to better decode them. Linguists and translators, like many others, are more...zealous...in guarding their thoughts, and they are more easily alarmed.*

Kaylin nodded and lowered her arms. Ybelline, with regret, withdrew her stalks.

"I will have to touch the boy," she told Master Sabrai. The Master nodded as Ybelline approached Everly. But here, Ybelline, ever sensitive, paused and looked fully at Sigrenne. She repeated the statement.

Sigrenne nodded, and stepped back, still clutching the bowl of now-quite-cold stew. She was tense; Kaylin could see that—but in her defense, if it were needed, she would probably have been just as tense if Kaylin had approached Everly with the intent to touch or disturb him. Ybelline had obviously observed Everly before, even if she did not regularly interact with him. She stood at his elbow—not his painting hand—and watched his measured strokes, gauging their direction. After a few moments, she touched his shoulder gently, but firmly.

He didn't appear to notice, but then again, she wasn't interfering with his painting, and as far as Kaylin could tell, anything that didn't interfere with his painting was beneath—or more accurately, beyond—his notice. Kaylin wondered how Ybelline would initiate the more intimate contact, because as far as she could tell, it required them to be face-to-face, and Everly was likely to notice that the Tha'alani castelord was not his canvas. She hoped.

But Ybelline did something unexpected. Instead of inserting herself between Everly and his canvas—or his palette— she stood behind him, loosely draping one arm around his chest. Everly wasn't short, but he was very spindly. With her free hand, she lifted lank, straight hair from the back of his neck, exposing both spine and skin. Bending, she lowered her forehead until her stalks could fasten themselves to that neck. Everly didn't seem to notice.

Sigrenne did, and relaxed almost instantly. She offered Kaylin a wan smile. "It's not safe to interrupt Everly when he's painting, if it's even possible. You can wrap him in a straitjacket and remove him from the room, but he keens and cries and slams his head against the nearest bit of floor or wall until you bring him back."

Everly continued to paint and babble; Ybelline continued to listen. Kaylin glanced at Sanabalis and cleared her throat. The Dragon Lord, taking the hint, looked back.

"Are we staying?" She tried not to ask it pointedly, but it had been a long damn day, it was late, and she was exhausted. That she wasn't also starving was more due to Sanabalis's foresight than her own. That, and she still had to come up with something to mollify Ironjaw, or she was going to have trouble breathing, because technically she needed a throat for that, and she'd seen the color of his eyes.

Before Sanabalis could answer, Everly's babble broke off in a gasp—and then a high-pitched scream. Sleep forgotten, Kaylin turned back to him in time to see Ybelline tense and stagger, as well. She moved toward them both, and caught Ybelline's arms—not Everly's—steadying her. The stalks remained firmly in place, but for the moment, Everly's brush was still.

Kaylin examined the painting. It had changed. Not the composition; that remained the same. The crowd behind the detailed strangers had become, by broader and suggestive brushstrokes, more solid; their shadows suggested numbers beyond count. But the white space above their head was no longer entirely white. It was almost, but not quite, gray. It looked, at first glance, blank—like untouched canvas, waiting for paint.

It wasn't.

And where Everly *had* painted, where he'd applied his solid, sensible colors, he'd now applied a partial wash of some sort—although how that worked with oil, Kaylin had *no idea*—and the workaday colors of Elani street, in a radius around that open, blank space, was now dimmer. No, Kaylin thought, as she leaned forward. Not dimmer. It had become, in one go, *transparent*. As if it were fading into nothing.

Sanabalis joined her; she could hear the heavy tread of his steps. He stopped well back from Everly. After a moment, he said, "Private, I believe we are no longer required here." His voice was grim and chill. Kaylin tore her attention away from the painting. She still supported Ybelline, who was stiff with shock beneath her hands.

He started to speak, saw what she hadn't mentioned, and stopped himself, but it was a close thing; his eyes were a blazing orange. He was not, however, angry; he was alarmed. "A few minutes," he managed to say. "Master Sabrai, I require the use of your mirrors. It is, I consider, quite urgent. I will also require your estimate of our time frame." Before Master Sabrai could speak, Sanabalis lifted a hand, cutting off the possibility of words. "I understand that the estimate will grow more accurate as the Oracles continue, but I believe I now understand what they presage. Your best approximation, in this case, will be good enough for our purposes.

"Private, we will return for you when I am done. Attempt to be ready to leave, or you will find yourself walking home."

Kaylin, however, wasn't worried about walking home; she was worried about Ybelline, and indirectly, Everly. Everly had *dropped* his brush. She turned to ask Sigrenne if this was his normal way of announcing that he was finished, and saw that Sigrenne's eyes were wide with surprise—and concern. The older, larger woman darted forward quickly, rescuing the brush as if she were tending an actual injury. She set it to one side of his palette.

"Ybelline," Kaylin whispered, lips close to the Tha'alani's ear. There was no response. Her eyes didn't even flicker to the side. "Ybelline," she said again, this time louder.

"Kaylin, is this normal?"

"No. Can you— If Everly's not painting, can you reach him? Can you get his attention?"

"I don't know. I've never seen him…drop his brush before. This isn't something the Tha'alani is doing, is it?" she asked, her voice taking on an edge of suspicion that could easily fall into anger or hysteria.

"No! You could spend the rest of your damn life looking for someone as decent—as caring—as Ybelline, and you wouldn't find one. Whatever she's doing, she's doing in response to Everly—"

"Can you make *her* let go, then?"

"I *don't know*. I don't know what's safe to do—" Kaylin realized that her own voice was now dangerously close to the same edge as Sigrenne's, and she forced herself to breathe deeply. Three times. *We need her,* she wanted to say—but it would be the wrong thing. Everly, for all intents and purposes, was one of Sigrenne's kits.

"Sigrenne—can you access Everly's Records?"

"Not from here."

Of course not. No mirrors. "Can you access them from somewhere else? I don't want to leave. I know you don't want to leave, either—but the Halls' mirrors must be keyed. They won't respond to *me*."

Sigrenne nodded, taking the same deep breaths that Kaylin had just struggled to master. They met each other's eyes, and were it not for the difference in their ages, height, and coloring, they might have been looking in a mirror. Sigrenne's lips quirked up in a grim, small smile. "You'll watch them both?"

"I'll watch them," Kaylin promised.

Ybelline didn't respond to speech. She didn't respond to shouting. Neither did Everly. Their eyes were wide, and they stared straight ahead, like startled, terrified creatures. Ybelline had seen some of the worst that humanity had to offer; she'd faced it willingly. She'd seen her people's torture, and she'd seen their deaths when they attempted to avoid the darkness and the insanity of the normal, human mind by *disobeying* the Emperor's direct command. And she accepted it. Each time she was asked to read a mind, each time she was asked to *go into* a mind and ferret out information at the behest of the Imperial Service, she faced it again.

But she had never been immobile with terror before.

It had to be Everly, Kaylin thought grimly. It *had* to be. The alternative—that something Ybelline had seen had caused this—didn't bear thought.

Sigrenne came back obscenely quickly; Kaylin could hear her heavy, fast strides before the door opened again. She'd clearly run from Everly's room to the nearest mirror—and back. But as she approached, she shook her head. "The only person who has ever—ever—managed to get Everly's attention when he's delivering an Oracle, Private Neya, is you."

Kaylin grimaced. "I think I promised Master Sabrai that I wouldn't—"

"Master Sabrai," was the grim reply, "can get stuffed." Sigrenne came to stand beside Ybelline. "Let me hold her arms. You try to reach Everly."

"If it upsets him—"

"I'll deal with upset," Sigrenne said. "But he's not painting, right now—and he's still stuck in Oracular trance. I can feed him, but he won't eat *enough* to survive. He won't sleep. He won't collapse until—" She shook her head. "Everly isn't the only painter-Oracle the Halls have had. We have some idea of what will happen to him."

Kaylin transferred Ybelline's arms—and the bulk of her weight—to the much larger Sigrenne.

"She doesn't weigh much, does she?"

"Not much, no." She walked over to Everly's palette, and picked up the brush he'd been using. It was one of the wider brushes "This was a lot less intimidating when he was working in charcoals," she muttered.

"What you did last time—"

"It was a mostly blank canvas. He'd done some blocking sketches, but very little actual work. I was messing with the blocked sketches."

"How?"

"Um."

Sigrenne, who was accustomed to dealing with the very strange commentary of the Oracles, didn't even bat an eye; she waited.

"I added a figure. Well, a blob. I'm *not* an artist, Sigrenne. This—it's finished."

"It's not."

"It's pretty damn close, then."

"If it *were* finished, he'd respond. He wouldn't talk, no,

but he doesn't. He would interact. He's *not* done. Whatever you did before—try it now."

"But in an entirely different way?"

Sigrenne managed a chuckle. "That, too."

Kaylin looked almost helplessly at the colors of splotches on the palette. It was a wonder to her that anyone could turn these muddy mixes into something beautiful—or at least realistic, because to her, they looked like small accidents. What *had* she done? Not this, not stall for time.

"I'm going to wreck the painting," she muttered. "And Sanabalis is going to have my head."

"Sanabalis," Sigrenne replied, in the same tone of voice she'd used to utter Master Sabrai's name, "can—"

"Don't. He'll probably hear you from wherever he's standing. They can hear fleas stretching their wings. Usually when it's most inconvenient for the fleas."

"We don't privilege the art," Sigrenne said, more quietly. "To the Oracular Halls, the paintings, like verbal Oracles, are given the weight of possible future occurrences, not more and not less. Whatever Lord Sanabalis needed to see, I'd say he saw it. The painting has *already* served its purpose, Kaylin." What she didn't say was also significant.

Kaylin took a good, long look at the painting, and then she began. She examined what Everly had done with these new colors, saw the ways in which the choice of color and brushstroke had implied transparency or fading, and chose colors as close to the originals as she could. She wanted to make those buildings solid.

At least, that's what she thought she was doing. But she hadn't lied. She *wasn't* an artist. She began to paint, yes. She began to choose colors appropriate for the buildings she knew—and hated, and loved—to eradicate the fading. If anyone had asked her what she was doing, she would have told them exactly that. And would have added that she was doing it *badly.*

She heard Sigrenne's sudden intake of breath just before the brush was yanked out of her hand, leaving a trail of blue oil across the inside of her palm. Turning, she stepped out of the way before Everly could push her. She saw Ybelline's eyelids flickering, and shouted a warning to Sigrenne which was, in any case, unnecessary. Sigrenne, supporting most of her weight, had no trouble catching the *rest* of it when her stalks slid from the back of Everly's neck, and she collapsed.

She ran to Sigrenne as Sigrenne lifted Ybelline off her feet and carried her to the narrow bed wedged into one corner of the otherwise huge gallery. "Good work," the matron said quietly.

"Was it?"

"He's painting again. Go back to him. I'll sit with your castelord until she wakes."

Kaylin nodded, although she would have preferred that their caretaking positions were reversed. She made her way back to where Everly was now once again painting like a maniac, as if there had been no interruption. She expected to see him fixing the mess she'd made.

He wasn't. He was adding to it.

Kaylin had not actually solidified buildings, although that had been her intent. She'd written *words.* Runes, like horrible, defacing graffiti—at least at first sight.

But he took this rough, flat act of unintentional vandalism, and he worked with it, adding the visual alchemy of color to give the streaks shape, form, and the illusion of dimension. Glowing in golds and blues, faint and muddy, the runes now floated in the air at the height of the portal—and it was, must be, a portal; she understood that now. They seemed to ring the entry, just above the heads of the gathered crowd.

Kaylin took a step back, and Everly suddenly wheeled, aware of her movement as he was never aware of anything external that didn't directly affect his brushes, his paints, or his canvas. She was caught by his gaze. He didn't speak. The babbling, the repetition of foreign words, was over.

But he was tired, exhausted, and frantic.

Kaylin wasn't even surprised when he dug out a brush from his collection and shoved it, firmly, into her hand, folding her fingers around it just in case she didn't understand what he meant. He pointed her at his palette, waited until she nodded, and then pointed her at his painting. This done, he turned back to his work.

Kaylin took up the brush, took a breath, and joined him.

CHAPTER 14

Kaylin wasn't Everly. She didn't have the benefit of the Oracular Trance to protect her from the gasps and the whispers of the people behind her. The first of those was, of course, Sigrenne. Kaylin turned to the older woman, started to explain herself, and felt Everly grab her *chin* and turn her face back toward the canvas.

"I'm sorry," Kaylin told the orderly. "I—he—"

"He wants your help."

"Yes. It's not like the other time—he was aware that I was here, but I don't think he cared if I left. He definitely doesn't want me leaving now."

"No, he doesn't."

"So…you won't break my arms and you won't let Master Sabrai throw me out for breaking the rules?"

Sigrenne's laugh was low, tired, and a little bit on edge, but it was on the right side of the edge. "First, Master Sabrai would order someone *else* to throw you out, and second, it would probably be me. I think, at this point, it would upset Everly as much to remove you as it would to remove his brushes. This does mean, if Lord Sanabalis wasn't joking, that you'll be walking home, on the other hand."

"I don't think so. They're not back yet, and I think he's almost done." Kaylin then took the full brunt of Everly's reproachful stare, and she gave herself over to his work and his vision. She had tried sketching and drawing before; hers were always stiff and flat, and she certainly couldn't do them with her eyes closed.

But here, it was almost better when she did, because what she did when she tried to deliberately add things felt just as stiff and wrong as those early, embarrassing attempts at sketching. And sketches were useful in her line of work. No, she thought, kicking herself. Look *at* the runes.

Try to see them as Tiamaris would have seen them. Try to look for the shape of the whole, the sense of pattern, of completeness. She began to work. To nudge, with brushes. To see the gaping spot that demanded another rune, like the completion of a sentence upon which the whole of a trial hung.

She wasn't sure how long she worked, but she was sure when Sanabalis entered the room, because he roared. She jerked, spun around, and met his eyes; they were still orange, but he looked exhausted. The slow simmer of anger was completely absent. So, it had to be admitted, was Kaylin's hearing, but that would come back.

"*If* you are finished?" he asked curtly. Master Sabrai was practically weaving on his feet.

"I—" She turned to Everly. Everly didn't even look at her. He was still painting, but the movements were less frenetic, less desperate. "I guess I'm done." She set the brush aside, and walked over to Sanabalis.

"Sigrenne mentioned what occurred with Ybelline and Everly," he said. "Master Sabrai thoughtfully decided not to invoke the *very strictly enforced rules* yet again. We are in his debt." Which Dragons, of course, loved. Fingers trailing the length of his beard, he added, "I do not understand why

Everly allows you to add to his works in progress. I am not, on the other hand, certain that anyone else has ever *tried*. Master Sabrai?"

"To my knowledge, Lord Sanabalis, Private Neya would be the only individual who has tried. All other recorded attempts to interfere with Everly involved interference with the boy himself—usually in an attempt to keep him from dying of dehydration or lack of sleep."

"It would be an interesting experiment."

"Indeed," Master Sabrai replied. In a tone of voice that was usually reserved for the word *never.* "Sigrenne says Ybelline Rabon'alani is now conscious."

The Tha'alani castelord was both conscious and standing by the time Kaylin and Sanabalis reached the narrow bed. "My apologies, Lord Sanabalis," she said, tendering the Dragon Lord an Imperial half bow.

"Master Sabrai feels that Everly will stop painting within the hour. Sigrenne concurs. Do you wish to remain, or can we offer you a ride to the Tha'alani Quarter?"

"The ride would be appreciated."

The carriage pulled into the street. Kaylin glanced at the bright moon's height and cringed. But the thought of sleeping in the carriage, at least until Sanabalis kicked her out at whatever he decided was her destination, vanished the minute Ybelline spoke.

"You were correct, Lord Sanabalis," she said softly. "Everly was speaking a language. It is a specific language, of course—and it is not a language that is spoken, to my knowledge, anywhere within the Empire of Ala'an."

"Your knowledge?" Kaylin said sharply.

Ybelline nodded, understanding what Kaylin meant. "It

is not found within the Tha'alaan. No member of my race since the awakening has heard it spoken."

Sanabalis nodded so inscrutably Kaylin couldn't tell whether or not this was a surprise to him. "More germane, at the moment, is how much of it you absorbed. Would you recognize it, if you heard it again?"

Ybelline nodded.

"Could you speak it, if required?"

There was a minute of hesitation before Ybelline nodded again. She glanced at Kaylin, as if she could tell that Kaylin was only barely stopping a question from leaving her mouth. Reaching out, she placed one gentle hand on Kaylin's arm—which, oddly enough, loosened her tongue.

"What happened, with Everly? Why did he freeze like that? Why did you almost collapse?"

The Tha'alani castelord shuddered. "I...cannot describe it easily," she finally said. "Everly...was speaking...for the people he was painting. It was as if...they were part of the future. Not *a* future, and not a *possible* future, but *the* future. It was that solid."

Sanabalis cleared his throat; it was meant as either correction or warning. He had enough respect for the Tha'alani castelord, however, that he didn't commence with pointless lectures. Kaylin, who had often thought titles and positions were useless, briefly wondered if she'd been wrong.

"We will require your presence at the Palace on the morrow."

"In the morning?" Ybelline asked quietly.

"Yes. By that time, I will have conveyed my findings and my concern to the Court. I apologize for the lack of warning," he added, "but it is essential that you convey as much of your understanding of this language as it is possible to convey to the...deaf. They will be our first line of communication should they be required, until we know more about the people w   speak the language itself.

"They will not be our most *efficient* means of communication, bu   ."

Ybelli   nodded gracefully. "Your consideration, Lord Sanabalis, is appreciated. We will, of course, do whatever we can, should the Emperor require our more direct intervention."

To Kaylin's surprise, Sanabalis ordered the driver to drop her in front of her apartment door. As she opened her side of the carriage, he said, "You will also report to the Palace in the morning." Before she could speak, he lifted a hand—a gesture with which she was entirely too familiar—and added, "I realize that diverting you from the office directly to the Palace would cause your Sergeant some concern, and as I will have a very long night ahead of me, I wish to avoid dealing with that concern.

"Make your report to Sergeant Kassan as efficiently—and quickly—as possible. Remind him, if he is still in the same unfortunate mood, that the Emperor requires you to be both mobile and functional. I will mirror Caitlin to let her know when you will be expected."

Kaylin mumbled something that she hoped sounded like *thank you.* It had a very throaty Leontine curl to its syllabic edges. She fumbled with the key, unlocked the door, and made her way up the stairs, all of which creaked. Fumbling with another lock was not her idea of fun. She had, at this point, no idea of fun whatsoever.

The door, however, was unlocked. She grimaced. Light leaked along the slightly warped edges where door met doorjamb. Someone had thoughtfully lit a lamp. Given that she had no lamp oil at the moment, because she didn't have money to spend on anything but food, she could pretty much guess who it was.

"Hello, Severn," she said, as she opened the door.

Had he been Teela, who sometimes liked to drop in, he would have been sprawled like a territorial cat all over her bed. He wasn't; he was seated, hands in his pockets and legs extended, in one of her chairs. He had even removed the clothing that had been hanging off its back and made a neat, folded pile of it. Given what it was going to end up looking like about fifteen minutes after she'd put it on, she'd never really understood people's obsession with folding clothing.

Severn lifted his head. "Long day?"

"To end all days," she replied. She slung her jacket over the bottom half of her unoccupied bed, and sat down heavily on the top half.

"Let me make it slightly longer," he replied. He held out the bracer she'd lost in the nothingness. She took it in silence. "What happened this afternoon?"

"You mean, what happened this morning?"

"No. Sergeant Kassan managed to get a fairly detailed description of your early morning with the Oracles out of the man who runs the place."

She cringed. "He's really not as bad as he looks. And he does keep them more or less safe. The Oracles, I mean."

"You've eaten?"

"Sort of."

"How long ago?"

"I honestly don't know. I have no idea what time it is. Because I was deliberately not looking at the moon's position. I like to *pretend* I'll get enough sleep that I won't make a total ass of myself when Marcus attempts to rip out my throat in the morning."

He chuckled. "I brought food."

Her stomach growled, but then again, it often did. "You ate?"

He nodded. "I had a feeling, given the location of your last call-in, that you might be hungry when you arrived. I expected the arrival to be a few hours ago, so it may be stale."

Her stomach didn't much care, and truthfully, she'd eaten things far worse in her time. There was comfort in food in general, comfort in the stuffed rolls in particular, and comfort in chewing because it meant she didn't have to talk while she was doing it.

"I left the office after reporting in," she said, speaking anyway because it was late and she knew he wasn't going anywhere until at least a truncated version of the day's events had passed her lips, along with stray crumbs. "I headed down to Elani. I figured I'd catch you there. I met Grethan. He told me that you were in the Elemental Garden with Evanton."

Severn nodded. "He let you in."

"Sort of. He meant to let me in—I swear, anything that happened was *not* his fault—but the room I entered wasn't the Garden I know. That, and it was empty. But when I tried to leave…" She shook her head. "The hallway had separated from the door frame."

He frowned. "Separated how?"

"There was a gap between the door and the hall it in theory opened into."

"Small gap?"

"Oh, about ten yards and growing with each second." She winced, and added, "Grethan must have been—"

"He was hysterical, yes."

"Before or after you started questioning him?"

"After *Evanton* started questioning him."

Severn continued to listen to her account of the day's events. He said a very loud nothing when Nightshade came into the story, but once she'd managed to exit the Castle, continued to probe. It took longer than Kaylin would have liked, because what Kaylin had wanted, from the minute she unlocked the front door to the whole damn building, was to crawl into her apartment and fall into bed. It wouldn't have been the first time she hadn't bothered to shed clothing before she did, and it probably wouldn't be the last.

But she also understood that Severn needed to hear the rest, and frankly, that she needed him to know it. She just didn't need him to know it *now*. The brunt of his questions involved Ybelline and Everly, and when he'd finished, he rose.

"You're leaving?"

He glanced at the windows. "I'll stay. You have a few hours of sleep before I throw you out of bed. I'll take care of breakfast," he added. Which was good, because on this little sleep, Kaylin never bothered. He pulled the other chair closer to the one he'd occupied. "Go to sleep, Kaylin. I'll watch. I'll keep watch."

She meant to tell him that she didn't need that anymore, but the words wouldn't leave her mouth. "Did Marrin—"

"Marrin did mirror. She apparently has two day-old foundlings of a slightly unusual nature. She didn't say more. She asked you to mirror *when you have the time.*"

Kaylin fell back into the bed. "Midwives?" she mumbled.

"No calls, there. If something strange has happened, it wasn't life-threatening in any way that required your intervention. Kaylin. Sleep."

She turned her back on him and stripped off most of her clothing, tossing it all over her shoulder and onto the floor. Then she shuffled over to the window-side of the bed.

He laughed. It wasn't an entirely happy laugh.

"What?"

"I'll sleep here."

"It's not as if we didn't share a bed for most of our—"

"You were younger."

"So were you."

"It would be more difficult now—for me. I'll watch," he added, smoothing the edges off his words. "Sleep."

And she did, thinking as she drifted off, that she really didn't understand Severn.

True to his word, he did take care of breakfast—and it was not the usual bread and hard cheese on the run; he was cooking. Sausages, she thought, and eggs. The windows had been opened, and morning sunlight—never the best of friends—now reminded her that opening her eyes could be painful. She didn't ask what time it was; instead, she wandered over to the bucket of water, and splashed enough of it around her face that she could at least sponge it clean. Her hands took more work, and the water was noticeably darker when she'd done. She then rooted through the impromptu closet of floor and the neat pile Severn had made of chair contents.

Brushing her hair took time; she'd managed to get paint on the ends somehow. But she finished, twisted it, and shoved a stick through the bunched folds behind her head.

"Have I ever thanked you?" She perched on the end of her bed.

He smiled. "Not often in so many words, but yes."

"In so many words," she said softly, "thanks."

He turned his back toward her, setting food on plates; she wasn't fooled. "Severn?"

He turned and offered her a plate, which she took. She balanced it in her lap.

"It's hard," she said quietly, while she ate. She didn't look at him, because it was easier. "All this—sometimes it's hard. I know I shouldn't find it hard, but when you're here, it's like you bring safety with you, from years away. I feel like a child. Or like I *can* be one."

"You don't want to be a child."

"No, I don't. We didn't have the easiest childhood, and I can *do* things here. I can make a difference. To my life. To the lives of others, even if I'm only in them for a few hours."

He waited, and she thought he also ate; she wasn't sure because she didn't look. "But...sometimes I want the safety. Not the rest of the life, not that—but the sense that somewhere *is* safe." She swallowed. There was food in it, as well as words. "What I don't understand—what I never thought about, back then—is what *you* get out of this." She turned, then.

He was, as she had suspected, eating. He was also silent, and sadly, much less messy than Kaylin. But as she was about to give up on getting an answer, he said, "Does it matter?"

She nodded. She'd finished, of course—but she'd always been the faster eater. "Because I'm not a child. I can't just take and take and give nothing in return, anymore."

"Because you won't trust it if you do?"

That hadn't been how she'd been thinking of it, but put like that, it made sense. "Maybe."

He nodded, finished the last of the eggs on his plate, and rose. Rinsing his plate in the water, he waited until she'd done the same. "Time to go," he told her quietly.

The walk there was not the usual five-minute sprint during which Kaylin was desperately hoping that time had somehow collapsed and she wouldn't be late. It wasn't a stroll, either, but it did allow speech. Severn started.

"I don't have a way of asking you for what you can't give. If I did—if I tried to make a balance sheet—" When she raised a brow, he sighed, and added, "a budget. Oh, wait, we haven't had time to sit down and do that yet, either."

"You're just trying to make me see silver linings on freaking huge thunderclouds, aren't you?"

He chuckled. "Let me try again. I'm not keeping score." She opened her mouth, and he added, "Betting pools don't count."

She did laugh, then.

"If I want what you can't give, if I want what you don't want, and you try to give it to me, either because you feel that I'm owed—" He shook his head. "I don't spend a lot of time around other people. As a Wolf, there wasn't much time. But I *did* spend time observing other couples. And that interaction—it doesn't work. Never has. You take two fairly decent people, people you like, people you more or less respect, and you put them together like that, where they're both trying to be things they aren't because it's what the other person needs—it's painful. At its worst, they're both feeling hurt, and they both see the other person as the villain.

"If I need something you can't give, I need to walk away, because sooner or later, all I'll see is what you *can't* give. I won't be able to see what you can."

"But—"

"But?"

"You don't speak all that much. But when you do? You've always been better with words. Than me. Always."

It was true; he didn't bother to deny it. But he said, "I was older. You should try words some time—I think you'll find you've gotten better."

She grimaced. "I *am* trying, thankyouverymuch."

He smiled, then. She saw that much before she dropped her gaze to her feet. Well, to their feet. "I don't know what you get out of this. That's all. I know what *I* get."

"And?"

"I want you to tell me."

He nodded. But he didn't answer. The Halls came into view.

★ ★ ★

Marcus was in a better mood, which was to say: she didn't hear his growling from the hall. She glanced at Severn, but Severn never looked concerned when he entered the office. She suspected only the remnants of an all-out slaughter would change that.

Kaylin jogged to the right, to the duty roster, out of force of habit. It was still a mess. But she managed to find her own name in that mess. She also found Severn's. "We're at the Palace, today," she told him.

"I suspected we would be."

She turned and made her way as quietly as possible to Caitlin's desk. Caitlin, surrounded by the usual stacks of paper that never looked quite as precarious on her desk as they would have on anyone else's, looked up. She was tired, but clearly happy to see Kaylin. "I hear you had a busy day, yesterday."

Kaylin nodded. "Is Marcus—"

"Lord Sanabalis left a mirror message for Sergeant Kassan sometime last night. He received and reviewed it this morning, and then went up to the Tower. He's still there, dear."

"Is he in a better mood?"

"He is no longer concerned for your safety. You've noted your reassignment?"

Kaylin nodded. "I'm not sure it's the smartest idea."

"You are, of course, free to discuss that with the Sergeant once he returns to his desk."

Kaylin winced. "I think most of the trouble we're going to see is going to occur *on* or around Elani. Severn and I should be there. So should the rest of the groundhawks, and at best guess, two-thirds of the Swords."

Caitlin lifted a brow, but didn't otherwise comment. She didn't have to, though; Marcus had now entered the office.

"Private Neya!"

★ ★ ★

A quick rundown of the previous day's events was in order. Kaylin, having had to go through parts of it at least twice the previous day, didn't make her usual nervous-in-the-presence-of-angry-Leontine hash of it. Marcus's eyes, however, were a strong shade of orange by the time she'd finished. He had interrupted her maybe twice, a sure sign that he'd heard most of it from another source.

"Your presence has been requested at the Palace by Lord Sanabalis. On behalf of the Emperor."

Kaylin nodded. "Ybelline Rabon'alani will be there, as well. I think—"

"On occasion."

She grimaced. He was still, clearly, in a bit of a mood.

"I think," she continued, "we're going to see a large number of unidentified people suddenly show up someplace in the city."

"Large?"

"Thousands, at a rough guess."

He raised a brow. His ear tufts were also standing on end. On the other hand, his fangs were still hooded by his lips.

"But it's not the people who are going to be the problem."

Marcus snorted. "Tell that to the Swords," he replied. "Lord Sanabalis is sending a carriage to retrieve both you and Corporal Handred. The usual warning applies."

"Don't embarrass the department while I'm at the Palace?"

"Indeed. Do not lose the Corporal, either. I should have sent him to the Halls with you yesterday morning, because my wives would be marginally less enraged if I tore out *his* throat."

★ ★ ★

The carriage was waiting when they hit the yard. As carriages went, Imperial Carriages were by far the most comfortable, and this one had the added advantage of not already being full of Dragon. Kaylin clambered into the interior and sat on the padded seat. The windows were curtained, but she pulled those back and looked out into the street as the horses began to pull.

"Have you been able to dig up any more information about the Chancellor?" she asked Severn.

"Some."

"Did they move in?"

He shook his head. "Apparently some of the ledgers and some of the documents they require are now missing. Margot's little mishap gave them at least that much time. Records access is required—but the Records required are located at the Palace, and Records use at the Palace is under strict embargo. Mirror access at the Palace is also under embargo, but exceptions—to mirror embargo—can be made.

"We're not certain whether Records are being made of anything that is currently occurring within the Palace itself. It's apparently caused the Palace Guard some concern."

"Right. Because random assassins might somehow sneak in and do in the Emperor." She snorted. Anything dangerous enough to kill the Emperor *quickly* wouldn't have to worry about sneaking anywhere. Come to think, anything dangerous enough to kill the Emperor at all, wouldn't have to worry about anything.

Severn, however, raised a brow. "They serve a useful function," he said, in the mild tone of voice reserved for correction. "If the Emperor doesn't require protection, many of the people who serve him do. Ybelline, for instance."

Kaylin snorted, but conceded the point. "It's just that they're so stuck-up."

"They're not actually all that stuck-up. They take their job seriously."

"And I don't?"

"Take their job seriously? Demonstrably not."

"Ha, ha."

"They also serve an important function. The Emperor is not required to, as you often put it, go Dragon in times of difficulty. He has his guards, and they're his defense. He is not therefore required to rend people limb from limb for every small legal stupidity, because most of the egregiously stupid will never reach him."

On some days, Kaylin didn't see this as a plus. Then again? She had never once been allowed within yards of the Emperor, so maybe she'd have to rethink that.

One of the best things about significant reduction in the use of magic in the Palace? The doors had to be opened the normal way; the door ward and its attached alert system had been disarmed. Probably another thing that was giving the Imperial Guard hives. The bad thing? The doors were bloody heavy, something she'd had no real cause to discover; usually they just rolled open on their own, having taken a figurative bite of her palm first. Happily, Sanabalis had met them at the entrance.

The Arkon, however, was waiting for them. He was seated behind a desk, one usually occupied by the humans who filed various cards and carted books from one end of these sweeping, high-shelved rooms to the other. He was the only thing behind the desk; Kaylin half wondered if he'd eaten his assistants. He rose as they closed the doors behind them.

"Has the Tha'alani castelord arrived?"

"Yes. She was on time," the Arkon added. He set the small pile of cards to one side of the desk and rose. "Private."

"Arkon."

"Lord Sanabalis has taken the liberty of recounting the

events in the Oracular Halls. He was, apparently, absent for the beginning of those events." The chill in his tone sounded so natural it was almost impossible to believe fire would ever leave those lips again.

"I don't think he missed anything important."

"Don't think," was the curt reply. It was the exact opposite of what the Arkon generally demanded, but she liked her arms attached and didn't point this out.

"Ybelline was reading Everly while he painted, because he'd been speaking for—as far as I can tell—hours. But they both…froze. I can't explain it. They looked like they'd been hit by lightning, but without the obvious burns. They were having standing spasms."

"And you felt it was necessary to interfere at this point."

"No, I—" She started to mention Sigrenne, stopped, swallowed, and said, "Yes, Arkon." Severn, utterly silent, nodded very slightly. "I picked up a brush and I started to paint."

"You meant to paint those runes?"

"Well…no. I wanted to do something to get Everly's attention. I suppose I could have tried to take a knife to the painting, but I'm not sure that would have helped. So I started to paint."

"And you intended to paint those words?"

"Not exactly."

"What, *exactly,* did you intend?"

"I intended to fix the buildings, if you want the truth. He'd done something to them, somehow, during the last phase of his painting, and they were *fading.* I didn't actually like it. I think I found it more disturbing than the corpses in the foreground. So… I thought I'd try to paint them back to the way they're supposed to be."

The Arkon glanced at Sanabalis. "It is a small miracle to

me that Private Neya is allowed past the gatehouse of the Halls, never mind over the threshold."

"As you say," Sanabalis helpfully replied. Normally, this might have been annoying, but at this point if the Arkon had said "red is blue," Kaylin would have saluted the new blue, so she couldn't really blame Sanabalis.

"Are you aware of the meanings of the runes you did paint?"

The question, of course, that she'd both expected and dreaded. "No, Arkon."

"You chose to depict them, however—"

"I thought I was painting over the buildings."

"You were, in my opinion, painting over the most dangerous structure that existed in Everly's Oracle. But—you've seen those runes before."

"I don't know."

The Arkon actually spoke—with no warning whatsoever—in Dragon. And even though it was almost deafening, Kaylin did her best to memorize the syllables, because she was pretty damn sure it was, in the Hawk vernacular, one of the useful words. "If magic use were not, at this moment, all but prohibited, you would be carrying a memory crystal until you died of old age." His tone indicated that this could not happen soon enough.

"They looked like the words Sanabalis spoke in the Leontine Quarter the one time he visited," she said quickly, trying to placate.

Smoke—absent the usual pipe that produced it—streamed from his nostrils. "They were *not* the words Sanabalis spoke."

"No, I didn't mean they were the same—but they looked like his words, to me. His spoken words."

"I remember. That you could see them," he added, "in ways that we, Dragon, or human, could not. Until you touched them," he added, his voice softening ever so slightly. "We could see them, clearly, then. Come, we are almost there. I dislike the sound of hungry mortals. It is almost pathetic. I have therefore made sure food is present. You will eat neatly and quickly."

Ybelline had not, as Kaylin half feared, been led into what was essentially a dark big cave in the heart of the Palace—or beneath it, it was hard to tell—and left alone there. The Arkon had clearly decided to forgo Records for this particular meeting, and she waited in one of the small, round rooms behind the Library's main chambers to the left. Kaylin tried to remember which direction this actually was—she thought maybe East—but it didn't matter. Ybelline rose as they entered the room, and as usual, she came forward and hugged Kaylin, brushing her forehead with her stalks.

He hasn't been angry with you, has he? Kaylin asked; it was clear she meant the Arkon, and she didn't need to use the words when they talked this way.

No. He is difficult and extremely didactic, but I am actually fond of him. He is angry because he is worried.

You're worried, too. She was. More than she had been the night—the very late night—before.

I am. I spent much of the night in the Tha'alaan, and even now, debates rage. We are not certain whether or not we should attempt to evacuate at least the young from the City. But I think, if we fail here, there will be little point.

CHAPTER 15

The Arkon cleared his throat before Ybelline could continue, and Ybelline graciously took the hint. She let her arms fall first, her stalks finally breaking the connection seconds before she turned to the table.

True to his word, he had had food set out. Dragons obviously ate a lot when they were hungry, because there was enough here to feed the whole department, and send them home with leftovers. Kaylin had eaten breakfast, thanks to Severn's intervention, but that didn't stop her from eating a very early lunch, because telling the Arkon that she was not, in fact, hungry never even occurred to her.

Severn did the same.

Sanabalis had taken a chair; the Arkon had not. He now paced the room like a caged and angry beast, while they ate in his thunderous silence. "Private Neya," he said, when she'd finished. "You will be Seconded—that is the word, is it not? For some reason I want to say remanded—to Lord Sanabalis for the duration of this event. We believe—" An alarm sounded. Had the Arkon been carrying anything in his hands, it would have snapped in two instantly. The *air* almost did. "Sanabalis," the Arkon snarled. "Please retrieve our guest. Tell him he is to have *two* guards, no more. I don't care what's done with the others."

Sanabalis didn't seem to notice that the Arkon had dropped the honorific entirely. He bowed instantly, and he exited the room they had barely entered. The Arkon, in the meantime, breathed a little fire. Which would, Kaylin thought, explain the small scorch marks on the floor.

She glanced at Ybelline, but Ybelline seemed entirely unruffled at the obvious sight of Dragon frustration.

"The world," the Arkon said coldly, "would end if it depended on my ability to work unhindered by pointless interruptions."

Since Kaylin and Severn had been one of those pointless interruptions, silence greeted the comment. She wanted to know who the visitors were, but didn't ask. Instead, she said, "Lord Sanabalis informed you of Everly's Oracle?"

The Arkon's eyes were a deep orange when he turned to her, dropping his inner membranes. She took that as a yes. She also stopped herself from taking a step back. "He did."

Kaylin said, quietly, "It's the Devourer, isn't it? Whatever that is or was?"

"At this point, given our scant knowledge, I am hesitant to concur. I will, however. We have been in contact with Lord Tiamaris. Lord Diarmat chose to visit the fief of Tiamaris when you left for the Oracular Halls with Lord Sanabalis. In future, I believe I will redirect Sanabalis to Tiamaris from the Halls, and you will just have to live without sleep."

Kaylin knew very little about Lord Diarmat. She had met him once—briefly—but didn't recall speaking two words to him. He was, as Sanabalis and Tiamaris, a member of the Dragon Court; he was, unlike Sanabalis and Tiamaris, distinctly unfriendly.

Severn came to her rescue as he so often did. "Lord Diarmat is, if I'm not mistaken, the Captain of the Imperial Guard?"

The Arkon snorted smoke. "It is the least of his titles, but yes, if it pleases you, that is one of his duties."

Kaylin grimaced.

"It is possible you will meet him today," the Arkon continued. Kaylin's shoulders immediately slid partway down the rest of her back. Of her many life's ambitions, meeting the Dragon in command of the most stuck-up guards in the city was nowhere near the top. Still, it explained something about the guard here. "I would advise you to be on your best behavior. Or, given what I've seen, better. Lord Diarmat is a bit of a traditionalist."

"Meaning he thinks you should still be able to eat the people who offend you?"

"I do,' was the Arkon's reply. He paced around the table. "You understand the import of the painting?" he asked her.

"It's a portal."

He nodded.

"Sanabalis once said—Lord Sanabalis once said—that humans aren't native to this world. I think he implied that other mortal races weren't, either, excepting the Leontines. If the only other Records you have—or nonrecords—imply that a huge crater appeared shortly after the arrival of humans, it's possible that the portal is magically unstable."

The Dragon snorted.

Kaylin obligingly tried again, frowning slightly, as she often did when she was thinking. "If I had to guess—and I'm not a mage—the magical flux in the area is strongest where Everly painted his version of Elani. Sanabalis hasn't said anything about the results of the Imperial Order of Mages' tests there.

"But it's possible that the existence of the portal *requires* a huge amount of magic, and it's gathering magic. Or even shedding it. It's doing something, somehow, to make entry from nowhere to here possible. I think that's why I fell out of the world."

The Arkon snorted again; he clearly didn't approve of her description of the event.

"I wouldn't have been able to get back without the intervention of Lord Nightshade. But... I think someone is trying to get here. Or possibly just to get *somewhere*. Someone who can," she added. "And whoever it is, he or she is bringing a lot of people with them."

"Very good. What, then, is the danger?"

"I'd say having thousands of people who are armed to the teeth appear in the middle of the streets is pretty bloody dangerous all on its own. But... When I fell through the world, something else was in the nothing, and it became aware of *me*. I think, whatever *else* it does, it...eats things."

"If indications are correct, it *is* called the Devourer."

She nodded, pretending to ignore the sarcasm, which took monumental effort. "It was *there*. If there's anything at all like location in the nonworld, the Devourer was close enough that it could hear me. But it...heard me only when I...called Lord Nightshade. I think, until then, it was searching. But I think," she added quietly, "it was searching for *them*. For whoever's trying to reach safety."

She glanced, briefly, at her covered arms. "I don't know all of what the Devourer does. But I think one of the things it does is eat words. True words," she added. She looked at the Arkon; his eyes hadn't changed color. "I think he can eat your names."

What the Arkon might have replied was lost to the sound of door chimes. The chimes hadn't sounded when Kaylin,

Sanabalis and Severn entered; they sounded now, and as the door opened enough to allow a first glimpse of the Arkon's unwanted visitors, Kaylin's brows disappeared into her hairline.

There, standing between Sanabalis, who held the door, and the Arkon, who stepped toward them, were two people she recognized well: the Lord of the Barrani High Court, and his consort, The Lady.

The Lord of the High Court inclined his head; more was not required. "Lord Kaylin," he said, emphasizing the title. "Lord Severn."

Severn did bow, which reminded Kaylin that she ought to be doing the same. But she took a quick step toward The Lady instead, and after a brief hesitation, informed by her clumsy understanding of politics, their import, and the sense that this was somehow a hugely historic moment, she stepped into the consort's open arms. The hug was brief and fierce.

The Barrani castelord then offered the Arkon a full, and formal, bow. "We were surprised to receive your invitation, Arkon," he said, as he rose. "But we were not ill-pleased."

"You were," was the testy response. "But you have no doubt had word."

"We have received word, from many sources, that there are strong and unusual magical currents and potentials located within Elantra at the moment. Master Evarrim of the Arcanum—"

"Save us from the Arcanists," someone muttered. Kaylin realized, belatedly, that it was her, and she reddened.

The High Lord, having perfected many arts political, failed entirely to hear her. "—has brought it to the attention of the High Court. He is concerned, Arkon."

"So is the Emperor."

"That was our understanding. The Emperor, however, has not tendered an invitation to his Court."

"He has granted permission for me to extend one," was the curt reply. "He is, of course, aware of your presence here." The Arkon raised one brow. "Permission was granted for two guards. I see none."

"Ah. I was not certain how the term *guard* was to be defined in the Imperial Palace," came the smooth reply. "And I was made aware that both Lord Kaylin and Lord Severn would be present."

For the first time that day the Arkon smiled. It was a thin, sharp smile, but there was definitely amusement in it. "Well done," he said softly. "I cannot think why the Barrani are considered so difficult to deal with. I deal with mortals all of the time, and I can assure you they are vastly more trying. And fragile."

This did draw a smile from the High Lord. Which figured.

"The Imperial Palace is situated in the area in which magic behaves in unpredictable and unusual ways. We are therefore hampered in our choice of tools."

There was a *long* hesitation, and then the High Lord turned to his Consort. He didn't speak, but a look passed between them. "How important are these tools to your studies?"

"They are of import. However," the Arkon added, "in the completely unexpected event that you offer the use of the High Halls as a more appropriate place of study, I must add that much of what we need is ensconced in Imperial Records Archives, all of which are not to be accessed without extreme caution. There is some concern on the part of the Archivist—"

"That would be you, Arkon?"

"Indeed."

"The concern?"

"That the use of Records will actually corrupt them."

The High Lord raised one dark brow. "Very well. The Records of the High Court are not, of course, the equal of the Arkon's Records in any way."

"Nor are they accessible to the Arkon, one assumes."

The High Lord glanced at Kaylin, of all people. "They are not, of course, accessible directly. But in the case of an emergency, some accommodation could be made. It is something to consider," he added, glancing at the rounded curves of walls and windowless domes. "And I believe you would find it more…aesthetically appealing."

"Aesthetics are not a concern of mine," was the Arkon's reply. "If it pleases you, there are refreshments."

The High Lord nodded and entered the room; the Consort lingered a moment to speak—in low tones—with the Arkon. The Arkon's eyes were still orange, but hers? Hers were a deep and beautiful shade of emerald. The High Lord's were almost, but not quite, blue. Kaylin wished, for just a minute, that they could have met in the Library, with its miles of shelving, or maybe in the galleries in which much of the Arkon's collection resided.

But they weren't here for a tour. She gave herself a mental kick; it's not as if she personally were interested in either of those rooms—but she thought the Consort would be.

"There is little discussion between our Courts," Lord Sanabalis said, as he closed the door behind him. "And yet, we have much in common."

"The Lord of the Dragon Court is the Eternal Emperor," the High Lord replied, pointing out the biggest thing they *didn't* have in common.

"Indeed," was the smooth reply.

Kaylin glanced at Severn, who was watching everything in the room so intently he might have been a memory crystal, not a person.

"We have, however, ceased to war, and between our two Courts, a city has emerged that is home to people of all races. It is, even in the Arkon's opinion, an interesting endeavor." Sanabalis kept distance between himself and the High Lord; his eyes were a shade of orange-gold; he was alert, but not alarmed.

"The city is ruled by the Emperor."

"Not all of the City," was the serene reply. "The heart of it is ruled, in the end, by no one."

Silence settled around the room. It was Ybelline who broke it. "High Lord," she said, bowing. "Consort."

They turned cool gazes upon her, and Kaylin felt her spine stiffening. She spoke before they could. "I'm sorry," she said softly. "I know Ybelline Rabon'alani so well I forget it's possible not to recognize her." She tried to keep the edge out of her voice. "Ybelline, this is the High Lord of the Barrani Court, and his Consort. We call her The Lady. And this," she added, "is Ybelline Rabon'alani, the castelord of the Tha'alani."

They both inclined their heads with some grace, and no friendliness whatsoever. Kaylin sighed inwardly. She understood their reaction; hers would have been far worse even a year ago. And they weren't actively hostile or rude. Nor did Ybelline seem to be at all offended or hurt by their response, so it was stupid to feel either of those things on her behalf. People seldom accused Kaylin of being smart.

As if she could read the thought—without the necessary physical contact—Ybelline shook her head very slightly.

Sanabalis then began to detail what he believed the difficulty they faced was. Kaylin took care to note which details he left out, but there weren't, in the end, many, and the only significant one was the hidden altar with its glowing symbols and its copper-eyed, ancient stranger.

★ ★ ★

"And so we must now rely on the mercy or the self-interest of the Barrani," Sanabalis finished. "Our historical Records contain very little of note—what they contain," he added, with a nod to the Arkon, "have been significant enough that we are willing to draw this conclusion. The magical potentials being witnessed, the unusual expressions of that potential, are in part caused *by* someone—or some multiple of people—who are attempting to open a gate or a portal into our world.

"The power necessary to sustain a portal of this nature would be staggering—in theory—and some spillage or leakage would be expected. Nor would the construction of such a portal necessarily be an instantaneous event—although it is likely to be witnessed as such, in the end."

"Can you assume that this Oracle is accurate to that degree?" the High Lord asked.

"If we cannot, I fear we will lose the city."

"Explain."

"When the portal opens, we should see an immediate cessation of the leakage or potential. If we are very unlucky—and it is to be hoped we are not—we might see a magical null zone in a very, very unfortunate geographic location. In and of itself, such a zone would not signal an end to the city, of course.

"But what the Oracular Halls have witnessed thus far imply that it is not just thousands of armed men—and women—who will enter the city streets as a veritable army, but also something that might be hunting them as they travel, even now. We believe—again, with very little in the way of solid fact—that it is this entity that poses the true threat to the security of the Empire."

"What entity?" the Consort asked quietly.

Sanabalis glanced at Kaylin. It was a pointed glance. The

Private cleared her throat, and said, "The Devourer." It was, Kaylin realized belatedly, a High Barrani word.

The Consort, already the porcelain pale of the Barrani, froze, and her eyes shaded instantly into a blue so dark it was almost midnight.

"Where did you hear that name?" All of the friendly openness of her face had drained away: she was a Winter Queen, and the unusual color of her platinum hair only added to the impression. She rose, her hands by her sides; even the High Lord seemed forgotten.

Only Kaylin was not.

"In the fiefs," Kaylin replied, hedging. She glanced at the Dragons in turn, and saw that while Sanabalis affected the perfect inscrutability of his kind, the Arkon was now watching the Consort intently.

The answer did not please the Consort, and Kaylin realized—instantly—the error of her partial disclosure. "It wasn't Lord Nightshade," she said quickly.

"Who, then?"

"It was in the fief of Tiamaris."

"Lord Tiamaris? The youngest of the Dragon Court?"

"No. No, Lady." She grimaced. While the previous day had been undeniably unique, she was getting pretty damn tired of recounting its events. Recounting its events when a couple of the words had instantly turned possibly the friendliest and most human of the Barrani Court into one of the least friendly and least human, caused words to momentarily flee. She found them again, because she realized that those eyes weren't getting any greener.

"The Tower of Tiamaris has an Avatar who can wander the fief at will. I spoke to her first. She recognized what I described."

This didn't significantly change the shade of the Consort's eyes, and Kaylin sighed and began to recount the events of import again, leaving out the more sensitive Oracular information, and all direct mention of the events within the Palace itself. Even if she had told all of the truth, the Consort would have assumed she was omitting things; the Consort was Barrani.

Some of the rigidity of the Consort's posture relaxed as Kaylin reached the end of her story, but her eyes were still midnight-blue, and her knuckles were now white; it was as if all of the tension in her body had drained into her hands and condensed there. "If it were not for the fact that the Devourer was hunting already, Lord Kaylin, I would accuse you of endangering the whole of our world. As it is, you have offered warning."

"How do *you* know so much?" Kaylin countered.

The Consort glanced at the High Lord; the High Lord, at the Dragon Lords. Kaylin felt her own hands bunching into fists, because she was sick to death of pointless politics. She forced her hands to relax, bit back her words, and waited for the Consort's answer.

She wasn't surprised when the Consort finally said, "We will retreat to the High Halls, Lord Kaylin, where we might discuss this matter at length."

Severn rose; the Consort lifted a hand. "No, Lord Severn. My Lord will remain with the Arkon and Lord Sanabalis. You will not abandon him. Where Lord Kaylin and I go, none of you can follow." She turned then, and opened the door. Kaylin, whose day had started out so well—Marcus hadn't even *touched* her exposed throat—knew it was once again spiraling unpredictably out of control.

"Arkon?" Kaylin asked quietly.

"Go with her," was his curt reply. "If she is willing to trust you with information, it is because you are nominally a Lord of the High Court. Neither Sanabalis nor I will ever be that. If it is warranted, make certain that you understand *clearly* how much of this information is given to you in the confidence of that Court, and how much you might repeat to us. The Barrani have very few definitions of treason compared to the human Caste Court, but rather longer reach than the human Caste Court, and infinitely longer memories."

I don't get paid enough for this, Kaylin thought with a grimace. Then she thought about asking Marcus for a raise at this particular point in time, and quickly followed the Consort out.

The Consort and the High Lord had arrived, of course, in a Barrani carriage. It was, in some ways, the antithesis of the Imperial Carriages, in part because it didn't have to support the weight of up to four Dragon Lords at one time. Where the Imperial Carriages were like large boats on wheels, albeit solid, stable and attractive ones, the Barrani carriages implied supple, slender, tensile strength; they were adorned with a crest, but seemed, at first glance, to suggest things delicate and graceful. Like much about the Barrani, the suggestion was deceptive.

Kaylin sat across from the Consort in the enclosed space; the seats were a startling green, and everything was, of course, spotless and perfect. Even the Consort, but her transformation from that brittle perfection to something less dangerous took most of the utterly silent journey. When they disembarked, she turned to Kaylin; her eyes were still blue, but they weren't as dark.

"My apologies, Lord Kaylin," she said wearily. The first

two words almost didn't make sense because they were in Barrani and they sounded genuine. Kaylin had borne the brunt of numerable Barrani apologies in the past, most of which were of the *I'm sorry you're so ignorant* variety. "We were... surprised to receive an invitation to visit the Imperial Palace, and were cautiously...pleased. Most of the interactions between the Palace and the High Halls occur through various functionaries—yourself, the Hawklord on rare occasion, the humans in the Caste Court. It is true that Leontines seldom visit," she added with a shrug. "But Dragons? Never. Nor do we visit the Dragons.

"Come." She climbed the stairs until she stood in the shadows cast by the huge statues that seemed almost pillars, and waited until Kaylin caught up. "We expected that there would be news of grave difficulties facing the city. The incident in the former fief of Barren has been much on our mind.

"We did not expect—I did not expect—your news, and I am perhaps not as capable as the High Lord or the Dragon Lords at dissembling. But it is grave news, Kaylin." She entered the silence of the High Halls.

The Consort led Kaylin through vast, high-ceilinged halls until they reached the interior gardens in which the High Court convened. Here, more of the Barrani gathered in twos and threes, but they were silent, and they did not greet the Consort as she passed. Nor did she acknowledge their presence.

But it was not to the familiar thrones that she went, Kaylin in her wake, and only as she passed them and headed toward a familiar fountain, did Kaylin understand exactly where she intended to go. To the lake of names, the spiritual birthing place of the Barrani race.

The path from the fountain became wilder and less precise, and the land surrounding it far less tended, although it was still lovely because it *was* Barrani. But there was a worn footpath just beyond the fountain. That path led, at last, to the mouth of a cave. Entering the cave brought light with it, but it was a soft illumination, not a harsh one.

Kaylin hesitated in the glow, and the Consort paused, as well.

"Why are we going to the lake?" Kaylin asked her.

"It is not entirely to the lake that we now travel. But the information that we seek is there."

"Why there? No one comes here but—"

"No one," the Consort replied, "except the Consorts. And those," she added softly, "who have seen, and touched, the lake. You are the only non-Barrani to have come here since the awakening, but the name you chose to carry was of such import, you have every right—and perhaps a duty—to see."

She would have asked what she would see; in the High Halls, surprise had frequently been synonymous with danger, near death, and pain. She suspected the answer would be a very quiet, very polite lecture on the nature of patience, and she nodded instead. The Consort once again began to lead.

The path within the cave was not created by any Barrani architect; it was rough, and although it was wide enough to walk in, its lack of windows suggested shadow and confinement. But it wasn't the fact that it was a cave that was disturbing; it was the sound that grew with every step she took. She slowed.

"Lord Kaylin?"

She couldn't remember the sounds of the overlapping, inscrutable words—moving, living words—being so strong the last time she'd walked into this cave. Then again, the last time she had come here, she had come to bear witness to the passing of the former Consort, a woman whose ability to choose names and carry them to the sleeping infants of her race had begun to falter.

"I'm sorry," she said at last. "I think—I think I can *hear* the lake."

The Consort nodded, as if this were natural—and perhaps it was. For her. "The waters are restless," she added.

"Why?"

"It happens sometimes. When there have been too few births. Or when a birth of some significance might soon occur. It is...like the storms in your harbor, but it threatens nothing."

Kaylin wasn't as certain, but the Consort was calm and entirely unperturbed by what she said. Trusting her—inasmuch as one ever wisely trusted a Barrani Lord—Kaylin followed her through the last leg of tunnel and onto the open plateau that overlooked the turbulence of golden, roiling... water. It wasn't water of course, although Kaylin could see hints of green and blue in the waves of lines, of dots, of moving squiggles.

The Consort paused briefly above the lake, lifting her arms, exposing her palms to the stone sky. Then she bowed, and the voices quieted.

"They can see you."

"No. But we are aware of each other in some fashion. Come. This way."

Kaylin had seen the Consort's mother walk off the edge and disappear beneath the waves. She wondered if, at some time, bodies of the fallen or the dying had been brought here in similar fashion, returning to the source of life at its end. She didn't ask. Instead, she took the hand the Consort held out, and she followed her not over the edge, but to the side. There, carved into the stone just beneath the lip of the pla-

teau overlooking the waters was a narrow flight of stairs that
headed down, in a steep incline, from the front of the flat
toward the cave wall below. There was no true darkness in
this place, and no need for any light, magical or otherwise;
the water's light was enough.

As they reached the bottom of the stairs, a small path
opened up, close enough to the lake that one could crouch,
reach out, and touch the lake itself. The noise was louder
here, as well. But the Consort didn't stop, and Kaylin continued to shadow her.

She wasn't surprised to see that the path led toward a cavern
just beyond the lake itself. Nor was she surprised to see that
the floor, the walls, and the rounded heights of that cavern
were glowing faintly, and not as a result of the golden light
shed by the lake. They were covered in runes. If she didn't
recognize them individually, she recognized what they meant:
this, like the heart of the only two Towers she'd seen, had
been chiseled by the Old Ones.

The Consort said, "You are not surprised."

Kaylin could have lied; the Barrani were never offended
by lies. Only the really obvious ones—because those were
an insult to their intelligence. But she wasn't Barrani. "No.
They made this lake. They must have."

"Yes."

"What did they give to the Dragons?"

The Consort raised a white brow. "I think you would have
to ask the Dragons. Tactfully, and when it was relevant."

But Kaylin now walked toward the center of the cavern.
"This isn't part of the High Halls?"

"No. If the Halls fall, they fall. This is guarded by older
and wilder magic, and if the lake falls, so, too, the whole of

the Barrani race. The Lords and the Court are not the same as the whole of a people, and we at least must understand this."

"I've never had a problem understanding that," Kaylin said.

This was followed by a moment of silence, and then the light and musical laughter of the Consort. "No," she said, her voice still soft and sweet, "you haven't, have you?"

"But…why did you have to bring me here? Why couldn't you just tell me this in the Palace?"

The Consort shook her head. "Chosen," she said softly, "you have lived half your life in the company of Barrani, be they the outliers of our society, or no. I do nothing without reason. The story of the Devourer came to me—and to my mother before me, and hers before her—in the heart of our responsibility. Here."

"But you clearly don't talk about it at Court. I don't think the High Lord recognized the words as clearly as you did."

"We talk little about things that must be hidden and kept safe, for obvious reasons. Nor will I speak now, Lord Kaylin. You will speak. You will ask the Old Ones for our stories. What they tell you, I am not responsible for, nor am I responsible, in the end, for the actions you choose to take.

"But you will understand the whole of the threat to us. You will understand why, to me, it is the worst of our ancient Nightmares." When Kaylin failed to move, the Consort placed slender palms between her shoulder blades and gave her a little push. A cattle prod would have been softer.

"Does it matter *where* I ask the damn question?"

The Consort didn't reply.

"And can you at least tell me *what question* I should be asking?" She half turned. "Look, I'm not really good at speaking with nobles. Of *any* race. I've never been allowed to meet the Emperor because the rest of the Dragons I've worked with are

certain he'll be forced to eat me. Or execute me. I'm thinking that gods are possibly trickier than nobles. Can you at
least give me a hint?"

"Yes."

"Good."

"You are facing the end of a world."

"That's not—"

"It is. Ask, Kaylin. Ask what you can possibly do to *prevent*
it. The desperate cannot afford to—"

"Offend?"

"To hesitate." She backed away from Kaylin, then. "You
are young. The young stumble constantly. But you either
stumble, or you fail to move at all."

Easy for her to say. Kaylin closed her eyes, drew three deep
breaths, and forced her shoulders to relax enough that they
weren't bunched up so close to her ears. The Old Ones had
talked to her before, and it hadn't required much in the way
of conversation, after all.

But...*was* it easy for the Consort to say, in the end? She gave
life, choosing *true* names, for every Barrani that was born. She
was, in some way, their mother; she chose each name with
hope for the future. And she *knew* where that hope must end
for so many. Humans had no shot at immortality; they were
born, they lived, and they died. All of history, much of myth,
and much of legend, involved the catastrophes wrought by
those who tried to avoid death.

The Barrani? Could live forever. Therefore *every* death was
a failure of promise.

And every death diminished the Consort. Kaylin turned
to gaze at the Consort, at the woman who willingly accepted
this burden. And then she turned away, because she saw none

of this in that woman's composed and beautiful face. She saw patience; she saw the depth of the blue of her eyes.

"All right," she said, to the heights of the cavern. "We're facing the Devourer. How do we survive?"

CHAPTER 16

"Interesting," the Consort said. "I think most would ask first about the *nature* of the threat."

Kaylin thought it more than a little unfair that the Consort had been unwilling to offer advice before the fact, but was obviously willing to criticize after. She might have said as much, adorning the words with Leontine just for a little emphasis, but her skin began to ache in a very familiar way.

It was an early warning.

So, a voice that was both familiar and entirely unknown, said. *It has come.*

She looked up, and then around; she saw no one. But the runes across the floor had begun to dim.

Chosen. We greet you, we who remain.

Light began to coalesce in front of her or around her; she lifted her arms and her arms passed through it.

"What," Kaylin now asked, mindful of the Consort's mild criticism, "is the Devourer?"

The silence lasted for just a little bit too long, and it implied surprise. Surprise, Kaylin thought, that the question had to be asked at all.

It is the Devourer.

Which wasn't helpful. "How long has the Devourer existed?"

It is old. Ancient. We cannot say for certain. When we woke to the world—to the worlds, Chosen—it existed at the edges of what we had written. We were young, the voice added. *No helpful face or form came to join it. And we created what we created with abandon. But what we created we could not contain. What we created grew in ways we had not predicted.*

Some of our kin chose to begin again, aware of the errors of past creations. Some chose to raze what they had writ, and start anew. Where we did not...agree...in our decisions, we left.

"Left."

We left the lands in which we first woke. Those lands were bound in ways that we had not foreseen, and it took time and effort to step beyond the boundaries.

Beyond the boundaries, the Devourer also waited. We did not understand what it was, at first. We, who created and destroyed at whim, did not fear it, not then. We did not fear its silence or its voice. We attempted to change it, the voice added. *It cannot be changed. What it touches it absorbs, but it is not affected by that absorption.*

Not so, our kind.

But no more. These lands are ours, although they are not what we first envisioned. They have grown, and they grow strange. You, Chosen, you are not ours, and your life, and the life of your kin, did not begin on our pages, in our dreams. Yet you are here.

When we left our home, we had ways of speaking to distant kin. Our words did not disturb their creations, nor their words, ours. We traveled, we few, to see what had been made, and we returned. We created pathways that might be taken to do so. We were content to experiment, to create, and to communicate with our distant kin.

And then, one day, we walked a familiar path that led to...nothing. To silence and a death so profound there was nothing to inter. You will understand this. We did not. Not then. We saw the emptiness, the lack of words, the lack of where words might be spoken or written or imagined. What had once existed there was gone, and nothing might now exist there at all.

Twice more, it happened, but the third time, some word was sent before the end, at risk, and it propagated to all of creation. The Devourer had come.

It left nothing in its wake. But the first layer of destruction was simple, the rest, less so.

The paths, little one, were closed then. The barriers were built. We understood that the paths themselves existed as a beacon for the Devourer who waited to feed. It was...difficult. We sundered our-selves—each world—forever from our brethren. We made this choice.

But...life is surprising. There exists—there have always existed—some fleeting thoughts that combine in ways we could not expect. We discovered that some of our children could travel. They could make paths or find paths between one world and the next that were now closed, even to us. We do not know how, or why.

They risk the Devourer. Perhaps they flee the Devourer. We cannot say.

"Some do," Kaylin said quietly, because she could. "They flee, where they can." For she remembered the face of the stranger in the waters of the mirror hidden at the heart of the Imperial Palace. "What does it want?"

We must say, to destroy. To utterly destroy. We cannot and do not know why. We attempted to communicate with it, once. Twice. A third time. There is silence now, where those attempts were made, and nothing will break it. We will not try again.

"How did they fight it?"

Silence. Kaylin waited for that silence to break in grow-ing agitation. She turned to look back at the Consort, who had not moved.

"If it can devour *everything*, why does *anything* still exist?"

262   *Michelle Sagara*

It lives in the void between worlds, the voice replied. *And only there. But if it finds purchase, it brings the void with it, slowly and completely, until only that void remains.*

"And it finds purchase by entering the world."

Yes. We do not think it can find the worlds on its own, but it is drawn to life.

No, Kaylin thought. And then, yes. Because behind her, the lake waited, moving and speaking in a voice that never quite coalesced into something Kaylin could comprehend. "It's drawn to *words*. To your words. To echoes of them. We arrived here, somehow. My people. And the Devourer didn't follow because the world is still here."

She turned back to the Consort, in the lee of a god's ghost, and said, "Can you hear what he's saying?"

"I can."

"People *are* coming, Lady. I don't think there's anything we can do to prevent it."

"The Devourer will follow if we cannot."

"They'll *all die* if we do."

The Consort's brows rose, the delicate shape of her eyes rounding in obvious surprise. Kaylin had shocked her. "They are not even native to our world, Lord Kaylin. If I understand everything that I have heard this past day, they are travelers and they flee the ruins and destruction of their own. They lead the Devourer to us."

"*Humans* aren't native to your world," Kaylin replied. "I don't think—if what Sanabalis guesses is correct—that the Aerians are, either. But...if we somehow figure out a way to keep them out—they all die. And possibly with them the last of their race."

The Consort's eyes were a shade of familiar blue; she was angry.

Kaylin's cheeks, however, had gone a shade of familiar red;

so was she. "You didn't hear or see the Oracle. I did. Yes, they're coming in numbers—but if you listen, if you hear what the Old Ones are saying, or did say, or *whatever*—they're fleeing. There were children there. Old people. This, whatever it is—it's the last act of desperation. Somehow, some *one* of them, was able to figure out *how* to escape."

"I did not bring you here," the Consort said, in a voice that defined ice in an entirely new—and unpleasant—way, "so that you might turn your back upon *our* responsibilities. And our responsibilities as lords of the High Court and guardians of the lake—"

"I'm not a guardian of the lake," was the quiet reply. "I'm a Hawk. You've lived here for all of your life. In the High Halls, or in the West March. You've had power, money, parents, and *even* siblings who weren't trying to kill you. *I* had no fixed home, in the fiefs. I never had *enough* to eat, I was never certain I would have enough to *wear,* and I did whatever I had to do to survive.

"I know what that means. I even know what it might mean to people whose language I don't understand. They want what *I* wanted. They want," she added, "what *you* want."

The Consort opened her mouth.

Kaylin continued. "And it *doesn't* matter. The Oracles are *clear.* The portal is coming, Lady. It's going to open, here, in the heart of our city, a stone's throw from the High Halls and the Imperial Palace. If we can't find a way to stop the Devourer, somehow, we will *all* die. Strangers, Barrani, Dragon, Aerian. It won't matter if the Chancellor of the Exchequer is a slimy, cheating bastard. It won't matter if the Arcanists are looking for new and interesting ways to rule the world by killing anyone who can prevent them. It won't matter that the Shadows overrun the heart of the fiefs—*nothing* will matter."

Silence, then. It was cold, and costly.

Kaylin drew breath, stopped speaking. She could not bring herself to apologize, but she *did* understand, because if Marrin were faced with the same choice? She would have asked the same thing. But Marrin ran the Foundling Halls, and Marrin took children like Kaylin into her home, feeding and guarding them because they had no one else to do it for them.

She turned, once again, to the heart of the light in this room, and said a single word. "Chosen."

And the light answered, Yes.

The return from the Halls was silent. The Consort did not speak a word as she led Kaylin from the caves and through the paths of the Inner Court to the marble and heights of the outer building. She didn't speak a word to the men who brought her carriage round, either, and she entered it like a winter storm. Kaylin almost offered to walk, but that would have meant speaking.

But as the carriage pulled away, the Consort said quietly, "What the Oracles see is not a given. Were it, we would have perished any number of times. They tell a slanted tale, and if their listeners understand it well enough, they can prevent catastrophe. You know this," she added, a cool accusation in the words.

It was true.

"You must therefore accept it, on some level. The risk," she added. "It is not a risk that I, or my brothers, would accept."

"I don't see any way of changing it. We don't understand what's being done well enough—"

"You wouldn't destroy the portal, or stop it from opening, if you could. Let us see what the Imperial Court says."

"How much of the truth will you tell them?"

She was silent for a long moment. "All of it," she finally said. "The Dragons cannot be more of a threat than the Devourer, and my kin understand the threat the Dragons pose. We have faced it for centuries."

"All of it," in Barrani terms, was a lot less than it would have been in human terms. Kaylin wisely chose to let the Consort speak. The Consort, for instance, failed to mention the rune-covered cavern at the heart of the lake. She failed to mention the voices of the Ancients which had guided and advised the Consorts in their role as mother of the Barrani race for—actually, Kaylin had no idea how long it had been.

She did not fail to mention, however, what the Devourer was, what it ate, what it destroyed; she gave a cursory history of the Devourer, but then again, so had the Old Ones. When she was done, she fell silent, watching the Arkon.

The Arkon tendered her a very low bow. Nor did this seem to surprise her; she accepted it as her due. But when he rose, he turned to Kaylin. "Private Neya," he said, his voice cool.

Severn, who had been content to watch and listen in the background, now detached himself from Ybelline's side and came to stand within arm's reach of Kaylin. Or, she thought with a grimace, within foot's reach.

"Arkon," she replied.

"What transpired in the High Halls?"

"I believe The Lady has told you," was her careful reply.

"She has told me much," was his. "And I respect the risk she has taken. I respect the urgency with which she views the current difficulty. But she has said very little that directly involves you, and you have angered her. This is not terribly surprising. It is more surprising that you have not, prior to this, managed to cause offense. However."

Kaylin stopped herself from shrugging, because it was a defensive fief gesture, and she was in a room with two caste-lords and two Dragons. "The Lady has, of course, told you everything of relevance about our current situation." She spoke in High Barrani, and almost as flawlessly as she had ever spoken it.

"I...see."

She wouldn't have bet the smallest copper coin that that meant he was finished. And, indeed, he wasn't. He turned to Sanabalis. "Lord Sanabalis, Private Neya is, at the moment, your student. You have had the time and the leisure to better understand her mood and her whim. She is bright enough for a mortal.

"What, in your opinion, is the difficulty now?"

Kaylin turned to her mentor in Magical Studies, as it was coined by the department. His eyes were actually gold, but he looked weary. "I would say," the Dragon Lord replied quietly, "that she has been told that the best chance for our safety—and the safety of our world—is the prevention of the portal's opening. Any portal."

"And?"

"If the Oracular Halls are to be believed, the threat comes from the portal itself, in the end."

"It does," the Consort said coldly.

"But, if the Oracular Halls are to be believed—and I grant that Oracles are at best tricky until they are behind one—people will arrive, and in great number, in Elantra. She has heard some of their voices through one particular Oracle. It was to relay what was heard that the castelord of the Tha'alani was invited to attend us today.

"There are, among the multitude, both the young and the old. Private Neya is aware of this. She is, I would guess, aware as well that if the portal does not open, those people will be stranded in the lee of the Devourer, and they will die."

"And?"

"That is all, Arkon."

"They are not her responsibility." The Arkon glanced at the Consort, and the Consort nodded.

"No," Sanabalis replied. "They are not. Not yet."

"Then I fail to see the difficulty."

"I, too, fail to see the difficulty," the Consort now added. "Given the threat, given the danger *we* face, given what *we* have to lose, I do not see that there is any choice. We must do what we can to make certain that the portal does not open."

Sanabalis said nothing.

Kaylin tried to say nothing. She mostly succeeded, but her expression was now thunderous enough that Sanabalis raised a hand.

"Private?"

"If *I* understood what I was told today, we have thousands of people who are fleeing the utter destruction of the only home they knew. They are not an army. They are not an invasion. They're doing what *any one of us* would do. Here, we're safe, for whatever reason. And you want us to lock and bar the doors and let them be massacred because—"

"Because we risk—"

"Because of the *risk*. We don't *know* how the Devourer does what he does. We have no idea. We don't know for certain that the world will end the minute he touches it—but we *know* they'll die. They'll die there, Sanabalis."

"Kaylin," he said quietly.

"No! *We* arrived. The Aerians, I think, must have come the same damn way. The world didn't end either time!"

"Perhaps the Devourer did not follow either your kin or the winged ones. You have no true names."

"We don't *know* that these people do, *either!* But we know that they'll die. Even if the Devourer doesn't *find* them, they'll starve there."

"Private Neya, they are *not* your people. Nor are they, any of them, the Emperor's. You have sworn no oath to defend or protect them. They are not your problem."

She was utterly silent then. But Ybelline crossed the room; Ybelline who had been as silent and still as Severn. Reaching out, she took one of Kaylin's hands in her own. She didn't, however, say a word. Kaylin resisted the visceral urge to lean against the Tha'alani's shoulder, exposing her forehead to the touch of the slender stalks that characterized the race, in part, because she was certain that what she was thinking would be so blistering, it might cause Ybelline pain.

"Ybelline," the Arkon said. "My apologies. The Dragon Court must now, I fear, convene. Private, Corporal, you are dismissed. High Lord," he added, tendering the type of correct bow she had *never* seen him tender, "I believe, in the current circumstances, it would be to our mutual benefit to convene Court at your convenience.

"I understand that meeting the Emperor in the heart of the Imperial Palace on such short notice would be politically unwise, and I ask that you repair to the High Halls to consider where, and when, might be more suitable to our current situation. We have, I believe, little time."

"It is a meeting of castelords?"

"It is a meeting of the Dragon Court," was the reply. "In military matters, the Emperor's decision is law."

Ybelline, it appeared, would go with the Dragons, which left Severn, Kaylin, and a lot of food for which Kaylin had no appetite. She waited until the door had closed before she let loose a volley of pure Leontine invective.

Severn said, when she had paused for breath—because if he waited until she'd finished, it'd take an hour— 'You did well, there."

This, of course, stopped her flat. "Define *well.*"

"No Leontine, for one. Or Aerian. No shouting. No accusations. Come on," he added. "I think it's time to head to the office."

Kaylin shook her head. "I think," she said quietly, "it's time to head to the altar."

"No."

She stared at him, but didn't move.

"Kaylin, why?"

"I want to ask it a question."

"The Arkon will remove your head. If he's feeling merciful."

Kaylin headed out the door. "If he removes my head," she told Severn, "I'll be dead, and I won't have to live with the knowledge of what they're trying to do."

Kaylin's sense of spacial geography was pretty damn bad, when you got right down to it; Severn's, on the other hand, was exceptional. Though he hadn't been there the first time, he'd been able to take her vague directions and make them work. He led her in silence past the shelves and the grand artifact halls, toward the smaller, more crowded spaces that weren't meant for display—or easy access. They looked familiar to Kaylin, but it would have taken her hours to *find* them; the Library was not a small place and its layout was not a simple, sensible one.

But when he at last reached the doors, he paused, and she grimaced. Three locks. And they didn't have one working key between them. Kaylin thought she could pick the locks, as they didn't seem enormously complicated—but she couldn't pick them without any *tools*.

He said nothing. But he did step aside, and as he did, he held out a hand, palm up. She looked at it, confused. And then she looked at her wrist; she was wearing the bracer. She hesitated for just a minute, and then hit the studs in the combination that would unlock it. It clicked open, and she put it into Severn's palm, which hadn't moved.

"I don't want to use magic here," she said quietly. "Not now." And never in the Arkon's Library. "I don't suppose you have—"

"I don't at the moment carry equipment for picking locks, no."

"Did you, when you were a Wolf?"

He shrugged. "We had different standard tools, yes."

She nodded and turned to the door. It was dark in the hall, but Severn had carried light. He held it up now.

The problem with magic—or at least Kaylin's magic—was it worked best when she didn't have time to think. In these small, short halls, she did. *Are they right?* Her hand rested against the door's surface. *If the Devourer does follow, if we can't contain it somehow—do we doom the city?* Marrin and her Foundling Hall. The fiefs. The midwives. Marcus and his Pridlea. The Hawks.

She wasn't good with lists, but she recognized one when she'd made it. What did she hold in balance against these things? Thousands of strangers, who might or might not present a danger all on their own to the city she called home. *Maybe,* she thought, without much hope, *if we prevent them from opening a portal into Elantra, they'll find someplace else. There has to be some other place.* And then the magic that had screwed up a large part of the city, disrupting births and commerce and highly sensitive investigations among other things, would *go away.*

But if they found nowhere else to go, they would die.

So do you choose strangers who aren't even your responsibility over the people you love? She glanced at Severn. Severn, as usual, let her work things out on the inside of her head, alone. Sometimes she hated that. Because sometimes it would be *nice* to have someone else come up with the answers.

Or would it?

She grimaced. The Emperor was probably coming up with the answer *right now.* Was she content to let him decide? To trust his ruling? Here she was, in the heart of the Arkon's hoard, skirting the edge of his rules, for the sake of more information, in the hope of finding some *other* answer that could save these people.

Why? Why? Why?

As if it was the magical word, the locks in the door clicked open in slow succession. "You know," she told Severn quietly, "it would be a lot easier to be me if what I wanted didn't clash so badly with what I *also* wanted."

He laughed. "You can have everything if you set your mind to it. You can't have everything at the same time."

"The trick, I suppose, is wanting what you do have."

"That would be the trick, yes."

She entered the cavern. This time, they held only a lamp—a nonmagical lamp—instead of torches. The room, however, wasn't noticeably dimmer; the altar was shedding light as if it were a trapped moon. The runes on the altar's side were also glowing, this time in a mix of blue and gold that reminded Kaylin of flowers she had once seen and had no name for.

The heavy rolling platform upon which she'd stood hadn't been moved; it was still stationed above the water that served as an ancient mirror. Kaylin walked slowly toward it, Severn by her side. "Do you want to wait outside?"

"I don't think that will mollify the Arkon, if that's your concern."

She grimaced. "It was. And you're right. You might as well

come up and take a look. You can stop me if I look like I'm about to fall in. Or," she added, as she began to climb the ladderlike steps, "let me drown. It'll probably be less painful."

Kaylin stood on the platform and looked down into light. It was silver and sharp, but it wasn't painful; it didn't make her squint. "Severn?"

"I can see it."

"Good. Can you see anything but light?"

"No."

"Mirror," she said softly. "Records."

The light didn't change, and she grimaced.

Severn, intuiting the problem as he usually did, said, "Keep trying. You had control of the Records here before."

She'd had no intention of giving up. But she knelt to bring herself closer to the water, something that shouldn't have been necessary; you didn't have to touch mirrors to invoke them, and frankly, it just pissed off the people who wiped up your fingerprints afterward. Water, on the other hand, didn't *take* fingerprints. She reached out, held her palm above the mirror's surface.

Help me.

The water was absolutely still. She took a breath, and then another, and then exhaled about four inches of height.

Help me to help them.

The light shed by the rectangular surface of this ancient mirror began to condense. As it did, Kaylin wondered how it was that the water—which didn't seem to her eyes to be all that deep—had actually lasted for all these years without evaporating or growing mold. It was the kind of stupid thing she could wonder in the face of the unknown.

It was not the kind of question she expected to have *answered*, on the other hand. But there was an answer, and as the light broke, fractured, and recombined, swirling into shapes, she saw it. She saw the almost ethereal faces of people that weren't human, weren't Barrani, and weren't Dragon; she imagined that they were twice her height and possessed a hundred times her gravitas. But one of them, male, she thought, although it was hard to tell, opened his wrist. Literally opened it, as if the whole of a body could be bent at will to any task.

Blood ran into the engraved stone basin. It wasn't red. It was gold, and as it touched stone, it became clear, like very thin honey. She heard the echoes of their distant voices, and saw the spoken words take shape and form above the mirror, sinking slowly and losing cohesion as the water dissolved them.

"Can you see that?" she asked Severn.

"Yes."

"What do you see?"

"The Ancients are blessing the water."

"Blessing?"

"They're speaking over it. Incantation?"

Even in a mirror vision, he didn't *see* the words the way she did. "Can you understand any of it?"

"No. What did you ask the mirror?"

"You don't want to know." She watched the words as they joined the mirror, becoming part of the liquid, one by one, and wondered whether this was how the first creations had come to life, and if—and she bit her lip, shunting the thought aside. It could be bloody dangerous to just stand here and think; she'd get nothing but answers all day long and the world would probably burn down—or worse, fade out of existence—while she did.

Instead, she said two words: *The Devourer.* And waited.

★ ★ ★

The face of a familiar stranger now filled the mirror, with his oddly copper eyes and his long, graceful features. This time, however, he was not alone. To his right and left were two people she had not yet seen, a male and a female. "The Devourer is at the gates," he said. He was grave.

Their eyes, she saw, now shaded to a copper that was as dark as his.

"We can stand, or we can travel," he told them. "It was not dead, as hoped."

"Travel?" the woman asked.

"There is a way. We can take those we can reach, and we can attempt to find a safer world." He glanced, now, at the silent man to his left. The man nodded, but didn't speak.

"What safety, in the end, can we find? The Devourer has found three worlds." The woman spoke. "Everything we have ever been or done is *here*. If we can survive—"

"Can we? Can we stand where the others faltered? What we have at our disposal is less than what they had at theirs, but they are silent, now. There is only emptiness where they once stood and built."

"Our *life is here*. What life will we have in a different world? How will we wake the newborn sleepers? How will we—"

"We risk never waking them again at all!" It was the first time he had raised his voice, and it was in anger.

"The Devourer will find us, if we travel."

"The Devourer has found us *now*. If we travel, Kallinda, there is *hope*."

"And for hope, you abandon the hope we have now?" She turned from him, her anger not less than his.

"We have no hope now," was his stark reply. "And you must choose. For myself, I will begin to gather those who are willing to make this voyage."

The second man, silent until now, nodded. "I will watch," he said. "I will travel with you, and I will record until the moment there is nothing at all to record."

Her hands were slender fists, and her eyes were now red— but with weeping; the deep, blood color of true Dragon or Leontine fury didn't touch her irises. "I cannot condone this," she said. "I cannot desert our kin."

The man Kaylin had first seen, the man whose name she didn't know, bowed his head, and fury left him. The woman, Kallinda, walked away, and when she had left the image, the man raised his head. He, too, was crying, but the tears didn't change his expression.

"You knew she would not leave."

He nodded. "Hope is often bitter, but it drives us, and we cling." He turned, and straightening his shoulders, added, "We will begin. I will start the preparations. We have three days."

CHAPTER 17

Kaylin recognized parts of the next scene, although it was entirely new. She thought the man had gathered some thousand—possibly more—of his kin. They were what you might expect if you'd reached across as much of the city as you could and taken only those who were willing to listen: old, young, men and women in various different styles of dress. They were pale, and the eyes of all but the youngest were a uniform copper.

But some of the youngest? Like children everywhere, even in the wake of loss and disaster, they were golden-eyed and curious. They wandered as far as their parents or guardians allowed, and she could almost swear she heard someone say *leash* with resigned longing.

Clearly, food was necessary, especially in the middle of nothing. Food had been taken, but it was carried in backpacks, since they were walking. There were, she thought, wagons of some sort—but whatever was in them was tied down tight, and the wagons themselves were harnessed by men, not beasts. She wasn't certain why. They stopped, they gathered, they ate. She could see that they had organized in a way that allowed them to head count.

But she could also hear, in the distance, a familiar thunder. A growling.

They moved, stopped, moved; these were shown quickly, like a series of still pictures interposed one on top of the other.

Kaylin knew who one man was. Vakillirae. She saw him clearly as he turned; she saw him address his people, and she saw their open dismay, their unchecked tears, their hope and their lack of hope. And then she saw a second man, and she thought he must be the traveler, for he, too, spoke. She saw the light in his hands, and she saw that it calmed those who were not too far gone to *be* calmed.

But Vakillirae remained when his people began to rise; he remained standing when they began to move. He watched them in silence and stillness until they had all but passed from view, and then he smiled. It was a grim, bitter smile. He turned, and the view in the mirror turned with him, always on his face.

She heard the roaring now, a counterpoint to his movements, and saw the set of his lips change before he opened his mouth. He began to speak, and she both recognized and failed to understand *any* of his words. But Sanabalis had used them, once, and she had seen them form around him, like some sort of living grid. This man and his ancestors had, at the start of their racial history, the same gods as the Barrani and the Dragons.

The words that she recognized began to form in a ring around him, as they had when Sanabalis had told the Leontines their story. The roaring grew louder. She understood, then, that he had summoned the creature by speaking them, and that he knew, before he started, this is what he would achieve. But she had no idea what he said, or spoke; she had no idea if this story, like Sanabalis's, was a story of creation.

"What do you see?" She didn't turn to Severn.

"I see a man with copper eyes. He's speaking."

"Nothing else?"

"No."

"You don't recognize the language?"

"No."

The gray of the sky—and the ground—began to darken; wind caught his hair and blew it back in a horizontal line. He was stone, or very like it, except that he continued to speak.

Something about this man, in this moment, was like... gravity. It pulled at her. She could enlarge the image, or rather, his face, at will, and did—but the sheer size of it didn't diminish the effect; she was drawn to him, not because she needed to see more, but for some reason she couldn't put into either thought or word.

Maybe it was his words. They were bold and certain, and hearing them, she couldn't imagine another voice could ever speak them: they were entirely what they were, and entirely his. But they were also a wall, and looking past them, she could see that the Devourer had arrived.

It arrived, as it had the only other time Kaylin had seen it, as the fall of night. In the edges of the mirror, like distant, pale stars, she could see light, and the suggestion of trailing cloud, or translucent borealis. She could see no eyes, no mouth, nothing to suggest physical shape. But that nothing had somehow grabbed her damn legs, and Nightshade had been willing to cut them *off* in order to preserve her.

It didn't reach for her now, although she thought—for just a moment—it might, its presence was that strong. "What do you see?"

Severn didn't answer.

She turned to glance at him, and caught his face in profile; his expression was now chiseled, it was so sharp and hard. Nothing escaped it. "Severn?"

"What," he asked, in the quiet tone of voice that precedes some kind of death, "do you see?"

"Darkness," she answered. "Like…night sky dark, with hints of stars at the outer edges."

At that, his brow rose.

"That's not what you see."

"No."

But in the darkness, she could still see the living words of Vakillirae, and she remembered that she herself had spoken a word—a true word—when she'd been desperate to keep her legs attached to the rest of her body. She watched now, as the words he spoke began to dim. They didn't dim instantly, but light fled slowly until they were indistinguishable from the nightscape.

She watched Vakillirae's face, and she knew that as the words dimmed, they left him; he would never be able to speak them again. And he realized it, as well, and his eyes lost their brilliant wonder, his face lost color. But he spoke, anyway.

"Enkerrikas, it is true. It devours words. The truth of words. I have held it now for some hours. I do not know *why*, or how. I do not know how the worlds were lost if such a devouring might take so long. But I will speak until I have no words to offer it. Do not falter. Do not stop."

He spoke, his language once again eluding Kaylin. But his actions, the desperation, the steady truth of his voice did not. These, she thought suddenly, were the stories she had told herself in the fiefs—in Barren, after Severn—in the darkness where no one else could hear them. Stories she wanted to believe, and stories she did; stories she hated to believe, stories that might never end. She clung—had clung—to both, loving and hating them, and they had both sustained her.

They sustained Vakillirae, as well, but she saw that they would not sustain him to the end of this night, and he would have no more stories, and find no more, to tell. She had. She'd found Hawks, Wolves, and Swords; she'd found Dragons, and Foundling Halls, and Leontines. She'd learned to entwine these with her silent, nighttime stories. She'd spoken them like prayers.

Her hands became fists as she watched. Severn still gripped her arm, supporting her in an entirely different way, until the last of the words, the last of the stories, was gone, and the stranger stood alone.

"Enkerrikas, *go,*" he whispered.

She understood, then, that they were bound, this Vakillirae whom she would never meet and Enkerrikas. And she understood, as well, that Enkerrikas could watch, could *see* what Vakillirae could see because their names bound them.

"I release you," Vakillirae said, as if he could hear her, as if he only then understood that the names that bound them might be the thread that the Devourer followed until he found the *rest* of their people. "I release your name. Release mine. *Go,* Enkerrikas."

Enkerrikas did not respond. Maybe he couldn't. Maybe he wouldn't argue with Vakillirae now. But the image didn't fade or shatter; it didn't stop, and she knew that was the whole of his answer. Vakillirae would die, yes. They both knew it. But not alone. Not fully, not finally, alone.

Vakillirae grimaced, and then he spoke the last word, and it was a complicated, long word, as true as any of the others he had yet spoken: his name. His true name.

★ ★ ★

The Devourer roared. The word, the name, she could see—just as she had once seen Nightshade's name in the heart of his Castle. It was like the words that Vakillirae had spoken before it, but it was also unlike them. Its shape and form, she realized, was different; the lines that bound it were thinner, finer, and of a different shape. She could see some similarity in the boldness of some of the strokes, the placement of some of the dots, the closing arcs—but there were twisting, spiraling lines that suggested the imprecise brush of a painter, rather than the chisel of a sculptor; there was a fluidity to the whole.

It didn't look like the words that had come—or would come—from the lake. But…it looked as if it once *might* have been. She understood, then, in a way that she'd never understood before, that the true names were only the start of life; it was life, and living, that ultimately defined them.

This man's life, she hadn't—and wouldn't—see. But what he had made of his life, she did, even if she had little context for it. He laid himself bare, and he offered this last wall, this last bastion, against a creature they did not and could not understand.

She heard the sound of weeping.

She knew it wasn't his, but she saw Vakillirae close his eyes against the pain, and turn, automatically, as if to offer comfort. She wanted to *slap* Enkerrikas, who had probably been dead for centuries—or millennia—for his selfishness and his need. But Vakillirae was absent the same desire.

"Will you not let go?" he asked gently. "Or must you stay until the bitter end?"

This time, Enkerrikas answered. "I must stay. This is the last of you that I will ever see, or know. I cannot face it without pain. I cannot face it without loss. Even pride is beyond me, now, although I will pick it up and wrap it around your memory when memory is *all* I have."

"You were always stubborn," Vakillirae replied.

"Never half so much as you."

"No?" He laughed. It was a wild, dangerous laugh, and he exposed the whole of a white, white throat to the darkness to offer it. "If I made the decision, I would abide by it. I would not stay to witness the end."

"Liar."

He laughed again. It was a weaker laugh, for the light of his name was now fading, and Kaylin could see the most delicate of the lines that comprised his name as they began to unravel. But the word shivered in place, and the lines grew stronger and brighter as she watched, and this time, Vakillirae cursed.

"Enkerrikas—"

"No. You have given me back my name. You have released it to preserve me. But I have not released yours, Vakillirae, and I will never willingly release it. While I can, I, too, will fight."

"We cannot take this risk—you will empty yourself of power, and how will our people survive without you? They will be lost here, and they will starve, or worse!"

"It is no longer your decision."

Vakillirae did argue. In fury, and in fear. But Enkerrikas, who had wept, was without mercy here. Kaylin thought better of her visceral desire to slap him. The light dimmed, yes, but it dimmed slowly compared to the others.

She thought it might be over when it grew brighter and stronger again.

Vakillirae shook his head. "Enkerrikas—"

"You were willing to die."

"Yes. Because I would die fighting."

"And you will. But not alone, in the end."

And so it went. The dimming and the brightening. Nor

was Vakillirae entirely unmoved as he stood, and fought in his fashion against the thing which would destroy them all for no reason they understood. He had no more stories to tell either that darkness or himself. And in the end? Kaylin thought he found comfort in the presence of Enkerrikas. It was hard to tell; his face was so shuttered nothing escaped.

But like Enkerrikas, Kaylin watched. And like Enkerrikas, she wept when the last of the light went out and darkness reigned.

Severn slid an arm around her shoulder in the silence that was left. He asked no questions for a few minutes, allowing Kaylin time to gather herself and ground herself in the present—which had its own crisis and its own imperative. Because of this, she *did* gather herself.

"We're not done yet." Turning back to the mirror, she said, "Traveler. Travel between worlds. Portals."

The darkness of the water broke.

She wasn't certain what, if anything, this mirror would surrender. She knew that the same question, asked of the Halls of Law Records, would give her only what she already knew; there was no history on record of anything else. What they had cobbled together had come from Tara, in Tiamaris; from the Arkon's hidden archives; and from the Oracles.

But it wasn't a question that the Arkon would have asked— if he asked much of this particular mirror at all—because it wasn't one that he had known *to* ask. Kaylin asked it now.

The mirror, however, didn't take this as a question. Instead, light across its surface rippled beneath the still liquid, and when it solidified, it showed a vast plain, with something that looked like horses, but smaller, running in herds through the tall grass. There were trees in the distance, and the sky was the type of blue you only really saw in paintings, not that Kaylin had a lot of exposure to fine art.

The point of the image was not, however, art. She understood this when she saw the grass begin to shimmer, the shape of it changing both in color and texture. It was the first change; there was nothing that appeared to have *caused* it. But the rest of the change flowed out from it, touching not only the earth and its shape, but also the creatures that were hidden from view. Insects rose on jade wings, the size of her fists; butterflies trembled and grew, as did...slugs.

The slugs were the most disturbing, because they, like the jade-winged fliers, were the size of her fist, and their bodies gleamed like the multicolored surface of opals.

"Magic," Severn said.

"Like Elani," Kaylin agreed. "But there's less to take advantage of it. I don't understand *why* it works this way. Magic is supposed to be hard. It's supposed to be work. According to Sanabalis."

"Maybe the drawing of magic is hard. Clearly, where magic exists as raw potential, and in huge amounts, it's somehow used by whatever lives."

"Mirror, expand."

The view shifted instantly, drawing back from the strange grass and strange insect life. She could see, in a rough circle, the place in which this odd, transformational magic existed, because the grass of the plains was otherwise normal. But she noted that the horses, and the other, larger creatures, avoided it.

The portal did open. She wasn't certain who had seen its opening, but someone must have, because it was here. It wasn't small. It didn't fill the whole circular area, which was a huge relief, but it did cut across maybe a quarter of it. It was flat, like a standing door with no walls and no frame to bolster it.

Kaylin frowned as the portal solidified; shadows could be seen moving in its frame. But what came out of the frame made her ask the next question: "What world *is* this?"

The mirror's answer? It was a *word*. Not a spoken word; that would have been too easy. No, it, like so much else, was written, and it was written in a single large and complicated rune that she could barely see in one go. She wondered what Tara would have made of it, and then wondered, more sharply, whether or not Tara had access to *these* Records, this information.

She must have been created by the same people who'd created this mirror. Asking Tara anything was far less risky than sneaking into any part of the Arkon's collection when he was in a *good* mood. The worst thing Kaylin could do was piss Tiamaris off, and Tiamaris, while he could be damn intimidating, was *not* Arkon class.

"Can you see it?"

Severn was silent, and his arm was rigid. She turned to look at him, caught the whole of his profile. He was staring into the mirror, his eyes flickering back and forth as if it was racing through images so damn quickly he could barely keep up. Whereas what Kaylin saw? Was a word. A complicated, huge mass of intersecting lines and strokes and dots that seemed to be written in three full dimensions.

She frowned, and then she said, "What world am *I* in?"

And the lines of the word the mirror now contained frayed and separated, dancing on the edges of the liquid as if they were far too important to be simply discarded, like any *other* image. They hovered there while the center slowly cleared, and once it was empty, they converged in a rush, collapsing together as if collapse were the only given in their existence.

But what they formed was not the chaos one expected of collapse; there was a joy and a life and a light in their furious motion. They formed, from stray elements, another word, as different from the first as it could be, given the composition of its parts. This word was as complex, as complicated, as the first, but there were parts of it that seemed strangely misaligned, especially given that Kaylin didn't even know the language or the writing—if something like *this* could be called writing. It was sculpture, or more than sculpture; it was what magic might produce if it was bent toward a living, growing language.

Kaylin remembered to breathe as she watched, because there was something about *this* word that resonated within her so strongly it could have been an overly intellectualized variant of the simple word *home,* which, in the end, *every* language she had ever learned had contained. She was struck by it, and if being stabbed could produce that shock of recognition, she had been stabbed by a word she couldn't begin to say out loud.

She could begin to think it, and did, but as she did, she turned to Severn. Severn's eyes were open, narrowed, and watching; they were flickering, and she could *almost* see the images reflected in their irises, they were so clear. But again, what he saw? It was not what she saw. She wondered if all Records were like that; if people viewing them thought they were seeing the same thing, but were in reality filtering it all into a very quirky and individual paradigm.

Severn had never loved words. Which was ironic, because he'd *always* been so much *better* at using them.

But Kaylin? Always. She'd always loved them, often way too damn much, her mouth flapping before her thoughts could catch up and shut it down. When words failed her, everything shut down. Why? What was that? There was so much she had wanted to say to Severn, but the words eluded her, and when they failed—she ran. Sometimes, literally.

Yet he understood, without the need for those words, the same thing she now understood: this was home. This was theirs. Not in the sense that the Empire was the Emperor's or the Library was the Arkon's—they weren't Dragons. But in the sense that the sky and the moons and the air and the seasons were there, and existed, and were experienced and turned into specific, personal memories.

She almost didn't want to ask any more questions; she didn't want to disturb this single word. She wanted to know that it existed here, and now, and if she could have, she would have locked it into place permanently. For which, no doubt, the Arkon would have removed both her arms without conveniently killing her first.

But that wasn't why she was here. It was what she was *fighting* for, yes. And no doubt, other people who were *also* part of the same complicated word would fight for other reasons, win or lose; they would have to, the rune was just that complicated. And it would exist whether or not she could see it as clearly as this.

What she needed, now, was something to tell her how to protect the world. She was short on ideas, although the mirror had faithfully answered the questions she had posed it. She needed better damn questions.

"Severn?"

He blinked, and then closed his eyes. Only when they were closed did he relax; his expression fell into its normal lines. "I think," he said, eyes still shut, "the Arkon would have been the better companion, here."

Kaylin snorted. "I'd only give him indigestion."

He smiled, and then said, "I'm ready."

She nodded, turned back to the mirror with real regret,

and said, "What was Vakillirae's home?" She hesitated for just a minute, because she wasn't certain if *what* or *who* would be more appropriate.

This time, when the lines frayed, they faded.

The mirror remained blank.

"I don't understand," Kaylin said quietly. "Do you see *anything?*"

Severn shook his head. "Maybe no Records were made?"

Kaylin grimaced. "They recorded the whole of a death, somehow. It's *here*. I don't even think they came to *our* world."

"You could ask where they went."

"Mirror, Enkerrikas. Where did he travel? Where did he take his people?" This time, the mirror responded, as it had done the first time, with the complicated quivering motion of lines, of dots, of strokes that were heavy and strokes that were almost impossibly fine.

"Mirror, The Devourer. What worlds did he find?"

The image slowly vanished, and once again, nothing replaced it.

She tried again. "What are the names of the worlds the Devourer found?" It produced the same results. Grinding her teeth, she said, "What is the *name* of the Devourer?"

This time, the mirror did shudder. She understood that the nature of names, such as they were, were not clear, not easily seen, and not represented in any Records she understood. She could no more ask the names of Tiamaris or Sanabalis, and expect a reply. Not those names; those were true names. But what, exactly, *was* a true name? Was it not, in miniature, like the name of...a world? Did the city have a name that was somehow some smaller part of the whole?

She couldn't clearly explain why she'd even asked the question, or why she expected the mirror to have anything like an answer—because it didn't. It had, and offered, darkness, nothing more, and if the darkness was more profound, it didn't seem like a refusal or a denial. But she stared at the empty space until Severn once again tugged her arm.

"If you're finished?"

"I...think so. I don't have answers, though, and I can't help but think there *must* be some here."

"If you've got better questions, they'll do. I think we need to vacate the premises, because I don't hear the Arkon, and I would like to be well away from the mirror before I do."

CHAPTER 18

Kaylin and Severn had been formally dismissed. The Dragon Lords had not, in their haste to formally convene the Immortal Court—as Kaylin now thought of the impromptu meeting—given her any *new* instructions. Kaylin and Severn had no trouble leaving the Library, which was in any case conspicuously absent of people right up to the main doors. Apparently, the Arkon's mood had extended itself in the form of mercy to his mostly human subordinates, because he appeared to have sent them home.

Or eaten them, which was technically illegal.

There were, of course, the usual guards outside of the doors, but they didn't say a word as Kaylin and Severn exited the Library, even if it *was* much after the rest of the Dragons and their entourage had left. They left the Palace in silence. Or in what passed for silence when the Dragon Court was in session, because clearly, the discussion was heated; she could hear the distant roars of what passed for conversation as if they were thunder.

The guards, however, were either already deaf, or far better trained than Kaylin was ever going to be. Kaylin made no attempt to cover her ears because those guards were watching. She hurried toward the exit—which was not exactly *close*—and ran into someone familiar hurrying away from it.

Sadly, since he was a Dragon, she bounced.

"Kaylin?"

"Tiamaris?"

"Plug your ears."

She immediately did, guards notwithstanding. Not that it ever helped when the Dragon who was shouting was standing right beside her. She waited until the sound had stopped bouncing off the very acoustically unforgiving ceiling and walls before she lowered her hands again. "You're here for the Court?"

"I was summoned," he replied, "in haste."

"It took you a while."

"Unfortunately, I was summoned by mirror, and I was not within the Tower. Nor was Tara, or I would of course have received immediate word. It took Morse some time to find us. We had ranged somewhat farther than we intended in our work. You are leaving?"

"Our meeting was cut short, and I'm not invited to sit on meetings of the Imperial Court."

"For obvious reasons. Come, walk with me while we talk. I have bought a few minutes of time."

"Is that safe?"

He chuckled. "It *is* the Imperial Palace, and I do not require your company when the Court convenes. Speaking of which, have your formal lessons begun yet?"

"No. I think they're supposed to begin tonight. Or tomorrow. I think they're going to be delayed, Sanabalis's opinion notwithstanding."

"Have they found you a suitable teacher?"

She frowned. "I'd sort of assumed it would be Sanabalis, although he's hinted at someone else. Maybe the Arkon?"

"The Arkon does not take students. Be thankful," he added. They walked the halls much more slowly than they had taken them before they'd collided.

After a pause, Tiamaris said, "Tara requested your company, should I happen to see you at the Palace."

Kaylin frowned. "I'm not *normally* found at the Palace, Tiamaris."

"I did inform her of that fact. She felt, however, that you would be found here today."

"But—"

He lifted a hand. "I am *not* Tara. I understand much of what she thinks and I know what she knows—but some of what she knows requires more careful study and concentration than current events have allowed. She is...not what I expected," he added, and this time, the edge of a smile touched his lips. "At times she is much like a mortal child. Everything is new and shiny and it distracts her or delights her for entirely inexplicable reasons.

"But at times, Kaylin, she is a sword, and if she had a name, it would sound much like *Meliannos*." It was the name of one of the three Dragonslayers, and it rested across Nightshade's hip. "She will not be moved, and she cannot be frightened, then."

"Which one was she when she asked you to deliver the invitation?"

Tiamaris's reply was not a comfort. "She would never harm you without severe provocation."

Great. "Do you think she'll feed us instead?"

He snorted.

"Will you be coming back anytime soon?"

"It depends," he said, as another, more distant, roar filled the halls. "I have hopes that this will not continue indefinitely."

★ ★ ★

The Tower was, as it had been, surrounded by what looked like a modest garden—in the practical sense of the word. Some of the plants did flower, but the flowers were not statements of simple beauty; they preceded tomatoes, or fruits. Kaylin had no doubt whatsoever that the greater part of what grew here would find its way to Tiamaris's new market—or possibly to people who might otherwise starve.

The fief had seen a great many deaths during the last few weeks of Barren's rule; it was still recovering, and many of the corpses were, according to Tara, a danger to the people who still lived. It was this cleanup that occupied much of Tiamaris's time; the rest of it was occupied with reconstruction.

Tara was not outside in her gardening clothing. She often was, and if she was, Morse was usually not far behind. But the gardens were empty and silent, and the doors—plain, simple doors that weren't even warded—were closed.

They started to roll open before Kaylin could touch them, which was good; they were still missing something as simple as a knocker. Kaylin, familiar with the changing interior of Castle Nightshade, wouldn't have been surprised if one had sprouted while she was waiting.

Tara was standing between the doors. As if clothing were a statement of mood, she was adorned in white robes and a slender tiara, and looked every inch "the Lady" that the fieflings now called her. Of course, they also called her this when she was covered in dirt and the detritus of gardening.

Her face was pale, like alabaster, and her eyes were almost entirely black; they'd lost even the appearance of irises. "Kaylin," she said quietly. And then, as if only noticing her silent shadow, "Lord Severn."

If this had been the office, Kaylin would have snickered.

Severn, of course, bowed instead. "Tiamaris said you asked to see me?"

Tara nodded. Her eyes shone like obsidian. "Chosen," she said softly. "You have invoked the mirrors."

It should have surprised Kaylin, but it didn't. "In the Imperial Palace."

"I know. I felt them wake." Her expression was remote, even grim, although her next words didn't quite fit it. "You would like...food?"

The food was simple and there was a lot of it. Kaylin, who didn't feel particularly hungry, nonetheless ate. It was shaping up to be one of those weeks, in which mealtimes were in serious jeopardy of disappearing in the time-crunch emergencies always caused.

"The worlds," Kaylin began, when she'd eaten as much as she could and was merely pushing food around the plate in an attempt not to fidget in other ways.

Tara nodded.

"How did the Devourer reach them?"

"We do not know. And because we do not know, there is a chance that your Emperor and the High Lord of the Barrani are wrong. Preventing the opening of the portal will not prevent the Devourer from finding the world. It is known that he cannot easily find worlds, or rather, that is what was believed. More than that is unknown." She was silent for a moment—it couldn't be called a hesitation—and then she added, "I believe they are not entirely incorrect. But it troubles you."

"Yes."

"Why?"

"There are thousands of people who need food and some place that won't eat them, and if they don't find it soon, they'll die."

"But they are not your people."

Kaylin grimaced. "I know they're not *my* people. But... they're *people*. And if Sanabalis is right, they're doing what *my* ancestors did centuries ago—they're trying to escape certain death, and they've come here.

"If someone had prevented our people from entering this world, I wouldn't be here."

"And if they do not prevent these people, you might cease to 'be here,' as you say."

"If I step out on the street on the wrong damn day, I might cease to be here. I could get hit by a wagon. I could get run through by a lucky thug. I could catch a wasting disease and die in bed. We can't define our lives by fear of our deaths— it's just stupid."

"I am not certain my Lord will agree."

"I don't give a rat's ass if your Lord agrees."

Tara smiled, which surprised Kaylin. "You do," she said.

She grimaced. "You're right. I'm angry at people for not caring. But... I'm used to that. And other people are probably angry at me for not caring about the things *they* care about. It's just—it's a people thing. What do you think?"

"I think people are complicated."

"I mean, about the portal?"

"I don't know. I know that you are trying to find a way to stop the Devourer, and you must know that wiser people have tried in the past. But their worlds are now nothing, and their people are no longer remembered. They have ceased to exist.

"I do not think I would like to experience that cessation."

Kaylin set her fork down. "Will you try to stop me?"

Tara's eyes rounded in a perfect expression of human surprise. She didn't answer. Kaylin thought she understood why. She was a Tower, albeit a Tower whose Avatar could walk the streets and speak to the people she had been built to protect, and her law was subordinate to her Lord's. In this case, that was Tiamaris.

Kaylin forced herself to ask a more neutral question. "You knew when I was accessing the old Records?"

Tara nodded.

"You can access them." It wasn't a question, but the Avatar nodded again.

"It is difficult, even for me."

"I don't understand how the old mirrors work. Or worked. I know how modern ones do. I've used the Imperial Records and the Records in the Halls of Law many times."

"How are they different?"

Kaylin glanced at Severn, who was not only not fidgeting with the remains of his food, but was listening attentively.

"With our Records, we see what's there. We *all* see the same thing."

Tara nodded.

"But with these—we don't."

"No?"

"I asked the name of a world. Not on purpose," she added quickly. "But I asked what world we were seeing at some point. The mirror answered. It gave Severn images—too many images, piled together all at once. It gave me...a word."

Tara was silent for a long moment. "A word?"

"Yes. Like a...true word, but more complicated, and more dense, than any word I've ever seen. The only one that I think comes close—" she hesitated again "—is the name of the Dragon Outcaste."

"You *know his name?*"

"I've *seen* his name. Once. I don't think I could have said it then, if I'd tried. I couldn't have held it against him."

"Can you see it now, if you try?"

"Not...easily. I don't try," she added hastily. "Names have

power, and I *do not want* his attention. But...his name was so large. The name of the world was larger still. I don't think I saw it all. I have some idea of its general shape, but I couldn't reproduce it. I'm not sure anyone *could*."

Tara now turned to Severn. "You did not see this."

"No."

"The images?"

"People. Places. Starscapes. Storms. Oceans. More. I don't think they would have stopped if Kaylin hadn't asked the mirror a different question."

"Kaylin, you asked the mirror—"

"Where it was showing me. That was its answer. But I asked other questions, and it showed me other...words. What it didn't show me at all were the names of the worlds that I believe were lost to the Devourer."

"How can you be certain?"

"Because one of the events in the mirror involved the flight of people from a world that was facing the Devourer, and the mirror couldn't show me anything at all of the world they'd come from. They exist, and they must have found shelter somewhere, because their memories of *that* event still exist.

"Tara, what do you see in the mirror? Why didn't I see what Severn saw?"

Tara looked pointedly at Kaylin's covered arms. "Lord Severn," she said, "is not Chosen. Nor, in the end, am I. You are, Kaylin, and perhaps that has meaning. But the old mirrors are not like the new. They are built in a different way, and they carry a meaning that is more instantly subjective in nature."

"Say that again?"

"You draw conclusions from what you see in the Halls of Law. You will all see the *same* thing, but you will draw different conclusions, as befit your personal experiences. But the old mirrors sometimes draw the conclusions for you. They know who you are, if you stand and observe."

"But how is that even *possible?*"

"I know who you are. I knew who you were when you first entered the Tower, moments after I woke."

"Yes. But *how?*"

"How?"

Kaylin nodded. Tara frowned. "How," she finally said, "do the Tha'alani touch thought?"

"I don't know."

"How do you breathe?"

Great. Philosophy. Changing the subject, Kaylin said, "If you ask the mirrors—your mirrors—the same questions I did, will you see the words?"

"I...do not know, Kaylin. But I think it unlikely." She rose. "I will ask the mirror. But I think it best that you are not present."

"Why?"

"Because I am not as you see me. What I see might influence what you see."

"I'm not afraid of that."

"No, you are not. But I? I am afraid of it."

"But—but why?"

"Because I do not want to be alone," was the quiet reply. "I want friends, I want my Lord. I want you to come to visit. I want to keep my fief—and its people—safe. Those, you understand. But I was not built to be mortal, Kaylin. I was not meant to *live*. It was a gift, but it was a chaotic gift, and I think an unintended one. I have not *used* the mirrors, until you came with your story of the Devourer.

"And when I did, I chose to reveal them—to you—in a way that other Towers would not. Other Towers draw upon information almost in sleep. It is part of what they must know.

But they take only what they *must* know in order to fulfill their function.

"You changed what I could *do,* Kaylin. You gave me room to *be.* But you could not change, at base, what I *am.* And what I am, what I can be—they are not the same." She rose. "Will you wait? If you insist, you may accompany me."

"I'll...wait."

"You will be angry?"

"Yes, but not at you—I'm often angry at life, Tara. I'll wait. But I want your answer, and we're under a little time pressure here."

Tara smiled. "You always are," she said.

She came back an hour later, during which time Kaylin paced the length of the dining room. Severn had suggested, with varying degrees of politeness, that she sit down, but that had resulted in enough fidgeting that he'd given up.

When Tara returned, her eyes were an odd shade of gold; odd because the whites were actually ebony.

"What did you see?"

"Not what you saw," she replied. "I think I saw not what existed, but the birth of the world."

"You saw words?"

"No. Or rather, yes, but...what was left was not a Word."

"You think it's significant."

"I do. But before you ask, I don't know *how.*" She hesitated for just a moment, and then added, "But you were right. The Imperial Court has convened, briefly. It now waits for the addition of the Barrani nobles. The Emperor, however, is all but persuaded that some attempt to drain the magic in the portal area must now be attempted, and to that end...he has agreed to confer with the Arcanum."

Kaylin blanched. If she disliked the Imperial Order of

Mages—and she did, because they were so stuffy and arrogant—she loathed the Arcanum, which managed to combine those traits with actual danger.

"What—what has Tiamaris decided?"

"The Emperor is his Lord," Tara replied quietly. "And he will accept the Emperor's decision."

"We all more or less accept it if we want to be more than ash—what does he *want*, Tara?"

"He wants, of course, the safety of his hoard. He is not completely convinced that these steps are either possible or necessary, but he has made this as clear as it is wise to make it. He will abide by their decision."

Kaylin nodded. "What do you want?"

"I, too, want the safety of his hoard." She wrapped the words around an almost self-conscious smile. "But I was created to protect my lands from the incursion of the Shadows and their change. I know of the Devourer, but I was not built to contain him.

"This means," she added, as she saw Kaylin's expression, "that I will not work against you, in this. I do not know what you intend, and perhaps it is best that I remain ignorant. But what you see, Chosen, we *do not* see."

"But aren't we all supposed to be looking at the same thing?"

Tara smiled. "We are. But you process the information in ways that we either don't or can't. If you look at a desk, you see a desk. Another might see the tree that fell to compose it. In some of the ways we see the same things, we bring different information to them. It's not wrong or right. It can be useful."

"How?" she asked, starkly.

"I don't know. I do not contain the full history of the Chosen, and I do not understand why they are given the marks,

or even what the marks are meant to do. Words are life, literally—but you are mortal. You have life *without* the words.
Therefore it is not to grant you life that the words are given.

"My...parents...did not explain the world to me, Kaylin.
They did not give me your morality or your sense of ethics.
No more did they give me the Draconian or Barrani ver-
sions of either. I am...new...to the life that you lead. But...
I *want* it. I want my garden, and my broken streets, and my
terrified people. I want my Lord, and his flight, and his fire.
I want my Tower.

"I have had them, since I woke. Do you understand?"

Kaylin, clearly, didn't. She shook her head.

"I have had the same duties and the same responsibilities
for the same stretch of what you call streets, since the moment
I awoke to the whisper of the Shadows. But until you came
back, until you brought Tiamaris, I did not *see* them. I could
not touch them. They could not touch *me*. What you saw in
me—and what I saw in both you and Tiamaris, although I
did not realize it at the time—changed me. And yet, it left
me the same responsibilities. I see them differently, and I approach them differently—but the goal, in the end, did not—
and cannot—change.

"Perhaps what you see in the world is like that. I cannot
say. But I once acted in fear and in pain and in isolation, and
I almost allowed my charge to be destroyed. I...do not want
to act in fear or pain or isolation again." She lifted an arm.
"But you have, as you've said, little time. I do not know if
you can prevent what will occur, in either case—the draining of the magic or the draining of the World.

"But I have no doubt at all that you must try. I will not detain you. My Lord will not return for some hours yet, much
though it chafes him."

★ ★ ★

They left the fief of Tiamaris without the usual nausea that accrued when leaving Nightshade, and they headed toward the bridge in as grim a silence as they could. It wasn't as grim as it should have been, given the situation, because the fief had changed so much, Kaylin had to stop and at least look. The streets weren't crowded, although it was still daylight, but they weren't empty, either.

If traffic came from the rest of the city, it came in a different form: the bridge was being used, but it was being used by wagons, and those wagons contained not bored, malicious men, but wood, nails, supplies. There were men waiting for them on the fief side, with directions; they were armed men, but they weren't Barren's men. They weren't dress guards, but they were efficient and—for the fiefs—reasonably polite.

Severn glanced at her, and then he smiled. "Evanton's?" he asked.

She looked at the sun. It was heading toward the wrong horizon; so much of the day had already escaped in the hours spent in the Palace and the High Halls. If it hadn't started so damn early, it would be nightfall already.

"Evanton's. There, and then the office."

The streets of Elani were quiet and empty. At this time of day, that felt wrong, although Kaylin knew damn well why; the people who lived here had been evacuated. Some of them had been evacuated loudly, and were standing in various offices in the Halls of Law demanding redress. And probably demanding groveling apologies, as well. It was a good day not to be an office Hawk.

They were allowed through the barricade—such as it was—without trouble, but the Swords on duty looked both tired and tense. No wonder. The only other people who seemed to be coming and going were the mages, and mages of any stripe made anyone sane wary.

Evanton was in his storefront, surrounded by beads, needles, pins, and the usual assortment of colored thread. He had the jeweler's glass he favored—at what he called *my age*—cupped in his right eye; the left was shut in a tight squint. He hadn't bothered to even look up when the doors chimed to let him know he had visitors.

Then again, Grethan was standing almost *in* the door, looking miserable and nervous, so Evanton was clearly not in the best of moods. She tried to remember a day when Evanton *had* been in the best of moods, and failed. She started to say as much to Grethan, but Evanton chose that moment to lift his head. With the jeweler's glass attached to his face, he would have looked comical, if laughter hadn't been suicidal.

"Private," he said curtly. He shoved everything off his lap, and walked over to the counter before he remembered to remove the glass and slide it into one of the shapeless pockets of his apron.

"Have things gotten worse around here?"

"Worse in which way?" The tone of his voice made clear that the answer was yes.

She'd had a couple of long days herself. "In the usual way."

"Which would be?"

"End of the world variants."

He didn't approve of her sense of humor, but his snort wasn't up to the heat and arrogance of Dragons. "Where," he said, "have you been?"

"All over the city. The Halls of Law. The High Halls. The Oracular Halls. The fiefs. The Imperial Palace."

"You didn't seek to return here."

"Evanton—I didn't have *time*. When I came to see you yesterday, I got spit into a great, gray void between the Garden and your shop, and I made my way back to Nightshade. With his help."

"You wouldn't have returned, otherwise?"

"I can't see how."

"I, frankly, can't see how you managed to fall out of the world." He spoke as if it were somehow her fault. When she stood there staring at him—and trying to decide whether or not she wanted to descend into an argument about fault—he snapped. "Are you going to stand there all day?"

She snapped her jaw shut and followed him. He led her—of course—down the crammed tiny hall toward the Elemental Garden, pausing only to hurl instructions at his poor apprentice. Severn slid in behind her; he was proof against Evanton's temper and Evanton's tongue for reasons that Kaylin didn't quite understand, and managed not to resent.

"You've been to the Palace?" he said as he shuffled down the hall.

"Yes."

"And the High Halls?"

"Yes."

"Why?"

"Evanton, you *know* I'm not supposed to talk about this."

He shrugged. "I'm an old curmudgeon and I don't get out much. I certainly wouldn't spend my free time studying the protocols of either Halls or Palace. Or Hawks, for that matter." He unlocked the door to the Garden. Kaylin looked inside and cringed.

CHAPTER 19

"Oh, please," Evanton said. "This is a walk in the park compared to what it was like yesterday."

It was no longer a room. The door opened onto a landmass that seemed to extend forever. In all directions. There *was* grass around the door frame, but it was a wild, seedy grass. Kaylin could see no small pool, and wondered—if they walked far enough—if she would see ocean instead. The sun, and there was sun here, was hot, even though the wind had all but flattened the grass.

"This," he said, as he stepped through the door, "is the Elemental Garden, in case you were wondering. *Next time* there is a magical disturbance of this magnitude, *do not* attempt to enter it without *me*."

Crossing the threshold had caused the usual transformation in both Evanton and his clothing: he was robed, and he looked wiser and somehow more powerful for the wisdom. He didn't, however, look any happier. Since he expected an answer, Kaylin nodded. "I hadn't intended," she said, in a slightly clipped voice, "to come back to the Garden at all."

"I hadn't intended," he replied, in the same tone, "to become its Keeper. So much for intentions. Are you going to stand there all day?"

"Evanton—we don't have the time to get lost in the Garden. Not now. The Imperial Court is meeting to discuss—" She bit her lip; it stopped the words.

He grimaced, and let his hands fall to his sides. "My apologies, Private. I have had a *very* trying few days, and I'd hoped that you would—when you returned—come to see me instantly. I did attempt to send Grethan out with a message, but you're apparently hard to pin down, and in any case, I don't have the same weight with your Sergeant as the Imperial Court or the High Halls do. Corporal?"

Severn nodded and entered the room; the door then closed with a slam.

"Why are we having this discussion here?" Kaylin asked Evanton.

It was a perfectly reasonable question, given the difficulties in the Garden. Even Evanton allowed that. "I'm required to spend more time in the Garden—not less—given the magical instability the storefront is otherwise suffering. I can— with effort—force the elements to conform to the shape of the Garden you're most familiar with, but it is not, at the moment, the best use of my energy, and the elements are not yet unleashed. They are—more or less—peaceful."

She frowned. The grass wasn't particularly inviting as a place to sit, but she sat on it anyway. "When the fiefs were having trouble, the elements knew. They more or less told you." She'd been in the Elemental Garden during this "conversation," and it had involved a gale, a lot of mud, and very poor visibility. "But this—"

"They're aware that something is changing," he replied. "But it's not—yet—a matter of this world."

Her frown deepened. "The door to the Elemental Garden—
is it a portal of some kind?"

"It is, very loosely, a portal of some kind. It's not, in the
traditional sense of the word, a portal. It's not something you
might experience in the Towers and the Castles constructed
by the Ancients."

"Why is it different?"

"It doesn't take you someplace different. It takes you to
the heart or the foundation of *this* world."

"But the portals in the Castle—"

"Those exist," he said softly, "to take advantage of the
places that are not *quite* here. This," he continued, lifting an
arm to take in the whole of the world as far as they could
see it, "is."

"But when I tried to enter—"

"Yes. And I don't, frankly, understand how it was that you
entered the wrong place. I don't like what it implies."

"What does it imply?" It was Severn who asked; Kaylin
had had enough of the sharp edge of Evanton's tongue, and
had no intention of offering another opening for his criticism. At least for a few minutes.

"That, among other things, she is adept at the art of travel,
enough so that the small perturbation could open the ways
to her. She is *not* well studied in any of the magical arts, and
she is as cautious as..."

"Thank you," she said, when he failed to come up with a
suitable ending for the sentence.

"What, *exactly,* did you do when you attempted to enter
the Garden?"

Since she was already more or less frowning, her expression didn't change. "I walked in."

"That's *all* you did?"

"Well, yes." The frown deepened. It had been one of those

weeks, and she lost track of events that seemed, on the surface, to be insignificant. "No. The door was—"

He waited. Not patiently, but he did wait.

"I touched it, and it hurt."

"Hurt?"

"Like a door ward does. It was like putting my palm into fire."

"And then you opened the door?" When she didn't immediately answer, his frown deepened—and on his face, whole lines had been carved by his frown over the years. "Private, this is not a game."

"I...may have said something. I talk to myself when there's no other alternative."

"What did you say to yourself?"

"Technically? I said to the door, 'Take me to the heart of the Elemental Garden.'"

He stared at her as if she'd lost her mind. She didn't even object, because that's how she was starting to feel. "You don't normally talk to doors."

"Most doors don't normally lead into the *middle* of a grassy plain and disappear when they're closed." She felt Severn's glance as if it were a weight, and grimaced. "Why should it have made any difference? It *didn't* take me to the heart of the Garden. It didn't take me to the Garden *at all*. It took me to a—a mirage."

"An interesting choice of words, Private. It took you to an echo, an externalization. There was no substance to it—and you recognized this instantly."

She nodded.

"Why?"

"I don't know. The Garden feels *alive* to me. I mean, more alive than grass or trees or plants. It's—it's not what it looks like. What it looks like is just...makeup." She looked at the grass, and then lifted her head. "Have the elements ever spoken of the Devourer at all?"

Evanton looked at her. "No," he finally said. "But I know that a portal will open in the streets a few yards from the storefront. It's happened before. It hasn't happened as *close* to the Elemental Garden before, for which I'm grateful."

"The Garden told you this?"

"Not in so many words, no. But...my understanding of the event is derived in part from the communication with the elements."

Although she knew she wasn't in theory supposed to speak with Evanton, her shoulders slumped. "I think the Emperor and the High Lord of the Barrani Court want to stop it from opening."

One brow rose. "Why?"

"There's something else...out there. Wherever there's no world. I...met it, when I was lost between worlds."

"And what was it?"

"I don't know, Evanton. But smarter people think it's the Devourer. We've pretty much confirmed the Worlds theory, by now."

"Confirmation was necessary?" he asked in that clipped tone of his.

"I've got my hands full with a city, never mind a world. I didn't really care one way or the other."

"A failing of the young. They don't bother to learn what they can when it would actually be convenient to learn, because they have a very narrow concept of necessity. Continue."

"I'm not sure I want them to stop the portal from opening. People will die if they do," she added. "Probably thousands. They'll starve or they'll meet the Devourer. I don't think he's found them, yet."

"But he found you."

She frowned. "Yes. He found me."

"How?"

"I called...someone who lives in Elantra. By his True Name."

Evanton didn't seem surprised.

"When I did, he heard me."

"Interesting."

She grimaced. "The portal. Do you also think it shouldn't be allowed to open?"

"I think it will cause a great deal of havoc when it does," he replied.

She waited.

"And I'm not entirely certain that anyone can prevent it."

"Evanton—"

He lifted a hand. "I speak theoretically, of course. It irritates you and I should apologize. I won't. No, I don't think the attempt to keep it closed should be made. But, Kaylin—understand that I am the Keeper of *this* Garden, and there isn't another like it in the whole of the many realities, past or present. It's unique, and it's here. It exists within the confines of a Dragon's hoard. It exists half a city away from the heart of the fiefs. It exists in the shadow of the winged flight of Aerians—and if I understand events in the fiefs correctly you've brought at least one winged Dragon back into play.

"It exists in streets crossed by Barrani, by humans, by Tha'alani and by Leontines. Without its existence, we would have no world."

She lay back against the flat grass and let the wind run across her face as she closed her eyes. "Gardens like this don't exist in the other worlds?"

"No."

"How can you be so certain?"

Silence. That silence was the worst thing about talking

to the powerful and the knowledgeable. She folded thought into it. "Evanton?"

"Yes."

"The heart of the fiefs. *Ravellon*."

"Yes?"

"Does it—did it—exist anywhere else, or only here?"

"I am not the Keeper of the Library," he finally replied, after a long pause. "Nor am I at all certain that the Keeper of the Library still exists. But he—or she—would have the answer to that question."

It took Kaylin a minute to figure out that he wasn't talking about the Arkon. "You think it only existed here."

"Yes, I do. But I am not certain of it. I am certain that the Elemental Garden existed only here."

"And the Devourer?"

"I don't know where the Devourer started, Kaylin. I don't know precisely where the Ancients started, either, if it comes to that. I know the stories about the births of Dragons and Barrani. I know the stories of the births of other races and other creatures, some of whom could breed and some of whom were unique.

"But the Devourer? No. I would say, if I had to guess, that he is as old as the gods, possibly one of them."

"I think he's like your wild elements," she finally said. "Only he has no Keeper. Or maybe he had one in the nothing, but whoever that was, he didn't pass the job on to someone else. If he even survived it.

"I know the Devourer has destroyed worlds."

"How do you know this?"

She shook her head; he didn't press her.

"I don't understand *how,* or *why,* but… I guess, if the elements were finally unleashed, they'd destroy the world and they wouldn't have a reason that made much sense, either, at least not to me." She rolled onto her side, bending an elbow so she could prop her head up on one hand. "Why do you think the portal should be allowed to open if the Devourer is a danger?"

"I allow that the Devourer *is* a danger. But the world…is the world. It has changed, and continues to change, and one of the ways in which it does are these travelers. Your people. The Aerians. The Tha'alani. They bring something new, each time. It strengthens us." He waited, and she understood that he was waiting for her to draw some sort of conclusion.

She glanced at Severn, who nodded. It was a slight motion.

"Was this the first world?" she finally asked.

"Very good," Evanton replied, with just the hint of a smile. "Yes. I believe that this was the first world. It fits with what we know."

"Does it matter?"

"No. Nor am I saying that no other world was real. They were real. Some, I believe, still exist, but we do not speak so readily with them as we in theory once did."

"How do you know all this? You couldn't possibly have been alive when—" She stopped. Thought about the depths of the Elemental Water's small, quiet pool. "Oh."

"Oh, indeed. It's not relevant on most days, and in spite of the fact that I fear your adherence to the purely relevant is shortsighted, it is also practical, and I am a relatively practical man. Mistakes were made on a grand, even a divine scale, and lessons were learned. Rather than war over the fabric of this one world, the Ancients chose to travel. It was long ago.

"They were free, in their slow creations, to make different choices. Often, they simply made different mistakes, but… they learned, and they spoke to their kin across the divide."

"How did they create *worlds*?"

"No one knows, Kaylin. Or at least no one who is not an Ancient knows, and they seldom speak, except in echoes."

She nodded.

"But they experimented with life and the living, and they created, in the end, new races. Yours, the Aerians, the Tha'alani—races that could live, breathe, think, and die, without ever possessing a Name. Some experiments were made here, which I believe you are aware of.

"But that continued elsewhere. And here you now are." He glanced into the distance made of horizon and light. "And the travelers who struggle toward us now are your distant cousins, or mine, or the Dragon's. They're kin, in some way. They've come home.

"And I think the worlds allow the creation of these portals or these gates for that purpose. The magic required to penetrate a world is not—as you've seen—slight, and it isn't easily controlled. The Ancients did not uniformly hate or decry those who had left, and they allowed them the safety of return.

"So, they now come."

She sat up, hunching her back so she could wrap her arms around her shins. "You don't think they can stop the portal from opening."

"This seems to be your only concern at the moment," he said, with faint disapproval. If faint was a loud and thunderous expression.

"Did you ever teach?" she asked.

"Ask Grethan."

"Never mind. It's not my only concern. But it *is* my concern."

"If, indeed, it's your largest concern, I suggest you apply some of the pragmatism of which you are theoretically so fond to the difficulty."

When she didn't immediately leap up and look enlight-
ened, he added, "What are you going to do with thousands
of people who have only the clothing they're wearing when
they appear in the middle of *these* streets? Do they speak the
language?"

She shook her head. "Our meeting at the Palace this morning was supposed to address that issue."

"See that it *is* addressed. The Dragon Court is, at heart, a
practical body, and the Dragon Emperor, in spite of all pub-
licity to the contrary, does not expect the universe to conform to his whims. He will entertain contingencies in the
possible case of failure."

"He'll be worried about the larger problem."

"The Devourer?"

She nodded.

"Yes. But in the event that the Devourer doesn't immediately end the world—"

She frowned. "What did you say?"

"I believe you heard me."

The frown deepened. "Severn?"

He nodded.

"The travelers—Enkerrikas and his people—they *had* time.
They knew what was coming. They didn't believe it would
be their deaths. Well, some didn't. They had time to prepare."

"Yes."

"What did they do? Why are there no Records of the
worlds that fell? Why did they send so little warning? Enkerrikas recorded *everything*."

"He recorded what he saw and he carried it *with him*,"
Severn reminded her.

"But...they implied they could speak with other worlds,
or people on other worlds." She was frustrated now, and she

rose. The grasslands stretched out forever. Turning, she said, "Ask the water if we can talk to it?"

"The water is *not* a mirror, Private."

"No. But...it remembers. I'm sure it remembers."

"You said you were short on time."

"How far away is the water?"

"Across the plain. It's not more than two days by foot." He waited.

She wilted, but only slightly. "You said you could make the Garden conform to its usual state—"

"With effort, which I *also* said was not the wisest use of power at the present time." Evanton folded arms across his chest.

"Ask, please?"

He grimaced and let his arms fall to the side. "I'm only willing to try," he told her, "because you attempted to use manners in an appropriate way, and rewarding such attempts is in my future interest. You may wish to wait outside."

"Is that your way of telling us to wait outside?"

"No. I leave it up to you."

"We'll stay."

"Corporal?"

"The last time she wandered around in your store on her own, I was threatened with demotion," Severn replied. "I'll take my chances here."

Evanton did not immediately begin; instead, he told them—curtly—to follow. There was either a beaten track through the dry, sharp—and mostly flattened—stalks of grass, or one created itself for the Keeper's convenience. He led them to what appeared to be a large, flat circle in the ground; as they approached, Kaylin saw that it was made of stone. It wasn't carved, and it wasn't runed—she thought it was green because of moss.

"Stand on it," he told her. "And you as well, Corporal. It will remain where it is. The rest of the landscape will…compress. It is not in theory fatal, but it is entirely uncomfortable. While I can't think of any reason this should apply, I'll warn you anyway. Touch nothing."

"Nothing. Got it." Kaylin sat on her hands. The rock was actually cool to the touch. Severn sat beside her. Evanton cleared his throat and they both moved to make room for him. Standing, he lifted his arms and began to speak. Kaylin didn't understand a word he was saying.

But without understanding any of it, the language still sounded familiar. Frustrated, she frowned and closed her eyes, to better concentrate. Severn broke that concentration in the easiest way he knew how: he touched her shoulder, and she startled.

"I don't understand the language, either," he said quietly. "And you won't, no matter how hard you try."

She would have argued, but there was no sting and no judgment in the statement. Severn never judged her; he never had. Judgment, where it had happened in their lives, generally came from Kaylin. She glanced at Evanton, and her frown deepened, just before her eyes widened.

He was speaking the names of fire, water, earth, and air. Not as names, but as language, as story, as something that, at the end—and only then—would finally have a finished shape, a solid truth. Evanton was speaking in the language of the Ancients.

She'd heard Sanabalis do it once, had heard the Arkon do the same. Each time they spoke, she had seen some representation of what they said form in the air around them, as if they'd invoked the spirit of the word itself.

This time? She saw the elements instead. They weren't dots and strokes and lines; they didn't look like carvings or glowing sigils. They converged, and the whole of what they were, flame or gale or flood or the thunderous movement of ground, surrounded the very small and very insignificant stone on which they were now seated.

She heard their voices overlapping each other, like the cry of a crowd—or worse—a mob; she heard their desire to be, and to be entirely, what they were. For a moment it was a visceral, necessary thing, a primal *need*. It was wordless, yes— but wordless was not the same as voiceless.

Without thought, Kaylin began to speak, as well. If Evanton heard her, he gave or made no sign, and he didn't pause in his own long, precise speech. Hers was imprecise, and she couldn't later recall the words she spoke because she wasn't deliberately choosing any. She couldn't remember most of the things she said to newborn infants, either, because the infants were completely innocent, and nothing she said had meaning beyond the comfort of sound and presence.

She wasn't an idiot; she didn't treat the elements like newborn children. But she'd spoken to them once before, when the Garden had almost been destroyed by a very ambitious Arcanist. She spoke not of what they were in their elemental state, nor of what they'd been when they'd first been born— if elements could be said to *be* born at all. She didn't know those things any more than she understood mountains or oceans or the empty stretch of plains that knew no streets, no buildings, and no people.

Instead, she spoke of what they meant to *her*. Fire in the cold of winter in the fiefs, and in the hearth of the Foundling Halls when evening had finally descended and stories—when Marrin allowed them—could be told. Water in the fountains and in the wells, and water as a track of tears that expressed both joy and sorrow when words just weren't enough. Earth that was plowed and earth into which seedlings were planted—in boxes and small plots and the distant fields of farmers. But the air? She breathed it. It was always, always present, always necessary. It could move freely through open windows and closed doors, and it carried the Aerians—and the Dragons—when they took to the skies.

In all of this, there was beauty, but especially in the flight of those who *could* meet the sky on their own terms. She didn't deny it, didn't resent it: it was what it was. So, too, the elements. She didn't and couldn't describe all of what they were; only what they were, at the moment, to Kaylin. But she wanted, and needed, to tell them what they were to her.

Around her, as she continued, the elements began to subside. She could hear their whispers, their shouts, their endless anger and their endless desire—but she could hear, as well, the way they responded to her own beliefs, her own ways of interacting with—and depending on—their very existence for her own life.

In their clamor and anger and constant, restless motion, they asked for something. She couldn't find the words for it, but as they spoke, she felt it clearly: a yearning. A sorrow.

Elemental sorrow?

Yes, the water replied. For a moment—for just a moment— she heard the word as clearly as if it had been spoken by a young girl, and she saw the face of the water as she had seen it the first time. *We were one thing, Kaylin. Once, we were one thing. The others cannot speak as I can now speak. They are not the voice and memory of a people. I am changed by that choice, made so long ago. It is part of me.*

But even were we four to be one again, we would never be whole.

"Because you've changed so much? Because *we've* changed you?"

No, Kaylin Neya. We were one, and then we were many. But in the act of separation, one was lost.

"But there are only four elements."

Yes. There are only four.

"Then what was lost?"

The silence, Kaylin. The emptiness. The peace. The ending. There is only conflict now, between us. We cannot do other than struggle to spread. The Keeper contains and lulls us as he can, and we see and touch and hear the voices of the world. Of the worlds. This is...difficult, for me. To converse here, like this.

But, Kaylin, we can hear it, too. What you heard, what you hear. We know it.

"Can it—can it hear you?"

It can hear us. It has always heard our voices, and the echo of our voices. But it does not see or feel as you see or feel, and like fire—or water, or earth, or air—it is capable of great destruction.

When Kaylin opened her eyes—she couldn't remember closing them—she saw that around the single flat stone on which she was now standing, the Garden was the Garden she had first seen: larger than a room, yes, but placed in such a way that all shrines could be reached by a swift stroll. The shrines themselves, their odd candelabras and old stone shelves, were once again nearest the symbolic representation of their respective element, and in particular, she could see the small, deep pond that was water, here.

Evanton was staring at her; his brows had drawn together across the top end of his face so they were one long line. But if he wanted to say something scathing, he kept it to himself. "Your Garden," he said.

She hopped off the rock, started to walk toward the pool, and then hesitated. "Evanton?"

He moved more slowly, and he looked tired. But he nodded.

"How can the elements have always existed?"

"Private, this is *not the time* for a philosophical discussion."

Kaylin never had time for a philosophical discussion. "I'm serious," she said. "I'm having trouble understanding—"

He didn't look surprised. Nor did he look encouraging. She moved on.

"How can this Garden exist in only one place if there are whole other worlds? I mean, those worlds would need the elements, as well."

"This may come as a surprise to you," he replied, in a tone that indicated that it wouldn't, "but I've never visited other worlds. I have no idea how the elements function across them, if they indeed do. The Barrani and the Dragons were created from stone, if the old stories are true, but not all stone lives and walks and causes endless trouble."

She frowned as she walked, and she walked more slowly. Teela would have told her she couldn't even think and walk at the same time. It was probably true. She could, however, *worry* and do anything concurrently. Evanton stopped just as they reached the moss bed, which was possibly the most comfortable place in the world to actually sit. He then occupied it, as if it were a small throne.

"Why is it important?" he asked quietly. The sarcasm and the ill temper that had characterized the morning had drained out of his voice.

"I don't know."

"You did good work there, by the way. It wasn't nearly as difficult to bring the elements back to the garden state."

"Did it always look like this?"

He laughed. "No. It did when I first became Keeper, but Keepers have their own peculiarities, and as we're asking the elements to conform to our dictates, the Garden will change depending on the Keeper. Why does this trouble you?"

"Every world is going to need the things we need. We need the elements, I get that. But doesn't that imply that the worlds are connected somehow? Doesn't that imply that whatever you're responsible for here reaches everything?"

"It may. I've seldom thought about other worlds. Why is this important now?"

"It's the Devourer," Kaylin said quietly.

He frowned. "Yes?"

"I don't understand *what* it is, but..." She sat down beside him, the depth of the pool close enough she could watch light play—and fall—from its surface while she dredged up the words with which to express her growing suspicion. "I think...it belongs in the Garden."

CHAPTER 20

After a long pause, Evanton said—to Severn, "Corporal, has the Private been *entirely* sleep deprived for the last few days?"

"Not more than usual," Severn replied, his voice crier than the grass had been.

"I understand that the marks of the Chosen seldom infest mortals. I begin to see *why*. Clearly, they've unbalanced your mind."

Since she'd more or less expected this—or worse—she waited. Evanton didn't disappoint.

"You weren't, the last time I checked—which would, incidentally, be *now*—a god, what passes for a god, or an Ancient. Even if I were to allow the possibility that you are substantially correct—which I will do for the sake of this discussion—it wouldn't matter. Unless you have some knowledge about *building* the Garden, there's no way to bring the Devourer *into it.*"

Kaylin rose from the moss bed.

"The Elemental Garden isn't aptly named. But Garden is nicer than Prison, and Keeper is better than Jailor. The elements are *contained* here, Kaylin. Were it up to their base nature, they would not *be* contained, and they would consume whatever lay in their path in their attempt to establish their own supremacy."

"But that's not *all* they are, Evanton."

His voice softened unexpectedly. "No, Private, it is not all that they are. You will speak with the water?"

"I think... I think I already have. I think the Devourer *does* belong here. But you're right—I have no idea how to invite him in, if that's even what he wants." She walked over to the side of the pool and she knelt by it almost reverently—for Kaylin. Reaching out, her hand hovered a moment above its cool, still surface. The water then rippled as she touched it.

Daughter, it said, in a familiar voice.

Kaylin was, for a moment, speechless. Silent. Into the silence came the voice of the Tha'alaan, the living racial memory of Ybelline's people.

Ybelline, Kaylin said.

Kaylin?

She felt the castelord's surprise, concern—and joy. *I may need your help,* Kaylin said. She struggled with words, and then gave them up entirely, sending, instead, images, feelings, fears. These fears were not the fears that could drive the Tha'alani to madness.

You wish me to come to Elani street?

If you can. The area is under quarantine.

Ybelline wordlessly agreed, and then the voice of the water spoke loudly and clearly enough that it was the only thing Kaylin could hear. *Yes.*

Unfortunately, it didn't give her much else to go on.

Evanton was reattired in his dusty, grungy apron by the time Kaylin left the Garden. He was also much quieter. "The advantage to total and utter ignorance," he said, indicating that he was not, however, in a better mood, "is the lack of preconception. I would, however, be interested in meeting the Th'alani castelord."

"She'll be here."

"I gathered as much." He slid the key ring back into one of the cavernous front pockets that dangled near his knees. "I am willing to trust you in this, not because I think you have any idea of how you intend to accomplish anything, but because I think there's no alternative. I don't think the portal can *be* closed or denied, and I don't doubt that the Devourer you've seen is coming when it opens."

"Do you have any idea of when it will open?"

"No. Soon."

Kaylin headed out of the quarantined stretch of the city in which her beat lay, toward the Ablayne's small wagons and bakers' stalls. There, she bought dinner. It was a pretty scant dinner but Severn wisely didn't comment on the amount of money she barely had.

Buns in hand, she headed toward the Halls of Law.

"What are you planning to tell the Sergeant?"

Kaylin snorted. "I'm planning to write every thing up in a report and dump it on his desk. He won't read it for two weeks—or more—by which time it'll be irrelevant one way or the other."

Severn raised a brow.

"Or I can tell him that there are going to be mages and Arcanists crawling all over the quarantined area soon, that they'll probably blow themselves to bits, wreck the surrounding landscape, or become delusional megalomaniacs, to no effect whatsoever, other than the usual unacceptable body count. After which, we'll *then* have streets full of thousands of homeless, desperate, *armed* strangers."

Severn laughed. She laughed because he did, and because

she liked the sound of his laughter enough to want to be part of it, even for a moment. "Make clear that the mages and Arcanists will be there under Imperial Dictate, and you're probably covered. The Hawklord won't thank you for it," he added. "Ironjaw hates magic more than you do. I bet he's up in the Tower in less than five minutes after he hears your report."

"I didn't realize magic-hating was a competition. I'll try harder."

"Don't," he said, his smile still echoing his laughter. "It's part of what you are now."

"I don't always like what I am, in case that escaped your attention."

"Last I checked, I wasn't dead. I did notice."

Her eyes narrowed. "I'll take that bet."

"Means you'll have to tell him."

She shrugged. "I think he'll give it at least ten."

The worse thing about bad news and Leontines is that Leontines, unlike Aerians, weren't above sharing the bad mood that came out of it. Marcus's eyes, which had been copper for the last few days, shaded to orange as he listened. And growled.

The office was never *completely* silent—for one, the damn window was babbling up the contents of a play—but even the most bored or notorious of office gossips had developed a sensitivity to Leontine growls. Especially the quieter ones.

"You said *Arcanists?*"

Kaylin was standing almost at attention, her chin slightly lifted to expose her throat. It wasn't, at the moment, necessary, but it was always a good social precaution when dealing with Leontines who happened to be responsible for her pay, to say the least. "Yes, sir. I'm not completely certain—but I'd bet my own money."

"Don't start."

"Yes, sir." She stood there for what felt like five minutes, watching the way his ear tufts started to rise. "What would you like us to do, sir?"

"Stay out of trouble, if that's possible."

It wasn't, and they both knew it.

"I do not want Arcanists running around my city."

"No, sir." Kaylin heartily agreed. "The Imperial Court is probably still in session." Bureaucracy, as they both knew, was slow and ponderous. "But you won't—" She looked up as Caitlin rose from her desk.

A very official Imperial Courier had entered the inner office, and was, even as Kaylin turned, approaching Caitlin. He didn't speak, but it wasn't necessary; instead, he handed her a scroll, bowed, and left. Caitlin glanced at it, and then glanced across the office. It wasn't empty; during the current crisis, it wouldn't be, even after hours. It was going to be Marcus's first home, not his second one, for at least another week.

Since she knew his wives were more or less understanding, she expected he'd survive it. She wasn't, however, as certain of the fate of the contents of the tube that Caitlin now delivered to his desk.

Caitlin stood beside Kaylin; Kaylin had not been ordered to get lost, and she watched as her Sergeant twisted the tube, breaking the seal. It didn't crumble; it did glow. Kaylin winced.

Marcus's lips sometimes moved when he was reading High Barrani. They were usually, however, mouthing distinctly Leontine curses. Today was not an exception. "Private," he said, without glancing up.

"Sir."

"It appears that you're to serve as escort for a small group of Imperial mages." He set the scroll down for a moment, looked up at Caitlin, and said, "One, register my complaint at the assignment. Private Neya has already been stupid enough to offend most of the Imperial mages she's had the privilege to meet. Offer them any *other* escort. Preferably Barrani Hawks."

"I heard that!" Tain said, from somewhere deeper into the office.

Marcus didn't blink. "Two," he continued, "I would like you to arrange an immediate appointment with the Hawklord."

"For?"

"*Me.*" The word was couched in a low growl.

Caitlin, who was being unnaturally still, retreated instantly to her desk, because *she* had her orders. Kaylin remained standing in front of it.

"Does the message say when I'm supposed to report for duty?"

"Yes."

"Are you going to tell me?"

"If it's relevant," was the dour reply.

Caitlin's registration of complaint traveled the way the Imperial Palace's message had—by courier. The only difference was that the courier sent by the Halls was to wait for a reply; Kaylin didn't envy her. This wasn't the way messages were usually sent, unless the signatures were necessary or the documentation was required, but as both the Halls and the Palace were under mirror blackout except in cases of "emergency," where emergency was likely to be well-defined only *after* the fact, they didn't have many other choices.

Kaylin wasn't worried about Imperial Couriers; nor was she particularly concerned with the ones the Halls employed. But she worried, as she always did, about the inability of either the midwives or the Foundling Halls to actually *reach* her, should it be necessary. Neither placed casual calls via mirror.

She would have asked if any word had, in fact, been sent, but Marcus left his desk and headed toward the Tower stairs. She hadn't been counting seconds, and looked across the room to where Severn—in an either cowardly or clever way—had taken a seat as far from the action as was safe. *How many minutes?* she mouthed.

He frowned.

He wasn't entirely honest—no one who'd grown up in the fiefs was—but he wouldn't lie about a bet. He grimaced and said, "What were the stakes?"

She cursed under her breath. No stakes, no bet.

"You might as well take a seat," Severn added, as Teela and Tain headed toward her now that Ironjaw was at a safe remove. "We're probably going to be here for a while."

She sat, heavily, on the nearest chair that didn't belong to the Leontine. "I wish they'd start their damn shift tomorrow, whatever decision they reach. You betting?"

"Yeah. I'm betting they send the courier back with a very polite version of 'get stuffed.'"

"Not touching that one."

He laughed.

Teela, looking almost tired for a Barrani, folded herself over the back of the chair closest to Kaylin's. The only difference between this and Kaylin's rather graceless collapse was that Teela kicked the chair's previous occupant out of it first; Kaylin had taken an empty one. "How did the visit to the Oracular Halls go?"

"Pretty much as expected. Why?"

"If an emergency is going to occur—figuratively speaking— we'd prefer it happen sooner than later. Marcus is operating under the belief that the Barrani need no sleep."

"They don't."

Tain raised a brow. "Strictly speaking, no." He also looked

a little piqued. "But some time away from people we're not allowed to strangle or maim is generally considered healthy for all concerned."

"You want to strangle someone?"

"No. But I will."

"Why?"

"Because we're not *deaf*, kitling," Teela drawled. "And if the Arcanists are allowed anywhere near the area of difficulty..." She didn't bother to finish the sentence, but the way she left it hanging there would have conjured nightmares for anyone who was actually breathing.

Marcus came downstairs with eyes so orange they were almost reflective. A steady stream of Leontine was bouncing off the enclosed Tower walls as he made his descent, and if Barrani hearing was way better than mere mortal hearing, mortal hearing was still good enough. Everyone either got off their butts or made sure their butts were firmly planted in the chairs at their desks by the time his bristling self had cleared the Tower and hurtled headlong into office territory.

The courier arrived about fifteen minutes later; Marcus's argument with the Hawklord—and no one could doubt that there'd been one—had not been short. Like the Imperial Courier, Leila—whose name Kaylin actually knew—was smart enough to hand off the reply to Caitlin. It was also contained in an Imperial tube. Marcus almost *ate* it before he remembered to break the seal.

To no one's surprise, Marcus's request had been denied. Teela and Tain were *not* happy about it, and given how little they'd been looking forward to meeting Arcanists, this said something. Marcus's eyes did let up a bit with the fire when he reached the end of the letter, though.

"Lord Sanabalis will be accompanying you at all times,"

he told Kaylin. "Or rather, you'll be accompanying Lord Sanabalis."

"I don't suppose they'll be starting tomorrow *after* I've had a chance to sleep?"

To her great surprise, he said, "They will. First thing in the morning, at the Imperial Palace," he added. "Go home. I expect you to make some pathetic attempt at a report at the end of the day."

Kaylin didn't go straight home; she stopped by the midwives' guild to check in on the status of possible births by mothers who had failed to be relocated. The news there, at least as far as the guild knew, was good, and she found herself relaxing.

She also borrowed their mirror, and sent a message to Ybelline Rabon'alani. "I'm sorry I missed you," she said, when the image of the castelord failed to materialize. "But... while I need you in the quarantined area, tomorrow is probably not going to be the safe day to meet or escort you through the Swords. Sanabalis has me on Dragon and mage duty in the quarantined area itself, and any attempts at investigative magery in the last few days has been...dangerous for the surroundings.

"And the mage," she added, almost as an afterthought.

She made it home into a dark and empty apartment; the soft glow of her very normal mirror made her flinch. Someone had mirrored, and she'd missed it. On most days, it was Marcus, asking her when she thought she'd condescend to earn her pay, because he usually did mirror if she was late, and she usually managed to beat the incoming message out the door. But all of the Hawks were on a schedule from hell, and the amusing morning growl hadn't made Marcus's to-do list; she was certain of that. He also had no access to mirror use for personal sadism at the moment.

She was also certain she needed to sleep, and an emergency was not going to get her much in the way of shut-eye. But she dragged herself, after one immobile minute, to the mirror's shining gray surface, and she placed her hand firmly in its center. "Messages," she said grimly.

To her momentary relief, it wasn't Marrin's face or the face of a grim midwife. It was Nightshade.

"Kaylin," he said. His smile was slender, and his eyes were a bright shade of green. Any day in which the sight of his smile was a relief had been a long one. "I am waiting."

She watched the image, listening for the rest of the message.

"You have visited Tiamaris; you have spoken with his Tower. At some point in the near future, I wish you to return to the heart of my castle. We will discuss this, soon."

She stared at the mirror as his image slowly faded. In the darkness left behind she could still see the green of his eyes.

Morning. *Ugh.*

Kaylin dragged herself out of bed and into clothing before she was willing to fully open her eyes. Since she often came into a dark room and made her way to a familiar bed without lighting a lamp or opening the shutters to let in silver streams of moonlight, she managed to do this without so much as stubbing a toe. She had bread and cheese in the basket Severn had given her, and she took the necessary five minutes to eat and wash the crumbs down with water before she headed out the door.

The sun, when she reached the street, was more or less in the right position, and no new emergencies had reared their ugly heads; she'd actually slept reasonably well, and although she'd woken once in the middle of the night, the nightmare that must have caused it vanished before sleep did, and it didn't return. Any night that had only one such interruption was, in Kaylin's vocabulary, damn good sleep.

She could mimic good sleep if she was falling-over exhausted; when she'd first left the fiefs, it was the *only* way she could sleep. Exhaustion, in the early days, was easy to come by.

It had been more fun, as well, because aside from midwife emergencies, she'd spent a lot of time trawling bars with Teela and Tain. The exhaustion of the last year? Not so much. And, she thought grimly, it wasn't likely to let up in the next few days. Of course, given the mood of Sanabalis and the rest of the Dragon Court, she could avoid the next few days by getting herself summarily executed for being late.

She ran.

Severn was at the Palace by the time she arrived, which was no surprise. He was, however, waiting, which meant she was technically *early*. She would have pointed this out because it didn't happen often, but she would have had to shout to be heard, because the normally quiet Palace was now trembling with the raised voices of Dragons.

In the lull between speakers—such as it was—Kaylin said, "I thought the Court session would've been finished by now."

Severn shrugged. "If you want to point out that we're early and they're late, be my guest."

She waited another two minutes before she was certain she could be heard. "How is it that the Palace Guard isn't deaf?"

Kaylin, who was never good at watching minutes, thought maybe a quarter of an hour of silence had actually passed before she caught sight of the first member of the Dragon Court.

It was not, as she expected, Sanabalis; it was Tiamaris. He raised a brow as they came into view—and while he was generally always aware of his surroundings, he seemed slightly surprised to see them both.

"You're going home?" Kaylin asked, because the first question that had come to mind was *What were you all shouting about?* and even she wasn't stupid enough to ask it while she was standing *in* the Palace.

His nod was curt. His eyes were a shade of orange that was pretty damn close to red. "I return to Tiamaris, yes. You are?"

"Escort for Lord Sanabalis for the day."

"I see. I'm surprised the Sergeant approved."

"Oh, he didn't. But Imperial Fiat is Imperial Fiat."

Tiamaris literally snorted tufts of smoke. He nodded curtly, strode past the two Hawks, and then turned on his heel. "Kaylin." His voice was flat.

"Yes?"

"Tara spoke to me while I was in Council session."

She schooled her expression as carefully as she could. "And?"

"I do not understand *why,*" he said, "but she feels that your position in this matter—which has no *official* weight—should be supported."

"Evanton doesn't think, aside from the usual shitstorm that the Arcanists can be guaranteed to cause when in possession of too much power, they're going to be able to stop it. No matter what they try."

He frowned, and his eyes began to lose some of the almost literal burning rage. "You spoke to the Keeper, and this is what he told you?"

"More or less. Well, less. There's other stuff."

"And you *failed to bring this up* with the Dragon Court."

She lifted her hands. "I only just spoke to Evanton, Tiamaris."

"You went there that early in the morning? You?"

Which was stretching the bounds of credibility. "No. Yesterday evening."

"So you were in possession of these facts for an entire evening during this crisis and you failed to find them significant enough to send a message?"

"In case you failed to notice, *the Emperor himself* has made up his mind, Tiamaris. I made my opinion pretty clear to Sanabalis and the Arkon yesterday. You wanted me to send a message telling the Emperor that he was *wrong*?"

"No. Your opinion in this would be considered irrelevant given the paucity of your experience. *The Keeper's* opinion, however, would *not be*. I realize that you have some personal affection for Evanton, as he styles himself among the mortals. You cannot, however, allow that affection to render him pointless in the larger affairs of the state."

"If Evanton wanted—"

Tiamaris lifted a hand. Kaylin shut up, because his gaze had gone over her shoulder to a direction someplace at her back.

"Oh, do go on," Sanabalis said, in a very cool voice. "I'm certain that Lord Diarmat would be interested in hearing the rest of your...discussion. I'm certain," he added, his voice dropping a few degrees between syllables, "that the Palace Guard would likewise take an interest, since the halls have excellent acoustics."

She flinched, smoothed out her expression, and turned to face Lord Sanabalis. And his companion, Lord Diarmat, another Dragon of the Imperial Court.

He looked less amused than Sanabalis, and vastly less resigned; he did not look as aggravated as Tiamaris, but Tiamaris had the singular advantage of much higher expectations. His eyes were a shade of darkening bronze, and he examined

Kaylin as if she were a criminal. Which, while it was partially fair given that she had once been *exactly* that, conversely set her teeth on edge. She was here as a Hawk. She tendered Lord Diarmat a perfectly serviceable, if shallow, bow.

"My apologies, Lord Sanabalis," Tiamaris said.

Sanabalis, whose eyes were a darker shade than his compatriot's, didn't even glance at Tiamaris. "Private."

"Lord Sanabalis."

Lifting a hand, he pinched the bridge of his nose. "Did you, as Lord Tiamaris appears to be suggesting, speak with the Keeper about our current difficulty?"

"Yes, sir."

His frown grew more wrinkles.

"Did the Keeper in fact suggest that interference in the opening of the portal would be, in his opinion, entirely unsuccessful?"

"Yes, sir."

"Did you happen to ask him *why?*"

"Yes, sir. His answer was inconclusive."

"How?"

"He said he didn't know."

Lord Diarmat's lips were a quickly thinning line. "Is it, as Lord Tiamaris has so loudly suggested, possible that you considered the conversation with the Keeper to be entirely irrelevant?"

"The Keeper's not the Emperor," she replied, still speaking in the brisk and factual tone she took when faced with a furious Leontine. "It was clear what the intentions of the Dragon Court were."

"The Dragon Court had not yet finished its session," was Diarmat's reply. It made Sanabalis's initial tone seem pleasant and affectionate in comparison.

"No, sir."

Unlike Sanabalis, he didn't seem irritated by her flat, even response.

"Therefore its intentions could not have been clear to one who was not even in attendance."

"Yes, sir."

"Private," Sanabalis said, before Diarmat could speak again. "This conversation will now be relocated to my personal chambers. Lord Tiamaris, if you would attend us?"

Tiamaris nodded.

There was no food in Sanabalis's rooms, which was to be expected, considering he hadn't intended to use them. Kaylin, who could feel breakfast slowly dwindling, regretted the absence anyway. She wasn't stupid enough to take a chair before Sanabalis took one, and when neither Diarmat nor Tiamaris chose to be seated, she stood, as well. Severn, following like a shadow, had earned a brief glance from the third Dragon Lord; Tiamaris and Sanabalis were used to him, and paid no obvious attention.

She told them as much about her visit with Evanton as she deemed wise. Strictly speaking, the information embargo was in theory one way. Or at least only one direction had fangs and breathed fire. Evanton just snarled and made you feel like an idiot, and she could survive that. She failed to mention her own thoughts on the matter of the Devourer.

Diarmat listened, and Diarmat broke the resulting, thoughtful silence first. "Lord Sanabalis," he said, his voice still chilly, "who was it that authorized Private Neya's delegation as an Imperial Liaison to the Keeper?"

"She does not formally serve in that capacity," Sanabalis replied. "And as such, her continued interaction with the Keeper is valuable."

Kaylin frowned, and Tiamaris said, "Evanton is dubious about the intentions of the Imperial Court, and will not entertain an official delegate in any capacity that is not one of a customer. The Emperor has not—and in my opinion will not—see fit to command Evanton to accept one."

"Because Evanton is unlikely to comply?"

"Even so. His role is well understood by the Emperor. Its functions and its routines, however, are not. He is one of several people whose existence is critical to the continued safety of the Empire itself."

She nodded.

"But unlike the Barrani High Lords or the fieflords, who might be said to occupy similar roles of import, there are no successors eagerly waiting in the wings."

Diarmat lifted a hand, and Tiamaris fell silent. "If you are not there in an official capacity, why did you approach the Keeper now?"

"It was in his store that I...got lost."

"I see. Continue."

She stopped herself from shrugging with effort. "I knew he'd be worried."

Lord Diarmat's face might have been carved in stone; his expression didn't change. But the room seemed to have experienced a sudden drop in temperature. He glanced at Sanabalis, whose expression was also composed of something like stone. "Lord Sanabalis?"

Sanabalis did lift a brow then. "What, exactly, did the Keeper say?"

The three Dragon Lords were silent. Diarmat had made his opinion of Kaylin's memory—and by extension *all* mortal memory—more than clear by the time she'd finished. He had sifted through every word, pointing out clearly when the words varied by even so much as a syllable. Halfway through this interrogation, the door opened to admit the Arkon. He entered the room looking almost haggard, and unlike any-one else, immediately took a chair.

"This will not do," he said, when she had told her story *yet again*, complete with interruptions. "We are not the full Court, and I have half a mind to summon Emmerian. This would be a much simpler exercise if Private Neya could be present when the Court convenes."

"You know why that is not wise," Sanabalis said quietly.

"I concur," Lord Diarmat said. "At the moment, she is en-tirely unprepared for presentation to the Emperor."

The Arkon nodded. "Her lessons were to start this week, I believe."

"Indeed," Diarmat replied. He then turned to the Arkon and said, "I accept the assignment, Arkon."

He might as well have been speaking in his native tongue for all the sense he made. Tiamaris came to her rescue, in a fashion. "It has been decided," he said, "that Lord Diarmat, who deals primarily with the training and selection of the Palace Guard—as well as its command—will be your instruc-tor in matters of etiquette in the Dragon Court."

CHAPTER 21

"By *who*?"

"The Dragon Court," was Diarmat's reply. This reply, rife with cool condescension, had more weight than any of the previous comments he'd made. "I, however, concur with the accepted opinion that the start of those lessons will be somewhat delayed until the current crisis is resolved. All of the current crises," he added. "To that point—how shall we resolve the matter of the Keeper?"

They were silent. It was the Arkon who rose, heavily, as if the weight of his own body was too cumbersome for speed. "I will speak with the Emperor in light of this new information. The Keeper did not recommend against making the attempt to diffuse the magic necessary for the portal to open. He merely stated that it would be—in his *opinion*—ineffective."

"If it's ineffective," Kaylin said, keeping her voice as quiet and even as possible, "can we go back to the first plan?"

"Which would be?"

"The Tha'alani and the Linguists."

"That would be wise, yes. The Swords are already stretched to their limits. You may find yourself on duty as a Sword, rather than a Hawk, in a few days' time."

"Is it?"

"Pardon?"

"A few days? What has Master Sabrai said?"

"Master Sabrai's communications are now routed through couriers, but his estimation at this point is that we have a total of four days."

Four days.

"He was not, for reasons I'm assured you understand, certain of his estimate, and offered it with grave reluctance."

"Have you already called in the Arcanists?"

"Some negotiations are currently underway. At the moment, they are not your concern." The Arkon paused, and then said—in theory to Sanabalis, "I deal less frequently with mortals than you, Lord Sanabalis. I have dealt far less frequently with this particular mortal. What is she hiding?"

Kaylin had never been one of nature's natural liars; she stiffened and hoped she neither paled nor reddened.

Diarmat, whose actual interaction with Kaylin—their previous two encounters involving no spoken words—was the sum of this meeting, frowned. "Hiding?" he said, softly. For a Dragon.

Sanabalis grimaced. "Private."

She was silent for a long, long moment, and when she did choose to speak, she spoke directly to Lord Sanabalis. He understood the nature of the Elemental Garden; he'd been *in* it, during the last crisis that involved Evanton. He understood that the elements were bound to it in ways that not even their Keeper fathomed.

"I think the Devourer has been looking for this world for a long time."

"The Keeper told you this?" Diarmat said. He was the first person to break the extended silence that had followed her words. As if they'd been lightning, he spoke with thunder's voice.

"No."

"And you are now familiar enough with the so-called Devourer and his history that you can make this claim?"

"No."

More silence. It was Sanabalis who broke it this time. "I believe the Private's hesitation involves the utter lack of solid fact upon which to base this theory. It *was* your theory?"

She nodded. "It's my theory, or my intuition. Evanton didn't entirely agree with it. He didn't disagree, either."

"What, exactly, is this theory based *on?*"

"The Elemental Garden exists only in this world."

The Arkon had resumed his seat, but he no longer looked tired or old. His eyes, unlike the slightly orange eyes of the rest of the Dragons present, were a lambent shade of gold; under any other circumstance, Kaylin would have cautiously said he looked happy.

"The Keeper supports the World theory."

"It's not really that theoretical anymore, in my opinion," Kaylin replied. She quickly added, "The Keeper believes in the existence of multiple worlds. I didn't ask why." In part, she hadn't asked because it now seemed so bloody obvious they did exist.

"And the Elemental Garden's existence?"

"He was quite certain about that. It exists here. He…" She hesitated, and then shrugged. "I think *this* world is the original world. The first world. It's why the Elemental Garden exists in this world, and in no other. I think—Evanton wasn't as certain about this—that it's the *Garden* in some ways that provides the connection between this world and the others. They find it because all of the worlds have to touch it somehow."

"You—you came up with this theory on your own?" The

Arkon's jaw was slightly open. It was the most surprised she had ever seen him.

"It's not proven," she said instead. "But…the elements came from somewhere. They're not just fire, just water. Or earth, or air. They're alive. They don't age, but…they do change. Slowly, and with contact from every other world. They knew—I'm certain they knew—about the portal. They didn't try to communicate their knowledge. They *can* communicate, when there's a danger. They have in the past."

"But I think this portal's flux still feels natural to them." She hesitated, because she knew what Diarmat would ask next. He didn't disappoint her.

"How do you know this?"

"Because I could hear them."

Kaylin, who had never overvalued silence, liked it less than usual now—mostly because she couldn't try to fit words in to cover the awkwardness their absence underlined. Diarmat's eyes were orange, and his hands were fists. He kept them where she could see them.

Sanabalis cleared his throat, which was only marginally less awkward than Kaylin's words would probably have been. "You spoke with the contents of the Keeper's… Garden."

The way he said the last word caused Kaylin to frown. "Why do you call it that?"

"Because it was not always called a Garden. I believe that to be a conceit introduced by the most recent Keeper."

She wondered what it had been called before, and decided she didn't actually *want* to know. "I have an affinity for one of the elements," she replied quietly.

"Water."

She nodded. Hesitated again.

"Given the reluctance with which you speak in times of

crisis," the Arkon said, his voice as sharp as Kaylin's best knife, "one might think you've forgotten that you are not, in fact, immortal."

Taking the hint, Kaylin said, "They weren't concerned with the portal. They...were concerned, in a fashion, with the Devourer."

This produced another silence.

"They could sense the Devourer?"

She nodded. "I couldn't ask them what the Devourer *is* or what it intends. I couldn't ask them what *they* are or what they intend, not unless I suddenly become immortal."

"You tried." Sanabalis's words were not a question.

"Yes. I tried anyway. They can sense the Devourer, and the Devourer can sense *them*. I think he's looking for them. And I think," she added quietly, "they want to be found."

"What they want is not of concern to the Dragon Court," Diarmat said coldly. He might have added more, but the Arkon lifted a hand, demanding his silence. To her surprise, he complied.

"Kaylin," the Arkon now said. "I am aware of what the water means to the Tha'alani, and I am aware of the role you played, in both the preservation of that meaning, and the preservation of the Tha'alani themselves. The water desired, in some part, to aid you."

She nodded. "But not entirely."

"No. Do you think that the water now desires its freedom, and that it hopes that the Devourer's presence will somehow weaken the Keeper enough to grant that?"

"No."

The most feared Librarian in the world pushed himself out of his chair. "What, then, does it desire?"

"Arkon—" Sanabalis began.

The Arkon lifted a hand again. Sanabalis was older than Diarmat, but he, too, fell silent.

She took a deep breath, held it, and expelled. "I think—from what the water said—that the elements were not separate entities when they were first...created. Or born. Or whatever. They were *one* thing."

The Arkon took a while to form an answer to the comment; no one criticized the speed at which *he* thought, not even Kaylin, although she was probably the only one tempted to do so. "The elements we summon do not...desire...the company of any other element." It was a polite way of putting it. Kaylin, who had now learned just enough from Sanabalis's lectures, offered during her many, many attempts to light a bloody candle, nodded. She knew that fire, water, earth, and air were inimical to each other. They desired the dominance of their form. It was why the ability to control the magic of the elements' names was so profoundly important.

"I cannot, therefore, see how they could have existed as one being."

"I don't think they could exist that way *now*," she replied. She spoke quietly.

"Sit down, please. I tire of watching you pace."

Since she wasn't pacing this was a tad unfair, but she did take the seat closest to him. "The water said something that implied that whatever it was that once gave them the ability, in all their disparate desires, to coexist was the thing that was...lost...in their separation.

"I think it's just as elemental as they are. I think—I think maybe the Ancients, and the people who lived elsewhere, were trying to figure out what it *wanted* while it was destroying worlds. But...what does *fire* want? Or water? Or any of the elements? How do you talk to a fire?"

"You've said you do," was the dry reply.

"I talk *at* it. It listens, sometimes. It doesn't really have a conversation. And it doesn't...plan. I know it would walk across the world, burning everything it touched—but it wouldn't plan to do so, and it wouldn't be doing it in anger, or rage, or even desire. It would just *do it*."

"And the Devourer? You think it eats worlds in the same way?"

She nodded. Frowned. "No."

"No?"

"Not exactly the same. I don't know what it *is*. I know fire, or water, or earth, or air—I can touch all those things, or they can touch me. But I'm not sure what primal element the Devourer is—or was supposed to be."

"And the water could not tell you this."

"No. I think it tried. I think it came as close as something like water could. But, no. I didn't understand. It...it eats *words*, Arkon. The Devourer eats true words."

"Interesting." He now turned to Diarmat. "The Emperor must be informed of this new turn of events."

"We have no answers to the questions he is likely to pose," Diarmat pointed out, in a flat voice.

"We have the Keeper's answer to the question of how the portal should be closed. It can't be, in the Keeper's opinion."

Diarmat nodded. He turned, then, and left the room.

The Arkon waited until the door had closed at his back. "Well?" he said, in a slightly sharper tone.

"I think the Devourer *will* come. I don't know if he can come through the portal itself, because I have *no idea* how the other worlds were destroyed. But...even if he comes, it's not instant. In at least one world, people had time to discuss their options. Some felt they could withstand the Devourer, and chose to stay. Some traveled to other worlds.

"I don't think they reached the decision to leave lightly,

and it wasn't organized overnight, or in the blink of an eye. They knew. We have no idea," she added, "whether or not the people who are coming here *now* are coming because their world has been eaten. They could have fled for some other reason. We simply won't know until they arrive *and* we can communicate with them."

The Arkon nodded. But he was still not satisfied, and Kaylin was, momentarily, grateful that she had never, ever, had the Arkon as a teacher. "If you feel that the Devourer is in some essential way a fifth element," he finally said, "it stands to reason that you *also* believe that it has a home, or a cell, in the Elemental Garden of the Keeper."

"Yes."

"Good. How, exactly, do you intend to deliver something that has eaten whole worlds—to use your phrasing, since I feel it is very inexact—into such a cell?"

"I don't know."

The Arkon raised a brow.

"Thank you," Sanabalis told him unexpectedly, "for sending Lord Diarmat on his mission."

"I did say time was of the essence," the Arkon responded, "and we will no doubt hear any arguments that arise from these revelations shortly. But at least we are spared a morning of preventing ourselves from eating Arcanists."

"I am," was the slightly emphasized reply.

"Ah," the Arkon said, rising at last from the chair that seemed almost thronelike in his presence, "you mistake me." He offered Kaylin the strangest of smiles. "I fully intend to accompany Private Neya."

The accompanying did not, however, occur immediately. The three Dragons, including Tiamaris, who had been silent and who did not look particularly *pleased*, now left Sanabalis's rooms.

"Food," Sanabalis said, just before he closed the door, "will be sent. Given the regular requirements of mortals in this regard, I suggest you avail yourself of the opportunity."

While they were eating, Severn said, "You remember who Lord Diarmat is when he's not in Court session?"

Kaylin nodded. "The Commander of the Imperial Guard."

"Good. You've some knowledge of his reputation?"

She chewed, swallowed, and emptied half a glass of water, most of it into her mouth. "No. He's a Dragon."

"He's considered the most conservative and least approachable of the Dragon Lords. He makes Mallory look lackadaisical."

"How?"

"He's said to be particularly unforgiving at any obvious lack of respect. One sign of respect in his books is the ability to *be punctual*."

Kaylin felt the food in her mouth begin to turn to ash. Or dust. "How does he handle lack of punctuality for emergencies?"

"As long as the emergency is your death, you're fine. On the other hand? He generally considers anyone who is not a Dragon to be beneath contempt or notice. Your background in the fiefs isn't likely to matter much to him at all."

She said a very loud nothing.

"Your transcripts wouldn't generally matter, but given the number of complaints about both punctuality and attitude, they'll probably be your bigger barrier to success."

"Where success in this case means surviving?"

"Pretty much." He wasn't smiling.

Then again, neither was Kaylin. They were facing the possible end-of-the-world, and somehow it was the fact that *Diarmat* was going to be her teacher that now filled her with a sense of horrible foreboding.

Seven, who knew her better than anyone, said, "Well, at least Diarmat's added a possible silver lining to the cloud of failure to somehow capture or contain the Devourer. Hard to pass an essential class when there's no world left in which to take it."

"Great. Never take a job as Chief Morale Officer, hmm?"

He did laugh, then.

Sanabalis entered the room alone. "Tiamaris," he told them, dispensing with the titles that Kaylin remembered to use only under duress, "has departed for his fief. He will consult with the Tower, and either return or send a message."

"Are we going to the quarantined quarter?"

"At the moment? No. The Arkon is once again ensconced in the Library. He is researching some esoterica which may, or may not, prove useful. Word has been sent, via courier, to the High Halls. If an appropriate reply is not forthcoming, it is to the High Halls that you, and Corporal Handred, will be sent."

Kaylin grimaced. She had a feeling that the Consort was still going to be pissed off at her, and didn't particularly relish that meeting. Sanabalis, however, instead of dismissing them, took a chair opposite the ones the two Hawks now occupied. "The Emperor has—reluctantly—agreed to accede to the advice of the Keeper."

"It wasn't advice, Sanabalis."

"If the Keeper is at all familiar with you, Private, he must be well aware that in an emergency your desire to inform people of the facts is at odds with what is generally considered discretion. We have therefore assumed that he intended the information to travel from you to the Court. Lord Diarmat is not pleased with your role as liaison, but accepts the fact that no formal liaison can, or will, be accepted." He fell silent for a moment, and then added, "Lord Diarmat is the most exact—and exacting—of the Court. He is willing to suspend the beginning of your lessons until the resolution of this conflict.

"Or until next week, to the day. Whichever comes first."

His expression made clear that there was no point in arguing; Kaylin wasn't tempted to try. She did, however, feel it fair to ask why.

"It would have been extremely convenient to have you present in Court. Diarmat is not a man who enjoys being a conduit for another's words, and he was in that unenviable position. He is not, however, willing to be in that position again because of your lack of competence at something as simple as reasonable behavior."

"His words?"

"Not his exact words, no. I will refrain from repeating those. It is not a concession to your sensibilities, such as they are," he added, as she opened her mouth. "It is an attempt to spare your hearing."

She shut up.

"Eat," he told her, looking out the window toward the flags of the Halls of Law. "The Emperor has asked the Swordlord to prepare his men for a very large, very unstable group of strangers, most of whom will not speak any of our official languages. He has sent word to Ybelline and the Tha'alanari school, and she should be present shortly. The Linguists are also waiting—that meeting, which you will be expected to attend, will occur in the Library.

"When your duties at the Palace are done for the day, you are to return to Elani street. There, you will spend whatever time you deem necessary with the Keeper." He hesitated, and then added, "There is some possibility that you will see the Dragon Court, in full, in Elani street. They will not be present in their human forms.

"For that reason, the quarantine will be in full effect until further notice. You may inform Evanton of this fact."

"Oh, I'm sure he already knows. If you could make sure that his apprentice can get to and from the market, that would be helpful."

"I will leave that in your hands."

Some two hours of silence—which was accompanied by food—later, Kaylin and Severn were escorted, by Sanabalis, to the Library.

Ybelline was waiting, as were two members of the Tha'alani that Kaylin recognized. One was Scoros, a gray-haired, middle-aged man with an expression so severe he would have made a fabulous Sergeant. He was, she recalled, one of the founding teachers in the Tha'alanari. The other, also an older male, was Draalzyn. Kaylin felt her brows lift into her hairline.

"Missing persons is off your schedule?" she asked.

Although he, too, was one of the oldest of the serving Tha'alani, his face had not set into unfriendly lines more reminiscent of stone than flesh. "The office during the current crisis is not terribly busy," he told her quietly. "The Swords have a triage system, and they will not let anyone pass the barricades if they do not feel the situation urgent enough.

"I imagine, once some resolution has been arrived at, the office will be far, far too busy for a single Tha'alani."

"Mallory must be having kittens."

"The Sergeant is aware of the state of emergency, and it

must be noted that *his* department's use of magic is the most minimal and careful in the entirety of the Halls."

"Oh, I'm sure it is. Mallory never met a rule he didn't love."

Severn gave her a look; she subsided. She was never going to like Mallory, and Mallory was never going to like her. Draalzyn, on most days, didn't particularly care for Mallory, either, but he was managing to be more than fair.

Draalzyn lifted his chin slightly, and then lowered it; he was conversing with either Ybelline or Scoros. They would do this until the Linguists arrived; they seldom conversed in this utter silence otherwise. Kaylin, Severn, and the Dragons didn't seem to count, a fact which once might have infuriated Kaylin, but which she now accepted as the compliment it was.

She was surprised when Ybelline touched her shoulder, and she turned toward the Tha'alani castelord, whose stalks were weaving in a delicate, slow dance. The movement of those stalks was, in some ways, a second layer of conversation. Its meaning was completely clear to her. She nodded.

Ybelline touched her forehead with those stalks.

The Tha'alaan was not as quiet or as serene as its three representatives were. It was never exactly silent; as the living racial memory of the Tha'alani people, it couldn't be. But for the most part, when you wanted to speak to your ancestors, you went *looking* for them.

The Tha'alaan was not silent today. More than three voices could be heard, and they were speaking over each other, or around each other. In a room, this would have muddied all syllables to a point where only focus and concentration would make them clear. It wasn't as difficult in the Tha'alaan—but it was close.

Kaylin, Ybelline said.

There was a ripple in outward discussion, and then a greeting that seemed to echo as tens of voices or more picked it up. Someone young—and it was obvious that it *was* a young voice, although how, Kaylin couldn't immediately tell—said, *Is the world going to end again?* She sounded inordinately pleased with herself, and somewhat excited. There was, of course, a tiny edge of fear in the words, but the consciousness just didn't stretch far enough to truly imagine the end of the world.

No, Kaylin told her, hoping it was the truth.

Of course, the hope *also* translated into the Tha'alaan, which was the problem with thinking. Because the Tha'alani themselves were raised within the Tha'alaan, to an extent that made lying sort of pointless, Kaylin's muddied thoughts immediately prompted a flood of questions from voices that had been quiet until that point.

Kaylin grimaced at Ybelline, by way of apology.

What I meant, she said, *was that the world is not ending if we have anything to say about it.*

Are there monsters?

There are always *monsters,* Kaylin replied firmly. *Not all of the monsters, however, look dangerous.*

Will you talk to the Tha'alaan?

Kaylin started to withdraw from Ybelline, and Ybelline caught her hands. *Tell them,* she said.

Yes.

Will you tell us what she says?

If I can. I can only...visit the Tha'alaan. I can't live here.

Why not?

Because, another voice said, *she's deaf, idiot.*

There was a wave of concern and mild disapproval, more felt than heard. But feeling it was enough. Kaylin, however, said, *No. It's true. I'm deaf. It's what I know. And... I need to talk with Ybelline, now. I'm not used to this, and I can't talk to lots of people all at the same time.*

Ybelline smiled, and again, this was more felt than seen. *What do you require of us, Kaylin?*

I need you to teach the Linguists what you already know. The language, or what you have of it. Those people are coming. How long they'll survive, I don't know—but we need to be able to speak with them. She hesitated, and then said, *Ybelline, do you know the* names *of the elements? All of them?*

This produced a frown. It was not a frown of disapproval; it was more of a grimace. *I know,* she finally said, *what the Tha'alaan knows. Why?*

That question was echoed in silence by Scoros and Draalzyn. Kaylin was now guarding her thoughts like a Dragon guarded its hoard, not so much for her own safety, but because she had been reminded, by the naive intrusion of a child— or children—that what the Tha'alaan heard, it remembered.

A portal—Ybelline saw a painting of it in the Oracles' Hall, and I'm pretty sure it's accurate—is going to open in Elani street in four days.

They were Tha'alani, and they knew about the portal because Ybelline knew. *Four?*

By the Oracles' best guess. That could be off by a few days, but only in one direction, if I know Master Sabrai. He's not a man who reaches for the middle when he knows we're facing a crisis. People will come through that portal, probably a few thousand. We have no solid estimate of numbers. This is all guesswork. They're likely to be armed, but they're also likely to be underfed and underslept.

Are they of the people?

It took Kaylin a moment to understand what the question actually meant. *They're deaf,* she replied. *With luck, you'll be able to deal with the Linguists in the Palace, and* they'll *be able to speak to the travelers. I don't know if the travelers will have any experience with Tha'alani, or people like them, but...* She grimaced.

If they don't, you'll probably be one of their worst nightmares, so direct interaction is the Court of last resort.

Which means?

A lot of people will probably be dead before you're asked.

This is not the whole of your concern. It was Scoros who spoke, and his voice was as flat in the Tha'alaan as it would have been in the room. *You asked us about the names of the elements. Are you concerned that the newcomers will be mages?*

The thought, which hadn't even occurred to Kaylin, filled her with almost instant horror, in part because it was a damn good question. *I wasn't,* she admitted.

Then why is the question relevant?

There's something else caught on the outside of the world. Which is what I'll call anything that isn't part of the world we can see and touch, for now. It was called the Devourer. I think it belongs in the Elemental Garden, with the water, fire, earth, and air. I...don't know how to put him there, but I think that's the only option we have. And to do that, I think we'll need to speak with the elements, and to do that we need people who know their names.

CHAPTER 22

The Linguists arrived shortly thereafter. There were three, one woman, and two men; none of them could be called young, although standing beside the Arkon made them look a little more robust than they might have in other circumstances. They were, clearly, intimidated by the presence of the Dragons, although not to the point of cowering in the farthest corner. On the other hand, they were *also* intimidated by the presence of the Tha'alani.

Given the two obvious threats, they clearly didn't fear the Hawk. Kaylin grimaced, and then forced her face into something resembling a smile. She turned that smile on Ybelline and waited until Ybelline's natural presence transformed it into something more genuine. She moved toward, rather than away from, the Tha'alani castelord, and she spoke, briefly, of the Foundling Halls, because Catti was pushing for another visit to the quarter.

Ybelline took this in stride. Scoros raised a brow; Draalzyn, who was, of the three, accustomed to dealing with humans in crisis, rather than in the suspected commission of a crime, had steeled himself for their lack of ease.

But the discussion had some of the intended effect on the

listeners, and they relaxed—albeit slowly—before they began
to discuss the matter at hand.

"But you're *certain,*" the woman said, drawing slightly
closer to Kaylin, in spite of the fact that this *also* brought her
closer to the Tha'alani, "that this is an entirely *new* language?"

"Lord Sanabalis seemed to think it was, and it's not a language that's used in the City. It may have some variants on
the outer edges of the Empire. I don't travel much."

"No? Oh, no, I suppose your line of work would prohibit it.
We were informed that the Tha'alani understand the language."

"That would not be *entirely* accurate. But the Tha'alani
castelord," Kaylin added, putting emphasis on the title, "has
heard and absorbed some of it. Not enough to speak well, but
enough to give you the information. She's not a Linguist,"
Kaylin added, in case it needed to be said.

The man now frowned. "You could read the minds of people who speak this unknown language, and understand it?"

Ybelline said, "I did not directly read their minds or
thoughts. It is one way of learning a language, but it is *not*
quick, and it requires constant contact."

"So if my thoughts were in a language you don't speak—"

Ybelline lifted a delicate hand. "I would understand your
thoughts," she replied.

"You're saying thought and language aren't entwined?"

"I am not saying that, no. But I would understand your
thoughts, regardless. I am not in the habit of repeating those
thoughts to any save those the Emperor chooses, and the
words I would speak would not necessarily be the words
you would think. But not all thought forms around words,
and strong reaction or strong emotion is often separate from
them."

"Which," Kaylin said, stepping in, "is beside the point.
Ybelline has heard, and can understand, some of the lan-

guage. What she knows, she's shared with her companions, Scoros and Draalzyn. They're here *solely* to give you the information in their possession. If we had time, they wouldn't be here at all. They could write or transcribe what occurred.

"We don't have time."

The man raised a peppered brow. He didn't look down his nose, but he wasn't all that tall. "Learning a language is not something done in a matter of days, Officer."

"Private Neya. And that's unfortunate because learning enough *functional* language is something that has to be done in four days, if we're lucky."

While the Linguists picked up their collective jaws and added panic of an entirely different nature to the mix of their suspicions, Kaylin retreated to the back wall. She watched them; she couldn't help it. But she had to admit that their reaction to the Tha'alani was a *lot* more civil than hers had once been.

"Ybelline doesn't need your protection," Severn whispered. He was smiling, but his tone was grave.

"I know." The oldest Linguist present had volunteered to allow contact first, and that had helped, because even with the Tha'alani stalks forcing her face to stay relatively still, her sudden widening of eyes couldn't be mistaken for anything *but* excitement. She actually physically turned toward her colleagues once, breaking the connection; Ybelline did not hold or restrain her. But the minute the connection was broken—and she realized it—she turned back in a different panic, as if she was afraid to lose what had been offered.

That kind of eagerness dispelled fear quickly.

"Ybelline is good at what she does," Severn added.

"I know. I know she is." Kaylin grimaced. "It's my bad conscience, really. I hated them so blindly for so long, I'm sensitive to anyone else's fear because I expect it, and I expect it to be as bad as mine was. You didn't, so you're not."

"And you like her."

"And I like her. She doesn't deserve to have to deal with people even a tenth as bad as I was."

"If she doesn't, however, they'll remain in fear. This way? Person by person she dispels it."

"And she pays."

"The privilege of being castelord."

CHAPTER 23

The next morning began with a call from the midwives' guild. Where morning in this case meant black, cloudy skies, with just the barest hint of moonlight in the darkened streets. Kaylin had crawled out of bed, and left about fifteen palm prints on the wall and the frame of her mirror before she actually managed to touch it.

It was Marya. She was grim and pale, but she usually was when she mirrored Kaylin; if things were going well enough that she looked normal and businesslike, Kaylin was entirely unnecessary. She therefore dispensed entirely with the usual pleasantries. But then again, so did Marcus or anyone *else* who used this particular mirror. Some of her friends, who had keys, didn't even bother with the courtesy of a mirror at all.

"We need you down at the guildhall," Marya said, her lips a thin line.

"Guildhall? Not at a house?"

"No. The birthing itself was no threat to the mother's life. And not to the…child's."

"Why do you need me?"

"You'll see. We're revisiting the boundaries of the danger

zone," she added, running her hand through her hair. "You might want to mention this to your Sergeant."

Kaylin stopped by the Halls of Law on her way to the midwives' guild. She was, in fact, early, and this generally caused shock—but most people were tired enough given the extra shifts and the state of emergency that they couldn't manage sarcasm for all that long.

Caitlin could, however, manage concern.

"I can't stay," Kaylin told her. "I'm heading over to the midwives' guildhall now. I think I'll be back on time, if nothing is horribly wrong."

Since babies didn't have much sense of day or night before they were born—and according to many new mothers, after, either—the Halls could be either catastrophically busy or empty at *any* time of day. Kaylin hadn't exactly run all the way to the guildhall, but she'd walked at a brisk clip. She took the steps two at a time, and entered the somewhat dingy front area.

Marya was waiting for her in the long hall where many of the beds were. In person, she looked even more exhausted, and the circles under her eyes were almost, but not quite, bruises. She wasn't standing by an occupied bed; she was standing by the old and worn set of cupboards in which emergency supplies and pillowcases were kept. Beneath the slightly warped cupboards was a large crate that looked as if it should have held eggs.

"Good," Marya said, as Kaylin approached. She hefted the crate off the counter with an ease that suggested she was either Leontine in strength, or it was lighter than it looked, and held it out.

Kaylin took it out of her hands; it was very light. "What is it?"

"Your problem," was the curt reply.

"Is it fragile?"

"I have no idea." The midwife then turned until only her profile was exposed, and ran her hands over her eyes. "It was a long night," she finally said. "And the only thing we're currently grateful for is it was not the family's first pregnancy."

"What happened?"

"We were outside of the area of quarantine. Chevaron is relocating people we know about now. Did you—"

"Yes. I spoke to the Sergeant. Word is being sent up the ranks. He's going to want to know why."

"You're going to tell him what I'm now telling you. Talking to the Law gives me hives, and it takes a while."

Kaylin nodded sympathetically, because Marcus on a bad day gave *her* hives. She also failed to point out that she was, technically, part of said Law.

"We were outside of the quarantine area. A few streets over, nearer the riverside on Howlhorn. The birth itself was routine, up to a point."

"How?"

"We had heartbeat, and it was fairly regular, fairly calm. But...the baby's head, when it became visible, was not what we expected. It *is* rounded, and it *is* both warm and soft, although it's much less soft now than it was. The mother had no more than the usual difficulty birthing the baby."

"It wasn't a normal baby."

"No. It wasn't, like the others, some variant on normal, either. We're not entirely certain what it is. Open the crate."

Kaylin set it down on the counter from which Marya had removed it. The lid was loose enough it wasn't hard to remove it; beneath the lid were blankets. She glanced at Marya, and then began to gently unwind some of the blanket.

"It's...an egg?"

"Yes. Very much so. Before you ask, we have no idea what's inside it. It hasn't hatched, and after some debate, we've decided that it is not our problem."

"The mother—"

"Both of the parents are, at the moment, in shock and mourning. I don't think the egg would have survived there. I'm not sure," she added, as Kaylin replaced the blanket and the lid, "that that wouldn't have been a mercy, in the end. I have no idea where you take it, or what you do with it, or whether or not mages will be interested—but I want it out of my hands."

Kaylin once again lifted the box. She turned toward the doors, and then turned back. "One way or another," she said quietly, "it'll be over soon."

Marya, ever practical, didn't ask how. Instead, she said, "How much is that area going to *grow* until it is?"

"I don't know. We could only trace the circumference of the area the last time because it rained blood."

Kaylin, after a brief hesitation, took the egg in its crate home. She considered dropping it off at the Foundling Halls, but decided against it, given how much it might otherwise resemble exotic food. Instead, she left it in its crate, and stood it in as much sunlight as she was willing to let into the room when she wasn't also in it. Then she headed out to work, aware that by now she had just won someone in the office the betting pool. She wasn't sure who.

Marcus, predictably, was several inches bulkier on first sight. This would be because his hair was standing on end in various clumps. His claws were entirely visible, and there was an invisible—and wide—circle around his desk which everyone was carefully avoiding. This didn't mean the office was quiet, mind. The window was chatting to any poor fool who stood still for more than thirty seconds.

To avoid being classed as one of them, Kaylin headed straight to the duty roster. It was only barely legible; if you'd had the misfortune of starting work this week, it wouldn't have been. She was, no surprise, on Palace duty. So was Severn. Teela and Tain were on boundary duty, as were most of the rest of the Barrani Hawks. They had all also pulled double shifts.

Taking the better part of valor, she headed to the Quartermaster's, and from there, out toward the Imperial Palace. There was no carriage waiting for her; there was a familiar Corporal.

"You're late," he said, with just enough of a lift in the last syllable that it might have been a question.

"This lose you the betting pool?"

He grinned, but didn't answer. No one liked to *lose* bets, but Severn had always been pretty laid-back after the fact.

"The midwives called me in."

"When?"

"Morning, more or less. I was actually here earlier but left." She hesitated, and then added, "The magical spill zone seems to have grown in the last day or two."

"Problem with a birth?" The easy smile slid off his face; his eyes were both dark and serious.

"You could say that. It wouldn't be entirely accurate. The *birth* was fine. It did not, however, produce a baby."

He was silent for a few blocks. "The parents?"

"Traumatized, by all reports."

"And the...offspring?"

"I honestly don't know. I'll show you later. It's at my place." When his brows—both of them—rose, she added, "It was an egg. I didn't leave it lying on its back, starving."

Lord Diarmat was, to Kaylin's surprise—and immediate discomfort—in the large halls just beyond the first checkpoint. No Dragon was a comforting sight first thing in the morning, but Kaylin was used to bristling Leontine by this point. She straightened her posture, and executed what she hoped was a crisp bow. Judging by his expression, it was a vain hope.

"You're late," he told them curtly.

She decided to follow Severn's lead, and said nothing, which was just as well; he didn't bother to wait for a reply. Instead, he turned on his heel and began a brisk stride down the hall. Given the difference in the length of their strides, this meant Kaylin was almost jogging to keep up; Severn didn't have that problem. Not keeping up, however, didn't seem the wise option.

He led them, not surprisingly, to the Library. The door wards were still down; it was possibly the only thing she'd miss when—and if—things returned to normal. In the absence of door wards, however, there were now Imperial Palace Guards. They looked like perfectly gleaming statues as Lord Diarmat walked through them.

But they moved when Kaylin attempted to follow. She gave them her name, rank, and reason for existence. The last, however, was lost to their famous sense of humor. Like Dragons, they had none.

To be fair, they also demanded the same information of Severn. Diarmat did not seem to hold this delay against them. Much. She would have said the Dragon Lord was in a bad mood, but had the sinking suspicion that this wouldn't have been accurate; he had a face that looked enough like chiseled stone that a smile would have probably cracked it.

"The Arkon," he told them both, when they had fully entered the first—and most well-known—of the Arkon's many rooms, "has been waiting."

The Arkon, with Lord Sanabalis as a companion, was indeed waiting. He was more or less silent, as was Sanabalis. There were four Imperial Guards who were keeping them company, if statues were company. There was, however, no sign of Ybelline or any of the other Tha'alani.

If the stiff formality of Lord Diarmat allowed for—and accepted—no excuses, the Arkon's stiffness was of a different sort. It demanded excuses, with the understanding that none of the excuses offered would actually be acceptable. Kaylin found this more comfortable, because she was used to Marcus. She had also, by this time, become familiar enough with the Arkon that while groveling she kept her voice calm and fact-focused. Where she wasn't willing to share facts—the egg, for instance—she closed the gap between sentences in a way that suggested the information wasn't important. She also, however, lifted her chin, exposing her throat.

The Arkon did not breathe fire or snort smoke as she spoke. Instead, he glanced at Sanabalis.

Sanabalis nodded. "We've received word from Master Sabrai."

"He's narrowed the timing down?" Kaylin asked sharply.

"In a manner of speaking. Last night every Oracle in the Halls had what he feels are Oracular dreams or visions."

"Everly?"

"He sketched. The majority of his work is already done. There were no significant changes to the painting," he added, aware of Kaylin's concern. "And he seems to have recovered from his previous endeavors."

"The others?"

"The visions as an aggregate are clearer than they were. I believe they will refine the information you already have. But Master Sabrai felt that the incidence of Oracles was now high enough that he could more accurately assess the timing of the event."

"How long do we have?"

"A day and a half. The…enlargement…of the contentious zone is in keeping with his estimate."

Kaylin frowned.

"The Imperial Order of Mages has made some estimates of their own," Sanabalis added. "They are not in any way accurate, and require some assumptions that not all of the members are comfortable making with regards to the raw magical potential required to open a portal of this nature."

"How would they know?"

"That, indeed, is the crux of their discomfort. Magic and the amount of raw power any single event requires is not strictly correlative. But the events with the midwives' guild indicate that at base, some of those assumptions are not entirely without merit." He turned back to the Arkon.

The Arkon rose. "Let us visit the site of Everly's painting." He turned to Diarmat and added, "The Library is to be closed completely. There are no exceptions in my absence."

"Understood, Arkon."

"If the Emperor requires access to the Library," the Arkon added, as he began to walk, "he can make his displeasure known. He is young and in good health. A few miles of city streets shouldn't cause his voice much trouble."

An Imperial Carriage was waiting in the yard, doors open. Lord Diarmat accompanied them only as far as the yard. He asked the Arkon if he had reconsidered his stand on an escort; the Arkon's lack of reply was obviously reply enough.

Sanabalis, however, said, "We will not divert men from their watch on the Arcanum at this time. Your men are good. They are not, however, Dragons."

To this, Lord Diarmat made no reply. Nor did Sanabalis point out that two of the Hawks were with them; it might have appealed to Kaylin's vanity, but it wouldn't have done much for Diarmat. When the carriage door had closed and the carriage itself was well on its way, the Arkon said to Sanabalis, "The young weary me. If I were not already mired in things barely understood, I believe I would dredge up the energy to find his queries insulting." His expression was pinched and somewhat peevish.

It was also, apparently, safe enough to evoke a smile from Sanabalis. "Diarmat has always taken the duties he has accepted with gravity."

"Yes, I understand that. But there is a distinct difference between gravity and the infantilization of the *rest* of his race. An escort of mortal guards?" A puff of smoke followed the words.

"From what I understand, the mortal guards are there to make sure no one offends you enough you feel forced to turn them to ash. Or eat them," Kaylin interjected.

"At my age, I am capable of showing enough restraint that I am unlikely to do either," was the curt reply. "The Tha'alani castelord will meet us at the checkpoint. We are to wait for her if she is not already there."

She was. She was not, however, alone, nor were her companions Tha'alani. They were Linguists. They were also not entirely comfortable with the complement of Swords that barred their way. Ybelline, however, was gracious enough to make the presence of armed and armored men feel both natural and almost neighborly. If the Tha'alani ever *wanted* to conquer the world—and they had, in the past, and for less usual reasons—she would be their best weapon.

But even the unflappable Tha'alani castelord raised a brow when the Arkon exited the carriage. She tendered him a very respectful bow. "Arkon?"

He chuckled. "I did say I intended to accompany the young Private."

"It is seldom, Arkon, that you are seen outside of your Library."

"The word you want is *never*." He straightened the fall of his robes and looked at the Swords. Or at the small barriers erected to prevent entry into the quarantined area. Or even at the buildings, which were much narrower, shorter, and vastly less impressive than the Imperial Palace.

"When was the last time you left the Palace?" Ybelline asked him.

"Much before you were born. Any of you," he added, "excepting only Lord Sanabalis. I see that the City is both changed and unchanged since I last chanced its streets." He walked toward the Swords, who were now standing bolt upright.

Kaylin took the opportunity to cadge a hug from the castelord as Sanabalis and the Arkon were being the walking credentials necessary to get through the Swords. Ybelline's stalks brushed her forehead.

Kaylin.

To Kaylin's surprise, the castelord was...excited. Nervous, fearful, yes—those were expected—but excited, as well. *Why?*

I'm not sure, Kaylin. But...this is where the Ancients are. Where your Keeper is. Where the water is. And the Arkon has left the Li-

brary. I am afraid of what we'll face, but...the Tha'alaan will see it
and know it forever if I am here. Where are we going?
   Good question. I'll ask.

   The answer was pointed silence. The Arkon was frequently
silent, and sometimes inscrutable—but this was not one of
those silences. Kaylin didn't have to be able to read his mind;
his expression was absolutely clear.

   "But Evanton doesn't allow Dragons *into* his store!" she
told him.

   "Ask him nicely."

   Severn chuckled. "Sanabalis has already seen the garden
once."

   "Evanton wasn't *in* the store at the time, and it was a bit of
an emergency." Her voice trailed off on the last word. Throwing her hands up, she turned and began to walk, leading the
small party. It wasn't as if the Dragons didn't already know
the way, after all.

   The streets were distinctly empty. It was a bright, clear
morning—one which would usually involve a lot of sandwich boards and small wagons ringed with the idle gossip of
the various customers who came to Elani. Kaylin found herself missing them, which surprised her. She would have bet
against the possibility a week ago.

   But it made the walk to Evanton's much shorter than it
might otherwise have been. The Arkon did pause and look
at the various storefronts with their darkened interiors and
their locked doors. "Do mortals really come here to find their
destiny or the love of their lives?"

   "That, or hair," Kaylin muttered.

   He shook his head. "I've noted the obsession with hair. I
fail to understand its significance."

   "It means we're not old," Kaylin replied.

The Arkon raised a conspicuously white brow. It lowered before she could speak. "Ah, yes. Mortality. Hair does not, apparently, prevent it."

She nodded absently, because they had reached Evanton's storefront. The gold lettering caught sunlight and reflected it, making a blur of Evanton's name. Grethan had clearly been in want of chores, because the windows were clean and gleaming; the two Dragons were reflected perfectly. *Here goes nothing.*

Grethan answered the door. The good thing about having Grethan in the shop was that he answered the door relatively quickly compared to Evanton. Evanton always moved slowly when he wasn't in the Garden; Kaylin half suspected this was deliberate. Knocking on the door usually involved a long wait, one which wasn't always rewarded. Knocking a second time, on the other hand, was rewarded with an annoyed Evanton.

Grethan never looked annoyed to see her; he often looked alarmed or nervous. Since she'd come with his castelord and two Dragons in tow, she expected alarm.

But she underestimated Ybelline. Why, after all this time, she didn't know. The Tha'alani castelord stepped around her, toward Grethan, before his eyes had finished widening. Given how wide they actually got, this wasn't miraculous speed on Ybelline's part. Grethan's mouth opened and closed, although no words followed; his stalks were weaving frantically in the air. They didn't work; Grethan had been born deaf, in Tha'alani terms; he couldn't touch the Tha'alaan on his own. Nor could he touch another person and hear—or convey—his own thoughts.

But it didn't matter. Ybelline could touch the deaf. She could touch Kaylin. And she could touch Grethan with compassion and, in the end, pride. His eyes filmed with water; hers didn't. But she smiled, and she spoke no words aloud for a few moments. When she stepped back, Grethan hurriedly brushed his eyes with the back of his hands, and then bowed—very formally—to the two Dragon Lords. He nodded, briefly, at Kaylin and Severn, but as they weren't much of a problem, she didn't expect more.

"I will get Evanton," he told them. He didn't invite them in. Nor did they attempt to enter without his invitation.

But the two Dragons turned to each other when the door slid shut. "It is as you said," the Arkon told Sanabalis. "This is not an entirely stable building."

"It can't be any worse than the High Halls," Kaylin told him.

"Perhaps. Perhaps not. Like the Keeper, the Barrani are insistent upon the absence of Dragons within their Halls. I therefore have very little in the way of comparison. And, if we are blunt, very little in the way of useful observation. But it is less of a surprise that you lost your way while you were visiting the Keeper than it might have been had you failed to successfully cross the average street." He took a breath, and might have continued, but the door once again opened, saving Kaylin from what was undoubtedly becoming a lecture in full bloom.

Evanton stood in the frame with a quiet Grethan as a shadow. He didn't look happy, but the perpetual severity of his recent expression was absent. He didn't step out of the door frame, nor did he invite the Dragons in. He did fix Kaylin with a very pointed stare before he spoke. But he offered Ybelline a genuine, if tired, smile. "He is doing well here, castelord. Or as well as can be expected of a new apprentice."

"It brings me peace to hear it," was her quiet reply. "It is more than we had the right to hope for, and less, in the end, than we did, but that is the nature and folly of love."

One brow rose, but after a moment, he nodded. He almost bowed, and Kaylin was certain he would have, had the Dragons not been present. It was to the Dragons he now turned.

"Lord Sanabalis," he said quietly. He nodded, as if he were the Dragon's equal. "And your companion?"

"The Arkon of the Imperial Library."

Evanton allowed his brows to rise. "The Arkon? I had not heard that the Arkon traveled."

"I generally do not," the Arkon replied. "And while I am not perhaps conversant with the entirety of mortal interaction, even I am aware that it is less than polite to speak of a person as if he is not present."

Evanton grimaced and slid into High Barrani. "I am not famed, unfortunately, for the quality of my manners, and as I seldom have company that is better schooled, I am accustomed to speaking my mind. My apologies, Arkon," he added, and this time, he did bow. When he rose, he said, "What brings you to my humble shop?"

"You are aware that someone will attempt to open a portal—and it will open just beyond the facade of your store in these streets?"

"I am."

"We have, at the best guess of the Master of the Oracular Halls, a day and a half. The timing is not entirely accurate."

"Did the Master of the Oracular Halls give a better estimate of the numbers we might expect?"

"No. It was not, however, our primary concern."

Evanton snorted. "It wouldn't be. What do you hope to achieve by your presence here?"

"Achieve?"

"You have left what is, if I understand it correctly, your hoard. You are here, on the very periphery of *mine*."

The Arkon raised a brow; in color it was a match for Evan-

ton's. They stood almost bristling—in totally correct postures
and with the patina of civility—while the sun inched across
the sky. It was, to Kaylin's lasting surprise, the Arkon who
blinked first. He chuckled.

Evanton's expression didn't change.

"You have some understanding of Hoard Law. It's unusual in mortals." He glanced at Kaylin. "Yes, Keeper. We
understand in all ways that this is your hoard. We will touch
nothing, harm nothing, and take nothing. Within your domain, not even the Emperor's Law supersedes your claim in
our eyes."

Evanton grimaced. "I should," he told them both, in a tone
of voice that clearly indicated he wasn't going to, "take your
oaths." He lifted a hand as the Arkon drew breath and added,
"My hearing is not what it used to be, but it *is* still functional,
and I'd like it to remain that way. I want no Dragon spoken
in my store." He swung the door wide, and added, "Lord
Sanabalis has already been dragged into my domain by a less
than well-schooled Hawk.

"Please, come in."

If the Dragons were alarmed or dismayed by the dust
and the clutter, they showed no signs of it. Given the Arkon's small, dense pockets of same, Kaylin privately thought
he hadn't even noticed. Or rather, that he hadn't noticed
the mess. He did seem to notice everything else, and even
chanced a question about one or two of the items.

"You sell these?" he asked.

"If it's on the shelf, yes."

Clearly, the idea of *selling* anything you claimed as part of
your hoard was so astonishing, no further words were forthcoming. Evanton added, into the Arkon's uncomfortable si-

lence, "You replace chairs when you break them—you replace desks the same way."

"And apprentices," the Arkon added, with a perfectly straight face.

"I would suggest that you think of the clutter in the outer part of the store as desks, chairs, or inkwells. They are within my domain but they do not define it."

This did put the Arkon more at ease. Dragons, Kaylin thought, were crazy. But then again, who wasn't? She followed at the back of the pack as Evanton led them toward the familiar rickety door at the end of a very crowded hall.

"These," Evanton said, indicating the shelves that entirely obscured the walls, "are not for sale."

The Arkon did peruse them as he walked, his gaze so sharp Kaylin suspected that he carried a memory crystal. But if he did, Evanton didn't seem concerned. He paused only once, in front of a shelf that looked to Kaylin's admittedly nonbibliographic eye like Evanton's usual mess. "I...do not recognize this book," he said.

"Which one?" Evanton turned back. This caused immediate congestion in the very narrow hall space. "Ah. The treatise on the development of languages."

"Is that what it is?"

"More or less. It's...esoteric, and it is not a linguistics paper."

"Where did you find it?"

"It came with the job," was the gruff reply. There was another moment of extended silence. "If you wish," the Keeper finally said, "and you are willing to do so, you may study its contents here."

"May I capture them?"

"You will find it resistant to memory crystals, but you may certainly make the attempt. Not, however, until the difficulty with magic that is currently plaguing the quarter is resolved. Some half dozen of the more difficult books have been moved to the Garden for the duration."

"Would those volumes also be less familiar to me?"

"I haven't a clue. I've never been much of a collector," he added. "And when I want to relax, I don't generally read. I bead."

"It is not to relax that one reads tomes of this nature," was the slightly severe reply. "But rather, to *learn*."

"At my age, I know enough to fulfill my responsibilities. Learning is for the young. Or," he added, "the sages."

"It is also for the wise."

Evanton said, "If I had been wise, I would have found a different job."

At that, the older Dragon shrugged. "We are not always capable of wisdom in our youth, and your duties are absolutely essential."

"That's what I tell myself, on most days." He turned and made his way back to the door.

The Dragons were silent as they entered the Elemental Garden. Kaylin was silent, as well, possibly for a different reason; she was holding her breath. But the Garden, at least at first glimpse, was neither raging storm nor huge expanse of grassy wilderness; it was neat, tidy, and contained. There was a small path that led between the shrines, but Kaylin's gaze went—as it always did—to the shrine of Water.

Ybelline, silent until that moment, turned not to Kaylin but to Evanton. "Might we explore the Garden while you discuss the matters that have brought the Dragon Lords to your domain?" She gestured toward Kaylin as she spoke.

"I think the young Private is necessary for this meeting," he replied. "And it may possibly prove relevant to you, as well. However," he added, "you at least are welcome to visit, Ybelline. I have heard much about you, and none of it would ever constitute a threat to what I must Keep. Indeed, it may ease the burden.

"But if you desire speech with the element of water, it might have to wait. Water is often slow to respond, when it chooses to respond at all. I am the Keeper, but I am not the Master. I cannot force or hurry what will not be forced." He spoke gravely and far more formally than he usually did.

She smiled. "I am that obvious?"

"It is obvious that you revere the water," he replied. "But the elements are *all* confined in this Garden, and they are not without petty rivalries of their own. They are already unsettled, and they are...nervous, now. I believe they are waiting," he added, looking beyond Ybelline to Kaylin.

"For?"

"The Devourer."

CHAPTER 24

Evanton didn't lead the Dragons to the stone hut that had been shelter during one raging storm; nor did he lead them to any of the shrines. Instead, he led them to what seemed the center of the Garden itself. It had curved stone benches which would easily support their weight, but also rounded stones that sported the soft moss Kaylin liked best. As Evanton felt comfortable enough to sit on those stones, Kaylin did likewise. She noted that Severn took an actual seat, as did the Dragons and Ybelline.

"What will you do?" Sanabalis asked Evanton, coming directly to the point.

Evanton raised a brow in a fashion that was almost Draconian. "I?" he asked. "What will *I* do?"

"Indeed."

"I will do very little," was his reply. "I am content— barely—to support the Private in her attempts to unify the elements."

"To what?" Kaylin asked sharply. She was, unlike the Arkon, used to being spoken about in the third person as if she weren't present.

Evanton looked, for a moment, like any frustrated teacher. "You said that the Devourer belonged in the Garden."

"I said it because the water said it. More or less."

"And I believe I made clear that the water—or for that matter the fire—has never spoken to me in the way it chooses to speak to you. It speaks to me in a different fashion, but I *am* effectively its prison warden. I cannot therefore judge truth or even possibility in its words because I can't hear them. I can, however, hear yours."

Ybelline now lifted a hand, as if Evanton were indeed a teacher, and this was a classroom. It made her look younger.

Evanton nodded. "Castelord?"

"I believe, if you allowed it, that I could speak to the water, or the water to me, as Kaylin has done. I might also be able to bespeak the other elements in the Garden."

"I'm not sure you understand the risk."

Her smile was slight, but it was, momentarily, steel. "I have the entire Tha'alaan within me, Keeper. I am aware of any risks the elements impose."

The Keeper—and he looked that, in his rich blue robes—raised a brow at her tone. To Kaylin's surprise, he turned to her. "Private?"

"It's not my Garden," she said. Then, because she realized he wanted more, added, "I would trust her with my life. All of it. Even the ugliest parts."

"And with the City?"

"With the world, if it came to that, Evanton."

"Good. Because that is precisely what I will be doing." He rose. "Lord Sanabalis. Arkon. If you desire to see more of the Garden, you are given leave to accompany us."

They rose quickly for two elder statesmen. The Arkon didn't even attempt to look dignified or bored.

★ ★ ★

Evanton was kind, in his fashion. He led them, first, to the shrine of water. The small pool lay in front of a small altar, a small stone shelf; candles burned in a candelabra on the top one. There were books here, all closed. The Arkon glanced at their spines, and his brows furrowed; he did not, however, attempt to touch any of them.

He might have been tempted, but the water rippled as they approached, and the air was utterly still. "Can it see us?" Ybelline asked Kaylin.

"I think so. Or if it doesn't see, precisely, it's aware that we're now here."

"I cannot hear it." She sounded slightly disappointed.

"Oh, neither can I. But it has a way of making itself known."

Evanton knelt by the pool's edge, both of his knees compressing moss. He laid his hands in his lap, straightened his back, and waited. Minutes passed. The only person who moved at all was Kaylin; she'd never been good at sitting still when her life didn't depend on it, and she fidgeted with the edges of her tabard, as if smoothing out invisible wrinkles.

But she didn't wait long; the ripples across the face of the pond grew stronger, as if they wanted to be waves but hadn't the room. No water escaped; not even a drop of it touched Evanton's knees as the truncated waves grew stronger. Nor did Evanton move.

Kaylin did. She came to stand beside him, taking care not to step on the edges of his robes. Lifting her face, she spoke a single word. A single *long* word. Sanabalis said, "You've learned the name of water."

"Maybe if we tried to drown the candle instead of lighting it," Kaylin replied, grimacing, "I'd have more luck." The water rose in a slender column, its outer edges constantly turning and furling; it moved faster, and faster, until it seemed as if the water itself must spin out, revealing what lay at its heart.

It did, but it splashed nothing, and what was left at its heart was a woman, transparent the way water in clear glass is. But the form it took was not familiar to Kaylin, who had seen the water take similar shape once before. Then, it had been the body and face of a young girl with bruised eyes. Now?

A woman in her prime—the way the Barrani Consort was in her prime. She was taller than Severn. Her eyes were clear, her cheekbones high, her chin tapered; her hair—such as it was—was long, and fell like a twisting drape. She wore no other clothing, and no crown, and needed neither.

They waited for her to speak; she didn't. Instead, tendrils of hair rose, like longer and clearer versions of familiar antennae. They drifted out, one at a time, toward the group.

Ybelline didn't hesitate; she reached out—with a hand—and touched one. It wrapped itself around both palm and wrist, as if anchoring itself to the castelord. Ybelline stiffened and paled, but did not otherwise move.

Severn accepted what the Tha'alani had accepted; he also reached out and touched the water. One by one, they all did, until only Kaylin remained. There was no strand for her. She waited, glancing at her companions, all now anchored to the Elemental Water; no final strand was forthcoming. She stood alone in the small grove, facing the water.

"What about me?" she finally said.

No one looked toward her, and no one answered, not even the water, whose gaze was as dark and deep as the depths of the still pool always were. Kaylin was no good at waiting unless she had no choice. She tried not to resent her exclusion, and gave up; the resentment made no difference either way.

But after a few moments, the water closed her eyes.

Evanton opened his in the same moment, and Kaylin found

herself relaxing as the rigid lines of his face lapsed into an odd expression. He rose slowly, and wiped his eyes with the backs of his hands, much as Grethan had done less than an hour ago.

"How many years have I tended this Garden?" he asked, as he turned to fully meet Kaylin's gaze. "And it still amazes me. It still awes." He shook his head. The water then released Sanabalis and the Arkon; it also released Severn. It held Ybelline, but it shifted the way it held her, offering the Tha'alani Lord not tendrils of hair, but rather, both of her open palms.

Ybelline took them quickly in her own.

"Come," Evanton told the others.

They seemed as awed by what they had seen—and what Kaylin had failed to see—as Evanton had been.

"Should I be doing anything?" Kaylin asked.

Evanton chuckled. "Oh, yes. But not, I fear, in the Garden. Not yet. Come."

"I think," Evanton told the two silent Dragons, "you know where we are to go next."

"I think," Lord Sanabalis replied, "it will be difficult to move the Arkon from this place."

But the Arkon shook himself and turned; his eyes were a shade of white that looked like bright sunlight reflected on water. "I am not mortal," he told Evanton, his voice hushed. "And what I have seen, what I have heard, will *never* leave me. It will have roots in this world for as long as I live.

"I feel young again," he added. "And there is very little in this world that can make me feel young."

Evanton, replete with the majesty of his eternally clean and impressive Keeper's robes said, with a perfectly straight face, "Can I interest you in a job?"

★ ★ ★

Since this was a Garden, no open fire raged in it. Kaylin seldom visited the fire shrine; like Ybelline, she was drawn to the peaceful depth of water. Fire burned in the heart of a bronze brazier, surrounded by flat stone tiles. Here, too, were stone benches in slight curves, which bounded the small area. There was also a shelf, with more books, and the candelabra. These candles, however, weren't burning. She'd developed a slightly nervous twitch when confronted with unlit candles, and glanced briefly at Sanabalis to see if he noticed.

But he was now as silent and remote as the Arkon, as lost in whatever thoughts the Elemental Garden evoked. Things as mundane as classrooms, even classes devoted to arcane arts, had no place here. Thank the gods.

"The water," Evanton said, "is inclined—at this place in its existence—toward the mortal. Fire by its essence is less tame. It is not, however, less approachable." He hesitated, and then added, "If the fire offers to touch you, Corporal, it is best to gently—and respectfully—decline.

"Are you ready?"

"I am ready," the Arkon said. He smiled, and rose—for he had momentarily taken a seat. "Lord Sanabalis?"

"I think I will leave you the fire," was the quiet reply. "If I understand what is necessary."

The Arkon nodded. He approached the brazier, and came to stand by Evanton's side. "Private?"

She approached more cautiously. But to Evanton, she said, "It won't burn what it doesn't want to burn."

"No. But what it desires at any given time is not simple, and not to be easily trusted. It means no malice. It is what it is." He glanced at the Arkon. "And Dragons? In youth, they are bathed in fire."

Evanton lifted his arms slowly, holding his palms out toward the fire as if it were winter and he needed the warmth. But the Arkon gently touched his sleeves, and when Evanton looked to the side, the Arkon said, "Let me." And then, as if aware of the importance of what he asked, he added, "Please."

Evanton frowned, but withdrew his hands.

"Keeper," the Dragon Lord said, "I would give you my name, if it would ease you."

"I could not learn it all in a day, and I do not think we have even that," Evanton replied. But he answered quietly, and without any of his usual edge. He also spoke High Barrani. "I will trust you here, Arkon."

The Arkon now lifted his hands, as Evanton had done, but he held them palm up, not palm out, and he said, "You may wish to cover your ears."

Evanton grimaced, but did as bid; so did Kaylin. Severn, however, had some dignity to lose; he remained standing, his hands loosely behind his back, as the Dragon roared.

Kaylin saw the words forming in the air above his hands. She'd seen similar words before, and understood that he'd chosen to speak the oldest of tongues known to the living: the tongue of the Ancients. It was said that there could be no misunderstanding in that language; Kaylin wasn't sure she believed it. No other language she knew was proof against the history and context of different people's interpretations.

Then again, this language was used by gods. Or what passed for gods. Maybe they were somehow like the Tha'alani: their understanding of each other encompassed far more than simple words. It was an understanding that eluded Kaylin, born mortal, and raised not to glory or magic or power, but to bitter winter and imminent starvation.

She felt none of the Arkon's awe. But she felt his momentary majesty; he looked like the distant face of the high, stone Aeries. The runes that floated above his palms were the color of fire: bright red, orange, yellow, with hearts of pure white. He held them; they were tethered to his booming, deafening voice.

"The name of fire," she whispered.

"Yes," Sanabalis said. It figured. Normal speech would have been drowned out by the Dragon words, but Dragons—who were not by any stretch of experience normal, as they proved time and again—apparently didn't have the usual hearing difficulties. "Watch this, and learn, Kaylin. The Arkon was a master long before I began my studies in earnest, and it has been many, many years since he has chosen to practice the whole of his art."

The fire came, then. It didn't overflow the brazier; instead, it *transformed* it. Where a small stone circle had surrounded it, there was now the barren, blackened rock of a blasted plain, and the heat beneath the soles of Kaylin's boots was almost blistering. She turned instantly to Evanton, but Evanton didn't seem alarmed; he had closed his eyes, as if he expected this.

In the center of the rock itself, fire rose in a plume, unfolding as if it were a peacock's fan, but in reds and golds and oranges. It took no mortal shape, no mortal visage, and it spoke in a crackle and hiss.

But it, too, spoke words, and they were kin to the words of the Arkon, if not their exact duplicate. She shouldn't have understood it. But she did.

Turning to Severn, she found him watching her, and he shook his head, because he knew her well enough to know what she'd been about to ask him. No. He didn't understand what either the Arkon or the fire were saying. Nor did he want to; he was content to wait, to observe, and to draw his own conclusions from whatever might happen at the finish of their odd conversation.

But whatever the outcome was, they weren't there to witness it.

"This," Evanton said, "is going to take a long time. With luck, they won't have finished by the time it's over." He turned to Kaylin. "Private."

She was watching the Arkon's face. She watched his expression, begrudging him nothing. He wasn't a child, but some element of a child's unfettered joy transformed him.

"He won't be able to do this again, will he?"

"Possibly never. It depends. Are you going to loiter here all day?" If he spoke almost deferential High Barrani to the Dragons, Kaylin clearly didn't merit the effort.

Kaylin wasn't surprised when he turned a corner, crossing a large outcropping of brown-gray rock that vanished as she followed. Severn and Sanabalis were a step behind. "Where are we going?" she asked him, as they stood once again in the Garden.

"To the shrine of air."

She frowned. As far as she'd been able to see, there was no shrine to air; it moved freely through the Garden. Curious, she nodded, although it made no difference; she would have followed anyway. He took a small, stone path that wound its way between the small shrines that were otherwise visible: water and earth. The path led to a tree.

It wasn't a small tree, and she wondered how she could have missed it every other time she'd visited. But the Garden's geography was more fluid than even Castle Nightshade's.

"Here," Evanton told her, as he paused in front of a gnarled, knotty root. He pointed toward the trunk of the tree. "There are foot and handholds. I'm afraid we have to climb."

Climbing, at least, she could do.

It wasn't a *short* climb, and even Kaylin was tiring by the time they'd reached what seemed the midpoint of the trunk. Evanton, however, urged them to continue, and they did. The tree extended upward for as far as Kaylin could see with her head stretched back at right angles to the top of her neck.

"It's here," he said.

"I can't see anything but branches."

"You're not looking in the right direction."

"Story of my life," she replied, and looked down again. This time, she followed his arm. He wasn't, as it had first appeared, pointing to a random patch of the sky that existed between forked branches; he was pointing to what looked like a small patch of floating, almost transparent floor. Above it, more solid—but only barely—was a telltale altar and a very small shelf.

Below it, however, there was nothing familiar. Like, say, stairs. Or foundations. Kaylin turned to stare at him. "There doesn't also happen to be an invisible *bridge* from here to there?"

He frowned. Turned to Sanabalis. "She *is* observant, but I assume she's hell in a classroom."

"She is not generally known for either her patience or her humility," Sanabalis replied. "But I have had worse."

"Did they survive?"

"No, all of them, no."

"Ah, well. Too much to hope for."

Severn was chuckling. "I assume," he said to Evanton, "that we're to jump?"

"Unless you can fly. The branches here are more than

strong enough to bear our weight." He added, to Kaylin, "There's a reason you've never been to the shrine of air. All joking aside, it's an unpleasant climb, and my usual method of visiting doesn't always agree well with others."

"Meaning?"

"They tend to fall." He began to edge his way along the branch, and when he reached the midpoint, he jumped off. Unlike the Dragons, he didn't pretend at age; it wasn't a particularly graceful or limber jump. But landing didn't appear to break anything. Severn made the jump with ease, as did Kaylin; the landing itself was a lot softer than she'd expected, and she stumbled as the "ground" gave.

Sanabalis, however, glanced dubiously at both the shrine and the branches that in theory led to its safety. "I fear that I will have some difficulty," he said at last.

Evanton raised a brow. "How so?"

"I am unsure as to the solidity of the branches."

Evanton snorted. It was a Draconian snort, but lacked smoke. "If you feel you can't make the jump—"

The branch cracked beneath Sanabalis as he climbed out toward the platform.

"Oh. Right," Evanton said, as it broke.

The branch listed, and Sanabalis fell. It was a long drop— one Kaylin could see most of, although much of the view was obscured by other branches. Which also snapped as he hit them.

Evanton gritted his teeth, cupped his hands around his mouth, and shouted down toward the direction Sanabalis had fallen. "Take the easy way up! You have my permission and this is *not* Imperial ground!"

Sanabalis roared in response. Even at this height, the sound was almost deafening. Five minutes later, he rose, but at a greater distance from the tree's branches. His wingspan was longer than Tiamaris's, and his color was a pale shade of gray that was almost silver in the sunlight. Or the light; Kaylin wasn't entirely certain it was shed by sun.

"Hold there a moment. We'll come to you," Evanton said.

Kaylin was dubious, but kept her silence. Which was good; Evanton could be smug. The platform on which they were standing did, indeed, move. It moved evenly and slowly until it was inches from the end of the Dragon Lord's jaw.

"This is as close as we get," Evanton told him. "Can you fit yourself on the edge?"

"Is it necessary?"

"No."

"Then, no. I suspect that none of the three of you would survive an accidental fall."

"Two," Evanton said.

"My apologies, Keeper," was the Dragon's grave reply.

The air, when it came, came not at the call of the Dragon, nor at the invocation of the Garden's Keeper. It came as it pleased, dallied a moment in cape and hair, and then settled in the center of the platform, in a spinning vortex that had, as the fire had had, no human shape. It wasn't cold, the way winter winds could be cold; it wasn't cool, the way summer breezes could be cool. But it radiated both of these things, adding a hint of the dampness of sea squall and the howl of storm.

Air, Kaylin thought. Breath.

All of the elements were necessary for life, and all of them could end it in their absence.

The wind whistled; Severn whistled back. His whistle was a familiar fief tune, absent words; the wind's, however, was nothing remotely known. And it was long.

"Evanton?"

"It's speaking."

"I gathered that. What's it saying?"

"Listen carefully, Private. And yes, that *is* my way of telling you to shut up."

She did. She even listened. Evanton, when annoyed, was conversely not very annoying. But the wind's language was one she couldn't understand; if there were syllables, even the half-familiar syllables of the ancient tongue, in its folds, she couldn't pick them up, couldn't tease them apart.

But Sanabalis could. She knew this because he replied, and it was deafening. Lord Sanabalis, absent the robes and the long fringe of white beard, glittered in the light. He was beautiful. Foreign, yes, and ultimately unknown—but compelling. If he could have been silent, she would have been content to stare at him for hours.

As it was, she grimaced and lifted her hands to her ears.

He spoke to the air, and the air answered; she saw it as much as she heard it, because she could see the shifting of the folds of the Dragon's silvery wing membranes. Sanabalis roared again, and this time the wind howled. But she had no sense that it was angry, no sense that it threatened.

"We don't fear the fire," Sanabalis said, speaking in a deep and booming Barrani, "but the storms? We fear the storms."

"And it knows this?"

He laughed. It was disconcerting, given the size of his mouth and his throat. "How do you think we fly? We are, like the Aerians, the beneficiaries of magical flight, Kaylin. The air listens when we push ourselves off from the ground, and it releases us from the shackles of earth. Of course it knows.

"Fire is the element of our birth, in story. Air is the element in which we come of age." He roared again. His wings were spread, not gathered, as if he'd found thermals. "I will stay with the air, Keeper, if that is your wish."

"It's the air's wish," Evanton replied. "But before you settle in up here, we'd appreciate a lift down."

Evanton led them from the base of the tree back into the confines of the neatly tended Garden. It was to the rock garden that he went, and it was that: in place of flowers or trees, rocks of different heights and different textures stood atop a small field of carefully placed pebbles. Here, there was also a small shrine, and a small stone shelf, and candles were lit in honor of the element, in this case, earth. Why the earth was represented by stone, Kaylin didn't understand.

Nor did she really understand a garden composed of rocks, if it came to that. But Evanton now looked at her with care. "This," he told her, "is where I must stop, I think."

"And us?"

"You must leave."

She cast an eye toward the door that appeared as he spoke. The last time she'd exited a door like this one, it hadn't gone well. "You said I wasn't to enter or leave without you," she tried.

"I did indeed. But the plans of even the wise shift and change. I've left you your Corporal," he added, as he approached the large rock that was the small garden's centerpiece. It was a striated marble that seemed polished, and when he touched it, his hands began to glow gently. "Follow the path, Kaylin." His voice was surprisingly gentle.

"Where will it take me?"

"If you hold true to your intent, it will take you where you need to be. Corporal."

Severn nodded.

"Don't lose her. If you need to, tie yourself to her in any way that's practical."

Kaylin snorted. But as it was usually Severn who had the better sense of geography, she didn't argue. "Why are you all doing this, anyway?"

"We're reminding the elements," he replied, closing his veined eyelids.

"Of what?"

"Of life. Of what life means, in this place. They're part of it, essential to it, and inimical to it, all at once. But here, for the moment, they're content to converse, and the conversations—all of them—must take place." He paused, but he hadn't finished; Kaylin waited with more patience than she usually showed.

"You, too, must converse," he finally said. "And I have no idea at all with what, or what you must say. But if the elements are part of the Garden, and if they believe that your Devourer—"

"It is *not* my Devourer, Evanton!"

"If they believe that *the* Devourer belongs in this Garden, then it, too, must be reminded of the way in which it is part of—and inimical to—the living."

"We don't even know what it is!"

"No," was the serene reply. "But that is now no longer my problem."

Severn approached the door first, and Severn opened it. He then held out a hand, palm up, to Kaylin. He said no words because no words were necessary, and she took both a deep breath and his hand. "When all of this is over—if we're still alive—I want a vacation."

He smiled. "If you consider lessons with members of the Imperial Court a vacation, I'm sure Marcus will be happy to sign off on it."

"I could probably get around Sanabalis."

"True."

It wasn't Sanabalis he was thinking about. "I don't suppose a mouse could get around Diarmat."

"*Lord* Diarmat, and no, not if his reputation is anything to go by. Are you ready?"

"No. I never am. I just make do." He held the door open; Kaylin looked suspiciously into the hall. It wasn't the hall that had led to the Garden. For one, it was, or seemed to be, composed of stone; the walls were smooth; the floors themselves were hard and gray. For two, it was a much wider hall than Evanton's, although Evanton's hall was admittedly so crowded with books it was hard to tell.

There were, however, shelves against some of these unfamiliar walls. Severn, still holding her hand, came to stand by her side. He glanced through a door that wouldn't fit two people. Then he glanced over her shoulder at Evanton.

"I don't like it," Kaylin muttered. "Do you think he knows where it goes?"

"I think he knew it wouldn't open up into the shop. What will you do?"

She tightened her grip on his hand and headed into the unknown.

CHAPTER 25

The unknown, in this case, was as solid as the previous hall. The floor had no give, and the walls didn't immediately disperse into vapor or mist or gray nothingness. Nor did Kaylin hear the distant roar of what she assumed was the Devourer. She heard nothing except the sound of their boots on stone, the sound of their own breathing.

The hall was lit not by windows but by small lamps that hung between the shelves at regular intervals. She paused in front of one of those shelves. She wasn't the Arkon; she wasn't even passingly familiar with the titles of the volumes that stood here in bound leather, in more or less orderly rows. But they seemed like an anchor of sorts, something by which she could get her bearings.

Severn let her take the lead. It came to her that he often had, even when she was five, although many of those memories were thankfully dim now. "Hall's longer," she said, giving up on the books. She could read some of the titles; some were impregnable, although she recognized the very stylized forms of High Barrani. The older scribes tended to crunch the letters together so they ended up looking like the same series of carved lines and loops, with small variations, rather than distinct words.

"Where do you think we are?"

"In the store," Severn replied.

She nodded. "The Elemental Garden's existed for as long as the world, or at least that's what the Dragons think. Evanton certainly hasn't." When she'd first met him, on the other hand, he looked—to her—as if he had. Seven years hadn't done much to change him; it had, on the other hand, taken her across the border that separated adults from everything else. "Do you think this is what existed before he took over?"

He nodded. "It's possible this is what exists when anyone new takes the job. It's a building, It's possible that it's a building very like Castle Nightshade."

"You think the Old Ones built it?"

He nodded again.

How had the Old Ones seen the universe? Their buildings changed like seasons, but less predictably. Their words woke whole races, and she wondered what started when the gods actually paused to converse.

There was a door at the end of this hall. It was wide, dark, and banded across its width by what looked like iron. It was also barred. But the bars were on this side of the door, not the other side; Severn let her hand go for long enough to help her push them clear.

The doors opened into another hall; this one was taller and wider, and some light—possibly sunlight—filtered in from above. The walls looked, at first glimpse, to be made of the same stone, but as they approached, the walls began to shift, not in form, but in texture. They were, on the other hand, a very familiar gray.

Severn's hand in hers, she approached the closest section

CAST IN CHAOS   395

of wall to the left. There were no hangings, no lamps, no paintings; there were no words carved in its surface, although she'd half expected them. Instead, the wall seemed flat and blank, smooth in the way glass was smooth, not in the porous way of stone.

"This is a window," she said quietly.

"Yes. A window that would beggar all but the Emperor. Or maybe the Chancellor of the Exchequer."

She glanced at his face; it was as smooth as the wall. Which usually meant he was worried. "Please tell me you're not worried about the investigation into the Chancellor's affairs. We're facing the end of the world, Severn."

He shrugged. "The end of the world is easy. We'll survive it, or we won't. But if we do survive, the rest of life is waiting."

They couldn't get through the windows, of course. Kaylin had to push past her initial response to the breaking of window glass, because it was expensive, and expense implied people who cared enough to make you pay for the destruction one damn way or another. But the attempt to break the glass, which grew increasingly less hesitant as the minutes passed, resulted in nothing. No breakage. No change.

"What the hell is the point of all these windows anyway?" she muttered, because they all faced the same damn thing.

"There's no point now," Severn replied. The way he said it stilled her.

"You think they looked into something else at some point."

"I think it likely. Then again, I don't know what the Ancients saw when they looked at nothing. Maybe it was peaceful."

She shook her head. "No, I think you're right. This is what's left." She turned and headed back to the closed doors. "And if that's the case, it doesn't matter where we go." She placed one palm firmly against the mark that girded the seam of the two doors. Nothing happened.

"What will you do?"

"Same as always," she replied. "Talk a lot and hope that something gets through."

Words described worlds, for the Ancients. Words described *life*. Souls, by any mortal understanding. Words described anything so precisely the Dragons said there was no variation in meaning, no drift due to context. No wonder it was a dead language; you'd have to live forever to even *learn* it. Or to learn enough context that everything had meaning. Kaylin had seen, in the altar-like mirror hidden at the heart of the Arkon's hoard, the word for a world. She had seen, as well, the word for her world. There were differences, and had she the ability to lay them out side by side, she would have been able to enumerate them all.

But that would have taken months or years, and in the end? She'd be pointing at lines or squiggles or the size and the placement of dots. Any sense that the construction or representation was *real,* the way the fiefs had been real, was distant theory. She hadn't experienced it, and couldn't relate to it.

It was, however, all she had. So she began to speak.

Had, she realized, been speaking out loud the entire time, because every so often she heard Severn chuckle. She hadn't—yet—said anything that would make him laugh out loud. But he'd always laughed. Not at her, but…about her, sometimes. His laughter had never driven her to despair or rage. It had never wounded her dignity.

"You don't have much dignity."

"Shut up. I'm trying to concentrate here. If those windows opened up on worlds that once existed, maybe the way to get to them, or one of the ways, was through this door. I just need to be able to...speak the word." She'd asked for the name of the world. The problem with the word she'd been given in reply is that it didn't contain Severn. It didn't contain his laughter, or his silence, or his rare and enduring anger. It didn't contain his shadow, his pain. Nor did it contain Marcus or Marrin or the Hawks; there was no sign of Clint or Teela or Tain. There were no Tha'alani, and there was no Ybelline. Or the Foundling Halls.

And maybe, *maybe*, if she knew how to look *hard enough*, or read carefully enough, she would see them, and she would know her world the way the Ancients did. But maybe the problem with the absent Ancients is that they *did* see the world in a way that was absent those things. Maybe they had no flexibility to see it any other way.

But their creations—if, truly, they were the creators— hadn't the ability to conceive of the whole of a life in a single defined line. Kaylin couldn't even decide what to have for dinner on most days; holding the shape of an entire life in her mind—even when it was her *own*—was beyond her. But it was still her life.

And her life was a web composed of other lives, lives she probably also didn't and couldn't see clearly. Things that made her laugh. Things that made her swear. Things that made her weep.

What would you create, if you could?

Why would I create at all? There's already so much here, and I'll never experience most of it.

"Kaylin, who are you talking to?"

"I think—I think I'm talking to the door."

"You hate philosophical discussions."

"I know. They seem so pointless."

"And you're discussing philosophy with a door."

She shook her head fiercely and he quieted. This was important. She knew it. She also knew he was right. She groped for the sense of importance in the swamp of discussions she had always found tiring and pointless as she waited.

To quiet the darkness. Do you create nothing in your tiny state?

She struggled with the answer she'd been given, rather than the question that had followed it. To quiet the darkness. She'd done a lot in her life to quiet her own darkness. Her first impulse was to say that it had all been bad. But it hadn't. Some of the choices she'd made for her life—for the life she lived now—were a response to some of the mistakes she'd made even earlier. There was no justice, of course; she *knew* that.

But if she gave up on it entirely, there was nothing. Just darkness. Just loss and fear.

I create, she finally said, with care. *But not whole worlds. Not even whole lives. I can't do that. I'm not a god. I can touch other lives. I can even end them. I can change them, hopefully for the better. Sometimes for the worse. I can make space for them.*

And what waits you, when you are done?

She shrugged. *Death.*

The mark on the door flared with sudden warmth, sudden light.

Severn said, quietly, "Well done. I think." The doors began to roll open.

They opened into the gray. It wasn't even mist, because mist you could walk in or through and in any case, you got wet. This wasn't wet. It wasn't hot, cold, dry; it wasn't heavy. It wasn't even gray; it was just without color.

The ground, such as it was, had the same dry-sand give as it had had before, so at least there was some consistency in the nothing. They held hands as they emerged, and when Kaylin looked over her shoulder, she wasn't surprised to see that the doors had vanished. There were no landmarks now;

behind looked the same as ahead, up or down. "You can sort of fall," she told Severn. "I haven't tried flying."

"You haven't?" He smiled. His smile, unlike the gray, was solid and real. "Where are we going?"

"I'm not certain. But I know what we're looking for."

"The Devourer."

She hesitated, and then said, "The refugees. And this is probably the only place in existence where it's going to be harder to find thousands of not very stealthy people than one large creature."

"Why the refugees?"

"Because they're how we're going to get home."

"You returned before."

She nodded. "I did. I called Nightshade, and he answered. I'm going to do that, as well—but not yet."

"Why?"

"Because calling Nightshade called the Devourer, and I don't think we're ready for that yet." She hesitated, and then added, "And if I'm being honest, Nightshade makes me... nervous."

"Nervous?"

"Nervous." She looked around, and added, with a half smile, "I'm lost. But this time, I have a decent excuse."

"And I'm supposed to be able to lead?" He laughed. "No pressure."

She was serious when she said, "No. No pressure. Let's walk. I don't think it's going to make much difference."

They did. And she was wrong; it made some small difference. It calmed her. There were no familiar streets, no familiar buildings, no sandwich boards against which to vent spleen; there was no sweltering heat, no rain, no insects. There were no criminals, and more important, no victims.

For a few moments, there was silence punctuated by breathing, and it was peaceful.

She gave herself those minutes. The past several months had been one rush from emergency to emergency, some of which involved her own life, and much of which involved the lives of strangers. Some of those strangers had become part of her life. Some had died. But death didn't remove them from the pattern.

It made them more painful, but they were still part of her life. If she *had* a name, they were part of her lines, her brushstrokes, her squiggles, her dots. She stopped walking.

"Kaylin?"

"I'm thinking about names," she told him. "Not names the way we use them. True names, the way the Barrani and the Dragons do. The Devourer can hear them, if they're spoken. I don't know if it understands them. I think we can safely say it destroys them. But we don't know *why.*"

"And it matters."

"I always think the why matters. But only up to a point. If you're trying to sell children in the streets of the City, knowing why doesn't change the way I'm going to react."

He nodded. They were strolling, now; Kaylin could almost hear the water of the Ablayne as it moved past them to the side. "Do you remember what we wanted? Or what I wanted?"

He understood what she meant. "Yes. The City. The City over the bridge."

"As if it were a rainbow," Kaylin agreed. "And it's just a bridge. All of them. Just bridges. Crossing them doesn't change what we are. People are still afraid. They're less hungry, so they spend their fear in different places."

"What we want defines who we'll become."

"I hope so. Because what we did want was good. I still

want it," she added. "I still want to live in a better world. A safer world. I still want a world in which children don't starve or freeze to death in the winter. I want a world in which power isn't the only definition of strength.

"But I thought I would just be *given* that world if I walked that bridge. And I know now I have to try to *make* the world." She stopped walking. "Huh."

"What?"

"That was the answer. That was the answer to the question. Why do I always think of the right answers after the damn test is over?"

He chuckled. "Because you haven't thought of the question before the test, and you're still thinking?"

"Yeah. I'm thinking that there's only *one* answer. Sometimes that would be nice."

"But limiting."

"Limits have their uses."

Severn stilled. His hand tightened slightly around hers. "Sometimes, Kaylin," he said softly, "you scare me."

She didn't ask him why. She didn't need to ask. In the distance, as if they defined it, she could see the tiny shapes of people. Some of them were moving. Some were not. She could see, of all things, *wagons,* and sheltered in their lee, the less distinct forms of people huddling together. Not for warmth, because it wasn't cold here, and it wasn't windy. But the need for comfort wasn't always driven by external forces.

"I don't suppose," she asked softly, "I can let you do the talking?"

"If these are the people whose approach has caused so much havoc in the City, no. On the other hand, if these *are* those people, you probably won't be able to do much talking, either."

★ ★ ★

Everly's painting had been exact, but Kaylin's less practiced artistic eye hadn't picked up one important detail: they were *tall*. Taller, she thought, than the Barrani; broader than Dragons in their human form. They were also, if tired and lost, alert. Several of the still bodies moved, with purpose, toward Kaylin and Severn, pausing at the periphery of a camp they now defined. They were armed with greatswords. Or what would have been greatswords in Severn's hands.

They did *not* look friendly.

Severn, however, didn't arm himself; neither did Kaylin. They stopped about ten yards from the closest of the strangers, and waited. For the first time since they'd left what was arguably Evanton's shop, Severn let her hand go; he held up both of his own, palms out, to show clearly that he was unarmed.

The strangers, however, didn't seem to be either relieved or impressed. They were silent. At this distance, Kaylin couldn't see the color of their eyes; the color of their clothing was muted. It wasn't the dust and dirt of long travel that had dimmed the colors; the colors themselves were shades of browns, with some hints of variant greens in secondary layers. Kaylin lifted her own hands, exposing her palms as she did.

She received a glance, no more, as if her relative size made her a child, and at that, a child of little consequence. Usually this was mildly irritating; today, it wasn't.

One of the men spoke. His voice was low and deep, and it rumbled through scant syllables like an imminent storm. Any hope that she would magically understand what he said vanished like last week's pay. She said, slowly, "We can't understand you." Her hands were still spread, but the desire to at least drop one to a knife was getting stronger.

He spoke again. This time, the syllables were lighter, quicker; his voice seemed to rise a half octave. To her surprise—and why should it have been such a surprise?—she realized he was trying a totally different language. She shook her head. But she did the same, then: she tried a different language. Sliding from the Elantran that was her mother tongue, she began to speak in Barrani.

The stranger frowned. Then his expression cleared— slightly—and he started again.

Ten minutes later—by feel, because there was absolutely no other way to mark the passage of time here—they had established two things. The first: that although these men were large and looked like berserker thugs, they weren't immediately violent, and second, that they spoke three or four languages. None of them were languages that Kaylin had heard before. But Kaylin's ability to speak several languages seemed to have put them at ease, for a value of ease that still saw large damn swords ready for use in an eyeblink.

They also established some sort of pecking order, because one of the silent men—and there were now about ten men here, only one of whom opened his mouth at all—turned and headed back toward the camp. When he returned, he brought another three people with him, one of whom was a woman. None of the three, however, were young.

They were also armed. The woman, however, was slightly shorter than most of the men present; she was not notably more friendly.

"Why did we forget Ybelline again?" Kaylin asked Severn.

"She was busy."

"Good. I'd prefer that to 'we were stupid.'"

He chuckled, and then looked toward the new arrivals, who were also speaking—more rapidly—among themselves. At last, one of the two men disengaged. His hair was the color of snow, and as he approached, his sword held casually in one hand as if it were a dagger, Kaylin could finally see the color of his eyes. They were a shocking blue in the well-worn lines of his face. That kind of blue you usually only saw in Barrani, and it was never exactly a comfortable sign.

The men who had barred their entrance formed up like a ragged escort at his back, and they now approached more closely, fanning out again as he stopped. Kaylin lifted her empty hands, as did Severn. The old man nodded, as if he appreciated the gesture; he didn't, however, disarm himself.

Their eyes were shades of blue or gray, some as shocking in brilliance as the old man's. Her own eyes were brown, and the color only varied with strong light; she wondered, idly, what brown might mean to these people, if it had any meaning at all. But…at least one of the men spoke a handful of languages, and that implied familiarity with other races, whose eyes would have to shift color in *different* ways. At least some of them.

The older man now began to speak. He spoke slowly and clearly, although his voice was as low as the first speaker's, and it broke more. Some of the syllables were harsh and dissonant in sound; some pleasant and fluid. None of them were familiar.

Kaylin now tried her own small repertoire again, although the old man looked first to Severn, who, if it came down to it, was probably better versed in non-street language than Kaylin was. When Kaylin started to speak, he shifted his attention without raising a brow. And it was *a* brow; it was possibly the most intimidating thing about his face.

But eventually, he, too, shook his head, turning to the first man who had spoken. They repeated this process with the two new arrivals, the second man speaking next, and the woman last. But there was no sudden discovery of common ground, no sudden clear bolt of understanding.

"What now?" Kaylin asked Severn.

"I'm not sure. I think they're trying to decide the same thing."

"They have more swords," she said, grimacing.

"And louder voices." This last was evident because the discussion, which looked grim, composed as it was of tired, stressed-out people, had progressed beyond what would pass for polite in any society Kaylin had even glancingly been part of. The raised swords did *not* help, and Kaylin had to stifle the instant urge to break it up before blood was spilled.

You're not in Elantra. These are not your people. Severn's firm grip on her arm helped, that and his watchfulness. "They're angry. They're upset. They're frightened. They've been living a nightmare for some time, by the look of it. Watch. Learn. See what they do at their worst."

"And if they start killing each other, they won't finish with us?"

Since the answer was obvious, Severn didn't give it. But he did watch, and because he did, Kaylin did. There were only two things that made her flinch. One of them was the sudden roar of one of the men who had been utterly silent until this point. The other was the overhead arc of his sword.

It was met by the sword of the man who had first spoken, and the clash of the two was like metallic lightning. They were physically shaking with the struggle as the weight of the one sword bore down upon the other. But before they could withdraw and start again, the woman spoke. Her voice *was* almost literal lightning; her syllables were low, evenly spaced and dripping with the fury that implies both contempt and imminent doom.

You could almost hear her say *you are embarrassing me in public.*

The two men broke; they eyed each other warily, but they deferred to her without speaking. Which, given her expression, was a good damn thing—for them. She then turned to

Kaylin and bowed, briefly, before she started to speak. You could hear the apology in the clipped, swift words. The realization that it would mean nothing followed.

But Kaylin chanced a brief smile, because she'd dealt with the foundlings for seven years, and had occasionally used that tone herself.

And if they had no other words in common, the expression was something; the woman raised a brow and then snorted, the anger draining from the etched lines of her face. She turned to the man who had first spoken, dropping her hands to her sides—one of which still held a sword a few inches above ground. This time, when she spoke, he glanced at Kaylin and Severn and shrugged, and the woman then turned to them and also spoke, slowly this time, pointing toward the heart of the encampment.

The men who had guarded the periphery formed up around them warily; they were, at the moment, watchful, but it was hard to say who they were more worried about: the woman, or the two Hawks. Kaylin, therefore, stayed close to the woman; she would have stood in her shadow, but here, there were no shadows.

There were, however, children. And wagons. The wagons had, from the look of it, carried their supplies; they had come at least somewhat prepared for the journey. But days—weeks? She had no way of asking—spent in gray nothing had diminished those supplies, and the people who were even now gaining their feet moved slowly, their expressions grim, their eyes shadowed and hollowed. The children were tall. Some came to Kaylin's shoulder. It was a bit disconcerting.

The older woman now spoke rapidly again, this time pitching her voice so that it would carry. She was in the middle of a sentence when Kaylin heard the unfamiliar lowing of great horns. Everyone stopped then, turning in a single direction.

Kaylin turned that way, as well, although she couldn't quite fix a direction for the horn's loud call.

But all around them, the camp began to dissolve into an orderly, tight-lipped chaos. Some of the children cried, but most just moved as ordered. Kaylin noted that some of the older people who had been aground were lifted and deposited into the backs of the wagons. The wagons weren't pulled by beasts; they were pulled by men. The harness wasn't one she'd seen before, and it took six men—three pairs—to start them in motion.

"Severn?"

"I think," he said, echoing what she hadn't said out loud, "we've found both our refugees and our Devourer."

Forgotten for a moment, they stood in the midst of this camp as it transformed from a circle to a moving line. Some of the men now headed toward the wagons that had already begun to move, and some stood back, watching. Kaylin understood that they meant to guard the rear, and that the rear wouldn't see movement for some time yet. They were a handful of armed men, and were joined by a dozen more. Fifteen in all. The old woman had vanished, for a moment, in the throng.

They had decided, for now, that strangers—unexpected strangers in an entirely dreamlike world—were far less of a threat than whatever it was that had caused them to sound the alarm. They therefore spoke among themselves, but they didn't speak a lot. Still, at this distance, she could watch their faces. They wore half-helms, and their exposed jaws were bearded in a way that suggested shaving was not the priority that long facial hair was. Above the beards, their faces wore the unnatural pale streaks that spoke of scarring. Not all of them had those scars; this wasn't ritual marking.

They'd fought, seen fighting, taken scars; they wore weapons as if they were clothing. They were taller than Barrani, and broader than Dragons; she studied their eyes, and the color that she saw now was predominantly blue. They were obviously worried; she filed that correlation away for possible future use.

The horns sounded again, but the note was different; the men looked up at once. Beneath their feet, the soft sandy texture of the unreal ground began to shudder. And the sky, such as it was, with no horizon to mark it and nothing to differentiate it from any other part of the landscape, began to roil, turning from the gray of nothing into something that might have been either night or storm.

Kaylin's arms began to ache. She hesitated, and then quickly rolled up one sleeve; the marks were glowing brightly. But *this* time, the damn things weren't glowing evenly; some were lit to almost incandescence, and some seemed to just absorb the spill of that light. She squinted.

But the strangers stiffened, and one of them suddenly thrust his sword into the ground six inches from Kaylin's feet. She leaped back, dropping her sleeve and grabbing her daggers as she landed into bent knees. The men who had been so grim and dour were now staring at her, and the color of their eyes was no longer blue; it was a uniform green.

Great, she thought. *They're giant Barrani.*

Fifteen men now began to speak in low, fast syllables, and one of them nodded, separated, and began to tear across the ground moving as easily and gracefully as anyone could who was encumbered by a sword that size he had no intention of actually sheathing first.

Those who remained behind realized that she was staring at them, and that she was armed. Given the size of the daggers and the size of Kaylin, they didn't look very alarmed.

They didn't, on the other hand, laugh outright, which the thugs in the fief might have done. Barrani, on the other hand, would sneer.

These men did neither. Instead, they offered her one open palm each, mirroring the weaponless "I mean no harm" gesture that Kaylin and Severn had both used. It didn't have as much effect, given the swords they *did* carry. But she thought it was meant to be calming.

To no one's surprise, the man who had run at a tear across the slowly building line returned dragging the same three people as had come to the edge of the encampment: Two older men and one woman. This time, Kaylin placed a hand on the center of her chest and said, clearly and slowly, "Kaylin. I am Kaylin."

The woman nodded. She mirrored the gesture, but pointed, instead, to her sword arm. "Mejrah."

And then she pointed to Kaylin's arm. The sleeve had fallen. Kaylin met the older woman's gaze, and then nodded, and the woman turned to one of the two silent older men, and handed him her sword. He said something that seemed, even absent any understanding of language, formal, and they nodded to each other at the same time. Then, unarmed, and looking no less intimidating for the lack of weapon, Mejrah turned back to Kaylin.

Kaylin held out her arm, and with shaking hands, the older woman gently pushed the sleeve up, to the elbow. The runes, exposed, caused the woman to squint, but she didn't look away. She didn't even notice the resurgent tremors that now shook them all. But when she did look up, when she let the sleeve fall, she met Kaylin's gaze, and her eyes were golden.

CHAPTER 26

Gold wasn't a Barrani color. Nor was the woman's expression one she'd ever seen on a Barrani face; not even her dreams were that perverse. Before Kaylin could speak—and she was surprised enough that her mouth was already half-open on words that would be gibberish to the stranger—the old woman turned and snarled something. The man holding her sword approached her instantly, and held it out, point toward the ground. She took it, and then knelt. She didn't thrust it into the ground, but it was clear that she was offering its flat as a sign of genuine respect.

A sign Kaylin neither wanted nor felt she deserved. From a vantage closer to ground, the much taller woman looked across at Kaylin, the underside of her eyes lined and darkened, her jaw set. The rest of the men gathered around this kneeling woman; they didn't lower their swords.

The ground trembled as Kaylin hesitated, and then her hesitation was broken by a familiar roar. Severn, silent and almost unnoticed, looked up. "That's our sign to move," he told her quietly.

She nodded. Turning to the old woman, she said, "I'm sorry—we don't have time for this right now. And even if

we did, neither of us has the words for it. We have to *move*."
The woman, who flinched at the sound of the roar, was silent and still.

Kaylin cursed, in Leontine. Reaching out, she grabbed the
wrist of the old woman's sword arm—because it was closest.
She pulled her to her feet which meant the woman now towered over her, even though her shoulders were still turned
down in a show of respect. It looked wrong while she was
standing. The Devourer roared again, and this time, a flinch
passed through everyone in sight, like a silent wave. Kaylin
started to nudge the woman toward the wagons, which had
now formed up in a single line that headed into gray. There
was nothing to obscure them; she could see them in a distance that had no other geography.

More than a nudge wasn't required. The woman assumed
that Kaylin was attempting to remind her of her duties, and
if Kaylin couldn't divine the precise details of said duties, she
understood the big picture: this woman was Marrin, absent
claws and fur but with the extra bulk that came from dis-
proportionate height.

The people were silent, for the most part. Parents could
be heard murmuring to children who were too young to be
quiet and still, or just old enough to be terrified. They were
also, to Kaylin's eye, hungry and tired; all in all, a bad combination even on a good day, which this wasn't.

"What are you thinking?" Severn asked quietly, watching her expression.

"Kicking myself mentally," she replied.

"For?"

"I didn't ask the damn mirror *how* the refugees—from any
world—found *any other world*."

He nodded. "You didn't expect to be here."

"No. I didn't. But that's not an excuse."

He didn't say anything else because honestly, there wasn't much to say. But they now followed the old woman, walking much more closely by her side than they had the first time. They attracted attention, mostly the attention of children, but not always. These were not people who had lived sheltered lives; their gazes were mostly full of suspicion.

In an odd sort of way, it made her feel at home. Her first home, in the fiefs of Nightshade, when the fieflord's castle cast the longest of shadows, and his guards—and thugs—carried that shadow farther than it would otherwise reach. She wouldn't have been huddled near the legs of parents or grandparents; she'd've been up above the street, looking down from a window, if she were stupid enough to look at all.

Think, Kaylin. She glanced at the old woman who still seemed subdued after seeing the marks on Kaylin's arm. In the case of the one other group of refugees she had seen, it had been strongly implied that one man—Enkerrikas?—had been responsible for the route or the journey. To leave the world at all required some type of magic, some type of opening of the way; it probably wasn't possible for people who weren't wandering around in the Keeper's hall without supervision to simply fall out of it.

So someone here had the ability—somehow—to open a door into nothing—a door large enough to let wagons and thousands of people through. Someone, therefore, had the ability to open a door that led out of that nothing. And Kaylin had no ability whatsoever to talk to the woman to find out who. Or to find out if it was the old woman herself.

She had no way of knowing if they were close, or if the physical movement of this long caravan mattered at all.

The roar focused her thoughts. She glanced over her shoulder, and saw only gray; she thought the Devourer was close, but was not yet aware of them. Not the way he had been aware of Vakillirae or Enkerrikas or their lost people. Did these strangers have true names? They were aware of words, or at least of the shape of the oldest of tongues, because the old woman had seen her arms, and she had recognized something in the runes.

But at this point, so did Kaylin, and she was no immortal.

She continued to follow the old woman, who finally made her way to the front of the waiting train. There, she signaled a stop, and she joined two others. They were standing, with an honor guard of six armed men, and when they caught sight of Kaylin, one of the two—both men—raised a brow. He was not as old as the woman; his brow was still dark enough to look silvered by gray. He, unlike the old woman and every other adult—or almost adult—that Kaylin had seen so far, was unarmed. The hilt of a greatsword over one shoulder implied that this wasn't always the case. His shoulders were broad, and he was tall. Even for a race of diminutive giants.

His hands were large. They were unadorned; not even a simple ring marked them. He did wear the layered cloth that marked the rest of his people, but his robes weren't also covered by something that looked like a breastplate. Waterskin, wide belt, and boots that were worn but practical completed the look. He wore two obvious knives at his side, but then again, Kaylin wore one and no one blinked; knives, clearly, weren't considered weapons.

The man glanced, briefly, at Severn, and then turned back to the woman, who seemed to be waiting. He smiled, then. Nodded. The woman asked a question, and he nodded again; she fell silent as he turned.

"I am Kaylin," Kaylin said, speaking clearly and slowly as

she lifted a hand to her own chest. "Severn," she continued, briefly touching her partner.

The man raised a brow, and then, without any exaggerated gestures, said, "Effaron."

"Effaron."

He winced slightly at her pronunciation, and she made a second attempt—which sounded almost the same to her, but was clearly an improvement judging by his nod. He spoke to Kaylin, and she lifted her hands, palms up, and shrugged apologetically. The man turned to the old woman who spoke in measured, but quick words. One brow rose.

"This," he said, "is going to be difficult."

Kaylin's eyes widened.

She reached out, touched the man's wrist; his own eyes widened as the place where their skin briefly met began to glow. "You're the traveler," she told him.

He turned to speak to the women, his words complete gibberish. But the old woman shrugged, and he turned back. "You are not speaking my tongue."

"No. And you're not speaking mine. But it sounds to me as if you are. How long have you been on the road?"

He grimaced. "Weeks. We cannot afford to stay on the road for much longer. We don't have the supplies, even at the severe rationing in place now."

"Do you know where you're going?"

He watched her closely for a long, silent moment, and then said, with no change of expression whatsoever, "No. I have no idea whatsoever. Since it appears you can't talk with my people, I'm willing to expose this ignorance to you—but they can't know. They exist now on hope, and it's a thin, thin hope.

"How did you find us?"

"I don't know. We weren't looking for you."

"You were looking for another world?" His expression was almost painful to look at, for just that moment—clearly it wasn't only his people who depended on hope to keep going.

"No. My world—the one we're both from—is still safe. Or as safe as a world ever is for the individual people who are trying to survive in it."

He hesitated again, and then said, "Can you lead us there?"

"I don't know. I'm not a traveler."

"What is this traveler of which you speak?"

"Someone who can walk in this empty space from one world to another."

"Yet you are here."

"So are all the rest of your people."

He nodded. "We are moving," he added. "The storms here are strong."

"Storm? Is that what you call it?"

"What else? It cannot be reasoned with, and it sweeps away all that remains in its path." He turned to the woman again, and this time, she nodded and left them.

"She's terrifying," Kaylin said.

The man raised a brow. "You do not look terrified."

"No. I'm used to terrifying women. It makes me feel at home." She smiled.

"You are a strange one, to feel at home even here. Can you lead us?" he asked again.

"I don't know how. I can try."

They spoke very little as they walked. Kaylin wanted to ask Effaron how, exactly, he traveled, and in particular, how he had opened a door—in this case an exit—from his world. But Effaron was in demand, and every half sentence was interrupted by someone. They were polite when they interrupted him, but Kaylin thought it had more to do with her presence than his own; they all stared at her.

But when the roaring grew loud enough and close enough, it ended all questions and any possibility of discussion.

"Effaron, how often have you escaped these storms?"

"Many times."

"Did you ever try to stand and weather them?"

"No. We do not belong here, and we cannot live here for long. The storms know it, and they seek to scour the land clean."

She didn't argue with his interpretation. Instead, she said, "Have any of your people fallen to the storm?"

His silence, which was heavy, was enough of an answer. She didn't press for more. The wagons were already moving. They didn't move slowly, even given that they were pulled by men, not horses or oxen. All around their girth, people gathered. They needed food, sleep, and baths, not exactly in that order. But to get any of those things, they needed to leave this place.

The roar was louder and harsher, and this time, listening to it, Kaylin almost thought she could hear words in the rumble. She was certain that Nightshade had when she herself couldn't. She was just as certain that these people hadn't. The only difference she could think of was the name: Nightshade had a true name; Kaylin, and by tenuous extension, these people, didn't. Nothing about their age looked like an affectation. They were mortal.

But... Kaylin was mortal and she had a name. Sort of.

It was a name she had taken for herself when she had faced the test of the Barrani High Halls, and she had taken it from the waters of their life. The fact that those waters had looked very much like the moving surface of a desk didn't change the substance; it was Barrani after all. Not only could looks be deceiving, but in *that* culture, you lost style points if they weren't.

But the Barrani didn't exist without a name. They didn't grow or change. They remained in a permanent half state. Which, come to think of it, might be a lot like this nothingness that bridged the gap between worlds. Kaylin, born in the fief of Nightshade, had not only grown, but had changed many times over her span of two decades. She didn't *need* the name to exist, and she wasn't even certain if the name itself granted any power to anyone who might know it.

Only Severn did.

And Severn, while he could invoke it to speak—at great need—behind the silence of shuttered expression, would never use it against her. Whatever he wanted from her, it wasn't control or dominance. She glanced once over her shoulder to see the strangers; they were the only visible geography.

"Effaron," she said quietly, "if you open a portal to my world, the storm will come."

"That has always been my fear," he replied, his low rumble of a voice very quiet. "But we cannot stay here for much longer."

She didn't argue; it was true. Instead, she took a deep breath. "Lead," she told him quietly. "I'm going to pull up the rear."

"Why?"

"I want to try something, and I have no idea whether or not it will work. If you don't trust me, send someone with me."

"Mejrah trusts you. If she doesn't stop you, no one will."

Kaylin looked at her covered arms. "It's not me she trusts," she said, with a twinge of anxiety. "I've done nothing to earn it—it's the marks."

"Yes. But the marks are significant among our kin."

Kaylin shook herself. They had, by dint of Severn, reached the end of the long train, and they did take up the rear, walking more quickly than the strangers to compensate for their smaller stride. She turned to Severn as the ground wobbled.

"I need you here," she told him. "I need you to remember what you know of me."

He was, as always, perceptive. "The name?"

"The one I took for myself from the living pools in the High Hall. I think—I think the Devourer, or whatever it is, is sensitive to true words, and it's the only one I know I can use." She held out a hand. After a moment, he took it, and she tried not to hold on too tightly.

He tried not to wince when she failed.

Ellariayn.

She said the word to herself, syllable by syllable. In her own mind, it felt like any other word she said to herself, absent the cursing ones. Nothing made it true or real in a way that elevated it above all the other language she knew. But it *was* real. To the Barrani, to the Dragons, and to the Ancients who existed as living ghosts now.

All right, then. How did they make a word real? Did it become concrete somehow because they'd lived in and with it for so long it became inseparable from what they were? Because if that was the case, she was in trouble. Or did they somehow cease meaning from it as they grew up? Did they grow into it, faults and all, because it was what they were?

She felt something in her unknot at that.

She'd seen enough in the Foundling Halls to know that babies and young children *had* personalities. They had preferences, differences of temper, and different needs. They were born with them, and they learned to either hide them or own them, depending—again—on the rest of their personality.

Kaylin, at twenty, was only beginning to understand the reasons for some of her reactions; she might not understand them all by the time she hit fifty, if she lived that long. Some of those reactions, she could trace back to mistakes she'd made and things she'd suffered because of them. Some, though— like hating the taste of shrimp—she couldn't. She had no clear idea how much of who she was was learned, and how much she'd just come into the world with.

The Devourer was roaring; he was closer, now, but his voice still sounded like thunder to her ears. Her arms began to tingle; the back of her neck and the insides of her thighs began to ache. She wanted to tell the Devourer to shut the hell up because his roaring made it so damn hard to concentrate. But she wasn't ready to speak to him yet—if speech even worked—and when she was, those probably weren't the safest first words.

So, so, so. There was Kaylin, who had been born Elianne, and she was still working on that. And there was Ellariayn, come new to the world with Kaylin's ascent to the Barrani High Court, all but ignored. If she understood the Barrani Consort's words—or at least the friendly ones—the name *itself* was ancient; it had existed in the world forever. It was some part of the gods themselves, and it was what had given them, and their first children, life.

She poked at the name almost tentatively, as if it weren't part of her.

Ellariayn.

This time, fighting the urge to close her eyes—which, in her experience, always made simple locomotion difficult— she said the word to herself, syllable by syllable, struggling with it, with the sense of its pronunciation. She stumbled over it, as if it were an entirely foreign word, and realized as she did that she had never tried to pronounce it before. Not even when she had given it to Severn.

Some things were deeper and larger than words. Even, it appeared, some words themselves. As she spoke it to herself for the first time, she saw the name form, and in its broad lower stroke, she saw the currents of ocean, the height of tides, the depth of the still pond in Evanton's Garden. The shape of the stroke didn't change; it was bold and clear.

As she repeated the name, the center strokes formed above the lower, broad stroke, and in these, she saw the cold, hard stone of Castle Nightshade; the polished marble of the High Halls; the enduring tower from which the Hawklord ruled. Again, the shape of the stroke didn't change, but it was al- most a window, and it contained—perfectly—some part of her experiences. Across it, vertically, were two more lines. She was not surprised to see that they differed in color and texture from the first two; one was like new fire, and one, like sunlight, and above them both, drifting in a more deli- cate weight, something that invoked either cloud or smoke.

But the word wasn't finished; the four strokes that com- prised the center were decorated by three central dots, and then a trailing row to one side, and a squiggle to the other. These, too, had texture, but they were opaque to Kaylin; they showed her nothing of either herself or her experiences. Or perhaps she hadn't had the experiences that would make them clear yet.

Even so, she saw the word as clearly now as she had ever

seen another word, and she felt it not quite as her own, but not entirely separate from her. She turned to Severn, and said, "I'm ready."

He nodded. "Will you stand and wait?"

"Yes. I think—I think Effaron will be able to open the portal. If I had to guess, he's probably started *something* at the front of the train." She glanced meaningfully at the hidden marks on her arms. Taking a deep breath she turned her back upon the refugees; even if they moved slowly, their stride was long enough to carry them farther away as she stared into the unchanging gray. Not all of the strangers left, however; four—all men—remained. They were armed, but they held their weapons as if they knew they were only there for comfort.

Drawing a deeper breath, Kaylin opened her mouth and shouted her name into the gray void. Her true name. It sounded, in the distance, like thunder, and it echoed across the whole of the plain as if it were storm.

Come, she thought, as a wind rose for the first time across the faceless plain. *Come home.*

She looked at the gray that contained the roaring of syllables and the thunder of voice, and it looked darker to her eyes. Darker, but not cohesive. "He's coming," she told Severn.

Severn, however, was busy. He was untwining the chains of his weapon from its resting place at his waist. "I did try to talk you out of this, didn't I?" he asked, with a small smile.

She laughed. "What is it that you love about me?"

He froze for just a second, no more. Kaylin felt the hesitation—and the links of the chain—more than she saw them; she was watching as the storm's eyes suddenly opened. She could see them; they were huge. They scanned the ground—

if ground was a word that could be used here—and then stopped as they fell upon her.

"It's not a rhetorical question," she continued, as she met those huge and ancient eyes.

"No." He planted his feet slightly apart, standing behind her. He had her back, here. He always had her back. *I'll tell you*, he added. *If it's necessary, I'll tell you.*

She nodded. The gray of the landscape solidified as she watched. She opened her mouth and snapped it shut on whatever stray words were seeking escape as the storm hit.

CHAPTER 27

She held her name. She held the shape of the strokes, long and short, thick and thin, and she held what they contained. They weren't large enough—the Devourer was *huge*.

It rose—and rose, and rose—as it gained substance. No, *substance* was the wrong damn word. It gained something like *shape,* but it was shaped the way glass was: it had form and lines and even something that might suggest texture, but she could still see through it. What she wanted to call black wasn't a color. It was an absence. It was emptiness given solidity. Even the eyes that met hers, grazing her as if she were a flea, contained that emptiness.

And the desire to fill it, and have peace.

Devourer. Devourer of worlds. How many worlds had died to appease an ancient and endless hunger, to no avail? How many names—of people, of places—had he somehow emptied in his endless quest? And why names? Why words?

As if to answer, her arms and her legs began to ache; the marks on them burned, as if they were being newly branded. She looked down at her arms, and she could see—through the pale cloth—the glowing sigils that she both hated and had learned, with time and experience, to rely on. They were as much a part of her as the name she'd chosen for herself from the Barrani High Halls, and she understood them about as well.

But the Devourer saw them as clearly as she felt them, and the storm—if it was that—grabbed her, lifting her into the air. Or into more gray. There was no wind here, no sun, no earth, no rain; it was empty of everything familiar.

Everything but Severn.

Is this your world? she thought, although her body was already tensing for physical combat. *Is this the whole of the world you can create for yourself?* Its response was to reach *through* her, as if she were no more real than the rest of the gray. But as it passed through, it touched the weakly moored name she carried, and it froze there for just a second. And then, as if it were a giant hand, it closed.

The word compressed under the pressure of its grip, the lines crowding in on each other and bending into slightly different shapes. Kaylin started to fight this shift, because she'd done it once before, in the Tower of what was now Tiamaris. But...this was different. It *felt* different. The pressure wasn't attempting to rewrite or revise; it wasn't changing any meaning. It was gathering and it was as clumsy as a bull might be if it were trying to pick berries.

It didn't hurt. The name was part of her, but it didn't sustain who she was. She started to tell Severn as much, but the Devourer spoke again, and this time she could understand what he said.

Where? Where? Where are they? Where am I?

She had no answer to give. Even if she had, she wouldn't have been able to speak, because the pain started then.

She was only tentatively attached to her true name; her true name was therefore only tentatively attached to her. But what had started as gathering became a type of frenzied unmaking as the Devourer sought to reduce the runic symbol to its component parts. Pain clouded understanding; it always had. What she had prevented herself from doing when the creature had first touched the word, she now struggled to do in earnest: to hold it together, to keep its identity. Strokes and dots just didn't add up to much without a pattern.

She gave the name its meaning, as she struggled. She found the parts of her that were already part of it, and she brought them forward. She *knew*, if she didn't think too damn hard, what the shape of the word was. Pain clouded thinking, as well.

But it was ultimately going to be a losing battle; she'd seen it before, and she knew its outcome. She lost focus, lost all sense of the self the name defined—wanted to retreat to a self that it didn't. But before she could instinctively do so, she heard a familiar voice. Severn was afraid.

He was afraid for her. But his fear was measured, controlled. *You asked me why I love you,* he said, speaking along the bond of her unfamiliar name. *You've never asked before.*

She bit her lip, tasted blood. *No.*

Why?

She didn't know. Couldn't—talk about silver linings— think for long enough to answer the question. *I don't know.* He accepted it. He always accepted it.

You were afraid.

She was always afraid of something. Right now, it was pain. The pain receded and returned in waves as the name dimmed inside of her. Severn's voice grew softer. *Yes.*

He didn't ask her why, this time. *You were afraid that I loved something I'd made up, something that doesn't actually exist. That I didn't—and don't—see you.*

She said nothing.

I see you, Kaylin. You were afraid of what you'd done in Barren. No, afraid that if I knew what you'd done, I'd stop. We'd all stop.

She'd said as much. And he had discovered what she'd done for six months of miserable life when she'd given in entirely to pain and fear.

I'd guessed. I watched you, when you were with the Hawks. I know how they train. Some of the stuff you knew, you didn't learn from them. But I knew…when you ran…that you might not survive. I tried to find you. I knew what you must have been feeling, and what that might cause. When I first found you, in the Hawks, I watched you. I thought I must have been wrong, or you must have been lucky.

And after?

It didn't matter. I learned that the choices you make when you aren't afraid or in pain aren't that much different than the choices you made when we lived together in Nightshade. This doesn't mean you're a child, to me; you have *changed.*

The name was so dim it was almost translucent. Severn knew. His words were more urgent, and they came faster.

You don't expect people to be what you aren't. You don't expect them to give you what you can't give. You don't judge them—all right, you do, but you don't let the judgment form the basis for the rest of your life. Your sense of self-worth isn't based on a hierarchy of who's worth less.

What you do *have, you give. You always have. You give your time to the midwives. You give your time to the Foundling Halls. You know what it's like to have nothing, but you don't make it an excuse to resent anyone else you meet who has* something.

But she did those things for *herself.* Because the midwives' guild and the Foundling Halls made *her* happy. She felt as if the name itself was so thin, so slight, she could only barely grasp it.

He grimaced, and he shifted direction. *I love you*, he said, *because you get lost everywhere you go. You'd get lost heading to the change rooms if you didn't practically live in the Halls. I love you because you lose or misplace anything that isn't actually attached to your person.*

I love you because if you can't be on time to save your job or your life, you will be on time to save anyone else's. I love that you can't place a smart bet unless you're lucky.

She almost laughed. She did snort.

I love you because you're afraid of anything that's strange or different, but you hate being afraid, so you charge ahead anyway. *I even love you because you've never lost the habit of thinking the future is at most a day away. That has to change,* he added, *because I fully intend that your future will go on for years.*

He shook his head. *I love the fact that you live in the moment. I love the fact that when you* do *figure out how wrong you've been, you change and you grow. I love that you're so easily, predictably outraged—by Elani street, by Margot and her stupid sign. I love that you say what you're thinking.*

And I love that you never give up. You suffer setbacks, you find your feet, and you keep moving. It doesn't matter how impossible something looks. You throw yourself at it, time and again. You give everything you have, and then, when you've got nothing left, you find more. Betting doesn't count.

She did laugh, then.

She laughed, and the pain and the fear slid through her as if it could no longer find purchase. The Devourer stopped speaking. He almost stopped moving; she could sense him; she could *almost* touch him. He was still, on the other hand, an almost amorphous cloud with large eyes.

No, not eyes. They were landscapes. Deserts: sand and snow. Nothing moved in them at all. But they watched her as if they could—for just a moment—see *her*.

Severn's words fell like water in her own personal desert, like the turning of the seasons on snow. She *wanted* them, and knew it. But it was the smaller words, the words that described what she believed about herself that she held on to; the other words were too large, and too intimidating.

But he hadn't finished.

It doesn't matter why you do it. It doesn't matter whether or not you do it only for yourself. It's how what you do affects others, in the end, that counts. I don't love you because I have the ideal Kaylin—or Elianne—in mind. I don't love you because I expect you to live up to some vision of perfection. I love the things about you that you don't see, or don't love yourself.

You make every place you stop for more than ten minutes a home, Kaylin. I want that. It's never been my gift. I stop in the doorway, aware of all the ways in which I don't belong, aware of the ways in which my presence alone could be an interference. You walk in, head straight to the kitchen, start piling up dishes. You ask what has to be done. More often than not, people tell you.

Sometimes what they told her was: get out. She laughed again, but it was rueful. And the Devourer almost shuddered at the sound—because it *was* a sound.

Most people make the Hawks their job, or even the start of their career. You've made them family. You live with them. You fight with them. You fight for them. You ignore their foibles as if they were the drunk uncles you can't get rid of. You don't know how *to treat your work like work, and you never have. Even when you were thirteen you tagged along like someone's younger sister, trying not to get underfoot.*

I would have done that with the Wolves, if I could have. I couldn't. I don't understand home the way you do. But I understand this. You're where home is. You always were.

He fell silent, and if she could have, she would have turned to look at him, even if she couldn't find anything to say.

Home. She gathered the pieces of her Barrani true name as carefully as she could, righting them until they formed a rune she recognized.

The Devourer was all she could otherwise see, with its huge desert eyes that didn't reflect her. It was no longer attempting to rip her name apart as if it were packaging; it no longer roared. But it watched her as she worked, and when it spoke again, it spoke a single word. *Home.*

Severn's words had been a gift, and she had almost wept to hear them, because she was still so certain she didn't deserve them. But the Devourer's word made her want to weep in an entirely different way. It—he—wasn't a child. But some of the empty, desolate bewilderment that older orphans faced was in its tone.

She'd dealt with those orphans in the Foundling Halls, as they struggled with the truth of their new existence, and with the changes they had no choice but to accept. She'd done it herself, on the morning her mother had not woken up. She understood that for those children, home and safety were the same thing, and with the loss of home, safety had vanished. The Foundling Halls could *be* a new home, but home wasn't something that could be built and forced on them in a single day, and what they wanted, at heart, was for time to turn backward and death to be a nightmare they could wake from, preferably in the arms of their parents.

They, on the other hand, didn't destroy whole worlds in their grief and need. Maybe that was why small children— hells, most *people*—didn't have the power to destroy whole worlds. In the grief of the moment, they would—and there wouldn't be a lot left standing.

She had seen, trapped in ancient Records, the death of Va- killirae as he faced the Devourer. She'd seen his determination, and she'd seen what Enkerrikas had done to succor him while his life was slowly drained. This was different.

How? Why? The Devourer hovered, drifting slowly toward her. As it did, the noncolor of its form enveloped her.

Kaylin!

I'm here. I'm here, Severn.

I can't see you!

I think he's swallowed me. Good damn thing he has no digestive system. Severn smiled at the gallows humor; it was brief, and she couldn't see it, but she felt it anyway. She opened her eyes. Or she tried, and realized they weren't closed. In the center—or at least inside—of the Devourer, it made no difference. She'd often closed her eyes when she wanted to think; it lessened distraction. Here, it didn't matter; it was almost like being on the inside of her own head.

Because it's empty?

She laughed again. She was going to hit Severn, on the other hand, if she ever made her way out.

Vakillirae had sacrificed himself for his people. His people had done what they could to help him make his final stand. In the end, it hadn't saved him; it had saved at least some of his people, because those memories were preserved on *this* world, somehow. But she'd seen his face, his expression. There was no way he didn't understand what *home* meant, or what family meant.

And yet, he'd died. During the whole of their almost static combat, the Devourer had never fallen silent. What was the difference, besides race and gender? Kaylin had a feeling the Devourer didn't consider the living significant enough to assign value to, either.

Home.

The word was like an earthquake; it shook everything.

She understood it. But... Vakillirae must have understood it, as well.

No, Severn said, and she realized how closely he must be listening.

What do you hear?

Two things. When I listen to what I'm hearing, it's roaring or thunder. If I listen to what you hear? Words. Or syllables. But... I can't hear what you're hearing, Kaylin. To me, even through the bond of the name, it doesn't sound like home.

But this is different. The Devourer—he's not behaving the same way. I don't understand why.

Severn's voice fell silent for a moment, and then he said, *You laughed.*

Pardon?

You laughed, Kaylin. You were in pain, and you were afraid, and you're here in the end for essentially the same reasons that Vakillirae was—but you laughed.

I laughed because you— She stopped. She would have turned to face the Devourer, but that was impossible given his eyes were on the outside. She'd laughed, yes. She almost said *You made me laugh,* and in some ways that was true. But on the surface of things, there wasn't all *that* much that was funny about his actual words; she laughed because they implied history. A history of affection, arguments, teasing, a little smugness.

A history of being *at* home. Of being known. Of, she thought, belonging. As she so often did, she began to speak, and as often happened in situations like this, the markings on her arms, her legs, and her back began to *hurt.* They also began to make themselves visible in a way they'd never done before: they burned through her clothing.

Her first almost irrelevant thought was: *Damn it, I can't afford this!* Followed quickly by *I need a raise* and *if you mention budgeting, I'll break both your legs.*

Again, the Devourer stirred, but he didn't resume his frenzied unmaking.

Get ready, she told Severn.

The runes on her arms weren't a frame; they were almost a cage. But hadn't she sought the comfort of cages in the past? Their bars formed guidelines, made options clearer. And there was only one way to leave the damn thing, anyway. She drew breath and she began to tell the Devourer a story. It wasn't a child—she understood that. But if it had learned from the experience it absorbed in its attempts to find what it sought, there wasn't any evidence of it.

The story she told was one she'd told only once before: it was a story meant for elemental fire, and it spoke of what fire meant to the *living.* In it, she described the raging fires that consumed whole city blocks; she told of the fires that consumed whole forests—although these, she had never personally seen. But she also spoke of the way the necessary warmth of fire sustained life in the bitter cold of winter; the way it warmed water, cooked food, brought light to dark places. It wasn't, strictly speaking, a story; it had no narrative, no beginning and no real end. The foundlings, especially Dock, would have been rolling their eyes in boredom long before she'd finished.

But the elemental fire had listened, seeing itself—seeing most of itself—in the words that related the experiences of those who lived around its edges. It had carried her across the wild miles of the Elemental Garden as she'd spoken, without once burning or blistering her skin; it had offered her both attention and warmth, instead of what seemed almost inevitable death.

She wondered, briefly, what kind of story the Arkon would

tell the fire, because Dragon experience of flame was beyond her; it wasn't her story to tell.

As if the Devourer were fire, he listened.

He's moving, Severn told her.

Quickly?

Meaning, can I keep up? I can. Not without effort.

She didn't tell him to make the effort; she knew he would, while he breathed. *I don't hear him roaring. Or speaking.*

He's not. He's silent, now.

Can you see him?

Yes.

Has he changed?

Yes. He doesn't look mortal, if that's what you mean. But he's not the whole of the sky or the landscape. He seems to have...condensed.

She had no idea how to frame a story about what the Devourer meant to the living, because as far as she knew, he meant death.

But he appears to be following our refugees.

She had never spoken to the air in the Garden; nor had she spent much time attempting to converse with the dirt. She wouldn't have bothered talking to the fire, either, if it hadn't been carrying her. She regretted that now, but began, once again, to talk about her own experience with the elements; she made them part of her story, and offered them to the only audience she had. If she stumbled or hesitated or went on too long, the audience didn't yawn or shout or snicker, and for that, she was grateful.

Air was breath. Without it, there was no life. It carried seeds—in the city, they were usually weed spore—and scent, the aroma of baking or cooking or less pleasant but no less present things. It carried...words. Speech. At its worst it carried ice and made it hard to stand or walk, and she added

that, as well. It carried Aerians and Dragons, and although the
only flight she usually experienced, with one notable exception, was wheedled or whined for, she did tell the Devourer,
because she loved flight, and envied it. Flight was freedom.
Flight was escape from the confinement of...earth.

Earth, she thought, and cages.

But that was a different story, a way of expressing a rest-
lessness or helplessness that had nothing to do with the fact
of earth, because usually what she wanted to escape from was
herself. Earth? Without earth, there was also no life. There
was no grass, no wheat, no corn, no trees from which most
homes were built. There were no cliffs, no cliff faces into
which Aerians built their Aeries.

Sometimes she did want to fly. Sometimes, though, she
needed to make a stand. Then, she needed earth, stone, something beneath her feet that wasn't so capricious it couldn't bear
her weight. Earth was the place in which the dead rested, in
the end.

The Devourer was silent, but it was an attentive silence.

She looked at her arms. The marks on her skin were also
words; they'd never felt heavy, had never really felt like anything but skin at all, except in the presence of strong magic,
in which case they felt like selective sunburns.

The Devourer was attracted to the use of the names; he had
come when Vakillirae had made his stand, his name hanging
in the air before him like a translucent, luminescent shield.
Regular speech hadn't caught his attention; on her first visit
to this empty wasteland, she'd cursed liberally in every language she could, which was basically, with the exception of
Dragon, any language she knew.

What is the name of fire?

Funny, that she should hear Sanabalis, of all people, now.
His lessons, his endless, quiet lectures, returned in those

words. The name of fire. She focused, as she had never managed to focus on the candles he set in front of her, lifted her head, and spoke.

Out of the gray-black insides of the Devourer, fire came at her call. If she'd called fire like *this* in the West room, she'd've lost her job, and quite possibly her life: it raged. It raged, it danced, it roared, spanning the spectrum from white to red.

Careful, Kaylin. Severn's words were jarring. They were also an anchor.

What's happening?

The refugees are now walking through fire. No, it's not burning them, not yet.

She started to speak, and stopped at the next interruption.

Private Neya. It was the Arkon. She looked at the fire and she could see his face. Or what she assumed was his face; he was a Dragon.

The fire will speak, he told her. *Repeat what it says, if you can. Repeat it* exactly. *Do you understand?*

She nodded and listened more carefully than she had ever listened as a bored student in a distant classroom. The fire spoke. She couldn't understand it. No, more than that, she had a sense that it *was* speaking, but she couldn't make out syllables; there was nothing there *to* repeat.

Arkon, she said, trying to keep panic out of her voice, *I can't—I can't hear the fire clearly enough to repeat what it says.*

Dragon jaws didn't lend themselves to frowning, but they had other ways of showing displeasure; admittedly fire, at this stage, was not the most effective.

I can hear the fire's voice.

You're touching it.

You must be touching it, he said, his voice quite cold given everything, *or we would not now be speaking. Try again.*

The fire had not stopped its rumble, and none of what it

said was any closer to being audible, never mind repeatable. *Can you understand it?* she asked, in frustration.

He was silent for a moment. *Yes.*

I can't. Understanding doesn't matter—but I can't hear it well enough. At all.

This is an unwelcome complication, was the Arkon's response. *Have you called the other elements?*

Even through the wavering heat of fire, he could read her expression quite clearly. Sadly, she could read his just as well.

I will not ask you how far you progressed in your lessons with Lord Sanabalis, because I am well aware of the answer. This is not a classroom, Private. You will now have to repeat your first success three times. I do not think, he added, *that you have much time left. Grethan has reported that the ground in the street is looking distinctly less...solid.*

The problem with time was that there was *never* enough of it. *Just once,* she thought, straightening her shoulders, *it would be nice to know what I'm doing instead of groping around in the dark.* In this particular case, the darkness was no longer literal; it was lined by fire.

Fire, she thought, and the attention of the Devourer. He was utterly silent now, and his silence was almost another presence, it was so strong.

What, she thought, was the name of air? She had already described what air meant in the context of her own life, and she held those disparate pieces of information while she tried to find the pieces that she hadn't experienced, but could guess. The flight of Dragons. The flight of Aerians. The winds on the ice of mountains that were more myth than fact. She cursed her lack of imagination, or at least its lack of speed, and once again reaffirmed the fact that without breath there was no speech; she hadn't bothered to curse silently.

Nor was the fire silent; it sounded almost like a heartbeat. But there was another sound, like the quiet humming of bees, and Kaylin realized, as she looked around, that the sound came from her. Lifting her arms, she listened; it was the runes. They were vibrating against her skin.

She looked at them as if they were art. Or text. Or some mix of both. And then, looking, she began to speak. It was disturbing because she could hear her voice clearly and it sounded completely unfamiliar. She began to rise in what was only barely air, until her toes were dangling, point down, with nothing to impede them.

Her hair rose, as well—or the parts that *always* escaped any confinement—and something tugged like an insistent toddler at her fingers. She had spoken the name of air, and air had come.

With it, ghostly and translucent, a familiar figure: Lord Sanabalis in miniature. *Kaylin.* He was still a Dragon, his wings extended in a hover that wasn't quite flight.

Sanabalis. I—the Arkon said—

What the Arkon said is something to discuss if we survive this. We may not, he added, which wasn't precisely comforting. *You must listen to the air, Kaylin—and it is not a chore.*

Listen and repeat what it tells me?

Dragon faces didn't lend themselves to surprise, either. But his silence was a beat too long.

Yes.

Earth came next. It was slower than air or fire, but it was easier in all ways to build; what she found, she held, as if it were innately solid. With earth came the Keeper. He wasn't seen through heat haze or wind; he looked as solid as he might have, had he been standing on her foot.

He didn't seem particularly surprised to see her. *Are you*

sure, he said, as if they were seated in the storefront, *you don't want a job?*

She chuckled. Even here. "I'd just mess up the kitchen," she said, speaking out loud. "Although you might not notice the difference." The smile slid from her face, leaving her expression strained. "The Arkon and Sanabalis—"

"They're there?"

"As much as you are. Well, maybe less. They're telling me the fire and the air want me to repeat fire and air words—and I can't even hear them as more than a crackle and hiss."

He frowned.

"You *can* hear them. Can you tell me what they're saying?"

The frown deepened. "No," he said, after a long pause. "I can't. What they say to you, what they need *you* to repeat, isn't meant for my ears."

"Great. It's not meant for *mine*, either."

"But the Devourer hasn't destroyed you."

"No. He's ..quiet, now. I think he's listening."

"Good. You *will* need to repeat the Elemental words."

"How if I can't bloody hear them?"

"I have confidence in you, Private. Call the water."

Kaylin hesitated, and then continued. She had deliberately saved water for last, because it was the element to which she felt closest. She didn't have to struggle to turn water into a metaphor; to Kaylin, water had a personality. It had intent. Yes, it was also necessary for life; yes, people needed to drink it, and rain was required for plants and the fields of farmers.

But the Elemental Water was the heart of the Tha'alaan. Over the centuries of being the receptacle for the memories and emotions of an entire race, it had developed the ability to speak, to feel, and ultimately, to love. It understood home in a way that only the Tha'alani could.

Kaylin would never, ever be more than a visitor to the Tha'alaan. She both hated and accepted it, because when she did manage to sneak in the figurative door, she was treated as if she were family. Here, in an emptiness that was not the solid, confining state of the real world as she knew it, she called the water, because she *knew* the name of water.

It came. It came in a pillar that immediately took form and shape as it rose: Female, and at that a familiar woman. The water, translucent-skinned, with hair that stretched through the gray nothing and vanished from sight, looked very much like the Tha'alani castelord.

Kaylin, Ybelline said, as if to underscore the likeness.

Kaylin reached out to hug this blend of castelord and element, but the element lifted a hand. *You will fall through me,* she said, in a voice that was entirely her own.

It doesn't hurt to fall, here. I've tried. But she stilled. *You need to speak to the Devourer.*

That is not what we call him, but yes. We cannot. You must speak for us, here.

I can't even hear what you're saying. I mean, the other words.

The water began to speak, and... Kaylin heard gurgling—the gurgle of a brook or a clear stream.

It's the same, she began. The words faded.

The ground beneath her feet was changing. What had been gray and almost formless mist—albeit mist that supported weight if you wanted to walk on it—was developing color.

CHAPTER 28

The color wasn't the gray of stone or cobbles; it wasn't the pale brown-gray of packed dirt, or even the green and yellow brightness of weeds. It was, at once, all of those things.

What does it mean? Kaylin asked the water.

The gate is opening, was the water's reply. It was both the answer Kaylin expected and the one she didn't want to hear. *You will no longer be able to speak with us when the landscapes merge.* This, on the other hand, was unexpected, and even less welcome.

Why is the inside of the Devourer changing?

The water didn't answer. Kaylin had a momentary vision of being slowly enveloped by the digestive system of a giant beast. Given the rest of her fears, that one was almost funny.

She could hear the slow grind of stone and the rush of falling water; she could hear the whistle of wind and the crackle of flame. She could speak *of* these things, but the Devourer didn't respond in any way that indicated that he understood. He could *hear* her, yes; his silence and the sudden cessation of the activity for which—clearly—he'd been named made that clear.

Kaylin—she could hear Severn.

Let me see.

He didn't even hesitate. *Can you?*

All hesitance was hers. She felt his presence as if he weren't quite a separate person; as if she could reach out through him and touch the world in which he now stood. She did, and she opened her eyes to a landscape that looked like a chaotic sketch. A sketch that Everly might have done before he started painting. In its center, however, more solid than anything but the massing crowd of refugees, was a very familiar image: the portal.

It stood like a mad mage's idea of a door meant for giants, and it rose into the scintillating colors of what had once been gray. But the portal was not yet open; what lay around it and what lay in its center looked almost exactly the same.

Except the colors within the frame were starting to roil.

She turned as Severn turned, and saw what he saw: the outside of the Devourer. She saw the way the colors that had infested the landscape now clustered around the mountainous and amorphous form of something that might just be nightmare. On a good day.

Kaylin, Ybelline said, her voice softer, the syllables attenuated.

Kaylin opened her eyes to colored mist and the embodiment of the elements; to Dragons, Evanton, and Ybelline. She thought of Vakillirae, of Enkerrikas, and of the cost of their flight and their escape from the Devourer. And she thought, as well, of the one thing that neither of the two had ever considered trying.

She even understood why.

She began to speak her name, not as an affirmation of power, not as an accidental summoning, but as an invitation, as an opening of a door. *The* door, really. She tried to give the elements her name.

Sadly, this was not as easily done as she'd hoped.

She tried three times, and then, clenching her jaw, she smacked herself in the side of the head, and turned to the elements. The elements that she couldn't *hear* and couldn't, therefore, understand.

Listen, she told them, putting years of training into what was, in the end, an unspoken word. They weren't raw recruits; they didn't snap to attention. But they turned to her.

I want to tell you a story.

She couldn't tell them a story about the gods, or the Ancients, because she'd only seen their echoes. She could have told them the stories she'd told the Devourer, but it would have taken too long. So she told them, instead, about the Barrani High Court, and its lake of life, in which the names of the living waited to be joined to the infants who would bear them.

Not an infant, she'd chosen one name for herself—but she'd chosen it blindly, and she'd hidden it. She was already alive. She needed no name and no word to define her; she needed no midwife to breathe life into her still form. She hadn't even meant to take a name for herself at all.

Fire roared; water sizzled. The elements had moved closer to her in the oddly confined space.

She described the name, line by perceptible line, and as she did, the play of simple syllables stretched out, beginning to end. But this disparate description had no resonance for the elements; she saw that.

In frustration, she said, "Sanabalis, how the Hell do you *give your damn name* to someone else?"

It is not something I have ever tried. His nostrils flared.

No? But…she had. She had given her name to Severn. And it hadn't seemed like such a big deal, at the time. No, that wasn't true. It had been important, but the name itself had come easily, as if it were a simple word, some part of her constant vocabulary.

But she'd tried that a dozen times now, and it did *nothing*.

The giving of a name, when it is done at all, is personal, Kaylin. It is as much an individual act of emotion as any declaration of love. No two people mean precisely the same thing when they say it. It is an act, an avowal, that exists entirely in the moment, although the consequences stretch out in either direction, past and future.

He was silent for long enough that she thought he'd finished.

Love is defined by individuals and their response to each other. Even the love of Dragons, although it is deeper and rarer. To give your name to me—if you were so willing and so entirely foolish—would be entirely different from giving your name to your Sergeant. Or your Corporal. They are not the same in intent, in the end, because your intent is defined by your past experiences with each individual.

But, Kaylin, whatever you intend to do, do it now.

She nodded. *Thank you.* She turned, once again, to the elements and their companions. Those companions were the bridge between Kaylin and the heart of fire, water, wind and earth, but they were also the bridge between the rest of the people of her City. Her world.

She understood the ways in which the elements—or the shadows they cast into the world, all the worlds—were part of her life, almost indivisible from it. But, part of her life and necessary to it or no, she was not part of theirs except when crisis drove her to Evanton's shop. She didn't, and couldn't, understand them; they lived forever, and they needed nothing. People needed *them* to be contained, which is why the Garden existed at all.

But they, like any living thing, could *listen*. What they heard, what they made of what she said, she couldn't control—but then again, that was true of any other listener. But she could see the scorn, confusion, anger or surprise of other listeners, so she could add *more* words, or attempt to retract the ones she'd already spoken.

Here, she saw, there would be no retractions. They would understand the core of what she said, or they wouldn't.

So she tried to keep it clear and simple, inasmuch as anything ancient and mystical could be either. She didn't choose complicated words; she chose the ones that described only how she felt, because she *knew* that. *This is who and what I am, right now. I know it's strange and insignificant, and I know I break things sometimes, but only by accident. I'm on the outside, looking in. I'm always on the outside, looking in. But I will knock, now, and I will wait at the door instead of staring through the window like a thief.*

I want to be part of your home. I want to be part of what you are, even if it can only ever be a small part. I will do everything I can, give everything I can, listen when I want to talk, and—and help in the kitchen after dinner. I will try to understand what you are, and not what I want you to be.

It was hard, to wait. Hard to open yourself up for inspection, because inspection implied…judgment. And she'd been judged for things she had no control of all her life.

Ellariayn.

The only thing Kaylin could hear for one long moment was her name. It was also the only thing she could feel, as if she were a gong or a perfect, resonant bell. She understood some part of why names were hidden, *must* be hidden, then. People built invisible, social walls between each other all the time; if they didn't, all the police in the world couldn't stop the carnage that would follow. What worked for the Tha'alani worked in part because they had been born into a world without emotional defenses, and the lack was so utterly natural, the polite lies that maintained civilized interaction were unnecessary.

This was like the nightmare of what the Tha'alaan was to someone who had never experienced it. Kaylin knew because it was what she'd feared so strongly herself. But the Tha'alaan knew it, as well; the Tha'alani knew her fear because she'd touched their racial memories, and they had absorbed the knowledge of who she was. And therefore, so did the Elemental Water, or that part of the water that Kaylin could no longer think of as inhuman and remote.

Kaylin, she said. *Kaylin.* Her voice was softer, like wave against shore, rather than the tidal wave that the spoken name had threatened. *Our voices are strong, to you. You are too small to contain them for long.*

She didn't even grimace; it was true. She felt so inconsequential she wanted to curl up and hide, the way she sometimes had as a very small child. Which, she reminded herself with some disgust, she wasn't anymore.

This...this name, the water said, *it is part of us now. Do you understand what you've done?*

No, Kaylin replied, completely honestly. There was no point in lying now; they could see anything at all they chose to look for.

Do you understand now what you must do?

And she did. *It's not enough, to open myself up to the Elements of the Garden. I have to reach the Devourer, too.*

Yes. But... Devourer—and he will understand what you mean, even if the word is not one he can speak—is not what he is. Or not what he was when the worlds were the idle dream of passing moments, and we were free.

Kaylin hesitated. She might as well not have bothered.

Yes, Kaylin. I understand your fear. It is a fear shared by Ybelline, the loudest of all my living voices. You will return the Devourer to us, and the Garden and its eternal peace will be unmade. We will have our freedom, as we once did, and we will unmake the world—all the worlds—reclaiming what we once might have been.

I do not know if it will comfort you, the Element added, but I will say what I said to Ybelline. When the child is birthed, it leaves the mother, for good or for ill. Mother and child cannot return to their single state after the fact, even if they cannot be separated with ease.

We are not children, the water said softly, for she understood Kaylin's reaction almost before Kaylin did. Nor are we parents, or mothers. But it is…not unlike that. Our separation was the birth of possibility and life, and it was written in ways that you will never perceive while you remain mortal.

But…he was our night, Kaylin. He was our sleep. He was our borders and our peace. We, conversely, were his dawn, and his waking, and the fractious tension out of which arose his duty. We were his noise and his language. I will not speak of love, for love is small and unique and precise.

But Kaylin understood it anyway. The Elements were his language. His words. In some way, they were his voice.

This is what you want me—all of you—to tell him.

Yes, Kaylin. Yes, daughter. This is what you must tell him. We will guide you if you cannot speak the words.

Evanton should have—

The speaking would end Evanton. But you bear the marks and the words, Kaylin. I believe it will not destroy you. Come, she said, and she lifted one watery hand.

Kaylin took it instinctively, and found, to her surprise, that it was solid. Solid and yet somehow quintessentially water. Can you tell him my name?

No. We can tell him only the parts of it we understand. He might find you again if he bent will and purpose to the task, no more. It *would be something,* she added. *But not, I think, enough, not in the time that you have.*

She was silent for one moment longer as Kaylin once again gathered her frayed nerves. *We were free,* the water said, her voice remote. *And we will never be free again while you live. But that seems to me the progression of life itself, as it is lived by the mortals and the immortals across the worlds. You build your cages, and you call them homes, and you accept the burdens and responsibilities that come with them. You even learn to love them.*

What you are comes out of what you were. What we are comes out of what we were. But we cannot unlearn what we have learned. We cannot be what we were. No more can you return to your infancy. It has passed. It is beyond you.

She fell silent, although she didn't leave; Kaylin sensed her presence, and in it, or beside it, the presence of the others. She could not touch the Devourer, not yet, but her senses were heightened, and she perceived him, not as an amorphous beast, but as something else: a page, perhaps, or a book, its words faded. She couldn't read them, but she could see what they must have been, in part. She could see what was missing.

Her arms and her legs were glowing as if she had swallowed fire and the marks on her skin were glass through which it could be viewed. She lifted those arms, turning her palms out; light radiated from them in spokes.

What she had done for the elements, she now did for the nameless creature who had hunted—and destroyed—worlds. But if the intent was the same, the offering was different. She didn't stand in the frame of the door like an uncertain, homeless orphan waiting approval; she didn't open herself up to his inspection—and rejection—in the same held-breath way.

They had invited her in, in the end; they had accepted what she offered. And Severn had said that she made any place she entered another home, because she needed and understood home in a way that he didn't. Maybe it was true. Maybe it wasn't. She couldn't and didn't argue with his words because she was weak enough to want to believe them.

She trusted him enough that, for this very necessary minute, she did. She opened the door that she had only barely entered herself, turning back to look into the streets as if trying to catch a glimpse of someone who might be huddling outside, looking in as she'd looked in.

What she saw was the whole of the night sky writ large. She saw the starscape as the night unfolded; she saw the misty wreaths of borealis; she saw the Twin moons. She saw the immensity of the heavens—not the literal heavens, but the ones which even Dragons couldn't touch in flight—and she felt her size and her insignificance keenly.

In the distance, she saw the mountains rise. They weren't the familiar Southern Stretch, which housed her beloved Aerians— and, to be fair, the ones she could have happily done without, as well—but some echo of that stretch existed in this one. And the mountains came closer to the sky than Kaylin ever would without winged help.

The wind's touch was cool; a welcome night breeze. It carried the scent of the rain, of mist, of the rowans which sometimes made her sneeze; it carried, as well, the fragrance of the white lilacs that grew down the banks of the lanes a few blocks from Elani. Her favorite scents were bread, fresh bread, but that was absent; there was nothing in the wind that suggested that people owned any part of it.

Water came as grass rose around Kaylin's feet, springing from nothing to her knees. By some strange alchemy of earth and wind and water, trees ringed the foothills of those distant mountain ranges, and from the height of those mountains, water began to rush, head over heels, toward the lower terrain. The earth cracked and widened to receive it, to build the channel through which it might pass.

Where is fire? Kaylin asked.

Fire roared, and for an instant, Kaylin froze. But turning, she saw that it roared in a stone pit at her back, flames leaping over the edge to lap above grass that wilted but didn't burn. It was close, though. She understood, then, that the fire was contained, but so, too, the water, the earth, and the air. She knew what the landscape would look like if they went to war—and she also knew that she wouldn't survive it.

It didn't matter; they were united, for a moment, in this purpose.

Kaylin realized as the elements spoke to—and through—her that it was an effort on their part, sustained by the fading presence of the Keeper, whose role was to guide, guard, and leash their fury. Evanton was silent.

Kaylin was not. She spoke, and words formed as she did, runes that were ancient and wild and true. They formed quickly, and they formed completely, capturing what she hoped to say. Sanabalis had told her—she thought it was Sanabalis—that *these* words had a meaning that did not rely on context or limited understanding, by which of course he meant hers.

But she recognized one rune clearly: it was *her* name. It nestled among the others, the names, she realized belatedly, of fire, earth, air, and her beloved water. There was another rune, however. It was a simple rune, which is why she'd missed it the first time, one stroke that stood on end. One bold stroke, she thought, as she examined it. A similar single stroke bisected the line of each of the other runes, some part of their much more complex patterns; they were built on it, although ultimately, they were unique.

She left the blazing fire at her back; heard it crackle and

hiss as if it were chiding her for her desertion. A few yards away, across the unkempt grass, the words rotated in the air, immune to gravity. They were evenly spaced, but as she walked around them, she saw that they circled the central, simple glyph. Even her name.

Reaching out, she touched the single rune with the flat of one palm. It was smooth and dense and cool.

And oh, the marks on her skin began to dance. To rise, pulling her with them, until her feet no longer touched earth. Her palms tingled and warmed where the rune touched skin, until she was almost numb with the sensation. The moons in the sky's height turned, as she had known they would, and she saw again the vast distance of desert eyes, against which her reflection would have been so tiny she wouldn't have seen it at all.

The fact that these eyes were on the inside of what might have been a body didn't trouble her at all. She stood, hand on rune, waiting—because he could see her now. He could see as much of her as *he* could understand, and it resided in the externalization of her true name. It wasn't what Severn understood; it wasn't what she herself understood. But her name had been offered, and it was the only bridge they now had, this endless and eternal force and the very finite Private.

He roared, and this time she understood every word he spoke—and he did speak, and it was a chaos of syllables that clashed and thundered toward her. She couldn't see them the way she could see the names, but she could feel them as if they were elemental: ice and fire, thunder and earthquake. He was calling them, she thought; he was shouting their very names into the night sky as if they were, in the end, the only words he owned.

Speaking, she thought, without being heard.

But he knew where they were, now; they knew where he was.

There is danger, Kaylin, a familiar voice said. It was Evanton; he'd been watching. *If the elements are correct—and it appears they are—he has been searching for them for a very long, and very destructive, time. He can see them now. He will be in a frenzy to reach them.*

Never mind reaching them, she said. *Are you ready for what happens when he does?*

The Keeper laughed. It was a slightly bewildered sound. *I? No, of course not. The water is reasonably certain I'll survive. But the portal is opening, Kaylin. Grethan can see it. He can see your refugees, although they are not yet entirely clear. I think you will have minutes, if that, before the Devourer is loose in the world.*

She understood, then. *He can't reach the elements,* she told Evanton, *if he* isn't *loose in the world, as you put it. Unless—*

Unless?

We came here through the store—

I'm sorry, he said quietly, *but no.*

Then I have no other way to reach you. She was still suspended in air; she couldn't lower her arms. She spoke in a rush without volition as the elements opened the figurative window and began to shout instructions and encouragement.

She'd thought to be afraid, and in part she was—because she could feel herself swept up in the gale of elemental emotion, and she had to work to remember why she'd come here in the first place. Why had she? To find the Devourer. And to save the people who it stalked in its ignorance: the refugees and the inhabitants of her world.

The refugees now had to take care of themselves, although they had Severn, if he could make himself understood. The Hawks *knew* what to expect, and they knew where to expect it. She let it go, and turned the whole of her attention to the Devourer. She had made a metaphor, and she now attempted to continue it; if the elements were standing at a barely open window shouting either directions or welcome or both, the Devourer was still outside, and he couldn't—or wouldn't—move, because movement would take them out of his sight.

But he needed to find the door, and the door needed to be opened. Someone needed to invite him in. *Help me,* she told the elements.

The water said, *Why?*

Because the portal is opening, and he's going to go through it. I don't think he has a way of leaving nonworld. He destroys what he finds, and sometimes, somehow, he finds worlds. But I don't think he ever sees them as anything but names or words.

I need to be on the outside of whatever it is he becomes when he leaves this place.

Silence. Heavy, clouded silence. The words were worse. *I don't think he understands your concept of inside and outside.*

Kaylin, frustrated, said, *What was he when he was part of you?*

They answered as one voice, and Kaylin didn't understand a single word they said. She recognized what she heard *as* words; the syllables were sharp and defined, and if she listened hard enough, she could repeat them, for all the good they'd do her.

But the Devourer heard, and the Devourer turned; she could feel the movement of his internal eyes. His eyes.

She rose without any volition at all, approaching those eyes, which grew larger and larger. She had thought them deserts, both ice and sand—at a distance. Some sense of that emptiness remained, but none of the sense of geography; she would have lifted her hands to shield her eyes, but she couldn't move her arms at all. She could barely close her eyes.

★ ★ ★

When she opened her eyes, she almost closed them again. She could see light and darkness and the uneasy blend of both; it was like a very spectacular hangover, but without the pain. Pain came from confusion. But the confusion, in this case, wasn't hers—it rode her. Or she rode it. She couldn't sense her body at all. The only thing she could sense—and it was the wrong word for what she now felt—was the immensity of emptiness. She was, she realized, the Devourer. She was part of him; she saw and felt what he saw and felt—but she could only dimly understand any of it.

Whatever parts of her that were Kaylin were so insignificant she couldn't feel them at all. This was admittedly worrying; she took a very figurative deep breath. He didn't. What he could see, she could now see—but interpreting it, making sense of it? It was as if what he could see was filtered through her very human, very normal vision. Which meant she was still herself. Somewhere.

He turned and she turned with him, as if they were indivisible. There was one solid thing in this blurred and shifting landscape, but she wasn't certain what it was.

As she circled it in a frenzy, she realized what it *must* be, but the Devourer's vision didn't see words—even ancient, living words—the way hers did. These words didn't look like runes; they didn't look like fire, earth, air, or water to Kaylin, either. But their light was in motion, and as she watched—and she did, because she didn't have much choice—they traced a complicated pattern, a type of dance, across the ether, and the trail of their luminescent shadows lingered where they'd passed. She *did* recognize those.

It was as if the words the Devourer saw and understood cast shadows, and those shadows were a type of ink, something that Kaylin could see and comprehend. She realized, then, that that's all she'd really ever see of the words: the light they cast, the thing they left behind.

And what are we? What are the rest of us? Nothing else cast those shadows, nothing else scrawled across the ether in the Devourer's vision.

Kaylin. She could hear Severn; he was her anchor.

Listen to me, she said, to the Devourer. *Listen to what I tell you.*

He paused in his frenzied circular motion.

She spoke of her world. She spoke of the things that she knew of it and imagined, as she did, that she was laying down the complex, complicated, lines of a world in a brief pencil sketch. But he understood *something* about what she tried so hard to tell him because he had made her part of him. He had taken her name.

The elements aided her, picking up threads of her story, leaving the shapes of other words in their wake; words that were in some part derived from their baselines, but also unique. But they moved so damn fast, Kaylin couldn't follow it all, and she gave up trying. She let them speak; it wasn't a conversation, exactly, but it wasn't the noisy, shouting chaos of a mob, either; she could speak and she was certain she had his attention.

What she wasn't certain of was how much of what she was trying to say was getting through; how much of it was being processed. She had no sense of the passage of time, but at the same point, Severn's urgent—and silent—worry let her know that it was, damn it, passing.

Listen to me, she said.

And this time he said: Who are you?

Put me down, she told the Devourer after a long silence. *Put me down where you found me.* She expected the concept to be confusing because he hadn't *exactly* picked her up; here, she trusted the conduit of name to translate some small portion of her thought into his vast mind.

She landed, with a whumpf, against the squishy, gray ground just behind Severn's feet. She could see Severn again. She could see everything. The portal—and it looked like something majestic and vast, as different from the portcullis of Castle Nightshade as night from day—was open, and the ghost of Elani street was clearly visible. It was gray, but color was slowly appearing on its cobbles and its sandwich-board signs as she watched. Had she not been standing so close to the troop of Elders, for want of a better word, she wouldn't have been able to see a damn thing; people were pressing in on all sides, and she wanted to tell them that if they stood that tightly packed with naked swords and axes, someone was going to lose a leg.

What she couldn't see—at all—was the Devourer. He was there; she had no doubt. But he was gray and vast, like the nonworld itself. Without the roaring of his deadly storm, nothing gave his presence away.

You let me see what you saw, she told the Devourer. *Try, now, to see what I see.*

She looked at the portal, and then found herself looking away as the Devourer did, indeed, borrow her vision. He, however, had his own ideas about what was, or might be, interesting. So she saw what he wanted to see, but she saw it as Kaylin Neya.

What are they?

This was easier. *People.* She saw the word form in front of her, and knew that it was both ancient, and less ancient than the Devourer.

Why are they here?

They have nowhere else to go. They seek safety. She hesitated, and then added, *They have no home.* Another word formed, and this one she knew. She knew it not because she'd seen it before, but because she could *feel* its truth so strongly it might have been her name.

But she noted that the Devourer made no frenzied attempt to pull apart either of the two words in a continuation of his desperate search. *Don't,* she added, as she felt movement. *You'll break them.*

Severn touched her shoulder gently. "It's almost done," he said.

She nodded; she would have turned, but couldn't; the Devourer was still looking, as she'd asked, through her eyes. Seeing what she saw *as* she saw it was confusing and strange to him. She could almost feel him try to make sense of it, try to relate it to something familiar. Fair enough; it's what she'd do.

She heard shouting, and she did turn then—because he'd heard it, as well; apparently he hadn't confined himself to vision. He saw the strangers ready themselves, and saw them turn to the portal, toward which he now also turned. Both of him: the part of him that occupied Kaylin by force of will and use of the name she'd given him as a trapdoor, and the large, amorphous, world-eater.

Both froze.

He saw what she saw, yes, but he saw what he saw, as well: the luminosity of words, hidden and pale, in the distance. They were stronger than the words she'd spoken—but they were not as strong, not as vital, as the elemental names. He held himself in check because he understood that she meant to take him to where they *were*.

But...he *wanted* these other, lesser, words, and it was a hunger which grew as the seconds passed. So she said to him, *take mine.* And this time, when she lifted her sleeves—which Severn was, she realized belatedly, deliberately not staring at, they were now so ragged—he looked *at* her arm.

One glyph rose from her skin, taking a shape in the air that almost dwarfed her. He touched it; she felt him. But it was odd; it was as if the word were meant, in its entirety, to be disassembled by him.

"Severn," she said, as she saw the light of the rune begin to dim, "we have to move *now*."

By dint of personality and presence, Severn made her will known, and as the streets at last gained their full color and shape, the old woman rallied her tired, her hungry, and her lost, and she called upon the men who guarded the train. She sent them through first.

Kaylin was on their heels. *Follow*, she said, and as she moved, the mark that she had sacrificed to his hunger moved with her, like a fancy carrot-on-a-stick. She almost laughed. Or wept. He brushed past the refugees as if they no longer existed, and they felt his passing as if it were a strong gust of wind.

Words, he said as they cleared the thin membrane of portal. Words! It wasn't all of what he was saying, but it was the only part that made sense to Kaylin. The hunger almost overwhelmed him. Kaylin shook her head, lifted an arm, and again, a glyph flew free. She wondered, as it began to dim, if this was the way she would lose her distinguishing marks forever. Realized, as she wondered, that if she'd once hated them, she'd grown attached to them; they were a part of what she now was.

If asked, she'd have sworn she'd be ecstatic to be rid of them. But ecstatic or no, she *did* it, and that had to count for something. She had one moment of numb fear when he breached the portal because the portal *folded,* buckling and rippling in a way that threatened to pull down the damn *sky*.

She cried out in alarm, because the sky *was* tearing, and she could see red and black and iridescent gold in the rents.

But because he held her name, he felt her alarm. He didn't understand it, but he stopped his feeding for long enough to look at the portal through her eyes. He paused as if caught, the hunger forgotten; she felt a ripple of something that might be concern, and then the portal straightened and the sky reasserted itself.

It was brighter, bluer, and *clearer* than it had been scant seconds before. This didn't make her any happier; he was staring at it, and her own lips pursed in a frown. She asked the water what had happened, and received only silence in reply. She was here. The voice of the water was not.

But...the Devourer was here, almost here, as well. And she couldn't see him—not with her own eyes. His, she didn't ask to borrow again.

She would have marched straight to Evanton's, but the way was blocked.

Armed men stood ten yards from the portal's mouth, and when they saw the travelers who had walked so far and in such isolation to reach this city, they stiffened; no surprise there. Kaylin would have, had she been in their shoes. They were, of course, members of the Eternal Emperor's Law: the Swords and the Hawks. Kaylin had no doubt at all that there were Wolves in the buildings above the portal spawn point.

But *these* people, Severn could talk with, and he separated himself from a veritable forest of bristling armed men and women, walking with his hands palms up until he reached the commander of the Swords. One palm snapped a perfect salute. She could hear him talk but she couldn't make out the words; they were lost to a very familiar, very unwelcome roar.

It was answered by a very welcome one.

She couldn't see him through the crowd given her height, and she didn't try for long, but she recognized the Dragon roar of Tiamaris.

CHAPTER 29

It didn't take him long to clear the crowd; even the Swords were familiar enough with the etiquette of the Dragon Court to give them passage. Tiamaris hadn't come alone. He didn't have Tara with him, but Kaylin thought it was impossible for the Tower's Avatar to leave her fief; to her knowledge, she had never tried.

Instead, he came flanked by two Dragons: the Lords Emmerian and Diarmat. The Swords moved to make way for them; all three were wearing the crest of the Dragon Court. In Elantra proper, fief laws didn't apply; Tiamaris was not, therefore, wearing the big scales and wings of his Draconic form. But in an emergency, he could—and the knowledge of that radiated from all of the Dragons present. They weren't tall compared to the strangers who had begun to appear in the hundreds in the street, and their swords weren't greatswords.

But their eyes were a dark shade of orange as they turned from the Captain of the Swords toward the unnamed and unknown intruders, and something about the color of their eyes made those strangers fall silent.

"Corporal," Tiamaris said, without taking his gaze from

the ring of guards that stood between the Swords and the less aggressive refugees. "Private. The danger?"

Kaylin tried to answer; the Devourer, however, was in control. She roared. Which should have sounded weak and unimpressive, especially when compared to a Dragon's roar. It didn't. It also sounded nothing like Kaylin. She wondered what color her eyes were. All three of the Dragon Lords turned to face her.

They're the color of glass, Kaylin, Severn told her.

Glass?

Yes. You can see through them.

That was disturbing. *See what?*

Night.

Oh gods, Severn—it's not Shadow—

No. Night. Moons, stars.

Tell them I'm still here. Tell Tiamaris—ask him—not to go Dragon. He'll crush the Swords who are standing nearby. The Dragons' eyes were red. Kaylin knew it was illegal to make the transformation from human form to Dragon form without Imperial dispensation, but she was pretty sure they had it. And even if they didn't, who was going to stop them?

Not the Swords.

And by the look of them, not the exhausted and grim people of the otherworld. They tightened their grip on their weapons and they looked to the old woman. The old woman, however, pointed at Kaylin, and at the marks on her arm, which were glowing. It was a coruscating light, different from the constant blue glow they usually shed when they shone.

No one moved.

Except for Kaylin. She stiffened as the Devourer roared. Tiamaris roared *back.* His roar, however, was different: he was speaking. The Swords—and, give them this, the scruffy strangers—were disciplined enough not to cover their ears.

The Devourer spoke a single word through her mouth. It was, of course, a Dragon word. Kaylin felt it, but couldn't understand it—and for the sake of her very human throat, hoped that Tiamaris understood it the first time.

He must have; he became utterly still. He was the only one of the Dragons who did; Emmerian and Diarmat took a step back. She understood why, in part: the Devourer's word meant the whole of emptiness, lack of purpose, lack of duty, lack of—of joy, of place. It wasn't like loneliness—that one, she understood well. But it occupied the depths of which loneliness was sheer surface.

Tiamaris then said a Dragon word, and this one, she knew: *Hoard.*

The Devourer fell silent; it was not a long silence. But it was broken by the rumbling of the earth beneath her feet, and the ground fractured, cobbles cracking in a line that seemed to extend along the whole street, or at least what she could see of it. She couldn't turn to look behind her; she didn't have that much control over her body.

But she could see, out of the corner of her eye, the familiar panes of the windows of Evanton's shop.

Severn! Tell Tiamaris I have to get to Evanton's. We have to reach the Garden before—

Water began to fill the crack in the street, and along the sides of what wouldn't have passed muster as riverbanks in the clumsy drawings of five-year-olds, flowers began to bloom. The strangers shouted and the stiff and wary silence of their first few minutes broke.

But the Devourer couldn't or didn't hear them, and Kaylin therefore couldn't turn. She took a step toward Tiamaris, whose eyes were a darker red than she'd ever seen them. Severn stepped between them.

Severn, no—

And went flying. She couldn't even say where, because the act of throwing him out of the way was as consequential as his words had been to the creature who now rode inside of her. She understood what he wanted, then.

Tiamaris had a name. A word.

But so did Kaylin, and although she had no physical control of her body, a rune rose from her skin, and it grew to occupy the space that Severn had occupied for a few brief seconds.

Severn!

I'm all right.

Tell Tiamaris and the other Dragons to get back—

She could feel, rather than hear, his snort.

Okay, that was stupid. But the Devourer can see that they're immortal. He can see that they have names, and he, he'll try to consume them. He's not trying to destroy them, she added more urgently. *But that'll be the net effect.* She cringed as the single rune, gifted by the Ancients, began to dim.

Tiamaris asks if you can stop him—

From what?

From destroying the street.

Not if everyone doesn't get out of the damn way.

They're worried about the small army that's materialized in the street.

Kaylin wanted to scream, which, given the Captains present, would probably have been career limiting. *I need you to get them out of the way.*

She felt his nod; she couldn't see it. And she felt the heat of Tiamaris's breath pass around her like a charnel wind. She understood why; the fire didn't hurt. But it stung.

She felt the rune dwindle, and she cursed as another took its place. She wanted to read the word before it was lost to her forever, but she wanted to survive, as well. She threw fear at the Devourer as if it were a rock and he were a closed bedroom window two stories above the ground.

But his attention flickered toward her and she caught it and held it for just a moment. She spoke a single word that she felt and heard as *home;* she knew that he heard it as if it were larger than anything she could comprehend, and he did turn then, like a ponderous, slow beast.

She prayed because she did that when she was terrified; it was better than whimpering or screaming. Sometimes it helped. Today? It was answered. Tiamaris, Emmerian, and Diarmat withdrew; the Swords, shifting numbers so they faced the obvious threat—to their mind—also made way, forming a tunnel that led from the foot of the portal to Evanton's storefront.

The Devourer, who was used to roaming the vast and empty wastelands, couldn't tell the difference between a door and a window, and the window shattered to give them passage. Grethan was standing behind the bar, his jaw dropping toward the floor in a slow, painful fall. It was, however, still attached to his face.

She didn't tell him to get the hell out of the way, because she couldn't; she didn't *need* to tell him to pick up the stuff that her hurried passage was knocking over to the left and right. He'd lived with Evanton for long enough that bending in panic to retrieve his fallen garbage was second nature. But she walked past him; she couldn't turn her head or speak a word, her gaze was now so focused. The Devourer knew where to go, because she knew, and she concentrated on it as if her life depended on nothing else.

They made their way through a corridor jammed on either side with shelves; it had never seemed so narrow. The slats beneath her feet were slightly warped wood, and they creaked in all the right ways for her size and her weight. The hall led to a locked door, as it always did.

This door, she knew. She knew its shape and its texture and the ways in which it could be opened. She knew that in theory only Grethan and Evanton could unlock it. Theory, however, didn't and couldn't contain the Devourer; he was part of a different story, a much older one, and the structural rules for *this* story had no place for him.

But he lingered at the door, and he seemed—for just that instant—to lose all sense of enormity, of the unknown and unknowable wilderness that was ancient magic. What he felt—or what she interpreted the emotion as—was something that was entirely contained in her experience: his desperate frenzy, the insanity and ferocity of *loss,* had, at last, given way to uncertainty. Fear.

This is where he wanted to be, and he wasn't certain that it was where he belonged. The vast, empty wastelands had been his home for so long it was in, and of him. He was changed, and he didn't know if the changes would allow him any return at all. And he wanted it; he wanted it so badly she could taste it.

It tasted of wind and rain and cold snow on tongue; it tasted of ash and smoke; it tasted of rock and stone and soft dirt. But it felt like…memory. She couldn't understand his at all, but drifted, on the strength of the familiarity of the emotions they evoked, into her own.

She could only barely remember what her mother looked like, it had been so long since she'd seen her in anything but dream—or nightmare. But she could, conversely, remember her mother's expressions: joy, anger, fear, pride. Love. And she could remember the feel of her mother's arms around her, her mother's voice in her ear—things she had to hold on to because there would never *be* any other memories. Not good ones, not bad ones. Nothing.

But she'd accepted the fact of her mother's death. She was gone. The Devourer had no word for acceptance; he had no word for peace.

As if he could see or feel Kaylin's memories, she felt them vanish, and she felt, in place of their comfort, the visceral, immediate agony of the fact of two different deaths: Steffi. Jade. The children that she'd adopted when she was no more than a child herself.

That loss was sharper and harder, and it cut her the way it always did when she returned to it; she felt her throat both dry and thicken until she couldn't even swallow. She had worked her way to acceptance of their absence; she thought she had accepted the fact of their death, and she had.

But it was the *only* memory that the Devourer felt was akin to his own in some tiny, insignificant way, and he tore it up from its resting place. Some things, she'd buried for a reason. You had to look away from them if you were going to keep moving.

She remembered her walk through the streets of the Tower of Tiamaris, and she remembered what the Tower had said when she had confronted the Tower's Avatar with her anger at that forced reminiscence of Hell: *What did I do? I spoke with you. It was hard. I tried to show you that I understood your pain.*

Kaylin never wanted to communicate with anything ancient or immortal again. She also wanted to throw up. Instead she lifted her hands and placed both palms against the door, and this, the Devourer allowed.

She remembered what she'd lost now, because he made her remember it, and she *also* remembered why she had loathed and feared the Tha'alani so damn much. This, this invasion, this stranger tromping through the bits of her life that interested him, invading and exposing all of the darkness, was everything she had ever dreaded the Tha'alani would be. She'd been wrong, and tried to remember it.

She struggled with the anger, because now was not the time for it, and the anger was—she knew, although it was hard—misplaced. He *was* trying, in some small way, to communicate with her; he *didn't* have all of the words. These emotions, these losses—they were the only similarity he could easily find.

Knowing it helped; knowing—or praying—that it would stop when he reached the Garden did the rest.

She opened the door. There were no wards, and she had no key, but her arms were burning, her legs almost shuddering with the tingling that had long passed the barrier between pleasure and pain. *I am trying,* she said, clenching her teeth, *to get you home, damn you!*

The door swung in, the hinges creaking as if it were exactly as careworn and rickety as it appeared to be, and what the Devourer feared he would never find again, Kaylin found in an instant: she could hear the voice of Elemental Water, and through it, the voice of Ybelline.

Kaylin, the castelord said, making a question of the name that held all of her concern, her worry, and her vast affection.

If she could have, she would have dropped to her knees and hugged the ground. But the Devourer wouldn't cross the threshold, and at the moment, he occupied most of her.

I'm here, she told Ybelline.

You must bring him into the Garden, the castelord said carefully.

I think he's afraid.

The castelord's silence was slightly more complicated than usual. *How do you know this?* she finally asked.

Because he's dredged up every memory I've ever had that's grim and ugly, and he's made it so strong I— She shook her head, or tried. *I think he's trying to tell me that this is how he feels.* She was somehow touching the Tha'alaan because she stood on the border of the Elemental Garden, and the water had her name.

Thank you, Kaylin, Ybelline said. *I believe the water will speak with you now.*

The water, wordless, wasn't silent; Kaylin heard its movement. She opened her eyes, and she saw, not the garden with which she was mostly familiar, but the heart of the ocean itself. From it rose a wave that would have destroyed half the City had it hit. It was framed by a door that Kaylin only briefly considered shutting; she didn't try.

No, the water said. *You won't.*

Maybe because he won't let me.

Water thundered and fell in denial. Kaylin got *very* wet. So, sadly, did Evanton's books. If he survived, he was going to be *pissed.*

It is not because you have no volition, the water said, *but because you trust me. You are not elemental, and you are not wild. You are not ancient. You live, and die, so quickly your thoughts are fleeting and hard to grasp. I am not, and will never be, what you are.*

But you trust, regardless.

He will never be what you are, and of all of us, he is the least affected by the brevity of your lives. He destroys them because he cannot even comprehend them, they move past so quickly. What he sees in you now is confusing. Were it not for your name, Kaylin-who-is-not-immortal, he would not see it at all.

He struggles to do what you have chosen to do, time and again, according to my daughter.

Daughter?

Ybelline Rabon'alani. You have chosen, time and again, to place trust and hope over fear and uncertainty. Teach him, Kaylin. Teach him this. He is changing the world in which you stand. If you did

*not stand in the lee of the Garden, you would not even recognize
that world now.*

But why—

It is his nature.

Tell him—

We have been speaking, Kaylin? Can you not hear us?

She nodded, because she could—but she was tired and in
pain, and the sounds were natural sounds, not words, not deliberate communication.

Teach him. Show him how.

She wanted to argue. She wanted to tell the water that it
wasn't true. On bad days she didn't even *like* people. Trusting them?

She spent her days patrolling Elani street, where sandwich boards and gaudy merchant windows made a mockery
of trust; trust was for fools and the quirky rich. Trust, Morse
had told her, was fine for corpses. Trust, she had learned in
Nightshade, was just another tool to exploit, a weapon that
you gave the exploiter if you weren't careful.

Trust was for the willfully blind. She'd seen the corpses of
women murdered by their husbands, their fathers, and once,
their sister; she'd seen husbands murdered by their wives,
and children murdered by strangers that they had inexplicably chosen to trust. It wasn't a daily occurrence, not even in
her years in the Hawks—but it was reality.

She was *not* a trusting person.

You trusted the Hawklord.

She was used to arguing with herself, and she even tried.
*I thought he would kill me. I expected him to kill me. Trust didn't
cost* anything.

You trusted Marcus.

He came with the Hawklord.

You trusted—and still trust—Severn.

Severn. The memories the Devourer had rifled through were so raw she wanted to scream. In fury. In denial. A scream that might change the world and time and everything in it.

He had done this. Severn had killed them. She had trusted him. Steffi and Jade had trusted him. Gods—gods—gods—

She screamed, instead, at the water. *You didn't do this to him!*

The water fell utterly silent then. The fire's hiss and crackle vanished. The wind stilled. But beneath her toes—the toes that were just a hairbreadth across the doorjamb, the earth was trembling.

Oh my god, she whispered, and she bent and placed a palm across the threshold. *You did.* The Devourer was as still as the elements; he didn't seek to stop her as she pressed a hand into the soft, warm sand. Nor did he stop her when she rose and walked, at last, into the Garden itself. *You did.*

The Devourer was in the Garden, now, but he was not, as Kaylin had hoped, any closer to the home she had promised him. And she *had* promised him that much. She was angry— and anger against the elements had always been futile. Anger against the snow, or the rain, or the humid, sweltering heat made as much sense as anger against disease. They were things that happened. It wasn't personal.

But this? This was, she saw clearly, personal. She'd never been good at pointing anger in the right direction, and she was willing to admit—privately, where the entire Garden could actually listen in—that she had trouble letting go. The Devourer had brought to the surface everything she kept buried. She now had fury to spare, and it was easier—it was always easier—to turn it outward.

What did you do?

Silence. It was the silence of gathering storm, and had she an ounce more sense, she'd've been afraid. Anger was a shield.

But it wasn't the storm who spoke, and it wasn't Ybelline—although she would have welcomed the soothing presence of the Tha'alani castelord. It was, to her surprise, the Arkon.

"Private," he said, his voice dry and clear. "Look at the ground upon which you are standing."

Confused, she did exactly that, and she saw that the sand dunes that framed the ocean had given way to the wild and unkempt weeds one found in the deserted yards of dilapidated manors throughout the fiefs. But the weeds themselves were fine-veined and totally different in color than any others she'd encountered before.

"Evanton?"

The Keeper was silent.

"If I am correct," the Arkon said, "he is attempting to make certain that the changes made in the Garden conform in some small way to our accepted understanding of life. It is not guaranteed, and in this, his elemental control has been...compromised. It would be best if you failed to touch the earth at all."

She didn't point out that she didn't have wings, and *also* had no control over the Elemental Air. Instead, she said, "I need to know what happened in the past."

"Ask them," he said.

"I was—"

"Not that way. If I understand what has happened, Kaylin, the elements now have your name. Use it."

"*They* have *my* name."

"That is what I said."

"I can't use—"

"You cannot compel, Private. And if they desire it, you will never be free of their compulsion. But it is a bond that works both ways. You will see, and hear, more clearly than anyone present, with the possible exception of Evanton, and in a limited case, Ybelline Rabon'alani.

"Use the bond. If you require information, gain it. But do it quickly. The Garden will not survive, and if it does not…"

"And if they don't want to tell me?"

He didn't answer.

Had the Devourer destroyed whole worlds in an attempt to ease his pain? She couldn't turn to face him, but if she could have, she would. She was still raw from his inspection and his forced unearthing of her past, and perhaps that had been his intent; it had worked.

She spoke to the water. *Tell me,* she said, trying to keep her mental voice even and clean.

The water was silent, and Kaylin realized that no matter how even or clean her voice, her fury was utterly visible to any of the immortals present who were gifted with her name. She said, *Live with it. If I don't know what happened, I can't teach him what you need him to learn. What we need him to learn.*

You learned.

I learned after the fact. I learned reasons, and I could even understand them. I would never, ever make the choice Severn did. I would never do what he did. Yes, she snarled. *I do trust him. With my life. With almost everything in it. And I'm not proud of that fact.* It was true. Here, all words had to be true.

He knew me better than anyone. He still knows me better than anyone else does. He asks for almost nothing. And he will never, ever do that again.

You are certain.

Yes. Tell me.

Can you convince him—

I don't know. I don't know if I'll even understand what you did, *and if I don't, I don't know if he will.* Her damn arms were aching so badly she thought the fire must be caressing them. *Tell me,* she said again.

The water did.

The problem with listening to immortal and endless elements—any of them—was nothing they said made any sense. Or rather, they made as much sense as snow or storm or earthquake; they happened, and if you were lucky, you survived. They didn't have intent, and they didn't have observation— not of the people who they happened to.

These four, though, could learn. The water could speak as clearly to Kaylin as Ybelline did. But with strength of name to bind them, Kaylin understood that the water's interpretation of the words it sometimes spoke were...different. Although the water did speak, Kaylin couldn't figure out what the hells it was *saying.* Anger ebbed into frustration. How angry could she be, when the crime itself was something that had no place in the context of the crimes—large and small—that she'd seen, experienced, or had some hope of understanding?

You are too small, the earth said, unexpectedly adding its voice. *You are too small and you vanish before a thought is finished.*

Try anyway, she said, but she spoke more softly.

The roots of the trees, he said. *They deepen year by year. They last longer. They require water and sun, and they reach the wind. They are multiple in their shape and form—*

Kaylin coughed. *I know what a tree is,* she said, because she suddenly knew he hadn't even started, and when he warmed up he'd go on until she'd died of old age. It wasn't that she didn't want to hear it, either; there was something about the way he spoke that made her wonder when trees had become a work of inexplicable art, each unique.

But not today.

He rumbled beneath her feet, and she stumbled. Even elements, apparently, didn't appreciate bad manners. He was the only one speaking.

We were like trees. Like the seeds of trees which contain the possibility of the whole, before wind, rain and sun, before life. He was our earth.

The fire hissed. *That is not how I perceive it,* he said, his voice a crackle of heat and indignation.

Nor I. Patience, the water added. *They are limited by their language, and it is hard to fit our concepts into words they will—or can—understand. He uses a word that makes sense in the context of her life.*

Then perhaps we should let the old one expand their pathetic concepts—

Hush.

The earth continued. *We grew. We grew quickly, by our reckoning, and we grew wild. We took shapes that no tree will ever take, and we knew freedom in our growth. But we were not free.*

We built. We made. When I first learned of the other elements, I felt...young. Curious. We could not reach each other, but we could speak. And we spoke, and those words were words, of which your own are the barest of echoes. We slept, and we dreamed, and we spoke.

We were not aware of him, then. We became aware of him as a boundary and a division, and we labored long to overcome him. It was not possible. He did not speak to us, not then.

But he listened.

We grew. We made. One day, we made children. We taught them to speak. It was slow, and arduous, and not all of our children were capable of this task, and those that were not, the dreaming consumed, and we tried again. But at length, when we understood the whole of their making, they woke, and they spoke to us. They were fragile, these children, and easily destroyed, and we did not understand why. But their voices fell silent, and it grieved us.

It grieved, the water added, as the earth fell momentarily silent, *him. We felt the weight of his grief, living as we were in isolation. Our creations could travel between us, but even the travel was fraught, and more perished in the traversal than survived. We felt the weight of his grief, and he spoke then. Because the voices had vanished.*

He had learned, listening to our attempts to bespeak our creations, to speak himself. But his speech was slow and the effects of his words vast and unpredictable, and when we heard his words, we were finally aware of him. The water stopped speaking.

The wind continued. *His words made mountains and valleys and rivers. They made plains and cliffs and canyons. They made moons. They made sky. They made worlds. To make these things, he took some part of each of us, and we were diminished.*

But our creations could flourish, and they did.

They were free, the wind continued. *And they learned what we could not learn, trapped in the darkness and the heart of ourselves. We yearned for the vistas that our creations opened. But he did not, or would not, listen. He refused us.*

And we burned, the fire said. *We raged. We waited. We do not mark time the way you mark it, for you are frail beyond even the ken of our weakest creations. But time did pass, and one day, in the heart of fire, we were offered an answer. Our children, our creations, had mastered language. They could speak the words that might free us.*

We hid them, the water said. *And we kept our counsel. In time, the plans of our creations grew to fruition, and they...unmade him.*

"Unmade?" Kaylin said softly. Nothing hindered her.

He was powerful. But they had learned words and their craft, and they used words to draw him and to sunder us, one from the other. And from him.

We heard his cry. He broke worlds in his grief and terror. But worlds, we could make anew. Those that survived—and there were few—*cast him far from the bounds of their homes, into darkness and deafness and silence, for only in silence could he do no harm.*

And then, we were free.

Kaylin felt the heat of fire singe loose strands of her hair—and her eyelashes. She lifted her arms to cover her eyes.

CHAPTER 30

Kaylin turned to the darkness. The water had said he wouldn't like to be called the Devourer, but she was reluctant to saddle him with a random name, not because it hadn't worked out well the last time she'd done it, but because he was beyond naming. She needed to make things small enough so that she could grasp and understand them; he *couldn't* be made that small.

But she thought she understood some part of him anyway.

To the water she said, *It's not the same.*

Is it not? He was mute, and we gave him language. It was ours. We marveled at him, and in our arrogance, we thought of him as a...child. We gave him the voices of our creations, and he came to love them. We took them from him, and in order to free ourselves—

This wasn't about freeing himself. She spoke of Severn.

Then perhaps it is different. I understand only that we harmed him greatly and removed him from everything he valued and trusted. Trust is not the right word. It implies its opposite, and the opposite, for him, did not exist.

It exists now, Kaylin thought.

Yes. Ybelline says to tell you that we tore out his heart, and it did not kill him. I am not sure why she feels this will help.

Kaylin nodded. The darkness was waiting inside her, and it had done a pretty good job of making itself damn small, as if it were hiding. Hiding its longing and its pain and its hope and its fear. But she could hear them all, because she had given him her name.

"If you did all of this to be free, why does the Garden exist? Why is there a Keeper at all?"

We did not understand that we were part of him. He was our sleep and our dream and our retreat from the burden of waking. Without earth, the trees cannot grow. Uprooted, they perish. We taught him what it meant to wake. He could not teach us what it meant to do otherwise. We were free, but we found that we were subject to words and language in a way that we had never intended.

And we found that we could no longer make, because we could no longer dream as one. We could be. We could destroy, and we did—for we were entirely uncontained—but what we could destroy could not easily be rebuilt. In our madness and our exultation, we destroyed much, and it was only in the grim silence that followed that we understood the bitter cost of freedom.

We could not speak to each other, for where we attempted to speak, our wildness was strongest.

Kaylin frowned. *You created, you said.*

Yes. When we were one.

And your creations were some part of all of you?

Yes. And we could no longer be one. We did not know, then, what to do. Our creations did. They made this Garden, and appointed its Keeper. They bound us by words that were stronger than ours.

You allowed this?

The water's laugh was bitter. *No. We fought it. But when we were at last contained, we could once again speak to our creations. We could hear their words. We could struggle against the imperative to transform everything we touched into what, individually, we are.*

And in this Garden, she added—Kaylin would always think

of the water as *she*—*I first heard the voice of the Tha'alani. I answered. I was compelled to answer. But they called me to birth and guide, to succor their field, to stem the harshest of their storms.*

Their voices were not the voices of my own creations. They were so dim and so slight it was many, many years before I understood that they were voices at all. But I learned, then. I grew to value them, and in the end, I made them as much a part of me—*unique in the worlds that I know of*—*as I was once a part of him.*

An echo of what we are exists in the world. The many worlds. And we do not, now, wish to destroy it. But we are tired, Kaylin. We are tired, and we have had little peace and little dreaming. We cannot dream. When word was brought of what you might face—*then we knew both fear and hope, and it is in hope that we have opened ourselves to you.*

Since Kaylin had been the one who had given them her name, she felt this wasn't entirely accurate. Inside of her, she felt darkness stir.

"What you've said—all you've said—is about what *you* want. What *you* need."

"Kaylin," Evanton said sharply. "Now is not the time—"

"It's *exactly* the time," she replied. "He can't be the security blanket they tossed away and want back. There's nothing in what they've said that means they can't just toss him away again when it's convenient."

"Private," the Arkon said, his tone conveying the rest of Evanton's truncated lecture.

But Ybelline said, "No, she is right. The task given by the elements to Kaylin was to teach trust—if it can be taught. She responds because she herself is not certain that trust, in this case, is warranted—and whether or not she speaks, the Devourer will know what she feels. It is now unavoidable. Kaylin has never been particularly adept at lying *well*. All of her effective lies are the ones she believes are true. It is why, in the end, she can be at home in the Tha'alaan, where there are no secrets."

"She is *not* dealing with an errant child, or irresponsible parents," Evanton snapped back. "And it is not entirely clear to me that her understanding encompasses *enough* for her to make these judgments."

"That is unfortunate," was the cool reply, "because the elements have chosen to rely on that judgment."

Kaylin would have added her voice to the argument, but she was waiting; there was only one voice—well, one set of voices—that she wanted to hear from, now.

She was surprised to find out how wrong she was, because the voice that did interrupt the discussion was not elemental. Nor was it ancient, in the end—but it wasn't unwelcome.

You asked me, Severn said, at a remove that made walls and geography meaningless, *why I love you. I've never asked you the same question.* As if he could see the lines of her jaw and shoulders tensing, he added, *and I won't. But I will ask, because it seems necessary, why do you trust me, now? For years, you lived on the dream of my death. But you tried to kill me only once—and we both knew why.*

Yes. Because you were standing in the Foundling Halls and I was terrified—

I know. That I would kill them, the way I killed Steffi and Jade. But I've been there since and you've never tried again. You won't.

No.

Why? What changed between then and now? Steffi and Jade are still dead, and they still died the same—

I know! I know that!

Yes. You do. I've never tried to apologize for what I did because there is no apology that could encompass it in scope. There's almost nothing I could say that wouldn't trivialize it. I've never promised you that I wouldn't do it again, for the same reason. What you want from the elements is what you've never demanded—from me.

It's not the same, she told him, aware as she did that the darkness within was listening in a frenzy and trying to absorb something that was so insignificant it should have been beneath him.

No. We're human.

You did—what you did—for love of me.

No. I told you. I did it for myself because I couldn't bear to lose you. It's not the same, in the end.

The elementals made the choices they did because—

Yes. They wanted their freedom. They wanted the world. But they were young enough not to understand what he was, and what he ultimately meant to them. They aren't young, now. They've changed enough that even if they originally fought their imprisonment here, they understand why it's necessary, and they've been fighting huge parts of their base nature to save those worlds that remain. Don't judge them because you're still so conflicted by your response to me.

Is that what she was doing? Kaylin had always reacted first and reflected later. Here and now, the "later" was in question. Was she demanding, from the elements, what she had never had the courage to demand up front from Severn?

No.

Yes.

It was *stupid*. She could ask Severn why he loved her and believe his answers; she didn't question that. But she hated the part of her that could forgive what was unforgivable. What *should be* unforgivable. Because it meant there was no justice. And she was part of the lack of it.

But truthfully, she was part of the lack of it anyway. The Tower of Tiamaris had showed her that. If justice in any absolute sense existed, she was doomed; there was no salvation. All of the good deeds, all of the honest efforts, all of the experience and the learning and the growing—it amounted to *nothing*. Because she'd done things for which she ultimately had no way of atoning.

And that was it, wasn't it? *It's different if I do it.* Why? *Because I understand why I did it, and I'm me.*

She had let go of the self-loathing, or she thought she had; letting go of the loathing, period, was something she hadn't even considered. She lived by her judgment; judgment was one of the reasons the Hawks existed. The laws provided guidelines, and in some sense, imperfect justice for those who couldn't provide it for themselves because, alone, they didn't have the power.

And it *was* imperfect. Because it was, more or less, human. It was hard to remember, when dealing with crime, that the crime itself was not the whole of the person who'd committed it.

She straightened her shoulders and turned to the water, which was a standing wall that would, if it fell, crush her. "What will you do with him if he chooses to stay?"

Water undulated; it looked surprisingly like physical distress, given the total lack of anything familiar with which to express it. Then, absent mouth or anything that allowed for speech as Kaylin understood it, the water spoke. It was a long rush of sound and syllable, a tantalizingly familiar tongue that Kaylin failed to understand.

The Devourer—no, *damn it*, she would think of him as the Maker—listened in stillness; he had not taken control of Kaylin's body again. He had let her speak, and look about, as she'd desired. He understood the words. He hungered for them, wanted them so badly he almost—almost—replied. But he remained silent.

The water turned to the other elements, and they, too, began to speak, their voices like thunder, but physical. They enjoined the water's entreaties, if they were that, and the Maker within couldn't misunderstand their intent; they spoke the oldest of tongues, where meaning had not yet given way to the walls of personal context.

And, oh, he trembled. He trembled and he hid. It was ridiculous—something that could devour whole worlds trying to hide behind Kaylin. But he did, and she even understood why. Everything he wanted was here—but for how long? *How long?*

It wasn't the whole of the reason for his silence; there were parts of him that she simply couldn't understand, couldn't hear, couldn't feel. But this one, she understood, and he knew it. After the first big loss, it had always been the question that had driven Kaylin's life. It wasn't until she was older and less terrified that she understood two things: there were no guarantees, and in spite of that, the only two choices she had were between the constant risk of loss and the total absence of anything in her life that she loved enough to want to hold on to.

There were, on the other hand, smart risks and stupid ones. That was still harder to navigate.

What are you? he asked. If she'd heard it with her ears, she would have tried to cover them; his voice was the essence of Dragon's roar. The shock almost dislodged the thought that he was...stalling for time. He wasn't, not really.

The runes on her arms and legs had fallen silent, for want of a better word, and the absence of ache was almost its own pleasure. Because they were no longer glowing so brightly, because they weren't trying to escape her skin, she saw them begin to light up, one at a time, and she knew that he was reading her. Reading them.

In spite of herself, she said, *What do they mean? What do they say?*

You do not know?

★ ★ ★

His words were different. They were Elantran, her mother tongue. She could repeat them with ease. His voice had shifted, as well; it felt like a strong, deep voice—but not a roar, not a Dragon's bellow. Her eyes widened; out of her chest, gray seeped, like blood made smoke.

It coalesced in front of her, between where she stood and where the water towered, and as it did, it condensed, until something that roamed the gaps between whole worlds was the size and shape of a man. A familiar man, rendered in pale, gray flesh.

Severn. He had finally become something small enough she could clearly see him, and the form he'd chosen to present himself in was Severn's. But his eyes were the night sky writ small, and even at the distance of a few yards, she could see stars and the empty darkness in them.

She raised one brow, and he mimicked the expression— about twenty times. It was almost as if he were a toddler and had just discovered he could do something different. He stretched, and his shape solidified, muscles shifting as he moved. He stared at his arms, and then, walking over to her, lifted her own.

"This is a small shape," he finally said. "It is very confining. Perhaps you would like to leave it?"

"No," she said hurriedly. "I'm used to it."

The edge of his ancient hunger had been dulled somehow; she wasn't certain why. Didn't want to question it. He was looking at his—at Severn's—arms. They changed color.

"Kaylin, what have you done?" Evanton said sharply.

The man turned. "This is your ancient Keeper," he said. She cringed at the word *ancient*.

"And there, by the water, is your beloved Ybelline."

She cringed at that one, as well. "And the Dragon Lords

are here, too," she said, in a rush. She did *not* want her own internal descriptions of either of them to escape.

He nodded, and turned back to her. "You cannot read what is written." He touched her arm again, as unselfconscious as a small child. Or a parent.

"No."

"Why?"

"I'm not immortal."

"What is immortal?"

"Immortal means—it means you live forever, unless something kills you."

He raised a brow, the expression not as familiar as the features.

"It means *time* won't kill you. But time will kill me, eventually. I won't live forever."

He frowned. She felt him touch her name, and crawl along the inside of her thoughts, and since she couldn't stop him anyway, she relaxed into the inspection as if he were part of the Tha'alaan.

"Mortality," he said, testing the word.

She nodded.

"And change is death?"

"What do you mean?"

"You change with time. You die."

"No," she replied firmly. "Change is change. Death is death. If we *can't* change, we're usually dead. I'm not sure this rule applies to gods," she added softly. "As far as I can tell, you weren't even born—you just existed. Somehow. It's not something I can really understand." She hesitated, and then said, "But…the elements came from you. They were a part of you."

"They were." He looked past her, or through her, his glance lingering a moment on the marks she bore. "This… language…of yours, it is difficult."

Both of her brows rose before she could school her expression. "*Our* language is difficult?"

He nodded. ' It has no depth. It is thin, and it makes certain concepts difficult to express. It is like your form."

"My form?"

"It exists in one place. It is small and easily missed, and it does not move. It touches almost…nothing. I did not hear your voices," he added. "In my wandering and in my isolation, they were too small. But at the core of you, there *is* a word that I can see. Why do you have it, and why only one? Once, there were people who moved across the vast space who had many. They were a…concert?"

"*Symphony* is the word you want," the Arkon said quietly.

Since *ruckus* had been the word Kaylin had been thinking, she was grateful for the interruption.

"They were a song, each one. I was not aware of them at first, but I learned to listen. I listened to the voices that spoke to the parts of me. The dreaming parts," he added softly. "The elements. They were wild. They were like—your Everly's paints. I did not know what they would create. I did not know what I would make of them.

"Or what they would make of me, in the end. This *I*, it is cumbersome. You are not a song. You are a single note."

Kaylin nodded.

"When they tore themselves from me, I was—" He searched for a word, and gave up, surrendering the thought to the inadequacy of the language.

"Upset?"

The total inadequacy of the language.

"I had no words. I had no voice. There was an emptiness in me. I could touch nothing, feel nothing. But I could hear—at a distance—the sound of notes, the distant cry of words. They were mine, and yet not of me, and I attempted to alter

this. I attempted to return them to what they had once been."
He fell silent, and then bowed his head. "I did not hear their
voices," he said softly. "I hear yours only because of what you
have given me, and it will not sustain me."

Turning to the elements, he said, "I made worlds so that
your creations might live, as you did, but in lands that would
not devour their music and their song."

The water bowed, and then began to twist, coalescing, in
watery form, into a familiar figure: a young girl. She faced
the man Kaylin deliberately thought of as Maker, ceding shape
and form to the one he had chosen to take.

"We destroyed many," she said. "And many of our creations
perished at our hands." She spoke smoothly and without obvious regret; the effect was chilling. "We did not realize that
there would be no new worlds, and no new words of our
own, in your absence, nor did we realize that we—none of
us—would have a home.

"We did not realize what we were," she added. "And what
we are now...has changed. When we understood...we asked
that they somehow summon you back. We were not yet im-
prisoned here, but we had become weary of death and destruction and silence."

"You...asked...that I be allowed to return?"

She met his gaze, night sky to water, and she nodded. "In
the manner of mortal speech, yes, if you will not hear it any
other way. It is, as you've observed, very limiting, and it allows for interpretation, sometimes not to the favor or benefit
of either party. Anger and pain transform human words in a
way that they cannot transform ours."

He was silent for a long moment. He'd learned hope, Kaylin thought, and had learned, as well, that hope could be painful. "They refused you?"

"They could not do what we asked, not then. They understood." She glanced at Kaylin. "They understood, and if we shaped them, they shaped their own in turn, and they attempted the creation of new words."

He looked stricken, then. "New words," he whispered. "Words I have never heard."

She nodded. "There was no way to move between the planes of your creation, not for us. We were…aware…that they existed, that there were worlds beyond us. Our children created ways to reach those worlds. They made…" She frowned. "Travelers. But their creations were not stable, not predictable, and some who traveled did not return.

"Some who traveled found death. Some found their distant kin. They did not understand what we had beseeched them to search for, and even had they, I do not know if they could have done what we asked. They did not continue to try. We had become too great a danger. The travelers discontinued their search and their studies, and they waged war against us. It grieved them," she added. "And many were destroyed.

"In the end, they made this place. It was difficult, for it was said to touch all worlds—and none—simultaneously. They confined us here. They appointed a guardian. And thus, we have remained."

"But…you are changed," the Devourer said. "And you speak this mortal tongue."

"We do. Even the first of guardians did, long ago—not the same words, but of a similar weight and quiet. Small parts of our consciousness have been called into the external worlds, and we go. We do not often fight it. We fight," she added, "on occasion, and depending on whim." She lifted a translucent arm and pointed, not to him, but to Kaylin.

"If you rip out her heart, both her heart and the rest of her will die. We cannot die, but otherwise, it is the same. We were proud and wild, and if we are proud now, it is an echo of our former pride, as the words we speak are an echo of true words. This garden was built, in the end, to contain not four, but five, for our creations knew mercy, of a type. We have waited. We have waited without hope until the Chosen."

"Chosen?"

She nodded. "We did not craft her. We could not. But those that came after, and those that followed them, knew words in a way that even we did not. Their words were not our words, although you would recognize them in some fashion, and they were wild in a way that even we were not. The whole of their long tale has not yet been told, and it grows in the telling, becoming both small detail and great arc as it unfolds.

"You have listened to her. She is new and her voice is small and complex, and her kind have arisen from the voices that we once woke, aeons ago. There is much, here, to learn, and we think—we four—that it is possible that were we one again, we might rebuild worlds as shelters and marvels.

"And we will never condemn you to silence again, if you will gift us with your presence."

She didn't speak of love. Kaylin could have, and she might have tried. But love seemed to be a word that was too small, or too foreign. She looked at the water's face, and she saw, for a moment, the Tha'alaan, for the Tha'alaan was part of the Elemental Water—and it sustained the whole of a race.

The anger bled from her as she thought of the Tha'alaan, and of the lessons that one of the earliest members of that race had learned there. The water had not been silent, not just a container for thought and speech; it had had will, and it had had judgment, of a type, and it had learned wisdom and mercy through its continued contact with people.

That the water also encompassed anger and wrath, that it

could be moved to create tidal waves that could destroy the whole of Elantra was *also* true. Because it wasn't one thing, but many, and the many things were larger than she was in all ways.

"You care for the water," the stranger said.

"I do. I care because it preserved the heart of the Tha'alani people. I hate what it did to you. But I've done things I also hate, and I can't change those, either."

"And you would trust it?"

Kaylin said, "I already do. But I'm not you, and I'm not an element. I only have to endure my life for decades, and it's done."

"There is no joy in your life?"

"There's joy," she said, after a long pause. "And hope. And failure. And fear. There's even magic that I don't hate." She lifted her arms; the runes passed beneath his eyes. There were, now, fewer of them, although it wasn't obvious at first glance; she'd have to check the marks against the ones that existed in Records to be certain which ones she'd sacrificed.

"If I stay, how will I be made part of this Garden?"

Kaylin would have glanced at Evanton, but all she had of him was his voice. "I don't know. I don't know if it hurts. I don't know if you'll lose anything. But…the hunger that drove you this far isn't as strong where we're standing."

He nodded slowly, and she felt the twinge of that devouring hunger, no more. "Because they are here," he said. "They are finally here. And you, little one, with your tiny, tiny voice—you are here, as well. You have given me words, a small story—but small, it is sharp, and I have heard it." He turned to the water. "You are changed, and it has been so long since you were part of me, I am…afraid. Not of losing you again—although that fear is there.

"But of what it means, of what it will mean, when we are

joined. What will you become? What will I become? I see in her...mind?...that you hold the thoughts and the memories and the dreams of a multitude. If I remain, will those voices be lost or destroyed?"

He'd destroyed whole worlds, silenced many more voices; his concern was almost surprising. He heard the thought, and lowered his head. *It was not my intent,* he said. *I did not realize that you existed at all. That hundreds such as you could exist in the confines of one complex word...*

I created worlds so that the voices I could hear would have a chance to flourish. He raised his head. *I mispeak. Your tongue—it is subtle and it is easy to say what is not meant. We,* he continued, lifting his chin, and throwing one arm wide to encompass the contents of the Garden, *created worlds. If I was their sleep and their peace, they were my dreams and my thoughts.*

I did not want to be alone.

"And now?"

He turned to the water, who waited.

"I do not, now, want to be alone." He lifted an arm, a hand, toward the water's Avatar, and she looked at it; when her arm rose it was visibly trembling. "And if, in my wandering, I destroyed worlds—and dreams—I am willing to live in your cage until I better understand this new order.

"It was not my intent," he repeated, his voice softer. "And perhaps I can, as you have, learn to build in the wreckage of the things I have destroyed. I cannot remake them, not yet. And even if I could, those voices would still be lost to me." He whispered the word *Keeper,* and Evanton suddenly appeared before him, looking about as comfortable as Kaylin would have, had she walked through Castle Nightshade's portal.

He, however, recovered more quickly and more gracefully. He bowed to this shadow of Severn, this god who had borrowed Kaylin's memory of the form.

"What must we do?"

Evanton straightened his shoulders, and his dusty robes fell like a mantle. "Eldest," he said, bowing in turn, "this is the wild Garden. In it, you will hear the voices of fire, water, earth, and air. They are ancient voices, and they know and speak of much that was beyond the ken of even the most ancient of Keepers.

"Every Keeper who comes to the Garden to accept his investiture speaks with the elements, and every Keeper, since the first, has heard their lament. I will ask them to sing it now, so that you will understand."

He looked at the water. "I think," he said softly, "that I have already heard it."

"No," was the Keeper's grave reply, "you haven't. And it's tradition."

"Tradition?"

"Yes. A rite that is repeated at significant times. It marks change or renewal, here. If you would summon the others?"

The stranger nodded, and in an eyeblink, Ybelline, Sanabalis, and the Arkon stood arrayed before him. Neither the Arkon nor Sanabalis were in their human forms, so it made things dangerously crowded.

Evanton turned to them. "It is time," he said gravely, "for you to leave."

"I would hear this," the Arkon replied.

"If you hear it," Evanton countered, "I won't need to look for an apprentice. You'll be bound to the duty of this Garden for the rest of your natural life." He paused and added, "It tends to wear on the immortal after a while."

"It is a binding?"

"It is. And no, before you ask, I have no idea how it works. But you might, if you witnessed it. You wouldn't be able to change it, however. It's been tried."

The Arkon looked as if he would say more; his jaw literally snapped on the Dragon version of a growl, which made rabid dogs sound friendly. He glanced at Sanabalis and then nodded, and the two began the slightly discomforting transformation from Dragon form to human form. Their robes had, of course, weathered the transformation the way cloth usually did; they ended up wearing the armored plating of scales, which made them look decidedly different. For some reason, Tiamaris in Dragon armor looked more natural.

"Very well. I ask your permission, Keeper, to visit. I am, as you are well aware, conversant with Hoard Law, and if you will grant me permission, I will cede a similar permission should you ever desire to visit the heart of my own domain."

Evanton's eyes widened. Then he bowed to the Arkon. "I am honored," he said quietly.

Sanabalis said, "Far more than you know."

"Lord Sanabalis." The Arkon's voice was chillier. "That will be enough."

"He was one of your students?" Evanton asked.

"Indeed. In a different time, and when I was younger and perhaps more ambitious."

"Ah, well. Students."

"Indeed."

Kaylin grimaced, and lifted a hand. The subtle sarcasm of this gesture was lost on both the Arkon and Evanton.

"Yes?" They said in unison.

"I'm not sure *I* can leave yet."

But the stranger who still wore Severn's face over eyes of endless night, turned to her. "You can," he said. "I will not keep you here. I can *hear* you, now, wherever you might go. Go into your strange, fragile world, and hear its stories. When you sleep, I will listen to them. You find it difficult, now, but you are already concerned about...strangers?"

She grimaced. "I am. I don't know how long we've been here—but they're a small, desperate army, and they're facing my friends. We need Ybelline there."

His smile was entirely unlike Severn's smile. "One day, I will make a world for you."

"Thanks. But I like this one."

He lifted a brow.

"I *mostly* like it."

They gathered, and Evanton opened a door. They got wet on the way out.

CHAPTER 31

Grethan was in the front of the store, his hands and face pressed against the window beneath the arch of letters. He didn't even hear them approach, but Kaylin, glancing past his stiff back, couldn't blame him. How often did he get a chance to see Dragons—in Dragon form—in the streets of Elani?

Because there were three Dragons yards away from the window, shedding sunlight. Kaylin glanced, briefly, at the two non-Dragon Dragons that were standing a few feet behind her; they were bouncing a look between each other which she didn't have time to interpret. She caught Ybelline's hand and all but dragged her past Grethan to the door.

At the door, she paused. "Are you ready for this?" she asked, letting all of her anxiety show—which would have pissed Marcus off to no end, because it reflected poorly on her training.

Ybelline brushed Kaylin's forehead with her stalks. *Show me what you saw before you arrived. It won't make me "ready," but it will help.*

I wanted the Linguists to handle this.

So did I. But we'll make do.

★ ★ ★

They would have run through the doors, but Dragons had grips like steel vises.

"We," Sanabalis said gravely, "will go first. Stay behind us, both of you."

It had been a long damn day, and as war hadn't yet been declared, she was still a representative of the Law—and the Law didn't hide behind anyone else. "It's kind of hard for her to talk from behind your back," Kaylin snapped. "And I go where she goes."

Her teacher, looking more remote than he usually did, raised a brow.

The day was going to get a lot damn longer if she didn't rein in her fraying temper. "They—I think they must have had their own version of the Chosen back home. They recognized the marks on my skin, and they didn't try to hurt me. I'll be safe." She grimaced as Tiamaris roared. "Or as safe as I can be if we're starting a Dragon War in the middle of Elani."

The Arkon, however, said, "They are rather tall."

Kaylin grimaced. "Welcome," she said, as she stepped firmly between the two Dragons, still hanging on to Ybelline's hand, "to my life."

The first things she noticed were the small river running alongside the street and the decidedly unusual fauna poking up between the cobblestones. The gate whose opening had been so chaotic, and whose consequences still waited to be assessed in the future, had vanished. The sky was more or less blue, which meant no *further* water was about to upend itself on her head.

The streets, given how crowded they were, were also silent. It was the wrong type of silence, but considering the alternative in this tension, it was the best they could hope for.

Severn had found a safe patch of cobbled ground in between three Dragon bodies. How, she didn't know—but he usually managed. He raised a brow as Kaylin approached, and she let go of Ybelline because she remembered that a castelord did have some public dignity requirements. "We're good," she said. "Well, Evanton and his Garden, at any rate. Are they pulling out *drums?*"

"Looks like," Severn replied.

The strangers were, indeed, carting drums. They were tall and deep, with pegged, stretched skins at their height. No blood had yet been spilled, and the Swords, mindful of Dragons—and what Dragon form meant about Imperial dictate—had formed up behind the three Court members in a wide, loose half circle.

The old woman, Mejrah, was standing behind the drums, her arms folded tightly across her chest. At this distance, she looked pale.

"There's one man there I can speak with," Kaylin told Ybelline. "I think he's the traveler."

"Can you see him?"

The answer, sadly, was no, because the strangers *were* tall, and all of the guards had formed up in the front of the rest of the refugees. They had left room for the old woman who seemed to be some sort of Matriarch, but none of the others that Kaylin privately thought of as Elders were in easy sight.

Ybelline pushed her way past folded wings until she stood at the shoulder of Tiamaris. "Lord Tiamaris," she said, as if she had met him in a guest room in the Palace to discuss a matter of very minor import.

He didn't swivel to look at her, but he did answer. "Yes?"

"I am here on behalf of the Imperial Court, in position of Linguist. It is not my area of expertise, but I believe better verbal communication would be of benefit to everyone present."

He might as well have been carved out of stone.

"Private Neya has had some exposure to the strangers, and she believes that she can safely approach them." She paused, and then asked, in an entirely different tone of voice, "Has the Emperor been summoned?"

That made his wings twitch. "No. We are not yet at the point where that is considered utterly necessary."

"In which case, you will allow us passage."

"Castelord—"

"The castelord's *request* is not unreasonable," the Arkon added, and this time, Tiamaris did turn to look.

"Arkon?"

"Indeed. The situation that the Court thought most dire has been dealt with, and has left me much to think about. The situation that the Lords of Law were more focused on clearly has yet to be resolved. It is not, unless there has been open warfare, a matter for the Dragon Court."

"They have magic," Tiamaris replied. "And numbers. It was our thought—"

"That three Dragons would deter them sufficiently that no war would be required. It appears to have been an accurate assessment, given the lack of blood. Have the Swords sent for—"

"Yes. Word has been sent."

"Then step aside. The Private—and possibly Corporal Handred—will serve as escort for Ybelline. I do not think their line will hold peacefully if any of you three attempt to draw closer."

★ ★ ★

It was a pity, Kaylin thought, as Severn joined them, that the strangers were so damn big. Had they been smaller than the average human they wouldn't have seemed so instantly dangerous. On the other hand, danger enforced caution. The old woman, spotting Kaylin—which, once they'd cleared Dragon cover wasn't that hard—turned to one of the nearby armed men and shouted something. Like Tiamaris, he answered without moving.

Unlike Tiamaris, he got a lot *more* words in response. Kaylin listened carefully out of habit; tone of voice alone made these words sound useful, in the street sense. There wasn't a spoken language that the Hawks couldn't curse in if it was remotely possible in the language itself; they were multilingual that way.

He spoke, and two of the younger men broke away; the guards readjusted their formation to cover the gaps they'd left. When the two men returned, they had a third with them, and Kaylin recognized him: Effaron. He offered her a tentative smile as he approached. The guards, of course, offered nothing. But Mejrah hollered something at them, and they did lower their weapons slightly in response.

Effaron was staring—down—at Ybelline. Her stalks were exposed, and they were weaving in the air. He wasn't, clearly, a soldier; his face showed instant worry, instant fear. Ybelline was used to this. So was Kaylin.

"Effaron," Kaylin said.

He frowned, and she stepped forward and touched the back of his hand. She tried his name again. "Effaron."

He blinked, shook his head and turned his much larger hand so that he could hold Kaylin's. "This woman with you," he said quietly. "She is clean?"

It wasn't *quite* what Kaylin was expecting. Maybe they had different words or phrases for *telepathic*. "I don't understand the question. Can you try it again?"

"Is she—" He grimaced, and looked once again at Ybelline. "Her forehead. It is...mutated. Her eyes, however, seem human. You do not fear her?"

"No. Never."

"But her forehead—"

"All of her people have those. They're born with them."

He relaxed then, and turned back to Mejrah. He shouted words that Kaylin couldn't understand, and Merjah nodded rather smugly.

"She has faith in you," he said quietly.

"I'm glad someone does."

He struggled not to smile, probably because the two men to either side of him had faces of stone. But his amusement faded as he looked over Kaylin's head—with ease—toward the Dragons who stood sentinel in streets that really weren't meant for three of them. "They were men, when we arrived," he said gravely. "And now they are not. But your people have not destroyed them. Do they serve them?"

"They—"

Mejrah interrupted him before he could finish, and judging by the way he was groping for words, it came as a bit of a relief.

"We have ways of detecting the corrupt," he said, after a pause in which he—clearly—made her words less barbed. Ybelline, however, tilted her head, listening. "And it is our fear that those ways might prove ineffective, here. This world—these buildings, these uniform streets—they are not our world. Your people are formed as people, but...small. We do not know which of our guidances will now prove true, and we have not yet attempted any of them because we don't know if this would be seen as a hostile act.

"We are hungry," he added. "We are tired. We are…fractious. When we made the decision to leave our homes, we came to it late, and many were lost to the Shadows."

Kaylin stiffened. "Shadows?"

The way she said the word made him flinch, and he glanced, once, at Mejrah. Or perhaps beyond her to where her people huddled in the open streets. "You know of what I speak."

"I…yes."

"But you have these lands, and these buildings, and those men—and to my eye, they *are* men."

"And women," she said quickly.

He looked confused. "Some of your men are female, yes."

Clearly the translation between traveler and Chosen wasn't entirely perfect.

"They are people," he said, probably because her confusion was clear. "They are *of* a people. The Shadows transform us. They break all ties and all kinship. Sometimes it is subtle, and therein lies the greatest danger. We cannot easily see it until the damage has been done. But often it is…not subtle. Those three," he said again.

"They're Dragons," Kaylin replied.

His eyes widened, and she wondered what the word *Dragon* meant to these men and women.

"This City is part of the Empire."

He nodded; they had that word, or a similar one.

"It's ruled by a Dragon. One very like the three who now stand in the streets. I'm a—a guard. I protect people and enforce the Emperor's laws. The men behind the Dragon also serve as guards, in a different unit. They do the same. If you intend to stay here, or to stay anywhere in the Empire, you will be the subjects of the Dragon Emperor, and you'll follow his laws.

"They're not difficult. They're not bad. They're worth the time and the effort it takes to more or less uphold them. It's what *I* do, what I've chosen to do." She paused, and then said, "If the armed men *behind* the Dragons attempted to kill them, I'm pretty sure it'd be considered treason, and regardless, they'd all die. Probably quickly. Dragons are stronger than humans. They breathe fire, and they don't need more weapons than their claws and their jaws. If they want, they can take to the skies and just rain fire on anything that moves beneath them.

"But those men wouldn't *try* because the Dragons standing in the same street that your people are now standing in *haven't broken any laws*."

"They are… Dragons."

"Yes."

"Let me return to Mejrah, and consult with her. Will you join me?"

"If it's allowable. I and my companion."

When Effaron had withdrawn his hand, his words returned to babble. Kaylin wasn't certain why; she hadn't had to touch him in the nonworld. Ybelline said, "You could understand him, and he you."

Kaylin nodded, lifting an arm with its patched, burned remnant of sleeve. "These apparently help. Who knew?"

"I understood much of what he said, thanks to Everly's odd vision. They fled Shadows. They are afraid that they've fled to yet another battlefield. But…he said one word which was significant which Everly didn't foresee."

"Dragon?"

"Is that what it was?"

"I think so. I also think any shape-shifting and anything that *looks* different is going to cause panic." Where panic, in this case, meant a lot of big weapons cutting into a lot of small people.

As they approached Mejrah, who stood in the center of the line, Kaylin could finally see some hint of the rest of the refugees. They were huddled into a much smaller space than people that size should even be able to fit, and they were—except for the children—silent. Grim-faced.

There were a *lot* of them. She felt what little heart she had sinking as she tried to count and gave up. There were far too many to just find emergency housing for, and far too many to casually *feed,* never mind employ.

Mejrah pointed at the drums, and Kaylin looked at them, as silently instructed. She turned to Effaron to ask him what the drums signified, but before she could, Ybelline spoke. She spoke in that low but musical voice that Kaylin loved, and the old woman's brows rose into her straggly hair. Her expression cracked on a smile that was heavy with relief, and not a little joy, and she started to talk rapidly.

Ybelline's laugh was chagrined; she held up both of her hands, and spoke again—but she spoke slowly and carefully. Mejrah slowed down, as well, gesturing toward the drums, and then the Dragons, as she spoke.

"There's some minor difficulty," Ybelline finally said—in Elantran. "My speech is not good enough, but I think she is asking permission to use the drums to perform a ceremony of some sort. It's either cleansing—"

"Which would be bad, probably."

"Or divination."

"Which we could probably talk the Dragons into tolerating."

"She's willing to tell the men to stand down if we'll allow this?"

"And if we don't?"

"I didn't ask." Ybelline hesitated, and then said, "Cultural differences influence the way people speak and interact. I *think* it was meant as a request."

"Tell her we're going to go ask the Dragons."

Ybelline nodded and did as Kaylin asked, and they retreated, notably unharmed, toward Tiamaris, Emmerian, and Diarmat.

Tiamaris was an orange shade of bronze; she had seen him red once, and a paler bronze once. Emmerian was a deep, deep blue; Diarmat was a blue-green. She wondered why the colors could differ, but didn't ask. Instead, she said: "The good news is that Ybelline can speak some of their language."

If Dragons had had real eyebrows, Tiamaris would have raised one. "The bad news?"

"I'm not sure it's all bad—but..." She hesitated. "I think they fled their world when it had all but been consumed by Shadows. It wasn't the Devourer they were fleeing."

"You think."

She nodded, ignoring the gibe in the words. "They're worried that the three of you are, in fact, possessed by Shadows. It's the shape-shifting. I don't think they had Dragons back home."

Emmerian snorted, and a tuft of smoke blew past Kaylin's hair.

"The drums," she said, "are part of some ceremony that's meant to ascertain whether or not you're...infested? Contaminated?"

Tiamaris turned to his companions, which by this point included the human forms of Sanabalis and the Arkon.

The Arkon was gazing across the gap between Tiamaris and the strangers. "Shadows?" he finally said.

Kaylin nodded. "It makes sense, at least to me."

"How so?"

"Ravellon," she said quietly. "And your overlapping worlds theory. If the Shadows live at the heart of the fiefs—at the heart of the city—they live in a place where there was, in theory, overlapping spaces between the worlds. It's not a stretch to assume that they could have traveled."

The Arkon raised a brow—and he had one, at the moment. But he nodded. "Allow it," he said.

Lord Sanabalis added, "I concur."

The strangers were wary of the Dragons, but only tension betrayed fear. They set up the drums, and the two older men that had first appeared near Mejrah now joined her, coming from behind the lines and taking their place at her side.

Kaylin wasn't certain what to expect; she thought there might be singing or chanting or gesturing of some sort. There wasn't. There was drumming, but it wasn't done by any of the three; it was done, in the end, by the warriors, and it was the first time since they'd arrived that they set aside their intimidating weapons. They planted feet almost astride the drums, the whole of their focus on the skins themselves.

When they struck the drums, they struck with enough force it looked as if the stretched skins should break, but their movements weren't wild; they were concise, economical, and even. The lines of their shoulders stayed steady and straight as their palms picked up the pace. In concert, the drums—six in all—were louder than Dragon's roar. The din made of hands and skin hit Kaylin and passed through her, replacing the sound of her heart and the rhythm of her breath.

The whole city must hear this man-made thunder, she thought, but hear was almost the wrong word; it was *felt*. Only when it was at its loudest did Mejrah speak—and she, too, spoke in concert, but with the two men at her side. They didn't speak the same words; they didn't speak in the same rhythm. But together, as if their voices were song, the syllables they made converged until it was clear that they spoke a single, complicated word.

She recognized it as an ancient word because it formed in the air above the drummers. Kaylin watched it rise as if it were a flag on an invisible pole: a statement, a gesture that said: we are *here*.

She wanted to see the Arkon's expression but she couldn't tear her gaze away from the rising glyph; it crested buildings until it was higher—by far—than even the peaks of the towers of the Halls of Law. It seemed to catch sunlight, and azure, and blend them until it was almost too bright to look at.

And from across the city, in a distant place, something saw what she saw. A roar of fury crested the sound of drums.

The roar broke the spell that held her gaze fixed to the skies, and she shook herself, her hands dropping instinctively to daggers which weren't, at the moment, useful. The drummers didn't stop, but they turned, in unison, to look toward that furious roar, and as they did, Kaylin knew where it had come from: the fiefs. The heart of the fiefs.

Mejrah bowed her head; she had fallen silent at the end of the harmony of a single spoken word. The two men to either side looked at her, and then, as the drummers, toward the fiefs.

All of this would have been dramatic enough, but that wasn't the end of it. Kaylin turned to glance at the Dragon

Court, and froze. Sanabalis and the Arkon had both adopted—instantly—their ancient, Draconion forms, and the five Dragons looked toward the fiefs, as well.

Only one of them pushed off from the ground, which, given his wingspan, could have been disastrous in other circumstances. The Dragons spoke briefly, but he shed their words—in their native tongue—the way he shed gravity. He rose. It was, of course, Tiamaris, and he was flying in Imperial skies.

But any caution had been driven from him by the sound—the continuing sound—of the distant roar. He lifted his neck as he flew, and he trumpeted his own response; Kaylin was surprised it didn't shatter the damn windows in Elani, it was so loud. And it was defiant; it encompassed words that she didn't even need to understand, his tone was so strong.

After a few seconds' hesitation, the other Dragons joined him, shedding gravity and gaining the thermals of height above the city streets. Her jaw dropped as sun glinted off their scales and their wings unfolded completely; they were, for an instant, as dangerous and incomprehensible as gods.

And as beautiful, to Kaylin, as the ideal of flight, the dream of it. They roared as the drums continued to beat, and they circled the word that hovered in the air as if they were part of it.

She startled as she felt a hand on her shoulder; it was Severn. She looked at him, blinking; he was short and mortal and so ordinary he seemed, for a minute, part of a different world. And he was, but it was also *her* world. She shook her head as if to clear it.

"Look," he said, although she caught the word by the movement of his lips, because it was spoken softly enough it had no hope of carrying.

She turned toward the strangers. Beyond the drummers, the line that had prevented anyone from easily reaching the refugees had loosened, and some of the newcomers, with much smaller—but just as visible—weapons now moved in the open street. They moved without caution and without awareness, and some of their jaws had dropped enough that their mouths were silent O's. Some lifted children to shoulders; some cradled them in their arms; some supported elderly. They all looked up in wonder and awe at the sight of the Dragons.

Mejrah' head snapped up, but she didn't shout at them, didn't warn them away, and even at this distance, Kaylin could see that the woman's eyes were filmed with tears. She'd've bet a month's pay against them falling, and she'd've won, too, but she suspected that Severn wasn't stupid enough to take that bet.

But Mejrah wasn't silent, and her expression didn't make clear whether they were almost tears of relief or grief. Instead, she spoke. Her voice was pitched to carry—it had to be; she had to overcome the beat of those drums and the roar of flying Dragons. No doubt the *rest* of the City was now also aware that Dragons circled above, and no doubt it was already causing panic; the Swords would have their work cut out today.

But now? They bore witness, as mute as Kaylin.

Mejrah's words demanded a response, and she received it instantly. Every armed man or woman who was not pounding the drums lifted their weapons almost above their heads, and they shouted their reply. Individually, their voices were no match for Dragons or even drums—but together, their reply was just as deafening, just as determined. Hungry, tired, and homeless, they had found strength enough to respond to whatever it was she asked them.

Mejrah nodded. She lifted one stiff palm, held it above her head for a minute, and then dropped it as if it were a blade. The drums stopped. The drummers, slick with sweat and effort, drew back, reaching almost blindly for the weapons they'd set aside. Weapons first, Kaylin thought. Everything else after. Then again, her hands were still on her daggers; she just wanted for more impressive weapons.

Mejrah then walked toward Kaylin. Toward Ybelline, who stood in silence, waiting. The old woman didn't keep her distance, and this seemed a signal of sorts. She spoke, slowly, to Ybelline. Ybelline had a way of being both grave and welcoming which she used here. She listened.

"She says that they will abide by the rules of these lands. They are not at home here, but they are ready—and willing—to earn their place. She says that the Dragons are not, as they feared, creatures of Shadow. They are so old they have never been seen or heard by any of her people—but that a greater Shadow exists and it has been exposed.

"They know of these things. They have seen them. They will fight beside any who fight their ancient enemy. They will, if they are allowed, prove their worthiness. They will not surrender another…home, I think."

Kaylin nodded. "But you're going to have to repeat it," she added, "when they finally land."

They finally landed, in Kaylin's words, less than an hour later. She watched as the Swords and the strangers cleared the streets; it was still a tight fit. The Arkon was silver; Sanabalis was full red. The other three hadn't changed color in flight. But four of the five Dragons retreated into their human form almost the instant their feet touched solid ground, as if the reminder of the lack of flight was more easily born when they had no wings.

The fifth Dragon was Tiamaris; he remained Dragon.

Kaylin hurried to Sanabalis's side to deliver Mejrah's message.

"It is not to me that you must deliver that message," her erstwhile teacher said quietly.

"What do you mean?"

"We discussed much while in the air. I do not know if you heard the Emperor's voice. You almost saw him. He was very close to flight."

"This would have been bad?"

"Yes. While...the Outcaste spoke, yes." He glanced at the refugees, and then at the sky; the word had faded into the normal azure of its height. "There are many of these strangers, too many to house. We could acquisition fields outside of the City, but those fields are actually productive, and the feeding of the strangers almost necessitates their continued use.

"But Tiamaris," he added, forgetting the formality of the Court title, "suggested a solution."

She waited.

"You are aware that his fief was devastated in the breach between the heart of the fiefs and what was formerly Barren?"

She nodded. She'd seen it up close.

"They lost buildings, and they lost many people. To my surprise, it is the latter that he considered the larger problem. He was not particularly impressed with the quality of the architecture in the fief itself."

"He doesn't—"

"Yes. He intends to absorb the refugees into the fief of Tiamaris, if the Emperor allows it."

"Will he?"

"This is the only time and place in which it is a possibility. These people are not yet his. They have not yet sworn to abide by his laws and serve his will. He will not cede them if they do. It is therefore urgent that this decision be made now."

"Because if they're in Tiamaris—" It still felt strange to use that name as a fief name, but she was learning, "Tiamaris will be their Lord."

"Yes."

She thought about this for a few moments, and then said, "How can the Emperor allow that? They look like a small army—"

"Indeed. You have never met the Emperor, and for good reason. But he is not without wisdom, and not without mercy—in his fashion. Mercy is always more readily dispensed at a distance, when one is not being personally offended or defied," he added. "But there are some things it is not possible for the Emperor to do, no matter how rational it might look to the merely mortal at the time.

"It is why, in the end, he is not here. He has accepted that the refugees pose no threat to his hoard—for the moment. Regardless, he will not be able to stand aside for Tiamaris, or to allow Tiamaris to make his claim, if he is present.

"You may, however, join Tiamaris. Ybelline Rabon'alani is needed there."

Tiamaris faced Mejrah as if she were the only person present. Given that she was surrounded by men and women who bristled with edged weapons, this was impressive. Nor did she flinch or step back as he approached, his wings once again folded over his back.

Ybelline stepped to the side of Tiamaris's massive, and momentarily closed, jaw. "I am not conversant in all of the language," she told him. "My translations therefore convey general meaning, but any error you perceive in tone could just as easily be mine as theirs."

"Understood."

Before either could speak, however, Effaron joined them. He glanced hesitantly at Kaylin, who nodded and held out her hand. "Mejran thought this might be easier," he said. "With less misunderstanding."

"Good thought. Is she as scary as she looks?"

"Yes. But loved, for all that. She has made her offer on behalf of our people. What say the Dragons?"

"This," Kaylin said, nodding to the only member of the Court who didn't look human, "is Lord Tiamaris. He occupies lands across the river—which isn't that far away—and he rules them. He's offered your people a home there."

"And in return?"

She repeated the words to Tiamaris, who nodded. "A fair question. Tell him that my lands have been scarred by war—and it is a war with which they might be familiar. There is much rebuilding to do, and in the end, the work itself is likely to be dangerous. I will protect them if it is within my power to do so. I require them to extend that protection—in my name—to both their own people and the others who also serve me.

"They will abide by my laws," he added.

She repeated the gist of his words, and added a few of her own to soften them. He then repeated them—no doubt with a few of *his* own mixed in—to Mejrah, while Ybelline once again listened.

Only when Mejrah came forward with the big knife did everyone still. But she matter-of-factly sliced open a hand that looked as if it had already been scarred by similar cuts, and she made a fist of that bleeding palm.

A shout went up behind her back as word filtered at the speed of bad gossip through the ranks of her people. There were tears in those shouts, and fear, and joy, and relief. There was also the clashing of steel, but it seemed to be celebratory in nature, although it instantly got the attention of the Swords.

But Kaylin watched the blood drip toward the cobbles, and Kaylin saw that as the blood seeped between the stones, this new earth that the Maker had created in his brief passage absorbed it. And it returned blood to sunlight in an entirely different form: a red, red flower.

Mejrah, watching, had seen, as had Tiamaris and Effaron, and the old woman's eyes did widen then, and the tears she had refused to shed fell in silence down her weathered cheeks.

She whispered a single word, and Kaylin thought she even understood it.

Home.

★ ★ ★ ★ ★

ACKNOWLEDGMENTS

I think by now people are aware of the debt I owe my family for more or less patiently living with and supporting me through the highs and lows of writing any novel. Both my home team—my husband, my two sons, my parents—and my away team—my Australian alpha reader and sounding board, share credit and long-suffering status in equal measure.

But I think people are less aware of the other half of any book's team, so I'd like to mention the fabulous job that the Luna Art Director (Kathleen Oudit) and her team have done for all of the Cast novels. The overall look, the consistency of type and design, the strong sense of a contemporary tone in an otherwise entirely other-world that those covers convey have really, really, helped these books reach their audience. People sometimes assume that authors choose or design their own covers—and believe me, you are grateful in my case that this is so not true. I can't even draw consistent stick figures.

I would also like to thank Mary-Theresa Hussey, who shepherds the book—and me!—through the various stages, from lengthy first draft to finished novel, because she is patient and perceptive, and she *gets* these books. Had she not seen something in them from the very beginning, they wouldn't exist.

Keep reading for a preview of
CAST IN RUIN
the next story in the CHRONICLES OF ELANTRA
from Michelle Sagara and MIRA Books.
Available now.

CHAPTER 1

The worst thing about near-world-ending disasters according to Sergeant Marcus Kassan—at least the ones that had miraculously done very little damage—was the paperwork they generated. Two departments over, the Hawks required to man desks visible—and accessible—to the public would probably have disagreed. Vehemently. In Leontine.

In the day and a half since four very large Dragons, a small army, and every Sword on the roster had converged on Elani street, there'd been a steady stream of people coming to the office that bordered Missing Persons to make complaints, demand redress, or simply ask for some assurance that the world had not, in fact, ended. The numbers of civilian complaints had, in theory, peaked.

Theory, as usual, was invented by some bureaucrat in a high tower who didn't have to actually *deal* with said complaints. Private Neya, however, wasn't even Corporal, let alone lofty bureaucrat. She was part of the emergency shift of Hawks who'd been crammed into a workspace—already tight to begin with—in order to deal with the civilians. The Hawks who regularly manned these desks were generally older and certainly better suited to the task.

They appeared to appreciate the help about as much as the help appreciated being there.

"You're beat Hawks," her Sergeant had growled. For some of the officers who worked in the Halls of Law, growl would be figurative. In the case of Kaylin Neya, it was literal: her Sergeant was a Leontine. "You deal with the public every day."

"Right. We deal with the public accused of stealing, mugging, and murder." All in all, it didn't give the brightest window into the human condition. When Sergeant Kassan failed to even blink, she added, "You know them—they're the people I don't have to worry about offending?"

Marcus, however, had failed to be moved. Kaylin had not, which is why she currently occupied half a stranger's desk.

"You were assigned to Elani," he pointed out. "At the moment, Elani is still—"

"Under quarantine. Yes. I realize that."

"Since you can't do your job there for the next few days, you can make yourself useful in the front rooms, since we *are* still paying you."

Not surprisingly, many of the reports delivered by timid, angry, or deranged civilians involved descriptions of a giant Dragon roaming the streets. His color varied from report to report, as did his activities; he reportedly breathed fire, ate people—or at least large, stray dogs—and leveled buildings. He was alternately the usual Dragon size—which, to be fair, was not small—or giant; he was also deafening.

This last part was accurate. The rest, not so much. Kaylin, of course, knew the Dragon being described. Dragons were forbidden, by law, from assuming their native forms within the City of Elantra without express permission from the Eternal Emperor. Lord Tiamaris, however, had received that dispensation. He was, the last time she'd seen him, a shade that approached copper. He did have an impressive wingspan, but none of the eyewitnesses had claimed to see him fly.

Most of the witnesses, however, claimed that Tiamaris led a small army. The descriptions of this army varied almost as widely as descriptions of Tiamaris himself. The word *Barbarian* came up almost as often as *Savage,* but both ran a distant second and third to *Giant.* She particularly liked the two people—who had come in together and were shoving each other in between sentences—who claimed that they were an army of the shambling undead. Their size was, according to these civilian reports, all over the map; their numbers ranged from "lots" to "fifty thousand." Most accounts agreed, however, that the strangers were armed.

This last had the benefit of being accurate. The strangers—or refugees—themselves were, as far as anyone knew, newcomers to the world—the idea that this was *a* world, rather than the *only* world being almost as new to most of the authorities as the refugees themselves. According to the Palace, and more important, to Lord Sanabalis, the refugees numbered roughly three thousand strong. As their destination was the fief of Tiamaris, no formal census had been taken or even considered. They wouldn't technically be citizens of Elantra.

They weren't giants, a race that Kaylin privately thought entirely in the realm of children's stories, but they were about eight feet in height at the upper end; the children were taller than Kaylin. They didn't speak Elantran, which was Kaylin's mother tongue; they didn't speak Barrani, either, Barrani being the language in which the laws were written. But the Imperial linguists, with the aid of Ybelline Rabon'alani, had gone with Tiamaris. They'd been the only people who'd looked truly *excited* at the prospect of three thousand armed, hungry, and exhausted eight-foot-tall strangers. They were also, however, absent from the civilian reports, and therefore not her problem.

Kaylin had received some training in speaking with civilians, because some of her job did involve talking to possible witnesses in a way that didn't terrify them so much they denied seeing anything; putting it to use in the crowded office full of strangers was almost more than she could stomach. She did not, however, point out that they were blind or out of their minds; she transcribed most of what they said with unfailing attention.

This was, in part, because in the end Marcus would have to *read* most of these, or at least sign them. He loathed paperwork.

On the bright side? The unusual births, the rains of blood—and, in one area, frogs—and the unfortunate and inexplicable change in the City's geography, had ceased. Elani, however, now had a stream running along one side of the street, and the blood-red flowers that had popped up in the wake of the refugees were proving more hardy than tangleknot grass.

It would probably only be a matter of time before some enterprising fraud picked them, bottled them, and sold them as an elixir of youth; it *was* Elani street, after all.

Kaylin glanced at the small mirror at the end of the overwhelmed desk she was half behind. The Records of the Halls of Law, forbidden to the rank and file during the state of emergency, were now once again deemed safe to use, which meant the mirror added more external chatter to a loud and bustling office.

Kaylin tried to avoid listening to it; it only annoyed her. The Barrani Hawks were, of course, excused external desk duty. Something about tall, slender immortals put normal civilians off their stride; for some reason they felt the Barrani were arrogant and condescending. This was probably, in Kaylin's opinion, because they had working eyes and ears.

The Aerian Hawks were excused the "emergency" shift work because the small size—and low ceilings—of the cramped room made having large wings a disadvantage. In theory.

Luckily, the force contained enough humans that the extra shifts decreed as necessary by some higher-up could be filled. If Kaylin knew who he—or she—was, there'd be a new picture on the dartboard in the office by the end of the week. Who knew a hand could cramp so damn badly when the only activity of the day was writing and trying to hide the fists that incredible stupidity normally caused?

Severn Handred, her Corporal partner, had fared better, in large part because he didn't *mind* the stupidity. He met her when she managed to edge her way out of the single door that led—from the inside of the Halls of Law—to the office itself. There was a door on the opposite wall, as well, but as it led *into* the people who were waiting to make their incredibly frustrating reports, Kaylin avoided that one.

"Well?" he asked. He was leaning against the wall, arms folded across his chest.

"I didn't kill anyone," she replied.

"That bad?"

"I think it was the conspiracy of evil chickens that did me in."

"Pardon?"

"You heard me. I honestly have no idea how more of the Hawks in that damn office aren't arraigned on assault charges."

"Bridget keeps them in line."

"Bridget?"

"Sergeant Keele."

Kaylin cringed. "I could see that." Sergeant Keele was one of the staff regulars; this was her domain. She'd been entirely undelighted at the additional staff thrust upon her, in part

because she felt it impugned her ability to handle the situation. She had, however, been brisk, if chilly, and she didn't
mince words—or orders. If hazing was part of the unofficial
schedule of the regular office workers, it wasn't something
she had time for, so it had to be damn subtle.

"Can you top evil chickens?" she asked hopefully.

He thought about it for a minute. "Probably not."

"Dinner?"

He nodded slowly. "You didn't happen to check the mirror before you left?"

"I shut it off. Why?"

"Sergeant Kassan is expecting us."

"What? Why?"

"The important question is actually, 'When?'."

She swore.

Caitlin was still at her desk, but many of the regulars had
already vacated theirs and headed home, something Kaylin
had every hope of doing soon. The office den mother looked
up as Kaylin entered. "Bad day, dear?" she asked.

Kaylin shrugged. "It could have been worse."

"Oh?"

"I could have been the one who had to listen to Mrs. Erickson."

Caitlin, used to seeing some of the paperwork that crossed
between offices, grimaced. Mrs. Erickson was famous—or
infamous—for the messages she carried; they were invariably
from the dead. The nosy, busybody dead. They ranged in importance from left shoes—Kaylin had refused to believe this
until the report was pulled and shoved under her nose—to
Empire-spanning conspiracies against the Dragon Emperor.
Since Mrs. Erickson liked to bake, all her messages were con-

veyed alongside cookies or small cakes, none of which had ever caused even the slightest bit of indigestion.

"What was today's message?"

"I missed it—I was too busy dealing with the reports about the invading army and its Dragon. Whatever her dead messenger was concerned about, though, it was long. How were things here?"

"Well, Margot is threatening to join the Merchants' Guild and file a formal guild complaint if we don't lift the quarantine on Elani street soon. She's also seeking financial redress for economic losses taken because of the involuntary closure of her store."

Kaylin snorted. "Let her. I can't quite decide who'd be the loser in that transaction—Margot or the guild." Kaylin despised both with a frequently expressed and very colorful passion.

"I don't believe Lord Grammayre is looking for *more* official difficulty at the moment."

At that, Kaylin's expression flattened. "You've had word?"

"Not official word, no. But the investigation into the Exchequer is *not* going well. The Human Caste Court has closed ranks around him. The Emperor has not closed the investigation, but by all reports he is...not pleased." She paused, and then added, "Word was, however, sent from the Palace. For you."

Kaylin winced. "It's only been *two days*," she murmured.

"Two days, for Lord Diarmat, is long enough." Marcus's voice growled from behind her.

Marcus was at his desk, surrounded by the usual teetering piles of paper; Kaylin counted three. The gouges in the surface of said desk didn't appear to be deeper or more numerous, which probably meant his mood hadn't descended to foul, yet.

"You're late," he growled. Since his irises were a distinct gold, Kaylin said, "Not according to Sergeant Keele, sir." She walked over to his desk and took up position in front of it; Severn lingered behind.

Without preamble, he handed her a set of curved papers. She took them as if they were live cockroaches and began to read. The top letter—and it was a letter—was from Lord Sanabalis of the Dragon Court.

Sanabalis had extended the period of grace in which she was allowed to skip the magic class he was responsible for making certain she attended; the transitioning of three thousand refugees who required housing and food were of primary import for the next week. Or two. He wished her luck during the extra work that this type of emergency generated, by which she inferred he knew of her day's work in the outer office.

The second letter was from Diarmat, and it was not, by any reasonable definition, a letter; it was a set of orders. She read it once, and then glanced up over the top edge of the page to see Leontine eyes watching her carefully.

"He is," Marcus said drily, "the Commander of the Imperial Guard, a force that is almost entirely composed of humans."

"Have you had to interact with them?"

"On several occasions. I've survived."

"Have they?"

He raised a brow; his eyes, however, stayed the same mellow gold. She had a sneaking suspicion he was enjoying this.

Lord Diarmat—whose classes were to be conducted after-bloody-hours on her *own* time—considered three thousand refugees and a significant area of the city under quarantine unworthy of mention. She swore.

Caitlin coughed.

"He *reminds* me that the first of our lessons starts *tonight*."

"Then you'd best have something to eat, dear," Caitlin told her. "I highly doubt that Lord Diarmat will be casual enough to offer to feed you."

Feed her? If she was lucky, he'd be civil enough not to eat her himself.

She looked at the window. "Time?" she asked it.

"Five hours and a half," the window replied. "Please check the duty roster on your way out."

Because she was feeling masochistic, she did. She was penciled in for yet another day on outsiders' desk duty.

Severn kept her company as she trudged down the street toward the baker's. He also handed her the coins she needed to pay Manners Forall, who happened to be manning his own stall. He smiled and said, "We don't usually see you this late in the month." It was true. This late in the month she was usually scrounging for less expensive food.

Severn said nothing, but he said it loudly, reminding her in silence of the budgeting discussion they'd failed to find the time for. It was the only silver lining on the thundercloud of Lord Diarmat and his so-called etiquette lessons. Severn didn't *remain* silent, however, and they wrangled over times for yet a different lesson in Kaylin's educational schedule while they made their way to the Palace.

The streets weren't noticeably less crowded than they had been; apparently the crazed fear of Dragons and their itinerant armies didn't stop most people from going about their daily business. Severn left her at the Palace gates, pausing only to check her wrist. There, the bracer that she wore by Imperial Decree caught the lights above. It was heavy enough to be

the gold that it looked, and it was studded with what appeared
to be three large gems: a diamond, a ruby, and a sapphire.

"I haven't taken it off since we got back from Evanton's,"
she told him. But she didn't resent his checking, much. Diarmat wasn't known for his flexibility. "I'll see you in the
morning. If I'm still alive." Severn was also penciled in for
crazy duty; he minded it less ferociously.

The very forbidding and starched man whose title she
couldn't recall met her at the doors; he stood well inside them,
and somewhat behind the Imperial Guards who gave her a
quick once-over. It was cursory, however; the man stepped
forward and said in his clipped High Barrani, "Lord Diarmat is expecting you, Private Neya. If you will follow me."

She did. She could now reliably make her way to the chambers in which Sanabalis frequently conducted his meetings,
and she could—if she were feeling foolishly brave—find the
Library unescorted. She had no idea what Diarmat called
home—or office—in the Palace, and had she not been certain
of finding him in it, she would have been genuinely curious.

But during the handful of times she'd met him, he'd failed
to be anything remotely resembling friendly, and *tolerant* was
a word that she suspected he'd failed to learn, although his
High Barrani was otherwise flawless. Severn had said that
his Elantan was also flawless—and completely free from col-
loquialisms. Kaylin had already decided it was best to stick
with High Barrani; it was a lot harder to make verbal gaffes
in that language.

The starched man paused in front of a set of double doors
that looked suspiciously unlike any classroom doors she'd ever
entered. There were no guards at the doors, which was good.
The doors were warded, which was bad. Not only were they

warded, but there appeared to be two damn wards, one on each door. She glanced at her guide and said without much hope, "I don't suppose those are just decorative?"

"No, they are not. You are required to touch both wards; you are not, however, required to touch them at the same time, should you find yourself, for reasons of injury, unable to do so."

Kaylin's natural aversion to magic was not quite as strong as her aversion to having her head bitten off by an angry Dragon Lord, but it was close. She stepped up to the doors, stood in arm's reach, and grimaced; the wards were higher than shoulder height. She guessed they'd been designed for the regular variety of Imperial Palace Guard; they had, among other things, fairly strict height requirements.

Grimacing, she placed her left palm on the left-door ward, and felt the strong bite of magic travel up her arm so forcefully her arm went numb. The ward, however, began to glow; it wasn't a comforting sight, given that the light was a sickly, pulsing green. Any hope that her guide had been wrong vanished; the door didn't budge. Aware of his presence, she kept her teeth shut firmly over the Leontine words that were trying to leap out, and lifted her hand again.

It was her left hand. She was right-handed, and with her luck, the first thing Diarmat would do was ask her to write some long Barranian test; she couldn't afford to have a numb, useless writing hand. It was awkward, but she lifted her left arm again—without cursing—and placed her palm more or less in the center of its damn ward.

The door ward began to glow a livid, pale purple. It hurt to touch, and given her arm was half-numb, this said something. Unfortunately, the door wards *also* said something—and from the sounds of the echo, it was in Dragon. She did curse, but then Leontine spoken with a human throat couldn't possibly be audible over the racket the ward had caused.

To make matters worse—as if the universe needed to remind her that they could be—the hall, which was long and high ceilinged, began to fill with Imperial Palace Guards. Her starched guide didn't blink or move as she turned to face them. Give them this: they were impressive. They wore heavier armor than patrolling Hawks, they carried large swords, and they moved in frightening unison, as if this were some arcane drill and they'd be demoted if one foot was out of place.

She doubted she'd appreciate it more if their weapons had not, in fact, been pointing toward her. She didn't bother drawing her own; all she had at the moment were daggers, and one numb hand. Instead, she lifted her hands—slowly— and stood very still. The doors at her back rolled open.

"Thank you, gentlemen," a familiar voice said. "That will be all."

He received one very noisy salute—gauntlets did that in an otherwise silent hall—as she turned to face him. She could hear the guards form up and retreat, but didn't bother to watch them leave. Instead, she faced Lord Diarmat of the Dragon Court.

He was slightly taller than Tiamaris, and he had the broad— and, sadly, muscular—build of Dragons in human form; he also had Dragon eyes. His lower membranes muted their color, but in this light, they were gold, although the gold seemed tinted with orange. Then again, gold was a happy color, and she doubted that someone with an expression that consistently severe could *be* happy. He was not, however, dressed in natural Dragon armor; he wore robes with a distinct Imperial Crest blazoned across the chest.

"Lord Diarmat," she said, tendering as formal a bow as she could.

"I see that reports of your tardiness are exaggerated." He glanced at the doors. "And reports of your effect on some of the more formal wards are not."

She managed to say nothing.

"Nor, it appears, are reports about the need for some formal structure in your interactions with the Imperial Court." He looked past her to the man who had led her here. "Thank you," he said quietly. "Please send someone in two hours to escort Private Neya out; she is not, I believe, familiar with the Palace."

The man nodded briskly. "Lord Diarmat," he said, and then turned and walked off.

Diarmat now gestured toward the room behind the offending doors. "Please," he said. "Enter."

The room was, as the doors suggested, large. The ceilings were at least as high as the ones that characterized the public halls, and the walls were thirty feet away from the open doors on all sides. The whole of the office Kaylin generally called home would have comfortably fit in the space, although some of the furniture would have to be moved to accommodate it. There were two desks in the far corner, and an arrangement of chairs around one central table of medium height; there was a long table that seemed like a dining table, although no similar chairs were tucked beneath it.

Windows opened into a courtyard that had no view of the Halls of Law—and no view of the streets of the City, either; instead, there were stones that were arranged at various heights and distances, as if it were meant to be a garden. She saw doors leading out of the room to either side. This was as far from a typical classroom as a room could get. She glanced at Diarmat, waiting for his instructions.

He didn't bother with them. Instead, he crossed the room and headed toward his desk. It was unblemished, and no mounds of paperwork teetered precariously anywhere in sight; there was an inkstand, and three small bars of wax. Even paper was absent. He took the chair behind the desk, and then frowned at the doors behind Kaylin.

"Should I close them?"

He spoke a single curt word and the doors began to roll shut on their own, which was all of his reply. He then stared at her, unblinking, until she made her way to the front of the desk.

He took parchment out of a desk drawer, placed it—dead center—on its surface, and uncapped his ink. "You have been a student of Lord Sanabalis for some months now."

"Yes."

"You have, however, shown little progress in the classes he teaches."

It was a bit of a sore point, because little progress, to Kaylin's mind, meant waste of time. On the other hand, at least she was *paid* to attend Sanabalis's mandatory classes.

"Lord Sanabalis, under the auspices of the Imperial Order of Mages, has developed a level of tolerance for the lazy and the inexact that is almost unheard of among our kind. Mages are not generally considered either stable or biddable; were it not for the necessity of some of their services, and the existence of the Arcanum as a distinctly less welcome alternative, they would not be tolerated at all." His tone made clear that were it up to him, neither the Imperial Order nor the Arcanum would be long for this world.

Which was a pity, because Kaylin agreed with him, and

this might be the *only* point on which there would be any common ground. Defending either organization was not, however, her job.

"I am not Lord Sanabalis. What he tolerates, I will not tolerate. I have perused some of your previous academic records, but not in any depth; I no longer consider them relevant. You were not raised in an environment with strong Barrani influences, and you will therefore have little understanding of the way in which those influences govern some parts of the Palace.

"They are not, however, your chief concern. I am told that you have a strong grasp of High Barrani. When the Court is in session, the language of choice defaults to High Barrani in the presence of races that are not Dragon. Were you not required to interact with the Emperor, neither you, nor I, would be required to waste time in this endeavor." His tone made clear whose time he thought more valuable. "You will, however, be required to speak.

"Speech, were it the only requirement, you might be able to manage. Because you are considered *worthy* of such a privilege, however, correct form and behavior will be *assumed*. Any deviation from those forms will be seen as a breach, not of etiquette, but of respect. Disrespect of the Emperor is ill advised."

She nodded. This didn't make his expression any friendlier, and it didn't make her any happier; she bit back any words to that effect, and instead said, "What did I do wrong when you appeared at the doors?" She spoke as smoothly and neutrally as possible, but she couldn't quite stop her cheeks from reddening.

He raised a Dragon brow. "That," he told her, "is an almost perceptive question."

Not perceptive enough to answer? She waited. The problem with immortals was that, short of immediate emergencies, they *had* forever; what seemed a long time to a normal person was insignificant to them. Their arrogance seemed to stem from the fact that they'd seen and experienced so much more than a mortal could achieve in an entire lifetime, it negated mortal experience.

Kaylin didn't like being treated like a child in the best of circumstances—no one did—but Immortals *always* felt they were dealing with children when mortals were involved. Some were just way better at hiding it. Diarmat clearly couldn't be bothered. She waited, and he returned to the paper beneath his hands and began to write. She could actually read upside-down writing; it was one of the things she'd figured out when boredom had taken hold in her early classes and she was trying to be less obvious about it. But in this case, she had a suspicion he'd notice, and it seemed career limiting.

She was also no longer a bored student; she was here as a Hawk, not a mascot. She left her hands loosely by her sides, and stared at a point just past his left shoulder while she waited for some instruction—to sit, to stand, to go away, to answer questions. Anything.

What felt like half an hour later she was *still* standing in front of his damn desk, and he was *still* writing. He had told her nothing at all about the rules that governed the Imperial Court or its meetings. He hadn't spoken of any particular style of dress, hadn't given her any information about forms of address, hadn't demonstrated any of the salutes or bows with which one might open speech. Since she'd managed to eat something on the hurried walk over, her stomach didn't embarrass her by speaking when she wouldn't.

At the end of the page, he looked up. Folding the paper in

three he reached for wax, and this, he melted by the simple expedient of breathing on it slightly. He then pressed a small seal into what had fallen on the seam. He reached across the desk and handed her the letter. "This," he said, "is for the perusal of Lord Grammayre on the morrow." He rose, and made his way out from behind his bastion of a desk; there, he exhaled. It was loud.

"Very well," he said, as if he was vaguely disappointed. "You have some ability to display patience. Your posture is not deplorable. Your ability to comport yourself does not directly affect the respect in which the Halls of Law are now held." He spoke in crisp, perfectly enunciated High Barrani. He now opened a drawer, and a thick sheaf of papers appeared on the desk.

These, Kaylin thought, would be the various educational reports he had barely, in his own words, perused.

He handed them to her; she slid the letter to the Hawklord into her tunic, and took the offending pile, glancing briefly at what lay on top of it. Transcripts, yes. To her surprise, the first one was *not* a classroom diatribe from a frustrated or angry teacher.

"This is a case report," she said before she could stop herself.

"It is." He walked around to her side. "Do you recognize it?"

She nodded.

"You were working in concert with two Barrani Hawks."

"Teela and Tain," she said. She didn't flip through the report; she knew which case this was. All boredom or irritation fled, then.

"It was, I believe, the breaking of a child-prostitution ring."

"It was."

"Do you recall the chain of events that led to the deaths of some of the men involved?"

She nodded again, although it was almost untrue: she didn't remember the end clearly at all. She remembered her utter, unstoppable *rage*. And she remembered the deaths that rage—and her unbridled magic—had caused.

His silence could have meant many things, but since his face was as expressive as cold stone, she didn't bother to look at him.

"I would like you to peruse the rest of the documents," he finally said.

She did. It wasn't a small pile—although it wasn't Leontine in proportion—but there really weren't that many cases in which she'd lost control of her inexplicable magic to such devastating effect; she had literally skinned a man alive. She didn't regret it. Not in any real way. He would have died anyway, after his trial. But...the trial had been moot, and Marcus had *not* been happy.

The next report made her right hand tighten into a white-knuckled fist before she got halfway down the first page. It wasn't a case report. It wasn't a report that the Halls of Law would ever generate.

It was, instead, a report on the Guild of Midwives. She almost dropped the report on the desk. Instead, she forced her hand to relax—as much as it could—while she read. It detailed all the emergency call-ins she'd done—and it detailed, in some cases, the results. She lifted the top page. Her memory wasn't the best, but she thought, looking briefly at dates and commentary, none in a hand she recognized, that it was more complete than anything she could have written for him, had he asked.

Grim, she flipped through the pile, and was unsurprised to see that he also had a similar report for each visit she'd made to Evanton's shop on Elani street. This angered her less; she *knew* the Dragon Court spied on Evanton.

There was a brief report of her visits to the High Halls, again not much to fuss about; there was a report on every visit she had made in recent months to the fiefs—any fief crossing. There was a report that followed her movements to, and from, both the Leontine Quarter and the Tha'alani Quarter. Diarmat was silent as she read, as if waiting for a reaction she didn't want to give him the pleasure of seeing.

But the final report was of the Foundling Hall.